BRINGING FORTH THE END OF DAYS

SIMON LAW

Eloquent Books
New York, New York

Eloquent Books
An imprint of AEG Publishing Group
845 Third Avenue, 6th Floor - 6016
New York, NY 10022
www.eloquentbooks.com

ISBN 978-1-60860-203-2

Printed in the United States of America

Book Design: Linda W. Rigsbee

DEDICATION

This is for everyone who gave me the inspiration

and support that I needed.

Thank you.

PROLOGUE

THOMAS HARVEY was a man of simple pleasures. He sat looking out into the distant sky thinking 'how funny things were.' It was funny to him how after all this destruction around him, after all the disease and killings, and even after all the hatred and bitterness that had consumed the world, how the beauty of an evening sunset in the distance could still take his breath away.

At the beginning of time when the world was new, beauty like this could be seen all around, in any direction you looked. The water was pure, the air was clean and safe, the ozone layer was flawless, and all of God's creations lived together in perfect harmony.

People had spent thousands of years debating the existence of God and would surely continue the debate until the very end of time.

People wouldn't accept the fact that the debate itself was pointless and we would never arrive at a satisfactory conclusion, as the only possible affirmation of its holy existence would come to us at the time of our death. It would be at this very point that some people may drift gracefully up to the euphoric ivory gates of heaven, to be greeted with open arms and smiles from all those that had passed before. There would be the sounds of children laughing, the smell of freshly baked cookies maybe, and that warm fuzzy feeling inside that you just cannot describe in words. Some however, may plummet deep into the burning lava of hell, spending the rest of eternity paying for their earthly sins. There was a time when these beliefs were held by the vast majority, which in themselves kept most people fearful and honest. But as the people's need for proof became more prevalent, atheism slowly gained majority rule over the population, leaving room for only one possible conclusion: that we would just rot away in the ground and become food for the worms.

Tom had spent much time in his life thinking about that very matter, never quite deciding which direction to sway. It seemed to him that most other people in the world had already acquired a firm point of view on the matter, although many of these were mere victims of parental brainwashing by overpowering figures that were too stubborn and ignorant to accept other possibilities. Others made up their own minds about what they believed from things that they had read, experiences they had, and what just felt right inside of them. Tom's mother's side of the family were very religious. They were old-fashioned people who always went to church on Sunday and ate fish on Friday. Tom's father had no family or strong influences in his life and had become completely agnostic. When Tom was born his parents decided that they wouldn't influence him in either way, letting him make up his own mind over time. But that was the problem, he couldn't. Tom was very bright as a child, and like most bright people he tended to question the unquantifiable and the unproven. Facts were real, undeniable, and irrefutable. They were certainties and absolutes which gave Tom reassurance and comfort. But facts were dull. They left no room for faith, beliefs, or possibilities.

Some people claim to have had experiences in their lives that reinforced their faiths. Maybe these were nothing more than delusions and misinterpretations, but either way these experiences seemed to empower the recipient, and give them hope and enlightenment. Tom remembered his Grandma Dunn and what she had said to him on her deathbed. She said that she had received a vision, a vision in which the Virgin Mary came to her in her sleep and told her that she had nothing left to fear. Grandma Dunn died in her sleep the following night, quietly and peacefully. Tom also recalled an old friend of his from college, a friend who was dying from an extremely rare brain disease. The doctors treating him knew almost nothing about the disease and all previous sufferers of the disease had been unsuccessfully treated and died. The friend had decided to undergo experimental surgery. It had never been done before and he came out the other side as fit as a fiddle, never to be sick again. The friend believed that God himself had watched over him that day, and had kept him on this earth for a purpose. From that day forward he began attending church again. He hadn't attended since he was young. Eventually he became a vicar himself, to talk of his experience and to reinforce the faith of others.

Tom had experienced nothing in his lifetime that would give him reason to have faith. But Tom wanted more than anything else for justification to believe. The whole concept of Christianity, or just religion in general was appealing to him. He liked the idea that we were all put on this earth for a reason, the idea of life after death, and a drive for honesty and morals.

His longing for a heaven was an unselfish wish too, as he longed for its existence purely for the sake of his loving family and all those who had passed before him. He wanted to think that everyone that he had loved and cherished were now in a better place, a place where they would be happy and at rest. It was an unselfish wish because he knew that even if a heaven did exist, it would undeniably refuse him access and there was no amount of good deeds or repenting that would save his soul from eternal damnation.

Regardless of what people believed, whether it was thunder and lightening and the creation of the world in seven days, or that the world and its inhabitants had grown and evolved over billions of years from random clumps of electrons, neutrons, and protons. Either way, Tom had found a common cynical agreement that the planet had first started to degenerate the day that mankind first set foot upon it. We stomped around with such arrogance that we caused the destruction and corruption of the world's once beautiful innocence. We polluted the water and the air, we destroyed the ozone, wiped millions of species into extinction, and spent the rest of our time killing each other and blowing random things apart to make a pointless statement. It felt inevitable to Tom that eventually we would completely destroy our own planet. It was only a matter of time. Be it Mother Nature, or God himself, someone had made a serious mistake when they invented man.

Tom believed this more than anything else, but could never quite pinpoint the root cause of our own destructive nature. He contemplated the influences that our own intelligence had on the matter. As it stood, we had arrogantly declared ourselves the most evolved and intelligent species that inhabited our planet. But maybe that was the problem. Most other mammals seemed to live a simple life contented with only the most basic of needs, to eat, breath, reproduce, and then die. Tom saw great beauty in its simplicity and grace and wondered why it was so hard for us to live the same way. Why did we demand so much more from life to keep us mildly satisfied? These animals never built contraptions of war. They didn't pollute and kill their own environment, and they didn't form armies and alliances to fight for supremacy.

It seemed to Tom that we as a species had been given the great gift of intellectual thought processes and the ability to design and create. But yet we did not have enough drive and common sense to use these gifts positively and use them to protect and encourage the fundamental things that made our very existence possible.

It was true that when we all envisioned alien life forms in science fiction books and movies, that we portrayed them as a nation unified—a nation of great wisdom and intelligence, perfectly evolved and adapted to suit their environment. Maybe we portrayed them this way because it was precisely how we longed to be ourselves but in reality could never quite achieve it. Tom considered the thought that maybe mankind was nothing more than a virus of the earth, consuming every natural resource in the area before multiplying and spreading to the next, until we had made our mark on each and every square inch of the planet.

Tom's thoughts came to a sudden halt at that point, as he could no longer ignore the pain from the sharp pieces of metallic shrapnel beginning to cut into his side. He shuffled around uncomfortably on the pile of rubble where he was precariously perched, rubble that had once been the walls of a college. It was the same college that he had attended when he was a teenager. He stared out emotionlessly at the sunset, watching as it slowly started to fade out, the final red and orange rays shimmering and bouncing off the top of collapsed buildings and burnt out cars in the far distance. The buzzer then started to emanate its annoying monotone beep from the oxygen canister upon his back, warning him that only ten more minutes of air remained. 'Damn thing!' He thought. 'Why didn't they last longer?'

The streets and alleys surrounding Tom were now littered with these discarded canisters and only a few remained functional. Normally after about nine hours of use they had reached the end of their lifespan and were deemed useless. Tom however, had recently devised a method of successfully modifying these old canisters to make them easily reusable. He would do this by hooking up the canister's air valve to the PGOGM (Photo-synthetically Generated Oxygen and Glucose Machine) at the house. Tom had now refilled his canister almost every morning since, giving him the freedom that he cherished to venture out into the open and experience the beauty of the sunset. He had also modified several other canisters in the house too, hoping that his housemates would someday join him outside and share the beauty of the sunset with him. But they had respectfully declined his offer, preferring to stay inside the house at all times. After all, the streets were not safe places to be anymore.

The dangers outside were not just from the deadly carbon dioxide pollution, but they had something else to fear now too. There had been numerous alleged sightings of the Jehovah's Enforcers in the area, and their intentions nowadays were a little more involved than just knocking on your door and inviting God into your lives. They were now more likely to slice you up into little pieces with a rusty implement. Even the thought of it inside Tom's own head sounded somewhat ridiculous and unbelievable to him, but he could understand how in desperate situations people would go to extremes.

Tom's own disbelief of these accusations was firmly put to rest a while back, when the fanatical group had ambushed him and an old college friend down a dark alleyway. Tom had managed to escape the brutal assault with a few minor scratches after having beaten his assailant to death with a lead pipe. His friend at the time was not so lucky and had quickly become the consistency of mincemeat. Tom had remained behind bolted doors for a long while after that, watching the sunset with longing eyes from his distant bedroom window. So he could fully understand the fear and hesitation of his new housemates.

It seemed that one key figure within the Jehovah's Witness faith had voiced his own interpretation of what was happening to the world, the poisoning of the air, the wars, and the growing sickness and death of the world's population. He claimed these events were the start of the upcoming apocalypse, the end of days. He said that God himself had spoken to him in a vision and employed him to aid in the final stages of the apocalypse. This talk caused immediate uproar from within the faith and he was branded a lunatic by many of his peers. They claimed his words were the voice of the devil and banished him from the faith forever. But his words had struck a bitter chord with many of the followers, who then left the faith to join him in a newly formed sect of the religion calling themselves 'The Jehovah's Enforcers.' Through either belief or fear they slowly converted almost eighty percent of the faith to their new sect, along with hundreds of previous atheists who now found reason and purpose to believe.

The new sect of the faith soon dropped their previous refusals to take part in blood transfusions in surgeries, enabling them all to undergo the 'Wagna procedure' (pronounced varg-ner), helping them to survive in the desolate world just long enough to finish off what they believe God had started. They believed this to be their final earthly task. They believed that sacrificing the remaining population of the earth (including themselves), would bring forth 'Judgment Day,' a time they believed would only occur once every soul on earth was free of its own human entrapment. They believed that our souls could then stand united in the presence of God to be judged. This was a day that the faith had been waiting for since it was first formed centuries ago, and now that the day was so close, they were certain not to let anyone stand in the way of it.

These interpretations and events brought up another key point in Tom's debate about religion and forced the question of how exactly each religion got started in the first place. Was the essence of these religions still what had been intended at the beginning? Exactly how much of each religion had been changed or left out over the years to suit people's own personal goals and beliefs? Religion and God had been used as an excuse for war from the very beginning of time, so surely becoming a member of a specific faith was just a means of persecuting people of a different one?

The buzzer sounded on the oxygen canister once again, warning Tom that only five more minutes of air remained. It was now very late for Tom to start walking back, especially as the house was a good few minutes away, even if he ran. The facemask was becoming increasingly uncomfortable at this point and the clear silicon air tubes were itching and irritating his nose, but he dared not remove it, not even for a second.

He reached down into his left trouser pocket and took out a shiny medal shaped in a cross pattern and embossed with the depiction of a lion mounting a crown. The inscription on the front of the medal read 'For Valour' and was suspended from a crimson silk ribbon. He caressed the embossed front with his thumb, wiping clear any dust and grime from its features. He then flipped the medal over to repeat the same action on the back. The engraving on the back read: Leonard Dunn, the name of Tom's grandfather. The medal was the Victoria Cross, the highest and most respected military award available, awarded only to the bravest men for acts of valour in the face of the enemy.

Grandfather Dunn had been awarded the medal for his courage and bravery in the Second World War, in battle against the Nazis. It was the middle of winter, with blistering cold winds, icy fields, and imminent snow. The rest of the officers in Dunn's regiment had either been killed off or taken prisoner by the Nazis and he had only managed to avoid detection himself by hiding underneath a mountain of rotting corpses for a day and a half. He waited patiently, smothered from head to toe in the blood of his fellow officers, until he was sure that the Nazis had vacated the area. He then followed their tracks to a nearby Nazi campsite and with the element of surprise; he single-handedly fought to take them all down. The brave soldier survived multiple bullet wounds and gashes to his tattered body and even when his left arm was savagely blown apart by an exploding grenade, he still continued to fight them, until every last one of them was dead. With his last ounce of energy he then freed all his surviving comrades from their decrepit jails cells and was hailed by all as a hero. After receiving basic medical care for his afflictions, he was then sent home to be with his loving girlfriend Suzie, who had been desperately praying for his safe return to her. He later went on to marry Suzie and they had two children together, Robert Dunn (Uncle Bobby), and Samantha Dunn (Tom's mother).

Tom was strangely pleased that his beloved grandfather had passed away just before the world had started to fall apart and would never know what had become of the world that he fought so passionately to protect. When he died he had left Tom the prestigious medal in his will. Tom had admired the medal all of his life. Even when he was just a small child he had repeatedly asked his granddad if he could hold it, and so it felt appropriate for Tom to look after it. Tom had cherished the medal and kept it close to him ever since, to remind him what honourable blood he had running through his veins. On many occasions Tom had considered actually changing his surname to Dunn, to match that of his grandfather's. The surname Harvey, passed down to him from his father, bore no honour, nor history. His father, raised in an orphanage from the age of two, never knew any of his family, though it was believed that his mother used to work as a prostitute in London back in the '50s, and that his father was nothing more than a common punter. Tom knew that none of this was the fault of his father, but still longed for the honour of being a Dunn.

Tom stared at the medal a while longer with a nostalgic smile on his face. The airflow in the mask's tubes then started to fall more dramatically and the sun completely disappeared into the distance. It would have been so easy for Tom to have just ended all his troubles right there and then. He didn't need to do a thing. Just sit, and watch as the world faded out around him. Never would suicide be quite so easy for anyone, and if it wasn't for his relentless conscience, he would have taken the option a long time ago. Yet he knew he was undeserving of such an easy way out, especially when so many others had suffered so badly, innocent people with promising lives and loving families.

He finally shook off these thoughts, as he had done many times before. He rose to his feet and ran back towards the house before it was too late.

CHAPTER ONE (A)

THE HOUSE where Tom now resided was a large four-bedroom place that he shared with three other survivors. The house was located on the top of a gentle hill in Maidenbower, an estate within the town of Crawley who's only claims to fame included its production of 'Pot Noodles' from its industrial estate, and its numerous appearances on 'UK Street Crime' on the Bravo channel. The house itself was close to the main M23 motorway which linked London to Brighton. The road was once infamous for its constant grid-locked traffic jams and the resulting exacerbated road rage that it caused, but had now remained unused for many years. Maidenbower itself was one of the newer and richest parts of Crawley and was filled with beaker-nosed snobs who looked down on the rest of the town with judgmental stares. At the time of its release, most residents of Maidenbower were able to go out and buy one of the new PGOGM machines without causing too much of a dent to their bank balances at all, while most other residents of the town struggled hard to raise enough even for a cheap budget version of the machine. It was ironic then, how Maidenbower seemed to have suffered the worst from the proceeding bombings, and that now there was very little of the estate left standing. From vandalism and looters, to missiles and bombs, there wasn't a great deal of the whole of Crawley left standing anymore either. The few things that had survived in Maidenbower included the house where Tom now resided, a few more houses on the same street, and some of the shops in the local parade, though even these had been vandalized and looted bone dry a long time ago. The train station in the adjacent estate of Three Bridges was still erect too, though a train hadn't been seen or heard on the rails in a very long time.

The rest of the estate, and indeed most of Crawley, now amounted to nothing more than rubble, with burnt out cars and rotten litter filling the once busy streets. The remains of the old college that Tom had attended as a teenager was a little way down the road from the house and was now nothing but a pile of bricks and metal too. The building still held memories for Tom, which was why it became his favourite spot to sit and watch the evening sunsets. The four by two metal plaque that bore the college's name had somehow survived the blast that destroyed the building, and now lay on top of the pile of rubble quite comically, as if it was put there to label the site. 'Oriel Community College' it read. The wording on the sign was not obvious at first glance. It was smothered in dirt and scorched badly at the edges, but after squinting for a while you could easily work it out.

The house where Tom's parents had lived was just around the corner as well, now in a similar state to that of the college. It was completely unrecognizable, no longer bearing any resemblance to the images in Tom's head of the loving home that once stood. Presumably amongst the rubble somewhere were the corpses of Tom's parents too, crushed to pieces under the bricks and mortar, slowly decomposing to nothing but brittle skeletons. Tom had wanted for a long time now to excavate the bodies from their tomb, pay his respects to them, and to bury the bodies to come to some form of closure. Yet the job itself was far beyond his capabilities. Maybe with the help of his new friends the job may have been possible, but he didn't want to ask. Even if he had asked, it would have taken weeks to actually find the bodies and it was possible that they weren't even in there. Maybe they had been going for a walk when the bombs hit. The energy it would take to dig through the rubble was energy that could be better spent. Besides that, there were plenty of other people that had their loved ones taken away in the bombings, and they had never asked him for help.

Of the houses that still stood on the street only two were still occupied. One was the house Tom now lived in and the other was on the opposite side of the road. The occupants of the other house were a couple in their late thirties who had cohabited now for more than ten years. The woman's name was Tina Smith and her partner was Tony Sheppard. Tom had known the couple since he was young and had always been on good speaking terms with them. The conversations were never anything deep and meaningful, just simple small talk about the weather and stuff, but pleasant nonetheless. Since the couple had become sick with poisoning they had become increasingly depressed, angry and bitter, which were emotions that they all struggled to fight off sometimes. But the couple had let the whole situation get the better of them and had become reclusive and closed off from the world to the point where they refused to even speak to anyone and kept to themselves at all times. They never left their house, and never answered their door to anyone. The only evidence that the couple was still alive was the occasional sighting of a figure walking past the front room window. He thought it a shame that the couple were treating him with such disregard, but understood that people dealt with situations differently. Maybe they had just found it too hard to come to terms with the situation and just wanted to be left alone to die together peacefully in their own home.

The house where Tom lived had previously belonged to a wealthy young couple with their little boy. Their names were Sylvia and Marcus Stevenson and their little boy was called Jacob. Back when life was still normal, Marcus had worked as an accountant for a high profile banking firm in London, and had earned himself a very healthy sum of cash. Although additional funds were not needed to support the happy couple, Sylvia had continued working throughout most of their relationship too, working as a midwife down at Crawley hospital. Sylvia enjoyed her time at the hospital immensely, but the time eventually came when she fell pregnant herself with little baby Jacob. It was at this point that she finally decided to quit work altogether, so that she could dedicate her time to take proper care of him. The couple had furnished their house throughout with only the finest designer products. The kitchen comprised of solid marble worktops, bread maker, blender, toaster, kettle, etc. The living room had a glimmering black marble fireplace, with solid brass railings and matching pokers. There were two three-seater sofas of pure leather, a genuine tiger skin rug in the centre of the room, and against the rear wall sat a seventy-inch flat screen television.

The four bedrooms upstairs were equally well-furnished. There was the main bedroom, with en suite bathroom and Jacuzzi. There was little Jacob's bedroom, and an office complete with a state of the art PC and single bed just in case Marcus got tired when he was working. And finally there was a guest bedroom with a double bed, fitted wardrobes, and real wood flooring. All in all, the house had been very respectable at one point. It now looked a little rougher around the edges than it used to, but it was still the most luxurious place that any of them could have hoped for.

The Stevensons had all suffered from asthma in varying degrees, and were therefore affected by the oxygen depletion a lot more severely than most others. When the incident first happened, they were the first to rush to the pharmacist and stocked up on every Tremoline healthcare product they could find, quickly buying new ones as they were released. They purchased boxes upon boxes of the stuff, and stockpiled it all in the spare bedroom. They bought boxes of oxygen inhalers and thousands of refill cartridges. There were tubes upon tubes of protective skin cream, about forty oxygen canisters, and every room in the house was fitted with its own carbon dioxide filtration unit. As time went on and the carbon dioxide levels started to rise even more, they quickly replaced all the filtration units with the new PGOGM machines. The PGOGM (Photosynthetically Generated Oxygen and Glucose Machine) used groundbreaking new technology that could actually mimic the act of photosynthesis itself. Three metal devices were attached to the roof of their house: the first was a carbon dioxide extraction device, the second were solar panels, and the third harnessed rain water and moisture from the air. These three devices were then connected to a bulky unit on the outside of the house which fed the components into the main PGOGM in the front room. The machine then converted the carbon dioxide, water, and energy from the sun into a breathable source of oxygen and a supply of food which was dispensed from a nozzle on the side of the machine. The Stevensons also fitted airtight seals on all of the windows and doors in the house, trying their best to keep the dreaded carbon dioxide out.

Despite all the precautions they took, their efforts seemed to merely slow down the onset of the poisoning. And so when the government announced the introduction of the 'Wagna procedure,' (named after Dr William Wagna who devised the procedure) the Stevensons rushed their little boy Jacob to the clinic to have the procedure done. Their understanding was that the procedure would exponentially increase Jacob's life expectancy back to that of a normal person. So they freely spent the last penny of their life savings to have it done, believing this to be the most responsible action they could take as parents. They never stopped once to think what Jacob actually wanted, or to consider the possibility that it would turn him into a complete outcast— a mutant, a freak.

Sylvia and Marcus had waited anxiously outside the operating theatre for the full six and a half hours of the lengthy procedure. In this procedure Jacob had all of his teeth removed, his gums surgically glued together and his lips and nasal cavities sewn shut. The surgeons would then open up Jacob's chest and insert silicon tubes into his lungs and his stomach. These were then threaded down his body and out through a biologically engineered umbilical cord which was attached to his belly button. The silicon tubes were threaded out the end of the umbilical cord and into the umbilical PGOGM unit. The umbilical PGOGM unit was the size of an old walkman and was made of stainless steal. On the left side of the unit was the carbon dioxide extraction vent, and on the right side were small solar panels. The unit worked in a very similar way to the large PGOGM machine they had for the home, with the added advantage that there was now no way for the carbon dioxide to enter the body and cause any harm. The machine would process the carbon dioxide and power from the sun, along with a supply of water, and store the created oxygen and glucose molecules in separate small compartments at the bottom of the machine. The oxygen would then be pushed down the silicon tubes, through the umbilical cord and into the lungs. This would happen whenever the body needed a supply of oxygen. Because the oxygen created in the unit was completely pure, the body needed to 'breathe' less often, as oxy-haemoglobin was formed in the bloodstream much more easily and satisfied the body's requirements. The glucose solution worked on the same basis, being stored in the glucose compartment of the machine until it was required, then passing down the tubes and into the stomach.

Once successfully attached to the machine, Jacob was then sewn back up again and a protective seal was placed around the end of the cord where it met the machine. This was to prevent the risk of infection. The boy was then sent to the recovery room for a few days for his body to heal and adapt to its new attachment.

Sylvia couldn't hold back the tears when she was finally reunited with Jacob, now realising just how deformed and frightening he really looked. The expression on his poor face was that of depression pushed so far to the limits that he appeared to feel no emotion at all. Even if Jacob had felt the urge to smile at his mother reassuringly, he had no mouth, and any muscular contractions on the face would surely rip apart the fresh stitches through his lips. Jacob's father now displayed a similar blank expression upon his face, for the bright and promising world that he had brought his son into was hopelessly crumbling down around him, and there was nothing that he could do to stop it. Marcus had worked hard for most of his adult life to ensure that his family would have financial security and a happy, worry-free life. He had never once contemplated that he would have to resort to such extreme measures, bastardizing his only son's anatomy, just to keep him alive in a world that would soon become too bleak and inhabitable to even obtain any happiness from at all.

Sylvia wiped the tears from her face and took Jacob into her arms, gently kissing him upon the forehead.

"You're gonna be OK now my baby boy. You don't have to worry about getting sick like everyone else, and you'll grow big and strong and healthy."

She started crying once again and waited for some form of reaction from Jacob, but there was nothing.

Tremoline healthcare had taken into consideration the lack of communication skills left behind after the 'Wagna procedure' and had designed the 'Text Talk' machine to be given out to patients. It was a lightweight titanium machine that could be worn on the forearm of the patient and was held in place with elasticated fabric. It was a device that could 'speak' for the patient. It had a speaker at the front and a 'qwerty' keyboard on the top. The patient would type everything he or she wanted to say into the keypad of the machine and then press the talk button. For quick responses the machine did have a selection of pre-programmed phrases which were customizable. These included: 'Hello,' 'Good-bye,' 'Please,' and 'Thank you,' etc. These were accessible by pressing down and holding one of the letters for three seconds. It was also possible to adjust the voice style and volume. It was strange that after so many technical advances in recent years that a more sophisticated method of communicating wasn't possible. It occurred to Marcus that maybe they were just working on a budget, or maybe the machine was just a quick afterthought when they realised the side effects of the procedure.

Jacob absolutely detested the machine from the very start and hardly ever used it. Maybe it was the sound of the computerized voice that annoyed him, a constant reminder that he would never speak again. Or maybe it was the fact that Jacob just had nothing left to say. Whenever Jacob really did need to say something, he would just grab the machine and use one of the pre-stored messages. His spelling was not good, and the machine would often misunderstand what he was typing, or it would pronounce it wrong, making him annoyed and frustrated.

Although the 'Wagna procedure' had claimed to guarantee the exponential increase of life expectancy to whoever underwent it, the guarantee was deemed void unless you stuck to a strict regime of maintenance. The patient needed to spend a minimum of three hours outside in the sunlight every day, in order for the solar panels to extract enough power from the sun, and so that the vent could extract sufficient carbon dioxide for it to process. The machine also required a supply of water to complete the photosynthesis process. The back of the machine had a flap that when opened exposed a funnel system. It was recommended that the patient pour between two and three litres of water into this funnel each day. Most patients would achieve this by simply hooking themselves up to a running tap and guestimating the intake.

The Stevensons followed this regime religiously right until their final breaths, teaching Jacob what he needed to do along the way so that when they passed Jacob would be able to look after himself. But when the day finally came that Jacob found his parents pale and motionless on the living room floor, he stopped doing it altogether. He stopped going outside, stopped filling up the funnel, and stopped wanting to live. It was a life without friends or family, a life without fun. A life where he would never again be able to eat, drink, or speak. It was a world without a future where he would forever be considered a freak by anyone who saw him. He curled himself up into a little ball and rocked back and forth on the spot, staring aimlessly at the lifeless corpses of his parents.

It was the same position Tom found the boy in two days later, pale and almost lifeless. Tom had moved back to the estate a few weeks earlier to be close to his parents after the first bombs had started to detonate. The day in question he had kissed his parents good-bye and taken an oxygen canister into town to try and find some form of military presence. Army officers had reached the town a week before and had offered the residents reassurance and hope, but that was before the bombs had started going off. There had been circling planes and explosions for days now. Most of Tom's neighbours had been killed in the blasts and the town was quickly becoming demolished. However hard he searched he found nothing but dead bodies and destruction. There were no signs of the army anywhere. Maybe they had been killed in the blasts too, or maybe they had just retreated back to safety like cowards. After his futile attempt, Tom headed back to his parents' house only to find it turned to rubble in a recent blast. The oxygen in the canister upon his back was now at critical level and sounding off its warning beeps. He needed oxygen quickly. Tom searched desperately for somewhere to go before it was too late. He tried Tina and Tony's house, but they just ignored his desperate cries for help as he had come to expect them to. He then turned to Jacob's house and started banging on the door. There was no reply so he tried the handle. It was unlocked. He flung open the door and the fresh burst of oxygen shot out at him like the back draft of a raging inferno. He quickly slammed the door shut again and ripped the oxygen mask from his face. A long, deep breath later his lungs felt good and rejuvenated. That was when he turned to see little Jacob on the floor.

That day was almost three years ago now and the war had long finished, not because of any peace treaty, or because either side had surrendered or reigned victorious. The war was now over because there was no one left to fight it. Because of disease and destruction the armed forces on all sides were either diminished or dead. Either way they physically couldn't carry on. The bombings died down, the planes stopped circling above, and eventually there was just silence.

Tom had felt such sorrow for little Jacob the day they met that it almost broke his heart. He couldn't even begin to imagine the deep depression that the boy must have felt, only that if it were him in little Jacob's shoes, that he would want someone to just put a bullet through his head. But how could he possibly ask a child if he'd like to die? And more to the point, how could he actually bring himself to go through with it?

Tom quickly removed the option from his mind and decided that he would do the only moral thing that he could, he would try and nurse the poor boy back to health again.

He helped little Jacob get back into his old routine and tried to make his life as happy and fulfilling as possible. He played with him, told him jokes, and tried to teach him how to read and write properly. Occasionally they would go outside during the evening and watch the sunset together as well. Jacob couldn't show his emotions very well, but it was obvious that Tom had made a real difference in his life. Jacob did his routine every day without fail, and without even being asked. He messed around and even started using his 'Text Talk' machine to talk to Tom, on occasions changing the voice setting to different accents to make Tom laugh. He would say silly things like, "How about a chicken tikka fajita amigo?" in a comical Mexican accent. Tom was pleased that Jacob was now in high spirits because of him, and it made him feel better about all the other things that he now felt so guilty about.

CHAPTER ONE (B)

THE DAY after Tom had first discovered Jacob and the house was the same day that he found two more survivors, Susan Brown, and Steven Norton. The two were not related in any way, but had grown so close that they now considered each other brother and sister. The Brown and the Norton families first became friends a long time before the whole mess had started, and had remained close ever since. It was back in 1990 when Susan's mother, Joanne had first met Steven's mother, Linda in a little coffee shop in the town centre. They had immediately got chatting about shoes and clothes. Linda had recently married a young man that she met in her hometown of Hove. His name was Andrew Norton. They had fallen madly in love a few years prior to that and had decided to move to Crawley to buy a new house and start a family together.

Crawley was a completely different place back then; a quiet respectable town, an ideal place to live and raise a family. Back then the estate of Maidenbower hadn't even been designed or contemplated and the land where it now stood was nothing but farmland with grazing cows and sheep. The forty-shop County Mall shopping centre had not been built either, nor had the twenty-screen cinema complex, or any of the violent nightclubs. The town of Crawley was a new town, built back in the '50s for the specific purpose of coping with the impending overspill from London. But London never seemed to stop overflowing and forced Crawley to grow bigger and bigger each passing year.

At the time the two women met Joanne was married to David Brown, and was pregnant with his child. She gave birth later on that same year and named the little girl Melissa. Joanne and David lived together with the baby quite content for a while, and seemed to have a happy marriage. But after just a few years things seemed to become quite edgy between them. David had become quite distant from his wife and child, spending all of his time at work or down at the pub. On the rare occasion that he was at home, he and Joanne would constantly argue and bicker about silly things, usually resulting in David storming out and going back down to the pub again. The initial spark had faded from the relationship and something serious needed to be done to rectify it. The idea of a divorce just seemed like failure to Joanne, so she decided that having another child might solve the problem. So she tried to get pregnant once again, this time hoping she would have a son. She thought that David would bond with a son more, would take him out to play football and talk to him about fast cars and girls. But Joanne knew that having a son was unlikely. Her family had a long history of only having girls. She had traced the family tree right back to the 1800s and most of the children had been girls. It was nearly impossible to trace back any further than that as there were very few men to keep the family name. On her father's side of the family the trend wasn't quite so bad, so she hoped that the genetic tendency to girls would finally be overcome. But in 1993 she inevitably had another baby girl and this one they named Susan Brown.

Even with another baby girl, the marriage did seem to gel back together again, and they were happy again for a while longer. But after some time it eventually degenerated to its previous state, and David started having an affair. He had become close to his secretary at work, and they had been arranging dirty weekends together in seedy hotel rooms, letting Joanne believe they were away on business trips. The affair went on for a good six months or so, until they were caught red-handed by Linda and Andrew, who saw them kissing in a roadside café along the A264.

In 1995 Joanne finally caved in and accepted her failings. She filed for divorce and won full custody of her two little girls. It was never easy for Joanne, coping as a single mother. David seemed to have upped and vanished like a fart in the wind and Joanne never saw a single penny in child support. Linda and Andrew, who felt some level of guilt and responsibility for the break up of the marriage, were very kind and loyal to Joanne. They babysat for her whenever they could, and always bailed Joanne out of any money problems she had. Joanne was grateful to say the least, for how good the two were to her over the years, and made them godparents to her children.

Despite not having a father in the picture, both Susan and Melissa were very happy children. The Nortons had given them more love and affection than their father ever would have, and they didn't miss him at all.

In November 1997 Joanne met an accountant named Mathew Douglas. He was a decent man with old-fashioned values and he completely swept Joanne off her feet. It was love at first sight, you could say, and Mathew absolutely adored the children as well. By that Christmas Mathew had moved in with them and the girls took to him like a fish to water.

Over time, the girls started spending less time with the Nortons, and after a while Linda realized how badly she missed the company of children. She decided that she and Andrew were now ready to have their own, and started trying for a baby. By some strange coincidence, the same week that Linda got pregnant with her first child, Joanne also got pregnant, though this time it was not on purpose. The two women were so entertained by the idea of giving birth together they started spending all their time together once again, watching 'Ricky Lake' on TV together every day, and discussing baby names. After the nine months was over the two women actually went into labour within a few hours of each other and insisted upon adjacent beds in the hospital. The fathers, Mathew and Andrew, had also become very close over the nine months, and had gone out to buy a video camera to record the births. The two were acting like excited little schoolboys when the women first started having contractions, getting every last moment on film. In the end Joanne was the first to give birth, beating Linda by just a few minutes. Joanne gave birth to another baby girl, and gave her the name Jayne Douglas. Linda also gave birth to a baby girl, and named her Shelly, after her grandmother.

The two babies soon grew inseparable as if they were twins or joined at the hip. The two older girls had lovingly taken them under their wings as well and began teaching them the ways of the world from a little girl's point of view.

In 2006 Linda got pregnant by Andrew once again, and this time gave birth to a baby boy they named Steven Norton. Everyone was besotted by him, especially Joanne. She was insanely jealous of Linda for a while, having wanted a baby boy all her life. But after a while the jealousy faded away and Linda let Joanne look after the boy whenever she wanted to. After all, they were like one big happy family and everyone got on like a house on fire.

In 2009 the house that was adjacent to Joanne's went up for sale and the Nortons moved in straight away. Within days of the move, the children had knocked down the dividing fence in the garden and played together every day. Life was like a dream come true for everyone. Everyone was so happy and content with their lives, and wouldn't have changed things for the world.

But like all things that were too good to be true, they were destined to come to a bitter end sooner or later, and they did.

On the morning of September 5, 2013, the two families awoke to find themselves covered in a thin blanket of green fog, with a pungent chemical smell in the air. It was also the same day that Steven was due to start middle school after having worried anxiously about it for months. But the strange ominous fog that lingered in the air forced Linda and Andrew to forbid any of them from leaving the house at all that morning. They locked all the windows and the doors and immediately switched on the news to find out what was going on. Joanne and Mathew had done exactly the same next door, as did most other people on the street, the town, and probably the country too.

The friendly anchorman gave a reassuring smile, and explained there was nothing for them to worry about. But it was obvious that the media knew next to nothing at this stage, and were trying to sound informed by using long complicated words with vague sketchy meanings. What they did know at this stage was that there had been reports during the night of mysterious crop dusting planes, dropping this weird green gas over the country. A few reports that came in had indicated that people had seen the Korean flag on the sides of the planes, though this could not be confirmed at this point. There had also been international sightings of the strange planes over America, Europe, Africa, and parts of Asia too. It had also been confirmed that the U.S. military had shot several of these planes out of the sky for air space violations, though they were not willing to make any official comment about it either. The anchorman then went on to say that the CDC [Centres for Disease Control] had analyzed the gas, and that its initial findings were that it had no detrimental effect to the health or well-being of the human body and that we had nothing to fear from it.

By midday all remnants of the fog had disappeared and everyone assumed that they were now safe. It appeared the CDC's findings were correct and the gas had no direct effect on humans or any mammal at all for that matter. But it would be months before anyone realized the true severity of the incident and the true purpose of the gas. The 'Green Cancer' had arrived.

The event headlined the news for many weeks afterward, but still no revelations were unveiled. The friendly anchorman had now begun to merely report on the various theories, accusations, and propaganda that surrounded the event (as the media always tended to do in the absence of any facts). After a while it slowly began to fade from the news altogether, to be replaced once again by ignorant celebrities making racially prejudiced comments and drunken models exposing themselves as they stumbled incoherently into taxi cabs. But yet, the whole situation had left a strange, bitter taste in people's mouths, an uneasiness to forget. Something was clearly amiss and nothing was as it seemed.

By this time, both Susan and Melissa Brown had both secured themselves full-time employment and were experiencing 'the real world,' as their mother called it. Susan had found herself a job as a hairdresser at the local salon and was excited over the prospect of being trained to do body piercings too. She had already gotten her own tongue pierced a little while before and was eager to share the experience with all of her friends. Melissa was now working as a cashier for Dorothy Perkins in town, but was actively searching for some form of job in the tourism industry, eventually hoping to become an airhostess or holiday rep, even a Butlins red coat would have been a great start at this point. Shelly Norton and Jayne Douglas were both fifteen at this point, and still the best of friends. They were both studying toward their GCSE grades at school, and their favourite subjects were music and drama. They had already made plans with each other to become cabaret performers when they were old enough, forming a cute double act routine that was sure to wow the crowds. Steven had eventually started his middle school classes and was now learning about the Aztecs and Romans, having now overcome the fear and anxiety he had once felt about his new school.

The parents all tried to carry on with life as usual, putting on smiles for the sake of their children, but they couldn't help feeling anxious. The green fog still played heavily on their minds and they could sense that there was something brewing, like the pre-emptive rumbles of a volcano on the brink of eruption.

In that December, when the younger children had broken up for the Christmas break, the effects of the green fog first started to slowly reveal themselves. Flowers and plants all over the country had started to turn a strange luminous green colour and then wilted and died. This had gone undetected at first as a certain amount of plant life was expected to die off during the winter months. But when the lack of greenery became suspiciously dominant, people finally started asking questions. Shortly after that, the friendly anchorman was back on the television again, trying to explain to everyone exactly what was happening. He explained that after the significant amount of plant life dying off in recent days, the government had ordered an investigation into the matter. He then went on to say that a group of organic biologists had found a foreign substance within the plant cells, and that this was a common factor in all the plants that had died. They compared this substance with the gas that was on file from the previous incident, and the two were an exact match. The substance appeared to contain a strange type of carcinogen that had previously never been seen before. The carcinogen was man made and appeared to have been designed to attack the cellular structure of a plant. It acted like a form of plant cancer, which spread throughout the plant, then deposited itself in the plants' pollen, to then be cross-transferred to other plants via bees during pollination. The effect of the carcinogen was that it mutated each cell within the plant and disabled the functional properties of the chloroplast glands, the glands primarily responsible for photosynthesis.

The anchorman had explained all of this to them with his usual friendly smile, and probably didn't even understand the severity of what he was reading on the digital cue card in front of him. He then went on to say that scientists were currently working on a formula that would reverse these effects, and that again, there was no cause for concern.

Despite the anchorman's reassuring tone and insistence not to feel concerned, the nation began to worry. They panicked and caused riots and protests in the streets. It wasn't long before it was apparent that the UK was not the only place plagued with this problem. It was now a worldwide epidemic and no one knew what to do.

What the anchorman had failed to inform the people was the fact that the majority of the world's oxygen supply came not from our trees and plants that grew on the land, but from the vast blanket of algae that grew on the surface of the sea. He failed to mention that these algae had been infected with the green cancer a long time before its presence on the mainland. He also failed to mention that this resource was depleting quicker than anything else, and that the government had been aware of this for years now.

In almost no time at all the levels of carbon dioxide in the air had grown astronomically, and the sales of Tremoline oxygen products soared through the roof. The company was almost unable to keep up with the public's demands for its products, and opened new factories and offices all over the world.

By early 2016 people everywhere were getting critically ill. It was at this time that Tremoline released the PGOGM, and all households across the globe purchased one. The scientists that had previously been employed to find a cure for the 'Green Cancer' had not progressed any further towards their goal, and the world's leaders were losing patience.

Due to the previous allegations that the crop dusting planes had borne the Korean flag, the Americans started to point their fingers at Kim Jong-il, the leader of North Korea (also known as the democratic people's republic of Korea). The position of president of North Korea had been abolished when Kim Jong-il's father died back in 1994. Since then, the highest position in government was head of state, a position that was actually held by Kim Yong Nam. Despite this, Kim Jong-il was still considered the leader of the Democratic Republic of Korea due to his many influential titles including: general secretary of the worker's party of Korea, and supreme commander of the Korean people's army.

Tensions had been high between America and North Korea since the end of World War II, when the country was first divided into the two states (North and South). This tension was heightened still in 2006, when despite sanctions imposed by the United Nations the North Korean army began detonating nuclear weapons in the ocean. The State was then labelled by the U.S. president of the time, George W. Bush, as 'part of the axis of evil', and from that point on the United States kept a very close eye on them.

The United States demanded an answer about the planes and the green fog, and threatened that if Kim Jong-il did not provide explanations and resolutions, that they would commence military action against them. Kim Jong-il did not take too kindly to the threats and vehemently denied the accusations. He warned that if the United States did not back down on their stand, then he would be forced to use their nuclear weapons to protect themselves. American military officers that were still stationed in South Korea following the Korean War, reported back to the United States that there were no signs of the 'Green Cancer' in Korea, and that the population was still fit and healthy. In response to this, the United States did not back down and began preparations for war.

Kim Jong-il then made an announcement to his people that the United States themselves were responsible for the 'Green Cancer.' He told them that the United States had been working on a new biological weapon that had backfired, and they were blaming Korea to save themselves from persecution. Because of this the Koreans gained alliances with Vietnam, Cambodia, and the Republic of China, along with Iran, Iraq, and many other countries that had previously been attacked and hurt by the United States. The Americans then called upon its own allies, including the United

Kingdom, Canada, Australia, and most of Europe. War was then declared.

It was in the months leading up to the war, that the German surgeon Dr. William Wagna, devised his procedure. At the time he was on Tremoline's payroll as the chief medical advisor to their inventors and product designers. He had a sudden brainwave after the PGOGM was invented, and endeavoured to make the machine portable. After realizing that is was not only possible to make the device portable, it was also very easy he realized that certain functions of the human body were no longer necessary. He realized that stopping some of these functions would completely prevent carbon dioxide from entering the body. It was at that point that he came up with the idea of the genetically grown umbilical cord as a medium for the body to receive the output of the PGOGM technology. The 'Wagna Procedure' was born.

Many of the most dedicated officers in the U.S. and British armies volunteered to undergo the trial procedure, believing it would make them stronger and healthier, and therefore giving them the advantage they needed in battle. The trials were all successes and the procedure was then offered to the public at an exorbitant price.

Neither the Browns nor the Nortons could afford this extreme price so the procedure was never considered for their children. Besides, Joanne and Mathew were scared enough for the health and safety of their girls without the added risk of some bizarre and lengthy operation as well. They were petrified at the mere thought of a third world war and the idea of a world with toxic air wasn't very easy to stomach either. Joanne and Mathew themselves were becoming extremely sick by this point, both suffering from shortness of breath, tiredness, and coughing up blood. But they put on a brave face for the sake of their little girls and carried on with life regardless. The girls at this point were still relatively healthy and this was a relief to Joanne and Mathew. They had been forcing the girls to take high doses of oxygen ever since the break of the devastating news. This was in the form of small asthma-like oxygen inhalers which were made by Tremoline and supplied to them free of charge by the NHS. Unbeknownst to the girls, Joanne and Mathew had actually been giving them their own ration of the oxygen inhalers as well, to reassure themselves that they were doing the best that they could for their children.

Next door at the Norton's house emotions were much the same. Linda's husband Andrew had already passed away, and her daughter Shelly was getting very sick. Jayne felt more desperation and worry for Shelley than anyone else. For her it was like losing her conjoined twin and there was nothing she could do to stop her from slipping away.

The friendly anchorman on the television had lost his smile by this point and was looking old and frail. He advised everybody that war had been declared, and to brace themselves for a rocky time ahead. It was at this point that the two families then decided to move into one house together, to offer each other care and support. The space inside was crowded and uncomfortable, but it was important for them to be close to each other at a time like this, when any moment could be their last.

It was North Korea that launched the first nukes, destroying a good part of North America and Canada. America then retaliated and completely destroyed North Korea and a big chunk of China at the same time. Bombs, missiles, and nukes relentlessly flew back and forth over the oceans, soon reaching the point when no one knew who was bombing who, but carried on regardless. But it wasn't until late 2017 that Britain first started to get blown apart.

It was during the air strike of 2019, the same one that took the lives of Tom's parents and the majority of Maidenbower, that the two families found themselves under attack. But there were no air raid shelters or bunkers for miles and miles, nowhere for them to hide. The best that they could do was to hope and pray. First came the noise of buzzing planes in the sky above them, and then the first blast exploded just down the street, completely destroying the local first school and the parade of shops. They all huddled together in one of the bedrooms and prayed to God that they would be spared. The second bomb then hit, much closer this time, the sound so loud that it vibrated violently in their eardrums. Hysteric sobs and tears echoed around the four walls that surrounded them in the small bedroom where they hid, as they clenched each other's hands tightly and begged that their willpower alone would save them. The next blast struck the Norton's house next door and blew it to pieces. The dividing wall between the two houses was also completely destroyed, letting the deadly carbon dioxide gush violently into the house. The bedroom in which the families were hiding was located on the far side of the house, so they were not immediately exposed. But the carbon dioxide travelled though the house quickly and was slowly seeping in under the door. It wasn't long before the PGOGM machine could no longer cope with the high CO_2 levels, causing it to overheat and conk out. At that point, while everyone else was screaming frantically, Mathew suddenly remembered the oxygen canisters that were stored in the living room downstairs. 'Maybe they had survived the blast, maybe not,' he thought. But he knew that they were the only chance for any of them to survive. He covered his mouth and nose with an old handkerchief from his pocket and quickly dashed out the bedroom door, slamming it firmly closed behind him. He ploughed his way through all the fire and rubble, becoming shorter of breath with every step, the sounds of explosions all around him. He reached the living room and scanned it for the canisters. Two of them lay on the carpet in front of him, smashed into tiny little pieces and useless to anyone. He then noticed the others out the corner of his eye. Three oxygen canisters, all intact and gleaming, looking to him like sparkling diamonds in a mine. With his last burst of energy he grabbed the canisters by their straps and made his way back up the burning staircase once again. But it was no good. His lungs were empty and badly in need of oxygen. He reached round in a desperate attempt to grab one of the oxygen masks from a canister, but all remaining energy had left his body. He began to choke on the carbon dioxide and collapsed lifelessly at the top of the stairs with a loud thud.

"Mathew! Mathew!" Steven cried out in shock, as he struggled free from his mother's clutches and ran out the bedroom door. At which point Susan immediately sprung to her feet and ran desperately after him. She found Steven standing at the top of the stairs, staring down at Mathew's corpse collapsed on top of the three canisters. Steven started to choke as Susan came running up behind him, grabbing his arm. At that very second they were deafened by an exploding missile, which sent them tumbling down on top of Mathew's corpse. The bedroom took the full brunt of the explosion which blew everyone inside to pieces, sending dismembered body parts hurtling through the air in a massive mushroom cloud of blood. Susan opened up her eyes again to see blood dripping down from the walls and the mangled body of her mother lying motionless at the foot of the stairs. An assortment of bloody limbs lay scattered down the hallway and a large fiery hole replaced the bedroom. Susan quickly came to her senses and blocked out the ghastly images, then turned to shove an oxygen mask on Steven's pale face, and then another onto her own. They mounted the canisters upon their backs and climbed over the rubble and body parts, out the front door, and ran for their lives. They ran as fast as their bodies would allow, explosions detonating all around them, until they could run no longer, and fell to an unconscious heap on the ground.

It was around this time that Tom was busy tucking little Jacob into bed and trying his best to make the boy feel somewhat safe for the night. He remained by Jacob's bedside throughout the duration of the explosions and prayed that somehow they would be spared. By the time that the morning sun had pierced through the distant horizon, all the noise had come to a stop and a deathly silence had engulfed them. Tom pulled himself up and took a long stare from the bedroom window at the death and destruction that now surrounded him. It was at this point that he realised just how lucky they had been to survive. Tom was so overwhelmed by the miracle that he felt it his duty to search the smouldering rubble outside for anyone else who may have been as lucky. He turned to Jacob in his bed and assured him that everything was going to be alright, before mounting an oxygen canister on his back and venturing out into the desolate aftermath.

After a few unsuccessful hours, Tom was almost ready to give up the search and head back to the house, when his attention became focused in on a faint beeping noise— a familiar beeping noise. It was the sound of an oxygen canister that was low on air. He carefully followed the noise and tried to hone in on its location. The noise appeared to be emanating from a small pile of rubble under a collapsed fence. He bent down and lifted up the wooden structure to find Susan and Steven, lying unconscious on the ground, badly wounded and desperate for oxygen. Susan was bleeding badly from a head wound and had shards of glass protruding from her back. Steven had deep gashes all down his arms and a chunk of wood imbedded in a gouging wound on his leg. Tom clambered over onto the pile of rubble and leaned over to check Susan's pulse, at which point she sprang back to life in a hysteric panic, thrashing her arms about and screaming at the top of her lungs.

Tom embraced her and explained that they would be safe now, but they needed to hurry back to the house before they ran out of air. Susan began to cry with her head in her hands as the memories of what had happened rushed back to her. But her sobbing and despair were shortly overcome with the sight of Steven lying beside her. She clambered to her feet. Tom lifted the unconscious boy into his arms and rushed them back to the house where he tended to their wounds and tried his best to comfort them for their losses.

CHAPTER TWO (A)

THE COMPLETION gauge on the front of the machine slowly ticked over to one hundred percent and the green light turned on at the bottom with a faint beep. The sky outside was a clear radiant blue as far as the eyes could see and the sun had been shining brightly and powerfully all day long. The PGOGM worked very efficiently in these kinds of conditions. The gauge on the machine had already reached one hundred percent twice that day and the air being pumped into the house was fresh and enriched with sweet tasting oxygen. Yet the lack of rain that day had made the mush quite dry and hard to swallow. The perfect mush was usually produced on 'rainbow days,' when it had rained recently but the sun was still bright and strong outside. Everyone knew that if there was a rainbow to be seen that the mush that day would be sweet and moist, like fruit salad mousse. But not today. Today it was going to taste like sprout-flavoured polyfiller. But still, it was important for everyone to eat.

"How much would you like my love? Just a bowlful?" Karen yelled toward the stairs, but her voice echoed away into silence and no sign of a reply returned.

"Jobe? Did you hear me? The gauge is complete . . ." She strained her throat shouting and began to cough, splurting out a few blood droplets into the palm of her hand, at which point the sound of footsteps began to emerge at the top of the stairs.

"Hey Karen, you alright my love?" a deep husky voice quickly replied. "You're supposed to be looking after that chest."

Karen continued coughing away uncontrollably, as more blood came spitting from her mouth.

"Well don't make me shout then!" She replied in a croaky gurgle and stood rubbing her chest uncomfortably. Jobe appeared at the doorway soon after and came rushing in to help her. Jobe was a tall, muscular black man with dark brown eyes, a shaven head, and looking distinctively like an x-gladiator who would no doubt install fear into even the most fearless of contenders. He gave Karen an affectionate kiss on the forehead and started to rub her back soothingly.

"I'm sorry, baby. I couldn't hear you upstairs. Are you alright?" He asked.

"Yeah I'll be alright, Jobe." She replied with a huff, composing herself and swallowing the gloopy blood congealed phlegm at the back of her throat.

"I fucking hate the taste of blood Jobe. It's horrible!" She continued.

"I'm sorry love. I'm sure you'll get better soon." He tried to reassure her, still rubbing her back gently. She turned to Jobe and gave him a strange disapproving frown.

"Oh come on, Jobe, for fuck's sake. I am an adult you know! I don't need you talking bollocks to me like I'm a bloody child whose pet hamster has just snuffed it! How the hell am I ever going to get better, huh? I'm not. I'm going to get worse and worse until I die. And so are you!" She ranted at him angrily.

"Why do you have to be so damn depressing all the time Karen? Have some faith for once!"

"I'll give you sodding faith Jobe! Ahhh . . . Look, I'm sorry, OK? I don't mean to be nasty to you, Jobe. I'm just . . . just . . ."

"I know, I know, it's alright Karen. What can I do to make things better?"

"You tell me Jobe. What the hell can anyone do anymore? We're fucked, and destined to live off that shit for the rest of our lives!" She muttered back at him, pointing over at the mush machine. Jobe smiled in return and gently kissed her forehead again.

"It doesn't always taste that bad you know. It's only on days like these. But I know what you mean Karen. You think I wouldn't kill for a juicy steak right now?"

"Southern fried chicken?" Karen added, starting to present a small smile at the corners of her mouth.

"Cinema hotdog, with fried onions and mustard?" Jobe responded licking his lips.

"Ergh! I'd rather eat this shit!" Karen told him, starting to laugh a little.

"Right, well come on then you silly girl, have a lovely bowl of mush and just imagine that it's a boneless bucket of southern fried chicken."

She smiled back at his persistent high spirits and wrapped her arms around his muscular body, squeezing him gently.

"I thank God that we still have each other. We've been blessed to have that much." He whispered gently into her ear.

"I know Jobe. I'm glad I still have you too. I'm just starting to feel like we really are the last two people on this earth. It seems hopeless you know?"

She broke free from his arms and strolled off into the kitchen, returning a few seconds later with two ceramic bowls and two spoons.

"You want some of this shit then, do ya?" she asked, holding one of the bowls up underneath the nozzle. She then reached up and pulled the cold metal lever down to the bottom. A brown gritty sludge came seeping from the nozzle and deposited itself into the bowl with a plop, 'like diarrhoea straight from a cow's asshole,' she thought to herself.

"Hmm, yummy!" He responded to her smirking, and took the bowl from her hand as she started to dispense another serving.

"No one is coming for us Jobe. You do know that, right?"

"Someone will come eventually Karen. We can't be the only survivors. It just isn't possible. If we've managed to survive this long then there must be more. There just has to be!" He chirped, sitting down on the sofa and scooping up a heaped spoonful of the brown mush.

"Jobe, we've been alone in this damn house now for years. I'm going stir crazy for God's sake. If there was going to be this big rescue thing that you keep imagining, then don't you think they would have come by now? Huh? The bombs stopped years ago, and there hasn't been an announcement on the television since way before that. I haven't seen another human being since Louise died next door."

"I don't know Karen, but we're not super-humans are we? There must be others with a strong immunity out there. Maybe all the other survivors are in the same situation as us. You don't see us going out and rescuing people do you?" He responded to her, before taking another spoonful of the mush into his mouth.

"Yeah, well I don't know. Maybe we should then."

"What are you suggesting?" He inquired with a frown, trying his best to swallow the gritty pulp.

"Well if we're gonna die anyway, why don't we just leave this shit hole behind us and go see what's out there? We have got the truck."

"There's no oxygen in the truck silly! We'll suffocate within seconds! We've only got one oxygen canister left, and that's only got about an hour's worth of gas in it. It would be absolute suicide to go out there."

"Well stop pointing out the problems, Jobe and start coming up with some solutions, would ya, 'cause I ain't prepared to spend my last dying days trapped inside this decrepit two bedroom semi!" Karen blurted out angrily, putting down her bowl and beginning to pace back and forth.

"I'm just as frustrated as you are my love, but it's too dangerous outside, and I don't want to lose you. I've already lost everyone else I've ever cared about and you're all I have left!"

She turned to him with an empathetic smile but continued pacing up and down the room. 'He is right though,' she thought to herself. She had lost everyone too and she knew exactly how he felt. She had lost both of her parents to the carbon dioxide poisoning and her brother had been blown apart in the bombings of 2019, but 'What is the point in being alive, if you have nothing to live for?' She asked herself. Contemplations of suicide had been fluttering in and out of her thoughts for a while now, as it was the only option she would have full control over, and the outcome of which would be certain. She had already made her first attempt at it a few months prior, but the kitchen knife had become too blunt over time to slice through her pulsating wrists and before she had the chance to replace the knife with something more suitable, Jobe had become aware of the situation and intervened. Jobe had been on his guard ever since that day and it was his prime reason for appearing so optimistic in Karen's presence, while just below the surface he was craving the easy option too.

Karen suddenly stopped in mid-pace, as an idea entered her head and she turned to Jobe with a look of impending inquisition.

"Do you have any idea where the Tremoline clinics are?"

"Um, yeah. They said on that commercial thing a while back. There's one in Glasgow, one in Manchester, I think, and one in Brighton. Why do you ask?"

"Well they have warehouses full of stuff— PGOGMs, oxygen canisters, inhalers. Don't you think there might be survivors there?"

"I don't know . . . maybe, I guess. That's of course if the clinics haven't already been destroyed in the blasts."

"Right, so then the nearest clinic would be the Brighton one, yeah?"

"Well, yeah I suppose so, but how the hell we gonna get there? Like I said, we've only got the one oxygen canister left and even if one of us went alone, you couldn't drive to Brighton in an hour, not from here, you'd run out of oxygen and die."

"We got any inhalers left?"

"Not anymore, you used the last one when you had that coughing fit last week."

"Shit! Fucking shit! There must be a way, Jobe! Come on man, think!"

She sat herself down on the couch next to Jobe and bent forward with her head in her hands, rocking back and forth trying to shake her brain into action. Jobe placed his arm around her waist and gave her a gentle squeeze, as he stared aimlessly into the spinning turbine of the PGOGM.

"Hey, I got one idea that might work." Jobe announced all of a sudden.

"What?" She replied abruptly.

Jobe then spent the next half hour clambering over the rooftop and dismounting all the solar panels and CO2 vent. It was hard work, even for a man of his size and the heavy oxygen canister on his back didn't make things any easier either. Eventually he managed to get them all detached and laid them down carefully in the driveway. The water butt that was connected to the PGOGM was far too big and bulky to even attempt to get down. Besides, it didn't look like it was going to rain much anyway. He finally returned through the front door looking sweaty and exhausted and removed his oxygen mask.

"Right, they're off. Now all I have to do is yank that bloody device off the wall, hook it all up and we're good to go."

"This is a great idea Jobe. I don't know why we never thought of it before!" She paused for a second to catch her breath and calm down her excitement. "So once you've disconnected the machine, how much oxygen am I gonna have left in the house?"

"Um, I'm not sure love, probably half an hour or so I would imagine. It shouldn't take me too long to fix it all up though." He replied reassuringly.

She gave him a warm thankful smile, before rushing up to him and giving him a long passionate kiss, her arms wrapped tightly around him like an anaconda.

"This is gonna work Jobe I know it. I love you so much you know!"

"I love you too Karen, I'm just hoping that when we get there the building hasn't already been destroyed, because when all the petrol runs out we'll be living in the truck for the rest of our lives!"

"Don't be so pessimistic. It's your turn to have some faith now!" She told him with a cheeky smirk. He smiled back, and nodded, trying to remember how long it had been since he had seen her this excited about something.

"I couldn't manage to get the water butt down from the roof I'm afraid, so eat up all your mush. I don't know when we'll be able to eat again."

She picked up the bowl from the side and looked down at the unappetizing brown sludge.

"Do I have to?" She replied.

"Yes, you do! And have you got any idea where the keys to the truck are?"

"Upstairs in the drawer I think— haven't needed them in a while now!"

"No, I know. I hope the truck's battery hasn't discharged too much, or we aren't going anywhere."

"Oh I've got faith in the old Dodge, had it for ten years now and it's never let me down once."

Jobe smiled back at her one last time and made his way upstairs for the keys.

"Which drawer?" He bellowed down the stairs.

"Bedside cabinet, third drawer down." She yelled back at him, feeling the pain in her lungs slowly return, but hiding it from his attention.

He came rushing back down the stairs a few moments later with the distinct jingling of keys in his pocket. He then proceeded to wrench the heavy machine from its wall brackets, leaving behind four gaping rawl-plug holes and ripped wallpaper.

"You ready then my love?" He asked, putting the oxygen canister upon his back.

"Go for it, and don't take too long."

"I'll be as quick as I can, promise." He assured her, pulling the oxygen mask back over his face. Karen covered her mouth and nose with the sleeve of her black cardigan, and opened the front door for

Jobe. He lifted up the PGOGM with all of his might, and staggered out the door with it.

Karen sat herself down upon the couch and patiently awaited his return while at the same time trying her best to keep her breathing to a minimum. The carbon dioxide levels in the room slowly started to rise, and she could feel it too. Jobe had been gone much longer than she had expected now. 'Maybe he was having trouble fitting the machine in, but he'd better hurry up, or he is going to run out of oxygen too.' She pondered to herself.

A few moments later she heard the reassuring sound of the old Dodge's engine revving up, and finally let out a sigh of relief. Jobe then appeared at the door again and declared the task complete. He placed the oxygen mask on Karen's face, covered his own with his hand, and rushed her out to the truck.

The red Dodge Dakota looked old and frail compared to Karen's memory of it, like it had somehow aged like everyone else. It was covered in dust and dirt and rust had started to appear around the rear wheel trims, but she was still happy to see it, like being reunited with an old pal. Jobe had fixed the solar panels and carbon dioxide vent from the house to the back of the truck with thick gaffer tape, and then threaded the leads into the cab through a small gap behind the seats. The Machine itself was sitting on the backseats of the truck and was pumping away as loud as a pneumatic drill. Even with the windows and doors completely shut, there was still not an airtight seal within the truck, so consequently carbon dioxide was slowly seeping in. Jobe had turned the machine up to full blast to compensate for this, making it vibrate and shake violently all over the place.

Karen looked at him and smiled with approval. She then said something inaudible over the sound of the machine and reached for something in her pocket. Jobe put the truck into first gear and began to pull away from the drive. All of a sudden 'Like a Virgin' by Madonna started pelting out of the truck's rear four-by-nine speakers at full volume. Jobe jumped with surprise and turned to Karen with a look of angry disapproval. Karen giggled back at him like an excited schoolgirl and started singing along to the song. It was nice to finally see her happy, even if just for a moment, so he laughed it off and continued on his way to the M23.

CHAPTER TWO (B)

IT WAS at 10.50 p.m. on the eighth of December 1980 that eccentric fan Mark Chapman discharged four bullets from his revolver into the body of legendary music icon John Lennon. This was a good three and a half years before Tom was even born, but strangely enough, John Lennon became one of Tom's favourite artists of all time. Tom sometimes felt annoyed that Lennon was the one to get shot when he was clearly the most talented and influential member of the Beatles. 'Why couldn't it have been Paul McCartney to get killed? He deserved to die for that rubbish he recorded with Wings back in the eighties,' Tom always thought. Lennon would have made a real difference to the world in Tom's eyes. With his idealistic views and opinions, his anti-war protests, and influential followings he may have even prevented the whole war on Iraq back in 2005 and maybe even the whole mess now. But Paul McCartney had done almost nothing good for the world at all, having wasted his later life married to a one-legged ex-porn star that eventually divorced him and took half of his multimillion pound empire.

Tom's Grandfather Dunn had been a big fan of the Beatles since they first stepped into the limelight back in the sixties, and even had the pleasure of seeing them live in Liverpool when they had first got together in a small underground club called The Cavern. Grandfather Dunn had such a great passion for the Beatles' music that he always tried his best to convert people to Beatle-mania. His wife Samantha, however, could not be converted. No matter how hard he tried over the years, she couldn't be lured away from her Elvis Presley obsessions. This tended to be the cause of a few mild tiffs over the years, but these were generally just laughed off and forgotten about.

Amongst the other things that Grandfather Dunn left Tom when he died was 'The White Album' on mint condition vinyl. It was then that Tom really got into the Beatles, having bought all thirteen of their albums by the end of that same year. He also got heavily into The Rolling Stones, The Who, and Led Zeppelin and appreciated their raw talent and passion for their work. He pretty much hated all the modern-day music that had emerged over the years. It all seemed like hashed together synthesised garbage and not like 'real' music at all. The singers and rappers just seemed to curse obscenities and promote drugs and violence, with nothing amiable to say. With the exception of the Brit-pop phase of Oasis and Blur in the mid-nineties,

Tom believed music had embarked on a degenerative one-way downward spiral into depravity.

It was lucky for Tom that Jacob's parents had a very similar taste in music. Aside from the fact that the house had breathable air and wasn't blown to bits, the thing that Tom was most pleased about when he moved in was the fact that they had the entire Beatles collection on CD. In fact, they appeared to have albums from almost every band that Tom loved, their entire collection amounting to over a hundred CDs.

Tom was also pleased that the power grids in the area had somehow survived the bombings, and that the house was still supplied with electricity. It was lucky for them that it had actually become illegal to switch off the electricity of an occupied house back in 2008, after a small child had died from hypothermia when his poor mother had failed to pay the bill. There was also a lot of commotion that same year regarding 'Carbon Footprints' and how we were damaging the environment. In response to this, all the main electricity companies started to source their electricity from wind farms and vast solar panels, which now made the process of supply fully automated and without the need for any human presence at all.

The house was still being supplied with running water as well. Though the supply was still plentiful, the quality and safety of the water was highly debatable. No one had manned the reservoirs in years, and consequently the water had not been purified or chlorinated since. They didn't like to think what kinds of things were now floating on the surface of the reservoir. It probably had an array of dead animals and pollution in it, but they all had to drink. Jacob especially needed a supply of water. To resolve this problem, they had all become accustomed to boiling and filtering the water every time they needed it. They were far from convinced that this was sufficient enough to kill all the germs and bacteria in the water, but there wasn't much more that any of them could do.

It was 'Happiness is a warm gun' from 'The White Album' that Tom had playing on the stereo that day as he scribbled away in his little black book. The book was a thick A5-sized notepad which was bound in a leather folder and sealed together with a brass popper clip. He had been writing away in the same book now for years, though it was a mystery to the rest of the group what exactly he was writing. It was one thing that Tom considered to be very private and personal to him and he became very angry and rude whenever questioned over it. He had finally relented on one occasion and had explained to them that it was kind of like a diary, or journal of events that he liked to jot down to keep him sane. Before the whole mess first started Tom wrote in the book quite often, having filled most of the pages before he had even arrived at the house. But as time went on he wrote in the book less and less. With every day much the same as the one before it, there didn't seem much left to write about. Tom usually kept the book in the inside pocket of his leather jacket, and never let the book out of his sight.

The fact that Tom was so possessive and secretive about the enigmatic book made Susan all the more eager to read it. She thought it was strange that a man would keep a diary and even stranger that he would become so emotional over it. Given the chance, Susan would have read through the book at her earliest convenience, but Tom always made certain that she never got the opportunity.

While Tom was busy scribbling away that day, the two kids were in the front room watching a DVD together. As well as the CDs, Jacob's parents also had an extensive collection of DVDs. They had everything from Hitchcock's 'Psycho' to Disney's 'The Lion King' to 'Friday the 13th part 16.' The kids seemed to spend most of their time watching the DVDs, and had probably watched each and every one about ten times over. Jacob had developed a taste for the horror films, his favourite being Steven King's 'The Shining,' about a little boy trapped inside a haunted hotel with his psychotic father trying to kill him. Tom and Susan were quite hesitant at first about letting little Jacob watch such violent and disturbing films and tried their best to keep them from him, but eventually they realized that he had probably experienced more horror in his lifetime than what could ever be portrayed in any film, and so they let him get on with it. Steven usually preferred to watch teen comedies and slapstick films from the turn of the millennium. It made him laugh at the thought of what mischief he would have got up to himself when he became a teenager, the wild parties that he would have thrown with his stupid college mates and the sticky situations that they would have to get out of. Because of their obvious differences in preference, it was very rare to see the both of them enjoying the same film, but at that moment they were sitting together watching the film 'Severance,' which blended comedy and horror together so faultlessly that it pleased them both to watch.

Susan during this time was upstairs having a bath. It had taken her over an hour to fill up the bath with boiled and filtered water from the kettle, and was barely luke-warm by the time it was full enough to get in. She bathed herself almost every other day to try and keep clean and nice smelling. But they had completely run out of deodorant, soap, and shampoo a very long time ago, so everyone had a slight degree of funky smell to them. Due to the lack of shampoo in the house, the men had all shaved their heads so that their hair didn't get greasy and horrible. Susan had refused to do this and tried her best to keep it clean, but it inevitably looked a little oily at times.

Once Tom had finished his journal entry he popped the folder closed and slid it securely back into his coat pocket. He then scoffed down a large bowl of gritty mush from the machine, before venturing out with his oxygen canister and starting his daily stroll.

He was just approaching the remains of the old Audi car showroom when he first heard the noise coming from the motorway. The world had become a very quiet place since the war had ended. All animal and bird life were now dead, there were no sounds of traffic, no people, nothing. Normally there was complete silence for as far as you could hear, but not today. The sound was clear and loud, and Tom almost didn't believe that he was hearing it at first.

'Beautiful Stranger' by Madonna was quietly radiating from the distance, over the hill and past the showroom where he was standing. A look of excitement and joy quickly replaced that of confusion and disbelief upon his face. He ran off in the direction of the sound, past the showroom and over the hill. At the peak of the hill he could look down on the motorway below and the red Dodge Dakota was just sitting there in the middle of the road, the music emanating from within the vehicle. Tom immediately noticed the solar panels and carbon dioxide vent on the back of the truck and was left astounded by the inventiveness. As he got closer to the car he could just start to make out its passengers: a big muscular black guy in the driver's side, and a chubby curly haired woman in the passenger seat, both of them appearing to be either dead or asleep. Tom ran up close to the truck and banged on the windscreen gently with his knuckles. The two sleeping passengers then awoke instantaneously in a confused daze and stared back at him with equal shock and disbelief. Once they came to their senses and realized that they had found another survivor, the smiles on their faces grew from ear to ear. They started waving at Tom through the glass.

"I'll go and get you some air," Tom yelled to them through the face mask, but the noise was muffled and inaudible. Karen quickly reached down for the stereo's volume control and Tom yelled to them again. Karen and Jobe understood this time, and returned a thumb's up to him with a grateful smile. He turned around and pelted back to the house, over the hill, past the showroom, the old burnt out pub, the piles of rubble, and in through the front door.

"I've found people! Real people!" Tom yelled out at the top of his lungs.

Susan was just drying herself down at this point and came flying out of the bathroom completely naked, quickly dashing back in for a towel once she had realised her mistake.

"You what? People? Where?" She blurted out excitedly.

"On the motorway, in a truck, two of them!" He replied, as he rushed about trying to find two more canisters.

"In a truck? How is that possible? Are they OK? How are they breathing?"

"They got the PGOGM hooked up to the truck. It's ingenious I tell you! I'll be back in a minute."

With that, Tom quickly popped the oxygen mask over his face and headed back out the front door again with the other two canisters over his shoulder.

"You hear that guys? We got visitors!" Susan called out to the kids and stood in the hallway for a while with a smile on her face, before then looking down at the towel wrapped around her.

"Shit, I'd better get some clothes on!" She then blurted out.

Darkness turned to light as the sun shot into the sky like a flare gun shot from the horizon, stopping dead in its tracks directly above and illuminating everything around. It was the most beautiful day you could ever imagine. There wasn't a single cloud in sight, nothing but pure blue skies for as far as you could see. The day was warm, not so hot that you felt uncomfortable and sweaty, but hot enough that you could wander around all day in just a T-shirt and wouldn't once feel the slightest chill. The air smelt good, fresh, like country air- full of the smells of wild flowers and the faint whiff of morning-baked bread rising in the oven. Noises then filled the ambiance in stereo sound all around Tom. Crickets buzzed around at his feet, ignorant to his presence. The sound of chirping birds echoed from the trees, singing away in a joyous high pitched harmonic tweet. A fat purple dragonfly then flew into sight, landing on Tom's shoulder as if he were a branch, and then fluttered away again into the air. A slight rustling in the bushes then drew his attention, as a big fluffy red squirrel grabbed a nut from the ground and scurried off to the top of a nearby tree to store it away.

Tom was stunned in disbelief, as a warm fuzzy feeling of content entered him and all he could do was smile. In front of him were fields upon fields of fresh yellow corn, each cob ripened to perfection and glistening under the warm sun. The smell of fresh bread whiffed past his nose again, and drew his eyes to a small wooden cabin in the middle of the cornfields, its straw rooftop peaking just above the cornrows.

His curiosity grew, as he started to gently push aside the corn and head off for the cabin. Before long he reached the end of the corn and emerged into a small rectangular clearing. Just in front of the cabin door sat an old man, swinging back and forth gently in an old rocking chair made of oak. His head was hung low and long silver hair covered his face. In his hand he was clutching something tightly. Tom hurried towards the man inquisitively.

"Excuse me sir, where am I? What is this place?" Tom asked, as he stopped in front of the man.

The man slowly lifted his head from its solemn hanging and gave Tom a stern look in the eyes. Tom recognised the face immediately. It was an old face from his past, a face that would normally only bear a smile, a face that would normally make you feel welcome and safe, but not now. Now the face was frightening and bitter, only showing anger and disappointment. The old man continued his judgmental stare until Tom's grin slowly sunk from his face, and he hung his head low in shame.

"Grandfather? How could this be? . . . You're . . ."

"DEAD?" The old man roared, his face red with anger and veins bulging from his forehead as if they might explode. Tom then raised his head again to bear his Grandfather's stare, a tear now forming in his eye. The old man then revealed what was concealed in his hand and threw it to the floor in rage. It was his cherished Victoria Cross.

"Grandfather, I . . ." Tom began beggingly. The old man then stopped rocking in his chair and suddenly started to choke, as if a cherry pip was stuck in his windpipe. Tom moved to help when suddenly the old man began to vomit out a luminous green fog from his mouth and nose. The old man thrashed about violently as the gas escaped his body. It expelled with speed and drifted up, like steam from a boiling kettle. It then faded away into the air as the man grew motionless and slumped forward in the chair.

"Grandfather?" Tom uttered worryingly and placed his hand on the old man's shoulder with a brittle crunching sound. With no response, Tom started to shake his grandfather gently, when the old man's body suddenly cracked open like a china doll, and then shattered apart to a fine dust upon the floor. A putrid smell then suddenly started to emanate from the man's ashes, a smell of rancid methane and stomach acid, which immediately shot up Tom's nose. He covered his mouth with disgust and stumbled backwards.

Lightening then crackled above him and the sky grew overcast with black clouds. The air quickly turned bitter cold and breezy and emanated the smell of car emissions and smouldering tar. The singing of the birds suddenly turned to screaming, as if the birds were in great agonising pain, screaming out for help. The rows of corn started to wilt over before suddenly bursting into flames, emitting thick black smoke that bellowed into the sky.

The sound of exploding gunpowder then startled him from behind, and he spun around, disorientated and scared. He saw blood dripping down slowly from a bullet wound in the forehead of a young Korean girl, a look of confusion and betrayal on her face. Her bottom lip quivered, as if she was trying to speak, but no sound emerged. Her body then dropped to the floor in a heap and began to melt away into the dirt, like water being sucked into a vacuum-like plughole. Tom suddenly spotted a pathway through the corn and took his opportunity to escape before he was consumed by the fire. But he couldn't run as his feet kept getting stuck in the dirt below, as if the ground were made of glue that gripped hold of him tightly. He struggled hard to pull each leg free and ploughed forward towards the edge of the cornfield. The flames were roaring loudly with life by this point, and towered above him on each side of the path. They crackled and blazed like a bonfire display, violently spitting out hot sparks of wood at him until he finally reached the end of the path, and out of the burning corn. He stopped to catch his breath but suddenly found the air too hard to breathe. His hair felt completely singed and frazzled from the flames and his skin felt burnt and blistered all over. He panted and panted, but just couldn't manage to catch his breath. He then looked up to see a figure appearing from the flames, a tall shadowy figure dressed in a dark hooded cloak and bearing a scythe. Its menacing eye sockets glowed red and yellow with the flickers of the flames, as it slowly started to approach him. Tom turned to run from the deathly figure, and the grass beneath his feet quickly crumbled away to dust, leaving behind a barren desert ground. He saw the figure getting closer and desperately tried to increase his speed, when the ground beneath him started to crack open, small cracks at first, turning to crumbling crater-sized holes. Tom leapt and bounded over the cracks at first, but they kept growing bigger and wider until they became the size of great canyons and he was forced to stop in his tracks.

An enormous thundering bolt of lightning then struck the ground in front of him, sending him crashing onto his back with a spine crunching snap. He was paralysed all over, as the shadowy figure appeared beside him and towered over him to pass judgment. The skin upon its ghastly face had all dried up and flaked away, leaving behind a hideous skull with maggots crawling from its eye sockets. Tom immediately urinated in his trousers with utter fear and tried to release a petrified scream, but his mouth wouldn't open. He reached up to feel his face to find his lips completely sown together with thick ragged cotton. The figure then laughed down at him and held the scythe up high about his head, when . . .

"Tom? . . . TOM!"

"Uh yeah, what was that?" He responded in a confused sleepy daze.

"You mind staying awake for our guests, huh?" Susan asked jokingly, giving him a little smirk.

"Oh, God I'm so sorry, you must think I'm so rude. I guess I don't have a lot of energy lately," he apologised to Karen and Jobe, rubbing his face. Karen gave him a little smile in return and placed her hand on top of his.

"Hey, don't worry about it Tom, you're forgiven this time but only because you saved our lives today. I guess we're all feeling a little unhealthy lately," she said, squeezing his hand a little then letting go.

"So come on, tell us everything. We haven't spoken to other people in years now. It's so exciting to have you here. Where did you come from? And where were you heading to in that truck?" Susan enquired excitedly.

"We ain't spoken to no one since about that time either. We were starting to think we were the last ones, ya know?" Jobe responded.

"Yeah we know that feeling well, I mean we actually do have neighbours over the road there, but they've turned a bit weird over the years and won't even speak to us." Tom added.

"We used to have neighbours at one point too. We were one of four houses that survived the blasts," Karen told them.

"So where are they now then? You didn't leave them behind?" Susan asked with a confused frown upon her face.

"No, no, we'd never do that. They've all passed away now. The girl that lived next to us, Louise was her name, we just found her dead one morning, lying lifeless on the couch. It could have just been the carbon dioxide I guess, but we found an empty bottle of sleeping pills as well, so we don't really know. And then there were the two Asian guys that lived at the end of our street, Rezwan and Mohammed, brothers. They'd already lost their whole family. Somehow they'd acquired loads of oxygen canisters in their house, so just decided one day to go out and search for help. We haven't seen them since." Jobe explained.

"So, you don't actually know that they're dead then do you? How do you know they didn't find help?" Tom asked, as he got up and headed towards the kitchen. "Anyone want a glass of water?" He added before Jobe could respond to the question.

"Yeah, I'd love one." Karen replied.

"Yes, please bro'." Jobe added, giving Tom the thumbs up.

"Susan?"

"Um no, I'm OK thanks Tom."

Tom then started to pour out three glasses from the jug of water they had boiled and filtered that morning. The water was normally boiled and filtered at least three times before they drank it, but Tom had been lazy and only done it twice that day. Consequently, the water had a slight yellow tinge to it, but it would have to do.

"Well we didn't know at first, Tom. Like you said, we thought they may be OK. They might have reached someplace, and that's what we liked to think." Jobe finally replied to the question.

"So what makes you think differently now, Jobe?" Susan enquired.

"Because we found dead bodies today, just a few metres from their house, and I'm pretty damn sure it was them." Karen answered hesitantly, obviously not wanting to talk about it anymore.

"It's alright, baby." Jobe whispered into her ear, giving her a little kiss on the temple.

"So what happened to them?" Tom asked gingerly, as he returned to the room with the water. "Did they run out of oxygen or something?" He sat down and took a sip from the glass.

"No . . . No, I don't think so I'm afraid." Jobe answered, trying to choose his words carefully.

"What do you mean? What happened?" Susan insisted.

"We left our house this morning for the first time in years, and like Karen said, we found the bodies a few metres down the road, except, it didn't look like they had run out of oxygen to me. It looked like they had been attacked, savagely." Jobe explained.

"Attacked? Attacked by whom?" Tom pried further.

"I dunno bro', but whoever or whatever it was didn't just kill them, it completely ripped them apart. There were parts of them everywhere."

"Jobe stop! Please, I don't wanna have to picture that sight again," Karen interrupted.

"OK, I'm sorry baby." He whispered to her, and then turned back to Tom and Susan. "So I don't know what happened to them, but it wasn't a lack of oxygen for sure."

Tom and Susan then gave each other a look that was a mixture of disappointment and confirmation before Tom turned back to Jobe to share his opinion.

"I think I know what happened to them, Jobe." He announced regretfully.

"What?" Karen replied with surprise.

"It happened a while before me and Susan first met, just after the bombings started here in the UK. I was out for a walk with an old college friend of mine when we were attacked from behind. It was these men in religious robes, their mouths and noses all sewn shut just like little Jacob over there. They spoke to us through those little 'Text Talk' devices and said they had been sent by God to kill us. The leader then got out a ceremonial dagger and came after us. We ran obviously, but they were too strong, too quick. I got sliced around the side with the dagger and fell to the ground. I saw a lead pipe next to me so I grabbed it and cracked the guy's head open with it. My friend by this point was already dead, so I ran for my life and didn't stop running until I was home again. When I went back the next day I found his body in the same state you were talking about." Tom explained.

"Jesus, I didn't believe what they had said about those guys, I thought they were just making it up— Jehovah Witnesses?" Jobe asked.

"Well, Jehovah's Enforcers, but yeah. I didn't believe it either until I experienced it. The thing is these guys have all had the Wagna procedure so they're all much healthier and stronger than we are. There are probably more of them that have survived things than anyone else. For once, we're the minority. Jacob said he saw some more of them out the window a few nights back too. He's probably mistaken you know, mind playing tricks on you and stuff, but I'd watch your backs anyway."

"As if there wasn't enough to worry about, right?" Susan added.

"So what's the deal with the kids anyway? Are they yours?" Karen enquired.

"No, the older one is Steven. He's my brother, sort of. And the one that's had the operation is Jacob." Susan responded.

"Jacob came with the house as it goes." Tom jumped in. "His parents were quite well off, as you can see by all the expensive furniture and stuff. They thought they were doing the right thing for Jacob by making him have the op. They died from the poisoning a few days before my home was destroyed, and I came here for shelter. I found their bodies in the middle of the room. Little Jacob was in quite a state, as you can imagine."

"Sounds awful, poor kid," Karen replied sympathetically.

"We're doing our best for him. I think he's quite a happy little kid now, as happy as possible anyway. So what about you then? Where did you say you came from again?" Susan enquired.

"We lived in a run down two bedroom semi up in Bromley," Jobe replied with a strangely proud enthusiasm.

"Oh right, OK. So where the hell were you going in the truck?" Tom asked.

"Well, Karen had this idea that other survivors may have headed for the Tremoline clinics, due to the fact that they store all the oxygen products and stuff in the warehouses. So we were trying to get down to the Brighton clinic." Jobe explained to them.

"Sounds like a good plan. So what happened?" Tom asked.

"The old trusty Dodge ran out of fucking gas, didn't it?" Karen replied and started to giggle, finally seeing the funny side of it.

"Ha, oh never mind. Hey, at least you had a plan. We've had no idea what to do." Susan replied, starting to giggle along with Karen.

"I tell you, it must have been an act of God for us to run out of fuel where we did though. It must have been a one in a million chance of breaking down where other survivors were. We're so grateful." Jobe announced more seriously.

"Nah, God had nothing to do with it Jobe, it was Madonna that saved our lives!" Karen quickly added, and burst out into full laughter.

CHAPTER THREE

TOM'S RECURRING dream haunted him again that night. It woke him up at 2:00 a.m. in a cold shivering sweat with the image of the bleeding Korean girl vividly branded in the back of his mind.

The dream had been recurring on and off for a good year now, but never grew less frightening to him. The scenario was mostly the same each time, without Tom even realizing that he was dreaming. He would normally be unable to stop himself from entering the corn-fields or from doing anything differently at all, but lately the dream had started to become more and more lucid to him. That was how it was that night. The sun shot into the sky and the birds and animals were bouncing about joyously. Tom knew from the start what was coming, he knew he was in the dream world, and he had full control of his actions. The dream always started off so pleasantly, and even though he knew it wouldn't last, he still revelled in the tranquillity of nature, if only for a few seconds. But before long everything started to burn, as it always did, and no matter how fast he ran, or what direction he headed off in, the skeletal figure in the black cloak always caught up with him.

He sat up in bed, trembling from the cold sweat and tried to calm himself down. Before long he came to his senses again and it was at this point that he noticed the banging noise coming from the bedroom across the hall. It was the bedroom that they had given to Jobe and Karen to stay in. The banging was constant and rhythmic, and before long the banging was accompanied by heavy breathing and it was obvious what was going on. He turned to look at Susan lying next to him. She was already awake.

"They've been going at it for almost an hour now," she told him apathetically.

"Really? Ha! They're obviously worry-free about things," Tom responded light heartedly.

"Bloody inconsiderate about things you mean!" Susan added grumpily.

An increasingly loud and husky moaning then started and was closely followed by female moaning too.

"Oh for God's sake!" Susan grumbled, and pulled the pillow over her head.

It wasn't long after Tom had found Susan and Steven crushed under that fencing, that he first started to feel an attraction for her.

She was sweet and nice and her natural beauty radiated through the effects of the carbon dioxide. Susan had felt completely overwhelmed by how caring and considerate Tom was to her and Steven and had fallen for him too. Maybe it was love, but more likely it was just comfort in a desperate situation. It hadn't been long before they'd started kissing and cuddling and sharing a bed together. They had enjoyed many passionate romps together at the start, but there was something in the back of Tom's mind that made him feel slightly uneasy about it. Maybe he felt it too unsafe to have sex without protection, for there would have been no means to prevent a pregnancy and he hadn't quite mastered the 'pulling out' technique. What would happen if she got pregnant? There was no morning after pill, no abortion clinics, no midwifes. It just seemed a very bad idea, regardless of his desires. Eventually neither of them cared about it anymore. It was just nice to have each other close. Despite this, the banging through the walls and the moaning was still an annoying reminder.

Tom soon managed to get back to sleep again without too much trouble and woke up again just after nine. Susan's side of the bed was already vacant by this point and her slippers were missing from the floor. Tom lay there in bed for a while longer, staring up at the ceiling and listening to the therapeutic tapping of rain against his window pane. He let out a long sigh and a yawn, before reaching for his jacket which lay next to the bed, and taking out his little black book. There was a lot that he needed to jot down that morning. The arrival of Jobe and Karen in the house was the most exciting thing that had happened in a very long time.

He popped open the leather folder and flicked through to an

available page near the end. He unclipped a black ballpoint pen from the spine of the folder and removed its lid ready to write. Recently Tom had found it hard to write anything in his book at all. His attitude and mindset had completely changed since that first day he brought it home from the hospital gift shop and this change had completely rendered the book's initial purpose redundant.

He remembered back to his very first entry in the book and how effortlessly he could fill the pages with such hateful rantings about people and the world. 'But those days were over,' he told himself. He had wanted so badly to just throw the book away and burn it, to finally put an end to that chapter of his life and remove the reminder of such evil thoughts that had once consumed his consciousness. But yet deep inside he knew that he would never be able to wash his hands clean so easily, and even if the book was gone, his memories would always remain.

He placed the black pen down onto the paper, scribbled down the date, and then started a new entry. After a mere few words in, the ink flow started to become intermittent and patchy. Tom pressed down harder on the page to compensate for this, but soon enough the ink completely ran out and left behind nothing but slight indents of the intended words.

"Oh for God's sake!" He moaned, and threw the pen on the floor with frustration.

"Tom? You awake now?" A voice called from downstairs. Tom let out a sigh of surrender and finally got up out the bed.

"Yeah, yeah I'm up," he replied, walking out of the room onto the landing.

"You looked out the window this morning babe?" Susan called from the bottom of the staircase.

"No, but I can hear it. It's raining at last!" Tom replied in a slightly patronizing tone.

"It isn't just rain smart-arse, take a look." Susan replied, and walked off out of sight. Tom let out another long yawn and made his way through the bedroom towards the window.

"Hey, look at that!" He exclaimed with an enlightened euphoric smile.

The powerful rays of the sun had pierced their way through the falling rain and split the droplets into a magnificent array of colours which covered the sky for miles. It was the first rainbow that had appeared in months and months of waiting. It was beautiful, and the mush was going to taste the best it ever had.

He pulled on a pair of jeans and a t-shirt from his bedside drawers and hurried down the stairs, only to find that Steven had beaten him to the dining table and was scoffing away at a bowl of mush.

"Morning Steven, so how's it taste this morning?" He asked.

"Mm, yeah! Best it's tasted in ages!" Steven replied with a mouthful of the stuff dribbling from the corners of his mouth.

Tom gave him a smile and then headed off towards the kitchen. He found Susan standing in front of the kitchen sink with the cold water tap gushing out a horrible yellowy brown fluid with bits of black grit floating on the top. He watched as she filled the water into a jug and started to hand pick out all the big bits.

"G'morning gorgeous!" He whispered from behind, as he crept up and landed a gentle kiss upon the side of her neck.

"Morning Tom, you're in a good mood now I see." She replied, turning round to hug him.

"Can you blame me with a sky like that? Have you tried some yet?"

"No, not yet. Jobe and Karen had some earlier. They said it was delicious, and Steven's having some now. Just waiting for the gauge to complete again and we'll have some together, wont be long now." She explained with a smile.

"It's silly the little things we get excited about, like little kids." He confessed as he wandered back off into the living room again.

He made a beeline for the Mush machine and peered up at the completion gauge, eighty-two percent. He was glad that he didn't have to wait long. He was too excited to be made to wait for ages. Jobe was sitting on the couch admiring Karen's bottom at this point, as she bent over to look through the large collection of CDs in the rack.

"Morning you two, how are we?" Tom asked.

"Hey Tom," Karen replied, turning her attention away from the CDs for just a second.

"Yeah, G'morning bro'. How you doing this morning?" Jobe asked in return.

"Bit tired ya know, didn't get a lot of sleep." Tom replied.

"Sorry bro,' we didn't keep you up did we?" Jobe asked, trying not to smirk.

"No, you're okay Jobe, just bad dreams ya know?" Tom replied.

"Bad dreams huh? Repressing something? Something on your mind?" Jobe asked.

"No, I'm good, thank you."

At that point the buzzer sounded on the completion gauge and Tom hurried excitedly back into the kitchen.

"Hey, come on it's ready! You can finish off that horrible water later." He gestured to Susan, giving her a gentle hug from behind. She turned to face him again and wiped her hands dry on her jeans.

"OK," she replied.

She grabbed two bowls and two spoons from the worktop and followed Tom back into the living room. Steven had completely finished off his bowl of mush at this point and was currently licking the remnants from the side of the bowl.

"That good is it?" Susan asked jokingly.

"It's amazing Suzie. Hurry up 'cause I want another bowl!" Steven replied, placing the empty bowl back down on the table and letting out a satisfied grunt.

"Calm down Steven, if the weather keeps up like this, we'll be able to stuff our faces silly all day!" She said, passing one of the bowls to Tom.

Tom pressed the green reset button on the machine and the gauge reverted back to zero again. Holding one of the bowls under the dispensing spout, he pulled down upon the metal lever on the right of the machine and the mush slowly began to dispense. The colour of the mush was a pale shade of pink and it had a light and fluffy texture like strawberry mousse, and it smelt sweet and delicious to him. Tom smiled at the glorious sight of it and filled the bowl up to the point of overflowing.

"There you go Susan, enjoy!" Tom said, passing the bowl over to her and taking the second one to fill.

Karen finished looking through the CD collection and sat down on the couch reading the track listings from one of the cases.

"It's disgraceful, over a hundred CDs here, and not a single Madonna album. What were these people like?" Karen asked, half jokingly.

"Yeah sorry about that Karen. I think Jacob's mum was more of a Kylie fan. She's got everything there from 'Locomotion' to all that new rubbish she made after her cancer scare. You not like Kylie then?" Tom responded sloppily between mouthfuls of the delicious mush.

"Oh come on, you can't even compare Kylie with Madonna. Madonna is a goddess!" Karen insisted.

"They're both a load of crap if you ask me!" Tom responded, gulping down the last spoonful of the mush. Susan giggled at the comment and gave him a slap on the wrist.

"That's blasphemy," Karen shouted at him in comical style, standing up from the couch with her hands on her hips. Susan burst out laughing at this point, splurting out bits of mush from her mouth. This triggered Jobe and Tom's laughter too.

"Alright, alright I'm sorry. Would you like me to fetch your Madonna CD from the truck later?" Tom asked in a sarcastically apologetic tone.

"Yes please, Tom." Karen replied smiling. It was the kind of smile that a little kid would display when asking mom for sweets.

"No problem, I'll get it when I go for a wander with Jacob. Speaking of Jacob, has anyone seen him this morning?"

"Still in bed I think, lazy bum," Steven answered as he got up from the table and took his bowl to the kitchen.

"Oh OK. Not like him to sleep in." Tom mumbled to himself in a slightly concerned tone.

"I'm sure he's fine Tom, he doesn't really get excited about 'Rainbow Days' like us, got no reason to really. I'll go check in on him if you like?" Susan offered.

"Nah its OK, I'll pop up there in a minute," he replied.

Steven returned from the kitchen and slouched down upon the other couch, pondering what he should do with the day.

"You can help me sort out that water if you're bored Steven?" Susan hinted as she noticed his obvious pondering.

"No I'm good thank you," he replied cheekily.

"I'll give you a hand if you like Susan?" Karen offered and got up from the couch.

"Yeah okay, thanks, Karen," Susan replied gratefully.

The two women made their way into the kitchen to start the filtering process. On the kitchen's worktop stood a clear glass kettle and four jugs of water. The water in each of the jugs was a slightly different shade of yellow to the one adjacent to it and were all labelled accordingly. The first jug on the right was almost empty and labelled '3.' It was the water they were currently drinking, having been boiled three times. It looked much more appealing than the other three jugs, but still retained an off-putting yellow tinge. The next one along, '2,' was slightly darker in colour with a thicker consistency, and the next one '1,' was so dark in colour that it was barely possible to see through it. The final jug at the end of the line was water fresh out the tap. It was gloopy, smelly, and was almost completely brown in colour, with various different items floating on the surface.

"So where you wanna start then Karen? Sieving or boiling?" Susan asked her with a sarcastic smile. Karen forced a smile in return and looked down at her options.

"Pass me the sieve. I'll start with this horrible shit!" She finally replied, gesturing down to the jug of so-called 'fresh' water.

She started off by sieving out all the black floaty bits on the surface of the water as Susan began boiling up the '2' water in the kettle.

"So you and Jobe didn't sleep much last night then?" Susan asked. Her voice was light hearted, but her face appeared judgmental and condescending.

Karen blushed and hesitated a little before responding. "I'm sorry Susan, were we loud? I forgot there were other people in the house. We've been on our own for such a long time now." She replied.

"Hey no, you did wake me up actually yeah, but don't worry about it. It's just..."

"Just what?"

"Don't you worry about things?"

"What do you mean?"

"You know, I mean, you don't have contraception do you?"

"Oh right, I get you now. No we don't. Jobe was sterilized years ago. We'd have never made good parents you see."

"Oh OK. That's lucky, I guess."

"So, do you and Tom not— um?"

"No. No we don't, I mean we did at first in the heat of the moment kind of thing but not anymore."

"Why not? Can't he just pull out?"

"I dunno. He makes excuses and stuff. I think he's just a bit paranoid about it, doesn't really matter now."

"Why doesn't it?"

"Well, don't really have much of a sex drive anymore. I feel too ill most of the time. We do care about each other though."

"Well that's the important thing I guess."

"Yeah, he's a nice guy. He's been really good to Steven and me"

"Yeah he does seem cool."

"So, is it true what they say about black guys?"

"I thought you said you heard us last night?" Karen smirked, as they both started giggling and carried on with the job at hand.

"So what was your life like before all this then, Tom?" Jobe enquired, leaning forward on the couch.

"It was alright, ya know, pretty standard I guess."

"What did you do for a living?"

"Um, dunno how to describe it, I was kind of like a chemist really. I worked in a lab."

"Oh right, sounds interesting. Big company?"

"Yeah, you could say it was a pretty big organization. How about you?"

"I used to fix clocks."

"Really? I assumed you were like a builder or something, given the size of your muscles!"

"That's a bit stereotypical don't you think?"

"Sorry Jobe, don't mean to offend, you just don't look like a guy that fixes clocks, that's all."

"Oh well, you're right as it happens. I didn't always do clock repair."

"Didn't think so. So what did you do before?"

"I was in the army since I was eighteen."

"Oh right, so what happened with that?"

"I just couldn't do it anymore. You're trained to blindly follow orders, not ask questions, and just do as you're told. But it got to the point where I thought, no, I don't agree with this shit anymore."

"So what were you doing at that point?"

"I was stationed in Iraq in 2004. We were there for years and it wasn't even our fight. That stupid Tony Blair, acting like George Bush's little rent boy. I resented it from the start. If America had a problem with them, then why couldn't they just sort it out themselves? Anyway, we were sent there to find these weapons of mass destruction right, which, by the way, never actually existed. And also to capture Saddam Hussein, which we did, and he was executed. But even then, when we had done everything they asked of us, they STILL wouldn't let us leave. They said we had to maintain the peace there. They didn't seem to understand that the Iraqi people really didn't want us there. They attacked and killed us at every opportunity. I had three of my good friends killed right in front of me. I couldn't take it anymore, so I quit."

"I don't blame you mate, I'm surprised you put up with it for so long."

"Well I'm not a quitter normally. I plough through the bad times. But this was just wrong."

"So why clock repair?"

"I don't know really, just seemed like a pleasant job, relaxing ya know."

"So how long have you and Karen been together?"

"On and off most our lives really. We knew each other from school. We dated and broke up a few times, didn't talk for a little while, then got back together when I came back from Iraq."

"You two married?"

"Nah bro' not that I wouldn't have, just never got around to it. How about you? You have a girlfriend before all this? A wife?"

"Yeah, I did have someone special, but she's gone now. Ain't no point living in the past though. Look, excuse me a minute, Jobe I gotta check on Jacob."

"No problem bro'." Jobe replied with a nod, as Tom stood and headed off out of the room.

"So how about you then kid, what did you want to do when you grew up?" Jobe asked, turning his attention round to Steven.

"Um . . . ?" Steven hesitated and thought about the question for a bit.

"I don't know to be honest with you Jobe, there were lots of things that I was looking forward to doing when I was older, but never really gave much thought about a job." He continued.

"Like what?" Jobe enquired.

"You know, just silly little things that kids think about, parties, girls, driving fast cars, getting my own flat, just little things. I wanted to get a tattoo for a start."

"Oh yeah? What of?"

"Anything really, just wanted to be rebellious!"

"What you think of this then?" Jobe asked, rolling up his sleeve. At the top of his arm was a tattoo of a British Bulldog growling.

"See, that's pretty cool," Steven replied with an approving nod.

"And what about your sister then? What did she do?"

"Susan? She's not really my sister ya know, we're just really close. She used to be a hairdresser down the local salon. She was training to do piercing too, which was cool I thought. I wanted her to pierce my nipple!" Steven explained with a nostalgic grin, before turning his attention round to the window. The rain outside had just started to die down at that point and the vibrant rainbow had slowly started to fade away.

"Jacob? You awake Jacob?" Tom called, knocking gently on the boy's bedroom door. No reply.

"Jacob?" He called again, but his words still returned no answer. He then reached for the handle and opened up the door to find the room in darkness and the bed empty.

"Hey Jacob? Where are you?" He called louder.

"In here, Tom," the electronic voice of the Text Talk finally replied. The noise had come from Steven's room across the hall, so Tom turned and went inside. Jacob was sitting at the computer desk playing Mortal Kombat on the PC. Jacob was fighting as an Outworld demon named Scorpion Inferno. His special ability was being able to burn his opponents to death with his bad breath. Jacob was very good at this game. He was wearing a pair of jeans and a baggy old T-shirt that used to be his dad's. His umbilical unit was clipped on to the jeans, and hidden under the shirt. Jacob seemed very engrossed in the game and looked quite content.

"Just checking you were OK, Jacob. I told Karen we'd get her something from her truck later, so come down when you're ready OK?"

Jacob reluctantly paused the game and held down the 'q' button of his Text Talk.

"Yes," said the electronic voice, and Jacob continued with his game. Tom grinned at him and shook his head. Jacob was starting to act as obnoxious as a normal kid but Tom didn't mind it. He started to walk out of the room and remembered his pen.

"Jacob, you don't have a pen do you?" he asked, peering into the room again. Jacob shook his head in response, his eyes not once leaving the glare of the computer screen. Tom turned and walked out of the room just as Steven appeared out of nowhere, and rushed past him into the bedroom.

"What the hell are you doing in my room again you little freak!" He shouted at Jacob. Jacob turned to him, giving him a look of disgust. Seconds later Steven felt an almighty smack in the back of the head and almost fell to the floor with surprise.

"How dare you be so disrespectful Steven? You treat Jacob with respect." Tom yelled down at him.

"But it's my room Tom!" Steven explained in his defence, rubbing the back of head.

"It's not your room Steven. This is Jacob's house and you should be grateful that he's allowed us all to stay here. Now apologize before you get another slap!" Tom replied angrily. Steven let out a sigh and composed himself.

"I'm sorry Jacob. You know I didn't mean it." He apologized. Jacob disregarded his flippant apology and once again turned back to his game.

"Come on then Steven, what's the matter? You're not normally this hostile. Get out the wrong side of bed?" Tom asked demandingly.

"No I'm sorry, Tom. I'm just getting really frustrated you know, there's nothing left to do around here." Steven explained, putting his hands into his pockets and shrugging his shoulders.

"Well why don't you go and watch a film?"

"That's all I ever do Tom. I've seen every one of them a dozen times, even the ones I don't like."

"Well there are a million books in my bedroom, and you haven't read a single one of them."

"Do I look like a geek? I hated books at school, and still do."

"Look, I know how you feel Steven, I really do, but we're just gonna have to make the best of things at the moment. We're all in the same situation you know. Why don't you play a game with Jacob on the computer and tonight we'll all have a game of monopoly together yeah? You like monopoly."

"Yeah, alright then Tom, I'm sorry."

"No worries kid." Tom said smiling, and continued back off down the stairs.

"Hey, what was all that about? I heard shouting." Susan asked, pouring out some water from the kettle.

"Oh it's OK. Steven was just throwing a tantrum, but I've sorted it out now." Tom replied, walking into the kitchen.

"Is he getting stressed out?" She enquired further.

"Yeah but it's getting to all of us. I promised him a game of monopoly later."

"Ha, yeah okay. I'll thrash your arse again like the last time." She replied, full of herself.

"You've got monopoly?" Karen interrupted.

"Yeah, Jacob's parents had a board in the loft." Tom explained.

"Oh cool! I love that game!" Karen chirped excitedly. Tom smiled at her enthusiasm and turned back to Susan.

"You don't have a pen do you my love? Mine's out of ink." He asked.

"Um, no I don't think so Tom, sorry. I haven't been able to get down the stationers lately, ya know?" She quipped. Tom laughed at her response and walked back into the living room.

"So Jobe, you reckon that that Tremoline clinic is still standing then do you?"

"Dunno bro', was the only place we could think of heading to, only place in reach anyway." Jobe explained.

"So how much more petrol you reckon you'll need to get there?"

"Well I think I heard the building was down near Brighton Marina, so I think a quarter tank would be plenty, but where we gonna get petrol around here?"

"Well I haven't wandered too far afield lately, but I'm sure that there must be a few cars around here that haven't been destroyed. We just need to break off the petrol caps and siphon it out."

"Good plan if we can find the cars Tom, but there won't be enough room in the truck for all of us to go."

"Well little Jacob can sit on the back. He doesn't need any air you see."

"Oh right, course not. A sound plan then."

"Yeah, I think that we should try and get at least half a tank of petrol first though."

"Why's that bro'?"

"Well, I'd hate for us to get there, only to find the thing has been blown to pieces and then not be able to get back. I mean we're safe here and I wouldn't want to put the kids in danger."

"Good point Tom, that's a lot of petrol we've gotta find though."

"We got plenty of time. Hey Jobe, you haven't got a pen have you?"

"Nah, sorry, Tom."

Footsteps soon came tapping down the stairs and Jacob appeared in the hallway. He was wearing his coat and carrying an oxygen canister in his hand.

"You ready to go now Jacob?" asked Tom. Jacob placed the canister down upon the floor and started typing into his little machine.

"Steven is rubbish at that game, let's go," read out the electronic message.

"Hey, you're not going without some water Jacob." Susan called to him from the kitchen. She walked out into the hall with the '3' jug of water in her hand. Jacob rolled his eyes, unclipped his umbilical unit from his jeans and passed it to her. Jobe and Karen watched on with curiosity. They'd never met someone that had been through the operation and were quite intrigued. Susan popped open the flap at the back of the unit and started to pour the water down into the funnel.

"I have to say, the guy that came up with all this technology is a clever bloke. He'd be the richest person alive now, if he was still alive." Jobe stated.

"Maybe he is still alive. Maybe he spent his fortune moving to Mars?" Tom responded jokingly.

"All done Jacob, you'll need a little more later tonight though, OK?" Susan told him, as she clipped the flap shut again and passed him back the unit. Tom reached down and grabbed the handle of the canister, swinging it up and onto his back.

"We'll see you all later then, OK?" He said, popping the oxygen mask over his face and twisting open the gas release valve. He gave them a wave goodbye and headed out the door. The rest of them covered their faces and held their breath until the two had gone and the front door was firmly shut once again.

They wandered off in the general direction of the motorway, keeping their eyes peeled for anything of use on their way. The hole in the ozone layer was so big nowadays that the heat of the sun was powerful enough to dry up the rainfall from the pavement in a matter of minutes and before long, it was as if it had never rained at all. Tom knew that come dinnertime, the mush was not going to taste as delicious as it had that morning. Jacob wore his coat unzipped and exposed the umbilical unit to the bright sun. The solar panels started to absorb the powerful rays immediately, and you could almost hear the machine starting up its process of making Jacob's breakfast. Tom often wondered what it felt like to have your meals passed down directly into your stomach. It must have been a strange sensation. The actual process of the umbilical unit was the same as the PGOGM, which in theory should mean that the food source would be the same taste and consistency as the mush. But as it was being delivered directly to Jacob's stomach, it must have meant that it bypassed all of his taste buds. Tom wondered if Jacob felt any pleasure at all from the process, or if he even noticed that it was taking place.

As they wandered down the road towards the remains of the old pub, Tom noticed a black Toyota van parked in the car park. It was parked on its own, a little way away from the pub and had appeared to have survived intact. Tom turned to Jacob and pointed out the van to him, as they quickened their pace and approached it. Tom hadn't paid much attention to the van before and didn't even realize it was there. As they got closer, Tom could make out writing on the side of the van. 'S.W.Carpets' it read on the side with a mobile telephone number underneath. Tom wiped away the dust from the back window and peered inside. There were rolls and rolls of carpet in the back, wrapped up in brown paper with tools of all descriptions scattered carelessly around at the bottom. He then looked around the side of the van for the petrol cap and opened up the metal flap.

"Oh bollocks," Tom muttered to himself and closed the flap back up again. The writing on the inside of the flap had read 'Diesel.' The abandoned Dakota would take unleaded petrol only and was therefore useless to him. It momentarily crossed Tom's mind that maybe they could just take all the equipment off of the Dakota and fix it all to the van instead. This would save all the hassle of the petrol search, but the idea would only be feasible if one of them knew how to hot wire a van. Tom didn't know how to do it, the kids surely wouldn't, and he very much doubted that either of the women had the slightest clue either. He wasn't too sure about Jobe though. He did look as if he'd probably hung around with a bad crowd when he was younger, but Tom didn't want to risk further accusations of stereotyping (even though he was right the last time).

Tom gave Jacob a shake of the head and disregarded his previous contemplation, as they continued on their way towards the motorway. The Audi showroom just ahead of them would definitely have a selection of unleaded cars, Tom reassured himself, as he remembered there being at least three or four cars that had survived the blasts. He was dubious however, as to exactly how much they would be able to siphon from them as display cars never tended to have much petrol inside them, if any at all. The cars inside the showroom were never intended to actually go anywhere, as any successful buyer would have a brand new model delivered directly to their door. When the showroom needed to acquire newer models for display, a big transport vehicle would arrive and take all the old ones away without the need to drive them anywhere. They ventured inside anyway to satisfy Tom's curiosity, climbing in through a gaping hole in the sidewall of the building.

Tom had always wanted to own an Audi in his lifetime, but just never got the chance. He loved the design of the cars. They were smooth and stylish and had a sense of prestige to them. He imagined himself driving down a long highway with the top down, wind in his hair and stereo to the max. He first fell in love with the cars when his mother's brother (Uncle Bobby) bought an Audi TT Roadster 1.8 convertible when he was just a kid. The car was second hand and had cost Uncle Bobby more than twenty-five grand. It had completely wiped out his life savings and his wife was not too happy to say the least. They had previously talked about using some of the money to go on a long relaxing vacation in the Caribbean. It was to celebrate their fifth wedding anniversary and she was really excited about it. After a few heated arguments over it and several bunches of flowers later, she gradually began to forgive him, but Uncle Bobby had never regretted his decision for a split second. He absolutely adored the car and showed it off at every opportunity he could. Tom remembered one time that Uncle Bobby took him out for a spin in it on the motorway. It felt like he was on a roller coaster ride at Alton Towers, picking up speeds of more than 140 miles an hour with the top down, the g-force pulling back the skin on his face beyond belief.

Tom stood there for a while, admiring the cars in the showroom with a little grin upon his face. He then leaned down at the side of one of the cars to find the reassuring green label of unleaded petrol. All the cars in the showroom were securely locked shut and so he started looking around for where the keys might have been kept. The reception area of the showroom had completely collapsed and was covered under a huge pile of debris. He lifted off a few bricks from the pile and scavenged around for a little while till he eventually found what he was looking for. It was a large metallic key safe, still attached to the part of the wall it had previously hung from. He pulled it out from the wall and ripped off the chunks of plasterboard from around it. The safe was locked. 'So where was the key to the key safe?' He wondered. 'Probably on the key chain of one of the dead employees, or maybe in the receptionist's desk drawer which was way down at the bottom of the rubble.' He continued to think. He decided it was probably a waste of time trying to look for it and passed the key safe over to Jacob.

"Here, you carry this kid." Tom told him, deciding that they could probably crack it open easier back at the house. Jacob's eyebrows furrowed in an expression that appeared disgruntled, but he took the safe regardless.

They then climbed back out of the showroom through the hole in the wall and carried on their way towards the Dakota to retrieve the Madonna CD.

"Did I hear right that you were a hairdresser before all this?" Karen asked, finishing off the last of the sieving.

"Yeah that's right, I used to love it. I got to chat with people all day and make them look beautiful. It was great." Susan replied smiling.

"I bet you had a few weird requests in your time though, right?"

"Yeah a few. It was the punk hairdo that made me wanna cringe, but you had to do what they asked."

"Like what?"

"Um, well there was this local girl I used to do. She was trying to be all 'Emo' and weird. She wanted this strange asymmetrical bob, with a short fringe and the roots dyed pink. It looked fucking stupid if you ask me!" Susan explained with a little giggle.

"You reckon you could have a little chop at mine for me? I've been trying to do it myself for a while, but . . . well, just look at it!" Karen said, waving her greasy curls about. Susan looked at the messy, uneven brown perm and tried to keep a straight face.

"It's not that bad." She replied.

"Not that bad? I've seen poodles with a better cut!" Karen insisted, starting to laugh.

"I'll see what I can do for you later Karen." She replied, trying not to laugh too much in return.

At that point they heard the front door starting to open and quickly took in a deep breath. They then watched as Jacob strolled in through the doorway and placed the key safe down upon the floor. Tom immediately followed and closed the door firmly shut again behind him.

"Hey! You've saved Madonna!" Karen exclaimed excitedly as she noticed the CD in Tom's hand. Tom pulled off the gas mask and quickly passed the CD over to her.

"Yep, all safe and sound," he told her.

"What's that you've found Tom?" Jobe asked, emerging from the living room and noticing the chunky key safe upon the floor.

"They're keys from the Audi garage. There's four cars in the showroom with unleaded, and the keys for them are in there." Tom explained.

"Oh excellent bro', they got much petrol in them?" Jobe enquired further.

"Not sure Jobe. To be honest I don't think there's a lot. But we won't know until we crack this open and have a look."

"Right, well leave that to me Tom. I'll have this bad boy open in no time." Jobe picked up the safe and walked back into the living room again. Jacob then threw his coat on the banister rail and hurried back upstairs to play his game, having now done his good deed for the day.

"So what's everyone else been doing?" Tom asked, turning to Susan.

"Not much, just finishing off the water for today. It's so much quicker when there are two of you doing it." She replied, hinting at him.

"Hey! I've helped you a few times!" He replied defensively.

At that point there was a loud crack from the living room and Tom hurried in to investigate. Jobe had cracked open the safe with a single strike and it was now lying wide open on the floor, displaying a range of Audi car keys, all new and shiny.

"That didn't take you long Jobe!" Tom announced.

"Did you think it would?"

"Not really, no!"

"You see, I've got some uses!" Jobe told him with a smirk.

"So I can see!" Tom replied, before strolling back to the kitchen again.

"I'm just going to pop down to the shops," He explained to Susan and Karen. "I might be able to find a pen or two amongst the rubble."

"You and your book! Is it really that important Tom?" Susan asked.

"Yes, it is to me anyway." He replied.

"So when am I gonna get to read it then?" She asked.

"One day maybe, when we're grey and old," He said smiling, and put the oxygen mask back over his face again. He gestured a friendly wave and dashed back out the door again.

"So what's this book then, Susan?" Karen asked inquisitively.

"Oh I dunno Karen, he writes in it all the time. I think it's like a diary or something, but he won't let me read it." Susan explained.

"That's very secretive don't you think?"

"Yeah I guess, but that's his right I suppose."

"Well let's go and read it!" Karen suggested cheekily.

"God no! He'd go absolutely mental at us! He exploded at me one day for just picking it up! Besides, there can't be anything that interesting in it, nothing ever happens around here!"

"That's true." Karen agreed.

As Tom paced down the pathway he decided that he would try once more to speak to his neighbours across the road. It had been a while since anyone had noticed them walking past their window and he just wanted to see if they were OK. He wanted to tell them about Jobe and Karen and maybe he'd finally get a conversation out of them.

The oxygen mask was really starting to irritate his nose at this point. He had ventured outside almost every day and the constant usage had started to leave a permanent indent on the bridge of his nose. It was quite tender sometimes and gave him little twinges on occasion. He tried his best not to think about it too much and approached the living room window of Tina's house. The window was almost completely steamed up from the inside and it was hard to see anything at all.

"Tina? Tony?" He called through the window, but there was no reply as usual.

"We've found more survivors. Why don't you come over and say hello?" He continued, but there was still no reply. He then cupped his hands around his eyes and peered deeper into the window. He could then just make out two figures upon on the living room couch, both motionless. He remembered back when he was a young boy, when his mother used to be really good friends with Tina's parents and they spent the day together regularly. Her parents had even babysat Tom a few times, letting him stay up late with Tina, watching the television and eating homemade cupcakes. He used to really like Tina. She used to be a really sweet girl. But now the life had vacated her body and she sat peacefully on the couch, hand in hand with her boyfriend.

Tom walked around to the front door and tried the handle. It was locked as he expected. He took a few steps back and gave the door an almighty kick and it flung wide open and bashed hard against the inside wall. The smell of rotting flesh hit him immediately and he tried not to think how bad that smell would have been without the mask on. He tried to blank it out and made his way through to the living room. The bodies looked so peaceful lying there on the couch, pale and lifeless. Tony's body was in such an advanced state of decomposition that his face was almost unrecognizable to Tom, and it was obvious that he'd been dead now for a good few months. Tina's body however, didn't look decomposed at all and still appeared to be stiff with rigamortise.

'She can't have been dead more than a day or two,' he told himself, remembering the brief period of time that rigamortise usually engulfed a body.

"If only I'd come sooner . . ." He whispered out loud.

It was at that point that Tom first noticed the noise, or rather the lack of noise in the room. The fan of the mush machine was completely motionless and silent, and the wires had been ripped violently from the side and left dangling in the air. It was then that it became obvious to Tom what had happened to them.

Tony had been sick with the poisoning for a long time now and Tina had probably spent most of her time looking after him and tending to his every whim. But despite her efforts, the day finally came that he inevitably slipped away. Tina would have been completely lost without him and may have even started to lose her mind. Her whole life and routine had revolved around him for so many years that maybe her mind just couldn't process the idea that he was now gone. She had obviously carried his weighty corpse into the living room at some point, and sat him down gently upon the couch, before turning away and carrying on as if everything was normal. The reality of the situation probably sunk in one morning a few months later, when she awoke alone in her bed. She experienced a single moment of clarity and knew exactly what she would do. She ripped out the wires of the PGOGM machine and sat herself down on the couch beside him. Tom could envision Tina giving him a gentle kiss on the cheek and holding his hand as the oxygen levels in the room slowly dropped down to zero and she was finally reunited with him.

Tina had left the house immaculately clean and tidy throughout. The floor had been vacuumed, the washing up had all been done, and all the furniture had been polished to a high glistening shine. Tom suddenly felt an overwhelming sense of pride and admiration for poor Tina. After everything that she had gone through over the years, she never once let things slip out of routine. It must have all seemed pointless towards the end, knowing that everyone she cared about was dead and that she would soon follow. But still she kept on, never once losing her pride.

Tom headed off up the stairs and was immediately drawn in by the silver framed photographs of the happy couple that hung from the wall on either side of him. One of the pictures depicted the pair on holiday together in Jamaica, lying on the beach in the sun. Another showed them in the local park with their Staffordshire bull terrier that they had named Bernard. Tom could then feel the tears swelling up inside of him and couldn't bring himself to look at anymore of the pictures. He hung his head low and calmly continued to the top. He opened up the airing cupboard door on the landing and took out a white bed sheet from the shelf before making his way back down to the living room again. He spread out the white sheet over the couch and enclosed the two bodies underneath. Tina wouldn't have wanted anyone to see them in that state and Tom had respect for her pride.

Tina and Tony had first inherited their house following the death of Tina's parents many years before. They had never been wealthy themselves and had even struggled to afford the cost of the now mutilated PGOGM. Tony had worked for the local council for most of his life as a general repairman, clearing blocked gutters and painting doors and such. Tina herself had fluttered from job to job for a long time until she eventually gave up and started claiming the dole instead. Consequently, they had both become very good with money and had acquired a tendency to ration things out and keep things stored away until they were desperately needed. It was therefore feasible to Tom that there may be a few things lying about the house that they could all benefit from, like soap and shampoo. He hesitated at first at the thought of being disrespectful to the late couple, but concluded that their situation was far too dire for such consideration, and so he started to carefully rummage around.

He started off his search in the kitchen and opened up the fridge door. It was completely empty except for a single bowl of mush on the bottom shelf. It was wrapped in cling film and was labelled with black pen. 'Rainbow mush' it read, with a date underneath. It made Tom smile at the thought of other people getting excited about the rainbow days too and the sweet fluffy mush that was produced on those days. Yet it had never crossed his mind to store up the excess amounts for those dreaded days that the mush was dry and horrible. He looked at the date again and decided that the mush was far from safe to eat by this point and closed the fridge back up again. He moved to the hanging cupboards on the wall and opened the first one on the left, exposing neatly piled stacks of crockery. Since the arrival of Jobe and Karen in the house they were short of a few bowls, so he took a few and placed them down on the worktop. He had no need of anything else in the cupboard. It had been a long time since they needed the use of any plates or mugs, and it wasn't like they ever had coffee and a fry up for breakfast. The next cupboard along was completely empty except for a few Tesco carrier bags and the one after that contained lots of pots and pans. The next one along comprised of two empty salt and pepper shakers and a bottle of ketchup that was more than three years out of date. He then moved to the drawer of cutlery and took out a few spoons to go with the bowls and placed them down on the worktop as well. He then moved to the underneath cupboards. The first one contained a half empty bottle of bleach, some shoe polish, a dustpan and brush, and a bar of imperial leather soap. He grabbed the soap immediately and placed it on the side. The bleach may come in handy as well he thought. It may help get rid of that nasty smell in the bathroom that had been getting worse and worse for months now. He picked it up and popped it on the worktop too. As he opened up the next door along he almost had a heart attack with excitement. It was like finding the Holy Grail.

"Fuck me!" He exclaimed, and stared at the item for a while in admiration.

It was a full bottle of Jack Daniels whisky covered in dust and cobwebs. He immediately grabbed the bottle and wiped the dirt clean with his hands. He really couldn't believe his find, it had been a very long time since he had drunk anything except that horrible water, let alone any alcohol, and Jack Daniels was his all time favourite. He smiled and placed it down on the side with the rest of the stuff. Behind where he'd found the bottle in the cupboard there was also a large brown cardboard box. After admiring the whisky for a little longer, he then got back down on his knees again and tried to pull the box out. It felt very heavy to him and was caught on the water pipe of the sink. He gave it another forceful tug and it finally came loose. He eagerly opened up the top of the box to reveal tins upon tins of food. There seemed to be everything from soup, baked beans, pasta, vegetables and even a few tins of cinema style hotdogs inside. Tom's look of excitement was then joined with that of complete confusion. How on earth could Tina and Tony keep themselves from eating all this up straight away? Surely they couldn't have been content with living off the mush for years? Maybe they thought that the machine may malfunction one day and leave them without anything to eat, or maybe they were saving it up for a special day, a birthday or an anniversary or something. The question seemed irrelevant now though and Tom dismissed it. He lifted up the weighty box and dropped it onto the worktop, overwhelmed with the idea of actually eating a proper dinner for once. His taste buds had become accustomed to the sloppy mush over time, but tonight they were in for a real treat.

Tom then started to feel sad for little Jacob not being able to join them in the banquet. He doubted that Jacob had previously been that jealous about not eating the mush, as it was pretty obvious that he wasn't missing out on much, but this was going to be the tastiest meal that any of them had eaten in years. It was entirely possible that Jacob couldn't even remember what real food tasted like. He was just a small child the last time he was able to eat and so maybe it wouldn't actually bother him too much. Tom hoped that Jacob wouldn't mind anyway, for the last thing he wanted to do was upset him.

Tom then started to make his way back up the stairs again, trying hard once again to not look at the precious memories that hung upon the wall. He reached the top and made his way into their bathroom. The bathroom was just as clean as the rest of the house, but seemed to contain nothing of use to him. There were a few old razors on the sink that had obviously been used over and over again until they were completely blunt, an old toothbrush, and an empty bottle of shampoo. He then turned and slid open the medicine cabinet hanging on the wall. Inside he found a few bandages, a bottle of Paracetamols, an electric toothbrush, and a tube of Canesten thrush cream. He picked up the tube to examine it and put it down again quickly once he realized what it was, with a slightly disgusted look on his face.

He thought the Paracetamols might come in handy and put them into his pocket. He gave the bedroom a quick scan and decided that there was nothing of much use in there either. It wasn't like he was going to start rummaging around in a dead man's underwear drawer or anything so he moved on to the last room. It had a desk with a computer, a chair, a printer, a pot of pens, and not much else. He left the room and made his way down the stairs again. He stepped back into the living room and almost jumped out of his skin with shock. Little Jacob was standing in the middle of the room, staring down at the sheet-covered couch.

"What are you doing in here?" Tom asked him, sounding angry and a little disappointed. Jacob pointed towards the front door that was wide open and shrugged his shoulders.

"Look, I'm afraid Tina and Tony have passed away Jacob. I'm sure you're quite upset." He explained. Jacob gave him back a blank look and reached down for his Text Talk.

"No." Replied the electronic voice and he shrugged his shoulders again.

"No? Well I guess they haven't been very nice to us recently have they? I tell you what Jacob, why don't you look through their DVD collection and see if they've got any movies that you'd like. I don't think they would mind you taking them now." Tom said to him, and gave him an affectionate pat on the head.

Jacob nodded his head in return and made his way over to the DVD shelves. Tom shook his head in disbelief of Jacob's blasé attitude and walked back into the kitchen.

Jacob scanned the collection carefully, specifically keeping an eye out for any horror films that he had not yet seen. Tina and Tony were obviously not the biggest horror fans and so pickings were very slim, but Jacob did manage to find a few films of interest to him. These included 'Invasion of the Body Snatchers', 'The Toxic Avenger,' and 'Stigmata.' Jacob's reading skills were still very basic and so his selections were based solely upon the image on the DVD cover, and these were the ones that appeared the goriest.

Tom returned to the room a few moments later with a Tesco carrier bag of his findings and the cardboard box with all the tinned foods. He placed them down upon the floor in front of him and turned to Jacob.

"Find anything good then?" He asked, looking at the DVDs that Jacob had taken out.

"You know, Jacob, you really should try watching something a bit more light-hearted!" He continued jokingly. He then turned to have a quick glimpse at the collection himself. There didn't appear to be much of interest to him. The collection was mostly made up of cheesy girly flicks and musicals. He then noticed a DVD at the end of the row which caught his attention. He took it out, looked at the cover and started smirking to himself childishly. It was the 'Madonna Confessions Tour' DVD.

"She'll love this!" He said to Jacob and placed the DVD on top of the pile that Jacob had selected. Jacob peered down at the DVD and gave Tom a scowling look of disapproval.

"Well it's not for me is it?" Tom replied. He picked up the pile of DVDs from the floor, dropped them into the carrier bag and passed it over to Jacob.

"Come on then Jacob, you can carry that." He said to him as he gestured towards the front door and picked up the heavy cardboard box.

"Oh God! Wait there a second," Tom said suddenly, before dropping down the box again and dashing up the stairs. Jacob waited for him patiently until Tom reappeared down the stairs, holding a handful of black Biros.

"I almost forgot a pen!" He exclaimed smiling.

"You weak pathetic fool, I've come for your soul!" Screamed a voice from the computer screen, as Steven frantically started pressing buttons upon the keyboard. He had finally got to the last level of the game on 'Easy' mode, and was trying to kill the end boss. The end boss was a seven-foot mutant by the name of 'Shoa Khan the Third.' He was wearing full body armour and a massive skull shaped helmet. In one hand he held a steel mallet, and in the other hand he held a fifty-inch machete.

"Ha, ha, ha, you suck!" The voice taunted him again, as Steven's character fell to the floor, decapitated. Big 'Game Over' letters then appeared on the screen and the game returned to the main menu.

"Stupid bloody thing," he complained, as he sat back in the chair and folded his arms in a childish tantrum.

At that point he heard the front door shutting again and wandered down to greet Tom and Jacob as they placed down their bags and boxes on the floor.

"Hey, you get all that stuff from the shops? I thought that place had been completely looted?" Susan asked them with a confused frown. Having overheard the conversation, Jobe and Karen then joined them as well, to satisfy their own curiosity. Tom pulled off his face mask for the last time and began to nurse the tender throbbing bridge of his nose.

"No, we never went down to the shop in the end." Tom explained.

"So where'd ya get all that, bro'?" Jobe asked, equally confused.

"I'm afraid our neighbours have passed away. I looked through the window to check up on them, and they were dead." Tom explained in a sorrowful tone.

"Oh well, had to happen sooner or later didn't it. So what stuff did you find?" Susan asked with eager anticipation, seemingly unmoved by the couple's demise. Tom picked up the bag and box again and took them into the kitchen.

"We've got a few more spoons and some bowls." He told them, taking the items from the bag and placing them down upon the side. "Some soap, some Paracetamols," he continued. "And feast your eyes on this!" He exclaimed, showing them the bottle of Jack Daniels.

"Ah sweet bro'! I think that's the most beautiful thing I've ever seen!" Jobe shouted excitedly.

"Oh really? Well take a look at this then!" Tom replied with a smirk, as he opened up the top of the cardboard box.

"Oh, Christ! Where did you find all those?" Susan asked with shock, peering down at the variety of tinned foods.

"It was all at Tina's house. God knows why they hadn't eaten it all, but it looks like we will feast tonight!" Tom replied to her, as she grabbed him and landed a long sloppy kiss on his lips.

"Oh, and I got a present for you too Karen," he claimed, reaching back into the bag and passing her the Madonna DVD.

"Oh wicked!" She exclaimed, giggling to herself.

"So, how's everyone feeling about a proper dinner, a glass of whisky, and a game of monopoly then?" Tom asked.

"Sounds good bro'! Anyone would've thought it was Christmas!" Jobe replied, nodding in agreement.

"I want some whisky too!" Steven interrupted, looking up at Tom with puppy dog eyes.

"Yeah, you can have a glass Steven," Tom agreed.

"Then afterwards, can we all watch a bit of Madonna, yeah?" Karen asked excitedly.

"Oh, I dunno about that Karen, maybe another time." Tom replied with another smirk.

CHAPTER FOUR (A)

WITH A gentle breeze and the pleasant chirping of birds in the air, Tom knew straight away that he was back in the dream world. The dragonfly landed on his shoulder and the squirrel ran up the tree. He looked around at the cornfields in front of him and even though he felt completely lucid and aware of what was coming, he still possessed a strange desire to venture over to the log cabin to see his beloved Grandfather. He composed himself and rubbed his face.

"It's just a dream. It's only a dream." He told himself over and over again. He took in a long deep breath and enjoyed the fresh air circling through his lungs.

"I'm not gonna move, I'm not afraid of this shit anymore!" He muttered to himself sternly and sat down under the shade of the apple tree, watching the fluffy red squirrel running about in the branches above him. He sat patiently, rocking back and forth on the spot waiting for the inevitable to unveil itself. As predicted, the fields suddenly burst into flames and turned the sky black. Still he sat, waiting for the man in the black cloak to appear. The tree behind him suddenly began to rot and within a few seconds it was nothing more than a pile of dust. He fell back, crashing through the cloud of tree dust and landed on his back where the trunk once grew, but still he retained his composure. He pulled himself to his feet and lightly brushed the tree dust from his trousers. Lightning then started crashing all around him and the ground began to shake and crack. Thick black smoke continued to bellow viciously from the corn field and slowly morphed itself into the familiar shadowy figure, eye sockets glowing red with the flickers of the flames. He slowly paced towards Tom, immune to the burning hot flames and dragging the scythe along the ground with a cringing screech. Tom began to perspire with fear and the heat of his approaching enemy, but still he never moved from his point of protest, right until the point that the deathly figure was mere inches away. The figure started to cackle at him through its rotten skull, the sound resonating all around and maggots falling from his face.

"You think you've nothing left to fear Thomas Harvey, but you are wrong, so very wrong." The figure bellowed in its deep husky voice. Tom began to feel the force of a cold shudder trying to enter his body but overpowered it with the gritting of his teeth and the clench of a fist. He brought his fist back and plunged it forward at the figure with all the strength he could muster. Yet, however lucid the dream had felt to him, it was still just a dream and the laws of reality were to be ignored. The air became dense and resistant to the force of the punch, like punching through water. It possessed no power, no speed and exhausted all of Tom's energy before even moving a scarce few inches through the air. The figure continued to cackle and grasped hold of Tom's flying fist with his skeletal hand and began to squeeze it. The sharp points of his bare boned digits perforated through the skin with a slight popping noise and buried themselves deep inside. Tom roared out in unbearable pain, tears streaming down the side of his face.

"There's a whole world of unimaginable horrors just waiting for you Thomas, and I will be your tour guide through the attractions. Not even God himself could save your soul now." The figure growled down at him as he buried his fingers even deeper into the flesh of Tom's hand, underneath the muscle and scraping along the wrist bone. He finally locked his grip like a tightened vice around the bone, twisted it around in the joint and wrenched the hand clear from Tom's arm, leaving behind a jagged bloody stump which showered out blood like a burst water pipe in the street. The hand spun through the air and hit the ground a few feet away with a gloopy splat. The pain was unbearable, like his brain had burst into flames from an implanted explosive. 'It's only a dream,' he kept thinking to himself, hoping that he could some how control the pain, blank it out, or wake himself up from the horror. The figure looked down at him with a cocky smile, staring deep into Tom's eyes and into his very soul, hearing every thought that was flashing through his mind.

"You can't blank me out Tom. I'm everywhere you go. I'm in your dreams and in your thoughts, and soon enough I will grow strong enough to invade your waking life once again and you will be gone forever!" He groaned in that deep husky voice, before taking the scythe in both hands and violently slicing at Tom's chest. It ripped apart his t-shirt and sliced half an inch through his flesh. Tom's weight toppled him over and sent him hopelessly onto his back again. He panted away frantically, squeezing his eyes tightly closed and praying that it would all be over soon.

"What's the matter Thomas? Isn't this the point when you're supposed to wake up in a cold sweat?" He cackled again in his menacing voice, before discarding his scythe to one side and kneeling down above him. He ripped off the ragged remains of Tom's shirt and buried both of his bony hands into the gaping wound upon Tom's chest, ripping the skin aside and exposing his bloody rib cage.

The white blazing pain flooded Tom's body again and his screams no longer carried any noise, just an empty breath upon a tormented face. The towering figure then wrapped his bony fingers around Tom's lowest rib on either side of the cage and gripped them tightly. He smiled down at Tom once again and then snapped the ribs clean off with a brittle cracking noise. He then continued to do the same with the next pair up and so on until he completely exposed Tom's pulsating bloody chest organs. The demonic cackles of the menacing figure echoed all around, shaking the ground with its deep husky resonance as he plunged his bony digits directly into Tom's beating heart, sending splatters of blood shooting back into his own ghastly skull. Lightning began to strike the ground vigorously from the angry black sky until the electricity began to channel through the ground and up into the glowing bones of the ghastly figure.

It was at that point that Tom finally regained consciousness with a bellowing scream. He was sweating profusely and in a state of traumatic confusion. The taste of blood was still prominent in his mouth and he could still feel residual pain from his rib cage.

"Hey, hey, calm down, Tom," Susan whispered to him, rubbing his chest gently.

"God, that was horrible," he confessed, panting frantically.

"Hey come on, it was just a dream," she assured him, and landed a kiss on his cheek. He eventually managed to compose himself and took a deep breath.

"Did I wake you up, love?" He asked.

"Nah, I was already awake, they're at it again next door. They're like a pair of horny rabbits!" She explained.

Tom hadn't noticed the noise until she had said that, then the banging of the bedposts became obvious. He let out a sigh and lay back down on the bed, his head cushioned gently in the pillow. Susan lay back down next to him with her head facing him on the pillow. She leaned in and landed a long sloppy kiss on his lips.

"I do love you Tom, you're a good man." She said, pulling herself away.

"I love you too, Susan, I'd be completely lost without you." He replied with a caring smile as they continued kissing gently. Susan rubbed her hand around his chest hair and slowly made her way down his body and into his boxers. Tom broke free from the kiss and started to nibble on her earlobes gently, planting little kisses down her neck.

"Make love to me Tom," she whispered to him softly.

"But . . ." Tom replied, trying his best to put a sentence together while sliding his hand up into her blouse.

"Look, I know my cycle, it'll be fine I promise," she pleaded with him. He grabbed her blouse with both hands and pulled it clean off over her head. Even though her body had become pale and aged from all the pollution, she had still retained a natural beauty that couldn't be described. She looked amazing to him, and glimmered in the moonlight. Her breasts lay pert and soft, as he leaned in and ran his tongue around each nipple in a gentle circular motion. He reached down and rolled off her knickers along her long smooth legs and dropped them to the floor as he knelt himself gently between her thighs. He leant forwards on top of her, feeling her breasts gently press against his chest and gave her another long passionate kiss on the lips.

The night sky was smothered in dark clouds, and before long it became stormy and violent, the wind so strong that it hit against the windows with force and started to shake them erratically. There was suddenly a loud scraping noise from the roof, followed by an almighty crash of metal upon the pavement. Tom immediately jumped up out of the bed in shock and pulled up his boxer shorts.

"What the fuck was that?" He yelled out with a worried expression.

"Oh, it's nothing Tom, it's just the storm." She replied with a disgruntled frown.

"Didn't sound like nothing to me?" he said, pulling up his trousers in a panic.

"Oh Tom! You can't leave me like this!" She cried out in a strop.

"I've got a really bad feeling about this Susan, just bear with me a second OK?" He replied, as he rushed over to the window and wiped the condensation clear with his palm.

"Oh Christ, fuck!" He yelled out hysterically, catching sight of the carbon dioxide vent smashed into a thousand pieces on the ground below them.

"What? What is it Tom?" Susan asked, finally starting to take him seriously.

"The filter! The fucking filter has smashed to pieces, we're gonna fucking die!" He screamed, running out into the hall. He bashed violently against Jobe and Karen's door then jumped up to open the loft hatch above him. The hatch immediately crashed open revealing a flimsy metal staircase. He jumped up again and pulled down at the last wrung of the ladder.

"Jobe! Get out here man!" He yelled at the door with another heavy knock and began to ascend the metal staircase.

"What the fuck are you making such a fuss about bro'? I'm kinda busy!" Replied Jobe's husky voice as he slung open the bedroom door angrily.

"Come on Jobe, we have to work quickly or we're all going to die!" Tom's voice echoed down from within the loft. He suddenly appeared back on the ladder again a few seconds later and handed down two oxygen canisters to Jobe.

"What are you talking about Tom? What's going on?" Jobe replied in confusion.

"The C-O-two vent has fallen from the roof. If we're not quick we're all going to suffocate. Now give one of those to Karen and the other to Steven, quickly!" He explained, and headed back into the loft for three more canisters.

Jobe paused for a few seconds to watch the PGOGM on the landing as the propellers of the fan slowly came to a grinding halt and the reality of the situation finally sunk in. He frantically ran back into his bedroom and dropped one of the canisters onto the bed.

"Put this on baby, the oxygen levels are about to drop! And don't you take it off 'til I get back, alright?" He ordered her and slid the mask over her face.

"What! What the fuck are we going to do?" She yelled back at him though the mask and jumped up out the bed.

"You and Susan just stay here right? Look after the kids." He called back at her, dashing out of the room and into Steven's room next door. Tom reappeared from the loft hatch once again and struggled down the rickety staircase with the other three canisters in his grip.

"Come on, Susan, you put this on too," he demanded, dropping the canister next to the bedside and handing her the mask.

"What on earth are you going to do Tom? This is serious fucking shit!" She screamed at him, snatching the facemask from him.

"Calm down Susan, it's OK. I'm just gonna have to take Tina's vent from next door and hook it up." He explained, gently caressing her cheek with his thumb. She wrapped the mask around her face and spun open the gas release valve, when the canister immediately started to beep at her.

"God damn it Tom, there's less than ten minutes in this damn thing. You'd better hurry up!" She cried desperately at him. He turned and dashed back out the door to find the rest of his house mates congregating on the landing.

"Jobe, we gotta get up on Tina's roof and dismantle her CO_2 vent and we've only got about ten minutes to do it, so let's go!" He explained and sped off down the stairs.

"I'm right behind ya bro'!"

"Jacob, you can help us too kid, let's go!" Tom called to Jacob as he emerged from his room.

"And what the hell are we supposed to do? Huh?" cried Karen from the landing.

"Just stay here baby and look after each other, conserve your breathing." Jobe replied.

"Oh God help us!" She screamed back, and ushered Steven into the bedroom with Susan.

"Right Jobe, the vent input connection is on the front of our house. It feeds the three PGOGMs fans that we have inside. We just gotta hook up next door's vent to our connection and we should be alright, OK?"

"Yeah I understand. You got a ladder? Tools?" He asked in return.

"Every thing we'll need is in the garage, so just follow me, and don't once remove your mask, no matter what!" Tom told him and burst open the front door. The hurricane force winds almost blew the door from its hinges and the carbon dioxide began to violently flood into the house. They rushed out together and fought against the harsh winds to pull the door closed again then made their way to the garage. Tom flung out some keys from his pocket and slid one straight into the lock, turned and sprung open the garage door.

"Spanners, wrenches," he called out, grabbing the items from an open toolbox and passing them to Jacob.

"Jobe, help me with this would ya?" Tom asked, struggling back out with a seven-foot wooden ladder. Jobe rushed to help and quickly grabbed the other end of the ladder. They struggled their way through the powerful winds and headed over to Tina's house. The violent storm fought viciously against them and the angry wind gushed mercilessly into their faces. It pushed the mask hard into Tom's tender nose and bursts of carbon dioxide penetrated in through the gaping holes in the sides.

They propped the ladder up against the garage adjoined to Tina's house and ascended it up to the first level.

"Right, pass me that spanner please, Jacob." Tom called. Jacob offered out the spanner and watched as Tom shoved it down the side of his trousers. Jobe then pulled up the ladder from the floor and aligned it from the garage roof to the side of the house. The ladder reached from the top of the garage to just above the top window of the house, leaving a two-foot gap to the plastic guttering on the roof. Tom began to climb the shaky ladder while Jobe tried his best to steady it from the bottom, but the ladder still continued to shake erratically.

Tom held on to the ladder as tightly as he could and barely managed to stay on. He climbed up further and leaped up to grab the guttering above him. He established a firm enough grip upon the plastic fixture and swung one leg onto the roof just as the flimsy guttering started to crack. He quickly swung over the other leg just in time before the guttering completely snapped in half and fell to the ground below. The canister upon Tom's back felt as if it weighed a ton, but still he persisted up the slanting tiles of the roof. He finally pulled himself to the peak of the roof and steadied himself against the breast of the chimney, briefly gazing out into the dark clouds of the night sky. Suddenly a bolt of lightning struck a burnt out car a few meters down the street and for just a split second, Tom caught sight of the dark figure from his dreams, looking back at him from behind the clouds. He momentarily lost his concentration and with a sudden gust of wind he lost his grip on the tiles and started to slide helplessly down the slope. He stuck out his foot towards the remaining section of gutter and jammed it right into the plastic grove. He steadied himself with a sigh of relief and as he prepared to restart the climb, the guttering suddenly snapped again. The weight of the canister upon his back pulled him down into the jagged edge of the plastic which cut deep into his ankle and buried itself underneath his skin. The carbon dioxide rushed into the gaping wound and stung like electricity through his body. Tom gasped out in pain and quickly pulled his leg free from the plastic.

"Hey! You alright, Tom?" Jobe called up, concerned. Tom nodded back lethargically and started his ascent again.

The carbon dioxide vent was fastened to the top of the roof with four large bolts and it took no time at all for Tom to loosen them with the spanner.

"No bloody wonder the other one fell off!" He muttered to himself. He threw away the last bolt and held the vent firmly in place to stop it from sliding off. Slowly, he backed away down the slope, holding the vent tightly behind him until he reached the edge. He swung his legs round, and dangled them over until he could feel wood underneath his feet, and slid down for a firm enough hold.

"You ready for it then Jobe?" He called down at him, and with a thumb's up he grabbed the vent with all his might, tried to untangle the leads, and lowered it down to Jobe's open arms. Jobe's arms were a few inches out of reach and Tom was going to have to drop it to him.

"Ready?" He asked, motioning to throw it.

"Ready as ever Tom, drop it!" Jobe agreed, as Tom let the box slip from his grip and watched it land perfectly into Jobe's open arms. Jobe stumbled back, adjusting to the weight of the box and almost fell off the other side of the garage roof.

"Right, I got it!" He yelled back up after regaining his balance, and then steadied the unit down by his feet. Tom rushed back down the ladder and repositioned it for the next level.

"Right Jacob, you gotta follow this wire and disconnect it from the front of Tina's house, alright?" Tom asked him. With a nod of understanding, Jacob then flew down the ladder and disappeared around the side of the house. Tom climbed down shortly after him and reached up for Jobe to pass him the box. Once again the reach was a few inches short and Jobe would need to drop it down to Tom.

"It's your turn now bro', you ready?" Jobe shouted down at him and Tom nodded. He gently released the box into the air but Tom failed to grasp a steady grip on it. He tripped over the bottom rung of the ladder and landed on his back with the box crashing down on top of him, the sharp corner of the metal box cracked into the side of Tom's rib cage.

"My God Tom, you alright?" Jobe called down in a panic, sliding down the ladder as if it were a fireman's pole and pulling the heavy device from off of him.

"I'll be fine Jobe. I just got the wind knocked out of me." Tom panted back to him through the mask. At that point Jacob came running back round the corner with the connecting plug of the wire in his hand.

The girls at this point were huddled around Steven on the bed, trying their best to remain calm. Despite her desperate attempts, Susan couldn't help but think about the last time she was huddled around in a bedroom, just seconds before her whole family was blown to pieces. She remembered how scared she was for her life, and the tragedy that followed. She knew that Steven would be thinking the same, as she gazed upon the terrified look on his face. She wrapped her arms around him even tighter and a tear formed in the corner of her eye. All three canisters were beeping like crazy at this point and the girls were sure that this was going to be the end. Karen's canister had turned out to contain even less gas than Susan's, and as the airflow started to die down she began to lose consciousness and black out.

Without warning, they were suddenly greeted by the welcoming sound of the PGOGM fans starting up again. Susan's tears of fright turned to those of unexpected relief as she fell back down on the bed with exhaustion. The front door then burst open again and the three men returned. Tom hobbled around the house checking that each machine was working properly, before he could finally feel safe again. He stumbled up the stairs, throwing his canister and mask to the floor and wrapped himself around Susan on the bed.

"We've done it my love. Everything's going to be OK." He gently whispered into her ear.

Jobe appeared in the bedroom doorway a few seconds later and carried Karen back off into their bedroom. Jacob got back into his bed with his usual blasé attitude to the situation, and Steven cuddled up to Susan and Tom on the bed. It wasn't long before everyone was fast asleep again, their weak and frail bodies completely drained from the stress and exhaustion of the event. The thundering winds outside were soon accompanied by rain and hail which poured away throughout the night and filled up their water butts to the point of overflowing.

Tom was the first to awaken for the second time that morning, as the sun beamed on to his face through the bedroom window. He carried Steven's sleepy body back into his own room and made his way clumsily down the stairs leaving Susan snuggled up peacefully in their bed. He grumbled at the ghastly mess in the living room and begrudgingly started to clean it all up. Susan had completely dominated the game of monopoly the night before, and by the end of the game had owned most of the properties on the board. She had sat with a smug grin on her face throughout the majority of the game, as the piles of money stacked up in front of her grew by the minute. They had all got a little too drunk that night and by the end of the game decided to leave the board and pieces scattered all over the table. Their tolerance to alcohol had completely diminished over the years of absence and it had only taken a few shots of the whisky to send them into a drunken stupor.

When they had opened the front door to retrieve the vent the violent winds had gushed into the living room without mercy and blown the paper money everywhere, like autumn leaves under an oak tree. Tom slowly began the task of gathering all the monopoly debris together and sorting it out into the cardboard box. Moments later there was a creaking from the staircase and Jobe appeared from the doorway yawning.

"Morning bro', how you feeling this morning?" He asked sleepily.

"Feel a bit drained, but I'll live."

"How about that chest? Does it hurt?"

"No, its fine, like I said, it just winded me a bit."

"Oh come on Tom, I saw the force that it smashed into you, it must have done some damage?"

"I promise you Jobe, it's fine. How's Karen this morning?"

"Dunno Tom, she hasn't woken up yet. I did manage to revive her for a while in the night, but she was just in a daze, confused. I'm sure she'll be OK this morning though."

"You could do me favour if you like Jobe."

"Sure, what is it Tom?"

"Could you charge up all the oxygen canisters, so we don't have to panic so much next time?"

"Charge them up? How the hell do you do that?"

"Have you never taken off the front of the PGOGM before?"

"Nah Tom, I don't tend to mess about with something that's keeping me alive, ya know!"

"Well let me show you."

Tom led him over to the machine and pulled off the front panel, resting it carefully down upon the floor.

"Right, well you see this tube here?" He said, pointing to a clear rubber tube coming out from a black square box.

"Yep."

"Right, well this is the processed oxygen supply that feeds into the fan."

"Yeah OK, I'm following."

Tom scanned the room and spotted a canister by the couch. He dashed over and grabbed it.

"Well if you pull out this tube from the fan connection, you can plug it into the canister here." He explained, pointing to a black plastic cap.

"That's really clever, I'd never thought of doing that." Jobe replied with an impressed grin.

"Simple really, you just need to remember to turn the dial here up to full blast, or the pressure won't be great enough to push the gas into the canister and it will discharge it instead." Tom explained further, pointing to a small black dial next to the tube.

"Right, I got it, but won't the oxygen levels in the room drop while I'm doing that?"

"Yep, they will. So leave it for a few minutes in between canisters to replenish it back up again."

"Cool, so what you gonna do?"

"I'm gonna clean up all this fucking shit everywhere." Tom

replied, looking at the state of the room again. He gave Jobe half a smile and carried on collecting up the monopoly money.

"Shall we go and check out that showroom later Tom?" Jobe called over to him, as he started filling up the first canister.

"Yeah, alright, Jobe. I'd completely forgotten about that to be honest. Where did you leave those keys?"

"The key safe should be down there by the couch, Tom."

"Oh yeah, well we can do that after breakfast then if you like."

"Sounds good to me." Jobe agreed.

It was about thirty minutes later when Tom was finally confidant that he'd found all the pieces of the game. He'd collected all the notes of money, the houses, the chance cards, and the entire set of playing pieces. Tom's favourite piece was the race car, as it was the most masculine piece on the board. After Susan had started to win game after game a few years back, she was forced to always play as the iron to compensate. Tom thought that maybe demoralizing her might make her lose, but it never did. Monopoly was one of their favourite pastimes and it was important to him that they didn't lose any of the pieces. It wasn't like they could go and buy a new set any time soon. Once the box looked sufficiently full and complete he put on the cardboard lid and slid the game back into a cabinet. The cabinet was full of board games and playing cards and such. There was Scrabble, Guess Who and Cluedo, amongst many others.

Poker was another great game that was in the cabinet too. Tom used to remember playing it with his father and Uncle Bobby when he was young and it brought back fond memories. His father and uncle used to meet up once a fortnight with a small group of other friends from the building site to play. Each of them arrived with at least a hundred pounds in notes, so stakes were always very high. The game they played was a fixed bet Texas hold'em, which basically meant that the winner would take the lot, no runners up prizes. Although there was a great deal of money at stake each time they played, none of the men took the game too seriously. On occasion they would even let Tom join in for a few hands. He had no idea what he was doing, but somehow seemed to win regardless.

Tom collected up all the whisky glasses, cleaned up the various spillages in the kitchen and then sat down on the couch.

"These are done now, Tom." Jobe called over to him, plugging the air tube back into the machine and replacing the front cover.

"Good job my friend, thank you."

"I'm gonna pop upstairs and see if Karen's OK."

"No problem Jobe, see you in a bit."

Jobe strolled off up the stairs again and left Tom alone with his thoughts. Before long he ventured back upstairs himself and sat down on the bed to transfer those thoughts to his little black book. He peered over and looked at Susan fast asleep next to him and gave her a kiss on the forehead.

"I really do love you," he whispered into her ear. A smile slowly appeared on her face and it was obvious that she was not asleep.

"I love you too." She replied in a sleepy voice. She opened her eyes and they exchanged smiles.

"You feeling alright, my love?" He asked her softly

"Yeah I'm alright Tom, just feel exhausted." She replied, and snuggled back into the pillow again.

"I'm just gonna check in on Karen, I don't think she's very well." He told her, and as he stood from the bed he accidentally knocked his little black book to the floor. As the book fell through the air, a folded A4 piece of paper fell from within the pages and floated gently underneath the bed. Tom picked the book back up and slid it into his leather coat that was hanging on the door, oblivious to the fallen piece of paper. He then walked out into the hall and into Karen's adjacent bedroom. Karen was still fast asleep in the bed. Her skin looked pale. Jobe was kneeling on the floor beside her and gently stroking her hand.

"How is she?" Tom whispered over to him.

"I can't seem to wake her up, Tom. I dunno what's wrong with her." He replied with a frown.

"Well Susan's only just woken up Jobe, and she's still feeling exhausted too. I think we should just leave them to regain their energy." Tom suggested to him.

"Yeah, maybe you're right Tom. What shall we do then?" Jobe asked him.

"Well, why don't we go check out the showroom? We do have the keys now."

"Yeah that's true, alright then." Jobe agreed, and rose from his kneeling position. Tom stepped back into his bedroom and grabbed his coat from the door.

"We're just popping out for a bit Susan, alright?" He called over to her. She replied with a faint grumble and pulled the covers over her face. The men then suited themselves up with oxygen masks, grabbed the Audi keys from the safe, and started their journey to the showroom.

It was about half an hour after that that Susan finally mustered enough energy to get up out of bed, and reached underneath for her slippers. The faint touch of paper brushed against her fingertips and her curiosity demanded she investigate further. She peered underneath the bed and caught sight of the paper that had previously fallen from the book, and so she reached underneath to grab it.

'**Procedure Summary Report**' was written at the top of the paper in bold letters with Tom's name written just below. Her curiosity then became too overwhelming to ignore and so she carried on reading through the text.

Procedure Summary Report

Date: 23/10/2006
Patient: Mr. Thomas Harvey
Condition: Diabetes
Treatment: Stem cell trial

Notes:

The patient (Mr. Thomas Harvey) has now completed the second stage of our trial stem cell treatment as a potential cure for his diabetes. Instead of injecting a concentrated amount of these stem cells directly into the patient's pancreas as in previous trials, we have decided to inject a large amount of modified stem cells into the patient's blood stream. In theory, these would travel around the body and heal not only the pancreas, but also any other organ in the body that had suffered damage from diabetes.

The procedure was a complete success. The stem cells have caused the pancreas to start secreting insulin into the body once again, and the stem cells also healed the damage to the liver and kidneys.

The stem cells themselves however, have not acted exactly as initially predicted. We previously believed that once the stem cells had reacted to the damaged tissue in the body, they would then bind themselves to the effected area and thus become part of it. But the stem cells appear to have obtained a self-replenishing property and have remained within the patient's blood stream. They now appear to be living as seemingly independent entities within the blood, like the single celled amoeba. From further tests we have observed the stem cells rush to a sight of damaged tissue, like antibodies, and immediately start working to repair the damage.

From the patient's perspective, this man has inadvertently become somewhat of an advanced being, being completely free of common diseases like the flu, malaria, and gastric infections. He also now possesses the ability to instantly heal minor wounds on his body.

Despite this, we do not consider this patient to be 'invincible' as anything fatal that may occur, like a heart attack or serious wounding, would cause the body to die quicker than the stem cells could repair it.

Other side effects are still being studied and observed from the patient. Until we are 100 percent convinced that there will be no long-term detrimental effects to the patient, we are terminating the trials.

We are currently testing a new formula on monkeys, to find out what would occur if we were to increase the dosage of these modified stem cells, whether the rate of tissue healing would increase to such a level that the patient would become completely regenerative and indestructible, remains to be seen.

Research continues.

Susan turned away from the piece of paper with a look of disbelief, before reading through it all again just to make sure that she'd understood it all correctly.

"That's not possible, surely?" She asked herself.

The look of confusion on her face soon turned to that of panic, and she quickly returned the piece of paper to the place she had found it. She knew how angry Tom would be if he found out what she had read and so she decided to pretend she knew nothing.

"Why would Tom want to keep something like that a secret from me?" She asked herself and started to wonder what other secrets could be hidden away within the bindings of the little black book.

She lay back down on the bed with a million different thoughts meandering through her brain and tried her best to rationalise them. Pretending to Tom that she knew nothing was going to be easy, but lying to herself was not. He had been so caring and considerate to her since the first day that they met that she immediately perceived him as an honest and trustworthy guy, but maybe it was all an act, maybe she knew nothing about him at all.

"Did he even mean it when he said he loved me?" She wondered.

CHAPTER FOUR (B)

IT WAS back in the June of 2000 that Tom was first introduced to an oxygen mask. He was sixteen at this point and finally allowed to play poker with his father and uncle for real money. His father, Jonathon, said that they would just play for a few pounds so that Tom wouldn't end up out of pocket, but the truth of the matter was that he had seen how well Tom had been playing lately and wasn't prepared to hand over all his money that easily. Tom had even joked that Uncle Bobby should throw in the keys to the Audi too, but the offer was declined with a smile.

It was just the three of them that night, gathered around the green velvet poker table. Uncle Bobby and his father had long since left the builders firm by this point and had gradually fallen out of touch with their old colleagues. Not that it mattered much to them, they enjoyed each other's company like a bunch of old school friends and laughed about while 'Abbey Road' by the Beatles played gently from the stereo system.

Bobby and his father were busy sipping Southern Comfort on the rocks while poor Tom sat there with a warm mug of Lemsip in front of him. He had been suffering with a sore throat for many days now, and it seemed to be getting worse and worse. His father had told him that it was all down to his smoking, and that he should quit before it did some serious damage to him. Tom was at a rebellious stage in his life and although he had a lot of respect for his father and had no doubt that he was correct in what he was saying, he still continued to smoke regardless.

Tom finished off his Lemsip, took a few aspirin and headed upstairs for an early night, finally giving the other two a chance to win some money from each other. He perched himself on his precarious window ledge and smoked one last rebellious cigarette out the bedroom window, before finally retiring to bed and drifting off into a drowsy sleep.

At 2:00 a.m. the following morning, Tom awoke with a shocking surprise. The tonsils in this throat had more than quadrupled in size and had almost blocked his air passages entirely. He thrashed about in a panic, knocking things over and banging against the walls. His nose was bunged up too, and he started to choke and slowly turn blue. His Mother burst through the door to find out what all the commotion was about and immediately called the paramedics for him. She gradually managed to calm him down enough to the point where he could just about breathe enough oxygen to stay conscious and held his hand gently while they waited for help to arrive.

When the paramedics arrived they put a mask over his face and hooked him up to a respirator. The gas was enriched with oxygen and blended with a saline solution. The saline made the gas taste sweet and it felt soothing against his jagged raw throat. Tom spent the rest of that night and the following morning in the accident and emergency department of Crawley Hospital, eventually being transferred up to a ward at about lunchtime. He lay there helplessly for hours on end, unable to get up or talk. Nurses came to check on him every so often, taking blood samples and attaching an intravenous drip to his wrist. At about dinner time a doctor finally approached him. He was a tall, friendly looking Asian guy who was the specialist ENT doctor (Ear, Nose and Throat). He explained to Tom that he was suffering from a severe case of tonsillitis and that he would need to drain some fluid to help him to breathe better. Tom was grateful and trusted that the doctor would be able to help him. What Tom didn't realise, was that the doctor was about to puncture both of his tonsils with an enormous lancet and squeeze the puss out by hand, and all this without the use of an anaesthetic. The doctor smiled and admitted, 'it may hurt a little bit.' But as soon as the needle perforated the first tonsil, the pain caused a common reflex reaction. Tom bit down hard upon the doctor's fingers and almost broke through the skin. Tom hadn't done it intentionally, but nonetheless felt a little chuffed at himself. The doctor then realised it may be a good idea to fetch some numbing spray, and proceeded with the other tonsil with caution.

Tom was allowed to go home a few days later, along with some strong antibiotics that he had to take. He waited patiently for a letter from the hospital, advising him of a date to have the tonsils completely removed. At the hospital, the doctors looking after Tom were a little concerned with how the tonsillitis had become so bad over such a short period of time. They ran several tests on the blood samples they had taken previously and looked out for any anomalies.

Tom finally received a letter with the NHS stamp on it a week later, but it was not what he had expected. The letter was very vague, but basically explained that they needed Tom to go back to the hospital for further tests. Tom had never undergone any kind of operation before and merely assumed that it was all standard procedure. When he arrived at the hospital they escorted him to the phlebotomy department and sat him down in a bulky metal chair. They extracted a small cylinder of blood, labelled it, and placed it into a rack. They then gave Tom a glass of sugary liquid to drink, and told him to come back in thirty minutes. Tom was very confused by this point, but drank the fluid anyway. He came back after the thirty minutes had passed and they took another small cylinder of blood.

It was the very next day that Tom received another letter from the hospital, advising him to attend a consultation of the test results. He went in nervously with his mother by his side, scared that he was dying of cancer or tuberculosis or something. The doctors then finally explained to Tom what was going on, that their suspicions had been true. They explained to Tom that he had type one diabetes and that to control the disease he would need to start giving himself intramuscular injections on a daily basis.

They explained to Tom that diabetes was an illness relating to the function of the pancreas in the human body. It came in two types that were inventively named type one and type two. The function of the pancreas was to supply the body with an appropriate amount of insulin which was required by the body as a form of skeleton key. It opened up the doors to each cell in the body to allow sugar to enter and to energise them. Whilst these doors remained locked, the cells and organs become deprived of energy and would slowly stop working. The sugar in the body would then remain in the blood stream, causing detrimental effects to the walls of the veins, and also causing blockages. These blockages can then cause serious circulation problems that could only be resolved by the amputation of limbs.

The type two variety of the disease was defined by having a 'lazy' pancreas. It supplied some insulin to the body, but not enough and needed to be aided. This was caused by excessive intake of sugar over a long period of time and was considered the 'self-inflicted' version of the disease. The type one variety, which was the one that Tom had been afflicted with, was defined as having a 'dead' pancreas. It was when the pancreas was not functioning at all, and the body needed to be supplied with the whole requirement of insulin. This was not a degenerative process, but more like having a pancreas with a built-in time bomb. This version of the disease was generally passed down genetically, from parents who were normally only carriers of the disease. The actual sufferers of the disease normally skipped a generation in the bloodline, so the culprits would have to be Tom's grandparents. He knew that neither his grandmother nor

Grandfather Dunn had ever suffered with the illness, so that only left his father's parents. With rumours that his father's mum had been a London prostitute, it was not at all unlikely that she had done business with a sufferer, and so Tom quickly placed the blame upon her.

Through ignorance and denial, Tom never took the illness too seriously at first, and apart from his injections, he carried on with life as normal. The injections felt very strange and unnatural to begin with, but it wasn't long before they became second nature, like breathing in and out. The doctors had provided Tom with countless leaflets and diet sheets that advised him exactly what he was allowed to eat and what he wasn't. The biggest things to stay away from being fizzy drinks, chocolate, and sweets of any kind, as these items contained dangerously high levels of sugar. Tom completely ignored this advice and thought that he could just carry on eating them and just compensate with a higher dosage of insulin.

It was about a month later when Tom first overcompensated with the insulin, and found himself in serious trouble. A normal healthy person would have a blood sugar level of about five milimoles per litre, but Tom had injected so much insulin that he was barely even reading one on the chart. This was called a 'hypoglycaemic attack.' The first symptoms of this were confusion and disorientation, so Tom had no idea what was even happening to him. The muscles in his arms and legs then became so deprived of sugar that they started contracting violently, causing severe cramp afflicting all his limbs with crippling pain. He then became pale, his eyesight turned to a white haze, and he fell unconscious on the floor.

Tom was a lot more careful with his injection dosages after that, but he never found it easy to get perfect. He suffered many more attacks like that afterwards, but eventually learnt how to predict them, and what to do if they came.

The diabetes was the first turning point in Tom's life. It changed his perception of the world and turned him very bitter. Despite this, Tom never allowed the disease to hold him back from anything, and achieved high in all of his A-level exams. He even got offered a place at Oxford University and took it without thinking twice. He took a course in advanced biochemistry, and it was during his studies there that he first met Dr. Richards. Dr. Richards had been invited to the university to give an inspirational talk about the importance of science. Tom had read up about Dr. Richards prior to his visit, and had found out that he was currently the head of a stem cell research project. After he had completed his thoughtful speech, Tom approached him and asked about the research. He explained to Tom that they had recently completed a batch of animal tests with the stem cells and that things seemed very promising. He went on to say that they were nearing the stage when they would be ready for the first human trial. Tom knew the potential that stem cells could have on his diabetes and begged Dr. Richards to let him be the first. Dr. Richards was very hesitant at first because of Tom's age, but after a lot of persuasion, he finally agreed that he would help Tom. Months later they finally performed the procedure on Tom and it was a complete success. Tom was free again, free from all the injections, free from hypoglycaemic attacks, free to go out and stuff his face full of as many chocolate bars as he could.

CHAPTER FIVE

"NO LUCK? Try this one instead Tom." Jobe called out thought the mask, selecting another key from the bag. Tom took the next key from his hand and tried it in the door lock. The key slid into the hole with ease and for a second Tom felt relieved, before realising that the key wouldn't turn and yanked it back out again.

"For God's sake, this is going to take bloody ages!" He moaned.

"Chin up bro', we're making progress." Jobe replied optimistically.

"I guess, though I'm not convinced that any of these damn cars even have any petrol in them."

"There was a bit in the first one. Every little bit helps."

"I know, but if all the cars have that amount of petrol in them, it will take about forty cars to fill the tank up!" Tom pointed out pessimistically.

"Well, hopefully they won't Tom. Here, try this key." He offered out another key from the bag, throwing the wrong one down in the reject pile. The key turned around in the lock and made a satisfying clicking noise.

"Oh, thank God for that!" Tom sighed out. He opened the door and swung himself into the driver's seat.

The car was an Audi A72 from 2015, one of the very last cars to come off the production line before the factory was destroyed. It had a smooth and curvy design and wind resistance was minimised everywhere. It was coated in a bimetallic paint that turned from purple to orange in the light. The car was very similar in design to the one that Tom's uncle Bobby used to have, with the obvious exceptions of the colour and all the gadgets inside. At the time, Bobby's new car was top of the range and came complete with all of the optional extras. Back then it was impressive to have an electric sunroof and central locking, but these were all pathetic and insignificant in comparison with the gadgets that the A72 had to offer. One of the amazing things that the A72 could do was automatically detect the weather around it, and then adjust itself to adapt. If the weather was cold outside it would put the heating on. If it was hot it would turn on the fans. If it was to rain, then it would put on the wipers, and if the windows were to steam up it would automatically demist them. It also had a voice activated navigation device and a built in 'Ipod inferno' stereo system, which came pre-set with over a million songs upon it.

He closed the door, slid the key into the ignition and placed his hands upon the leather steering wheel. He'd heard that on an open road it could obtain speeds of up to 200 miles an hour, and the urge to put the car to the test was so tempting.

"Hey bro'! Stop day dreaming would ya!" Jobe shouted at him, shaking a petrol can and tube at the window. Tom quickly snapped out of his dreamy daze and peered down at the petrol gauge.

"About quarter tank." He replied back.

"Excellent, we'll have that!" Jobe replied, and gestured to take the keys from him. Tom let out a sigh, and begrudgingly took the key from the ignition.

Jobe took the key and strolled around to the side of the car, turning it into the petrol cap and pulling the cap free.

"It's your turn to do this shit bro'." He called over to Tom, as he placed the can on the floor and threaded the tube into the hole. Tom gave up his comfy seat and joined Jobe by the side of the car.

"I thought you liked the taste of petrol Jobe?" He said to him sarcastically.

"Well, we'll see if you like it now won't we," Jobe replied defensively. Tom gave him a cheeky smile and grabbed the other end of the tube. He composed himself, held his breath and removed the oxygen mask from his face.

"Take your time and don't panic." Jobe said, watching him attentively.

Tom knelt down on the floor and brought the clear plastic tubing to his lips and gave it a short suck. The taste of fumes entered his mouth immediately and the sight of fluid in the tube appeared shortly after. He quickly removed the tubing from his lips and shoved the end into the can. He slid the mask back onto his face and was finally able to breathe again, while the petrol siphoned itself out into the can.

"Not a single drop in my gob Jobe!" He taunted him.

"You the man Tom, just means you'll be doing all the sucking from now on!" Jobe taunted back.

The flow of petrol stopped just before the level reached the top of the can, and Tom screwed the cap back onto it.

"You sure there's no more petrol cans in here Jobe? Under a pile of crap somewhere maybe?" Tom asked.

"Don't think so bro', but if you fancy fishing through all that shit then be my guest." He replied.

"Well we're gonna have to empty this in the truck then before we can do anymore." Tom told him.

"Yeah that's alright. The truck's only over the hill. Let's go." Jobe suggested. Tom nodded in agreement, as they climbed their way out the building.

"So what cars have you had then Tom?" Jobe enquired, as he strolled along swinging the petrol can.

"Well I had a blue Fiesta when I was young. My parents bought it for me when I passed my test." Tom replied.

"A fiesta hey, sophisticated!" Jobe sniggered.

"Hey don't mock, it was a good car. It survived a lot of battering over the years, through bad driving and too much alcohol and it never broke down on me once." Tom explained.

"So what did you have after that?" Jobe enquired further.

"That's the only car I've had. It was with me until I finished my university course, then when I moved away I didn't really need a car. How about you then? You like trucks do ya?"

"No, not really Tom, the Dakota is Karen's truck. I'm more of a bike guy."

"Oh right, what did you used to have then?"

"I used to ride around on a big Harley Davidson."

"So what happened to it?"

"A Stupid fucking Mini crashed into me and the bike was a write off."

"Really? Were you OK?"

"Broke both legs and a few ribs, but I was more upset about the bike!"

The mush that morning was almost as good as the rainbow mush had been the day before. The rain and the sun had made their appearances on separate occasions that morning, therefore the machine was unable to instantaneously fuse the two sources. But despite this, they had appeared in equal amounts within a short period of time, which made the consistency almost perfect. The taste however, was not quite the fruit salad mousse taste of the rainbow mush, but more like slightly stale rice pudding. On a normal day this would have been more than satisfactory for anyone to eat, but the tin of peach slices in the cupboard seemed much more appealing to Steven that morning.

Steven sat there at the dining table eating them slowly, savouring every mouthful. Jacob had woken Steven minutes before by creeping into the room and tapping away at the computer. Steven was not in the mood for an argument, his lungs still felt a little sore from the events in the night and it felt like he had just smoked a whole pack of twenty cigarettes. He gave Jacob a scowling look and released a sigh of surrender before descending the stairs and raiding through the cupboards. The sound of Jacob's relentless tapping on the keyboard could still be heard from all the way down in the living room. Steven was surprised he hadn't broken the thing yet, but still he persisted.

Susan and Karen were either busy in their rooms or still fast asleep and Steven had no one to talk to. He finished his tin of peaches and started examining the DVDs that Jacob had taken from Tina's house.

"Crappy, sodding horror films!" He complained under his breath and put the cases back down again. 'Why the hell did Jacob have such a morbid taste in films?' He asked himself. He weighed the idea of venturing over to Tina's house himself to see if she actually had some decent films, some comedies or science fiction maybe. Anything but stupid teenage girls having sex, taking drugs, and then getting sliced to pieces by a maniac in a mask. He peered over at the full oxygen canister sitting by the PGOGM and the idea became increasingly tempting. He wasn't normally allowed to go outside by himself, and if Susan or Tom found out they wouldn't be happy with him at all. He wondered how long he would be left alone. Maybe he could pop over there and be back before anyone would even notice his absence. After all, it wasn't going to take him long, five or ten minutes maybe. And he'd been sitting on his own in the living room for a good fifteen minutes already. He eventually decided that the venture was worth the risk and mounted the oxygen canister upon his back. He tiptoed over towards the front door, minding the creaky floorboards and gently prised open the door.

He dashed past the newly acquired carbon dioxide unit that had been placed in the drive, over the road, and into Tina's house through the open doorway. The smell of rotten corpses hit him immediately and made his stomach start to churn. He breathed deeply and tried to compose himself, knowing that if he were to throw up in the mask he would surely drown in his own vomit. He felt the peaches in his stomach start to dislodge, churn, and rumble. He swallowed deeply and took a few more long breaths. His stomach finally started to settle down so he walked over to the DVD collection, pretending he didn't know what was underneath the white sheet on the couch. He knelt down and started fingering through the collection. It was then obvious why pickings had been slim for Jacob the day before. Tina and Tony were obviously not horror fans at all, as most of their collection was formed of comedies and dramas. Steven felt like he was in heaven and wanted to take every single one of the films back with him. The others would probably not pay too much attention to the odd new DVD here and there, but they would surely ask questions about a whole new bookcase full of them. They would know he'd been over there. They would tell him off, shout at him. Steven considered whether he actually cared about being told off. What was the worst they could do to him? They couldn't ground him, or tell him that he couldn't play with his friends. They couldn't refuse him dessert with his dinner. All they could do was shout. Steven decided that he could cope with shouting, that it was no big deal and headed off into the kitchen to get a carrier bag for his newly acquired DVDs. Steven was getting increasingly excited over the selection of films and filled the bag up very quickly, returning to the kitchen for another which he also filled to the brim. Steven soon realised that he wouldn't be able to manage a third bag and accepted his losses, before sneaking back over to the house again.

He immediately noticed a noise from the en-suite bathroom above him and knew that someone had gotten up. Maybe they had just woken up and had been unaware of his absence. He might not be in trouble quite yet. He removed the mask and the canister, and set them back down where they came from hoping nobody would notice it had been used. He then took the carrier bags up the stairs and into his bedroom. Jacob was still sitting at the computer in the same position that Steven had left him earlier, playing the same game.

"Hey Jacob, you alright?" Steven asked with a pleasant smile. Jacob was so surprised by Steven's friendly tone that he actually paused the game for the first time, and turned to face him with a confused look, nodding in response to his question.

"Can I ask you a favour please?" Steven continued, placing the bags down by his feet and sitting down on his bed. Jacob looked down at the bags and started to type into his machine.

"You've been to Tina's house." Read out the computerised voice.

"Ha! There's no fooling you I guess!" Steven replied cheerfully before continuing. "Well, 'cause you got that umbilical thingy, they don't mind you going outside and stuff, so if they ask who got these, can I say it was you?"

Jacob thought about the question for a bit with a slightly smug look on his face, enjoying the power bestowed on him. After a while he started to type into his machine again.

"One condition." The voice read.

"What's that Jacob?" Steven asked.

"You're not watching any of those rubbish films when I'm around." The voice replied after a few moments of tapping. Steven gave a sigh of defeat and agreed to the terms.

It was Susan who was in the en-suite at this time, brushing her teeth with an old filthy toothbrush that she'd acquired when she first arrived. The bristles were completely bent out of shape and the lack of toothpaste made the experience less than satisfying, but it was the best attempt she could make to be hygienic. She rinsed her mouth out with some of the triple distilled water that she kept in the bathroom and then slipped herself into a pair of jeans and a jumper. She stretched her muscles out with a yawn and could hear the faint creaking of her joints.

She then started contemplating how many people she would murder for the sake of a strong black coffee. It had been years since she'd satisfied her cravings for caffeine, and although her body had recovered from the withdrawal symptoms, her brain still reminded her exactly what she was missing. She shook off the thought and made her way down the stairs.

"Where the hell is everyone?" She muttered to herself, before recalling her sleepy conversation with Tom earlier. The beeper started to sound on the mush machine so she leaned over and pressed the reset button. She strolled off into the kitchen for a bowl and spoon and found herself staring longingly at the stack of tinned food. They had already consumed quite a few tins the night before and maybe they should start to ration themselves to it. She didn't want the delicious food to all be gone in a few days, but then again it was pointless just keeping it in the cupboard forever like Tina had. She started to rummage around the tins in search of the peach slices that she had noticed the night before. Before long she noticed the empty tin lying by the sink, the remnants and juice spilt over the draining board.

"Oh, bastards!" She said to herself much louder than she had intended, and decided to just settle for a bowl of mush instead.

Tom and Jobe came in through the door a few moments later to find Susan just finishing off the bowl.

"Honey we're home!" Tom called out in comical fashion. Susan returned him a funny look, suddenly remembering the medical report she had read earlier. She quickly shook it off just in case he could somehow read her mind, and replaced it with a warm smile.

"How did it go?" she asked.

"Yeah, not too bad my love. We managed to get just over a quarter tank in the truck now. Still got a way to go though." Tom replied, taking the heavy canister from his back.

"Well at least it's something, Tom," She encouraged.

"Yeah, it's a start, and we've only done the showroom so far. I'm sure there must be other cars about." Tom replied.

"Is Karen still not awake Susan?" Jobe interrupted with a concerned slant of an eyebrow.

"No I don't think so Jobe, I've only just got up myself though." She replied. Jobe gave her a nod and placed his oxygen gear on the floor before starting to ascend the stairs.

"Where are the kids then?" Tom continued.

"Upstairs playing on the computer I think. Steven's eaten the peaches as well! I was looking forward to them!" Susan responded in a disgruntled fashion.

"Karen? You awake babe?" Jobe whispered, gently knocking on the bedroom door. He waited a few seconds and could hear a faint murmur from inside. He opened the door and crept in. The curtains were still drawn closed and the room was in complete darkness.

"You feeling alright my gorgeous?" He whispered again.

"I feel really bad Jobe," replied a weak faint voice.

Jobe walked to the window and drew the curtains slightly so he could see what he was doing and the midday sun beamed in through the small gap. It partially illuminated the room and Jobe could make out Karen's figure in the bed. He sat down beside her softly and started to stroke her hair.

"My chest hurts so bad Jobe." She said, struggling to talk.

"Oh baby," Jobe replied affectionately. He put his hand down on the pillow next to her to steady his weight, and leaned in to kiss her on the cheek. He immediately felt his hand become wet and pulled it back to examine it. The room was too dark to establish what the gloopy liquid was and so he stepped back over to the curtains to pull them wide open. He looked down to see his hand dripping with blood and as he turned back to the bed, he could see the whole pillow below Karen's head was drenched in it, and completely covered the side of her face. At that point she started to cough, spluttering out more blood vigorously from her lungs. She let out a whimpering cry of pain and rested back down again on the pillow panting.

"Oh Christ baby, it's alright, you're gonna be fine." He replied in shock, and rushed back over to her bedside.

"It hurts so bad Jobe, I can't take it anymore." She cried.

"Just try and relax baby, I'll see if Tom's got anything for you, OK?" He whispered, before giving her another kiss and dashing out the room in a panic.

He ran down the stairs faster than he'd ever moved before, bounding two or three steps at a time. He missed a step and almost tripped and fell, but grabbed on to the banister at the last moment and rushed into the living room.

"Tom! Tom! You gotta help me bro'. Karen's very sick, she's coughing blood everywhere." Jobe yelled at him.

"Really? Jesus! She must have taken in loads of that carbon dioxide last night." He replied, throwing down a bowl of mush and getting to his feet.

"She's been kinda sick for a while now Tom, but never like this. Please, we have to do something for her, what have you got?" Jobe asked fidgeting like crazy.

"Um, -er, God I don't know." Tom replied shaking his head, in too much of a panic to think straight.

"We've still got that box of inhalers in the loft Tom, they'd probably help." Susan interrupted abruptly.

"You still have some of those? Perfect, they work wonders." Jobe replied in a hopeful tone.

"Oh yeah, I forgot. Come on, let's go get them." Tom announced and followed Jobe back up the stairs again.

He jumped and released the loft hatch before dashing up the rickety ladder. Jobe waited anxiously at the bottom as Tom passed him down a heavy brown box. Jobe took it and rested it on the floor. He ripped off the sticky tape and opened it up, revealing packets upon packets of the inhalers and cartridges. He tore one from the packaging and slid a cartridge inside with a reassuring clicking noise, before walking back into the bedroom looking calm and composed.

"Hey Karen, have some of this baby, you'll feel much better." He said with a smile, and placed the inhaler into her hand. She smiled back at the pleasing sight of the device and inserted both of the plastic tubes into her nose. She pressed down on the button at the top and inhaled the oxygen deep into her lungs. The gas felt soothing to her discomfort like ice cream on a sore throat, as she let out a sigh of relief.

"God that feels nice." She finally announced, her voice starting to sound a little stronger.

"Tom's got a whole box of these baby, so have as much as you like, alright?" Jobe assured her, starting to stroke her hair again. She inhaled another burst of the gas and raised her head up to look around. Tom was standing by the doorway looking in with concern, just as Susan appeared from the landing and came in holding a glass of water and a wet cloth.

"Hey Karen, how you doing girl?" She asked caringly, sitting down on the other side of the bed from Jobe.

"Feel much better now Susan," Karen replied, as colour started to return to her skin.

"Here, have some water Karen. It'll take away that nasty taste in your mouth." Susan put the glass in her hand. Karen took a sip and washed away the remnants of blood from her mouth and throat.

"We're all here for you Karen. You're going to be fine," Susan continued, as she took the cloth and wiped away the blood from Karen's face.

Jobe stayed alone by Karen's bedside throughout most of that afternoon, comforting her as she drifted in and out of consciousness. It was just after four o'clock that she eventually managed to climb out of bed, as Jobe helped her get down the stairs wrapped up in her duvet.

"Hey you're up!" Susan called over from the dining table.

"Yeah, I'm feeling much better now." Karen replied, faking a smile and sitting down on the sofa. Jobe then sat down at the table, his face looking riddled with worry and guilt as he slumped forward with his head in his hands.

"Hey, she'll be fine." Susan whispered over to him and held his hand comfortingly. Tom appeared from the kitchen, holding the bottle of Jack Daniels and two glasses. He leaned into the chair next to Jobe and sat the bottle down on the table.

"Fancy a glass Jobe?" He asked him, having already started to pour it out.

"I can't think of anything better to do." He replied softly, giving half a smile and took the glass from Tom.

Karen lay there in a daze, wrapped up tight and snug around the soft duvet covers. She rested her head down gently upon the arm of the couch and lay there feeling sorry for herself. She had known the inevitable result of her health for quite a while, but the conclusion now seemed so much closer. Her death had been a certainty for a long time now and she had come to accept the idea. It was not her death that she feared, but more what she would be leaving behind. She had been at Jobe's side for most of her life and crumbled at the thought of them being apart. Not just for her own comfort, but for Jobe's sake. She knew that the deadly carbon dioxide would soon enough claim his life as well, but didn't like the thought of him being alone in the world in the meantime, just waiting to die. He was a good man with a caring heart and he didn't deserve any unhappiness. But her passing could not be prolonged much longer.

If it wasn't for all that playing on her mind, she'd actually be quite happy with the idea of passing away. It would mean an end to the suffering and destruction, and she would be greeted with open arms by all of those she once loved. Her beloved mother would be the first to embrace her. She would be waiting there at the gates sitting down in a sturdy old rocking chair. She'd be wearing her chunky bi-focal glasses, resting half-way down her nose and have a crossword puzzle in her hand.

"'Ello my dear! What took you so long?" She would say with cheery old-fashioned enthusiasm, before rushing off to make everyone a nice cup of tea. Her father would be standing close by as well, looking slightly nervous and twiddling his thumbs. He'd give her a warm smile and a hug and ask her if she'd had a safe journey. Her little brother would probably make an appearance too, when he wasn't too busy trying his corny chat-up lines with all the departed singles.

The images in her head made her smile and any fear that she may have had surrounding death had been long washed away. She sat there on the couch for a long time, with this weird smile upon her face, completely oblivious to any conversation going on around her.

It was the same images floating around in her head the day she tried to end it all. Her friend Louise used to live in the house to the right of her with her pet cat Joey at the time. The two houses had a joining wall and the two front doors were just a mere few meters apart from each other. Louise had got the mush machine installed upon her wall, but was too poor to afford any additional oxygen products. Luckily enough for Louise, she appeared to be quite resistant to the carbon dioxide in the air and remained quite healthy for a long time. Because of this, she was brave enough to hold her breath long enough to dash over to Karen's house on a regular basis. They had all talked about having Louise move in with them to save her the risk all the time, but the house was small and Jobe was not too keen on cats. So Louise stayed next door with little Joey and came round to visit them every Tuesday and Thursday. It was one Tuesday morning that little Joey decided that he was bored in the house and wanted an adventure, catch some mice maybe, or chase a bird, oblivious to reality. Louise had not checked where Joey was and when she held her breath and opened up the front door, Joey went dashing out into the open. Louise was left absolutely helpless to save him and couldn't even call out his name without gushing in the carbon dioxide and suffocating. Joey went leaping and bounding around for at least five seconds before he realised he should have stayed in doors. He stopped running and fell on his side. He started coughing and heaving like he was bringing up a hairball, but soon enough became motionless and died. Louise found herself standing in the middle of the street for at least a minute or so, with her hand covering her mouth and nose. All she could do was to watch the cat die and tears started to stream down her face.

Her body started convulsing, in desperate need to breathe, as she finally turned away from the dead pet and knocked against Karen's door. Karen opened up the door immediately, as she normally did, covering her face in the same way. Louise collapsed in the doorway in uncontrollable floods of tears, as Karen closed the door up again and tried her best to console her. It was a good twenty minutes or so until Louise could compose herself enough to explain to Karen what the matter was. She felt terrible for Louise. She had looked after the animal for almost twenty years now and it was the very last remaining part of her family unit, the last reminder, the last thing she had to care for. It was almost like having your own baby die right in front of you. It was devastating to her. Louise spent the rest of that day with Karen and Jobe. They watched films and listened to Madonna in an attempt to cheer her up, but nothing seemed to work. Louise slept on the couch and had a big bowl of mush in the morning. She then decided she needed to go home and be alone for a little while.

Karen and Jobe were concerned, but thought they'd give her some space until she was due to come over on Thursday. Thursday came and went and there was no sign of Louise. Come Friday morning Karen decided that she needed to check up on her and took a gas canister over to her house. She found Louise dead on the couch, clutching a picture of her and the family. The photograph had been taken when Louise was just nine and depicted the family eating Christmas dinner around the table. Her mother and father were pulling apart a cracker, her brothers were pulling funny faces at the camera and Louise was sitting with little Joey on her lap. He appeared tiny in the picture and couldn't have been more than six months old. The rest of the family were seemingly unaware that Louise had the cat on her lap, as she sneaked bits of turkey off the dinner table for him. It was a nice picture and Karen could imagine how Louise felt when she looked at it. She carried Louise's body upstairs to the bedroom and tucked her up underneath the covers. She then walked to the bathroom at which point she noticed the empty bottle of sleeping pills.

Karen fell into a pit of depression after that and couldn't find the will to get up in the mornings. She started to think about her own family and how badly she missed them all. Jobe was his usual caring self to her, but didn't seem to be able to empathise. He had lost all his family too, but was too manly to show it, and remained calm and composed with his emotions buried deep inside. Karen started to feel like she couldn't talk to him anymore and made her way to the kitchen. Jobe was in the middle of having a bath at the time and never noticed her leave the bedroom. She searched through the kitchen drawers frantically, until finally she found a ten-inch carving knife. It was the kind of knife that you need to sharpen every six months or so with a grinding brick. The knife had not been sharpened in a very long time now, as there was no need to use it. Karen was oblivious to this and rested the blade against her wrist. She took a deep breath and bit down upon her lip, before pulling the blade across with force. The blade had almost no affect, and left behind a mark similar to that of a cat scratch.

"Damn it!" she screamed, and searched the drawers again for the brick to sharpen it. By this time Jobe had dried himself and got dressed. He heard Karen's scream and came dashing down the stairs. Karen had found the brick and had just started to sharpen up the knife, when Jobe came pelting into the kitchen and snatched the knife from her grip.

"Don't even think like that Karen, I need you! I love you!" Jobe screamed, and started to cry for the first time since she had met him. It changed her opinion of him instantaneously and she started to smile. She realised that Louise hadn't been half as lucky as her. She had something more than just a cat, she had a loving man that she adored, and he adored her back. As long as he was alive, then she had a reason to live as well.

Karen finally snapped out of her dreamy trance a while later with the sound of Jobe calling her name.

"Karen . . . Karen?" He called.

"I'm awake Jobe," She finally replied with a gentle smile, her senses livened up by a seasoned aroma.

"Here, we've made you some tomato soup." Jobe replied, holding a bowl of the creamy orange substance. The soup looked like heaven to her with bits of herbs and vegetables blended into it and croutons floating on the top. Her smile grew larger as she sat up in the couch and took the bowl from his hands.

"Oh, thank you babes, it smells gorgeous." She said to him, sounding forever grateful.

"That's OK my love, you enjoy it." He responded with another warm smile and gave her a gentle kiss on the lips. He then returned to the dining table and rejoined Tom and Susan.

"She alright?" Susan whispered over to him with a little smile.

"Yeah she's OK. She's a fighter." He replied with optimism.

Karen was about half-way through her bowl of soup when Steven and Jacob first made their appearances downstairs. Steven approached the table with a DVD case in his hand and perched himself next to Jobe, while Jacob carried on through to the kitchen and began to fill up his funnel with water from the jug.

"Afternoon Steven, how you feeling?" Jobe asked.

"Lungs feels feel a bit rough but I'll live Jobe. How's Karen doing? I heard all the coughing earlier." Steven asked with concern.

"She's not too good kid. Why don't you try and cheer her up for me?" Jobe requested quietly, giving him a rub on the shoulder. Steven gave him a nod and a smile and stood up from the chair. He walked over to Karen on the couch, carrying the DVD in his hand and caught her attention with a little wave and a grin.

"Hey Karen, how you feeling?" he asked, sitting down beside her on the couch. She swallowed the spoonful of soup and mustered a response.

"Hello, Steven, I'm alright, thank you."

"You fancy watching a film?"

"Yeah, OK Steven, what you got there?" She enquired, as Steven passed over the case for inspection. 'Summer Camp 7: The Geeks Get Laid' read the title in bold friendly letters and underneath the writing was a picture of a greasy teenage boy with spots, buck teeth, and glasses. He was wearing an adult nappy and posed in a compromising position. Karen let out a short burst of laughter and insisted that Steven play the film immediately.

"You know how to play poker Jobe?" Tom asked, taking a mouthful of whisky from his glass.

"Do I know how to play poker? I'm the grand master of the game Tom." Jobe responded with cheeky confidence.

Tom responded with a disbelieving frown and a little grin, before walking over to the game cabinet for the poker set.

"What we having for dinner Tom?" Susan asked, stealing the last sip of his Jack Daniels.

"Um, dunno Sue, what does everyone think?" He answered, walking back to the table.

"Well we can just have mush if you want, if you wanted to save the food for a special occasion." Susan suggested.

"Occasion like what? Christmas?" Jobe added with sarcasm.

"Yeah you're right Jobe, let's just sod it hey?" Tom said with agreement.

"Alright then, I'll see what we've got left," Susan replied with excitement and scurried off to the kitchen.

"Right then Jobe, five card draw or Texas hold'em?" Tom asked, taking out the cards and the poker chips from the cardboard box.

"Gotta be Texas hold'em aint it bro'. You ready for a thrashing then are ya?" Jobe asked with playful arrogance.

"Yeah right, we'll see!" Tom replied and started to deal the holding cards. Jacob then reappeared from the kitchen and tapped Tom on the shoulder.

"Huh? Oh Jacob, are you alright to go by yourself today? I'm kinda tired from earlier still, do you mind?" Tom replied. Jacob shrugged his shoulders and started tapping on his machine.

"No problem." It read out, as Jacob motioned towards the door.

"Hey, keep you eyes open for any petrol while you're out kid, but don't go too far." Tom called over to him. "And we'll watch the sunset at dusk, alright?" He continued. Jacob replied with a nod and a thumb's up, before finally disappearing out the front door.

Susan remained in the kitchen for a while longer, excited about all the food like a child in a sweet shop, her eyes wide open and an eager smile upon her face. There were still at least a dozen cans on the side that comprised of everything from beef stew to baby carrots, and hotdog sausages to banana rice pudding. It took her a long time to decide what she fancied, but in the end it was the spaghetti and meatballs that won her over. She emptied the contents of the tins into a big saucepan and turned on the hob.

"I'll see you're ten, and I'll raise you another fifty." Tom announced, stacking up a large pile of blue plastic chips in the middle of the table. Jobe looked up from his cards and tried to read Tom's face. Tom was better at this game than Jobe had expected, his face remaining completely emotionless and calm. Jobe returned a look of frustrated confusion and peered back down at his cards again. Tom noticed the confused look and started to smirk.

"What's funny?" Jobe asked.

"Nothing mate, so what you gonna do?"

"I'll call your fifty Tom."

Tom acknowledged his courage and dealt out the river card on to the table. It was the queen of spades. Tom made an agreeable 'humming' noise, while Jobe remained looking nervous.

Steven and Karen were starting to giggle quite loudly at the film by this point and the noise was starting to make it hard for Jobe to concentrate.

"Check," Jobe finally declared.

"Check? You stingy bastard, I'll bet another fifty then." Tom replied.

"That's it then, I fold." Jobe moaned and slapped his cards down on the table.

"What did you have Jobe?" Tom asked.

"A pair of queens and a pair of tens," Jobe replied unhappily

"That was a good hand. You should have carried on with that." Tom advised him with raised eyebrows.

"Well you've obviously got a better hand than that, don't ya?"

"Nope, I ain't got anything actually!" Tom replied and started to snigger.

"What? You were bluffing me the whole game?" Jobe asked with surprise.

"I told you I was good!" Tom reminded him, and gathered up all the poker chips with a contented grin.

Susan called out from the kitchen a short while after to announce that diner was now ready. It was far from an elegant meal in comparison to what they were all brought up on. In reflection, it would have been the kind of meal that your mum would cook you on a Monday evening when she was too busy and stressed after a day's work to conjure up any better. But in this situation the meal to them was comparable to a knight's banquet, and everybody's mouths were beginning to water. Steven soon smelt the sweet aroma drifting over to him and joined the others at the table to munch away at the delicious tomato drizzled beef meatballs and spaghetti, making agreeable noises throughout the entire meal.

Jacob returned from his daily walk-about just after they had finished off the luxurious feast and had gathered around on the couches to catch the end of the movie. Normally at this point Jacob would have kicked up a stink at having to watch such a mushy feel good comedy, but decided to keep his thoughts to himself this time for he knew that his opinions would be far from welcome and would make him look increasingly arrogant and intolerant.

On Jacob's travels that afternoon he had spotted an old Ford 'Ka' parked just the other side of the college. Its exterior had been knocked about and dented all over and had started to look like a glossy sweet wrapper that had been unfolded and pressed flat. The vandals responsible for the crumpling had also smashed in the glass from all the windows and had ripped apart the foam from within the fabric seat cushions. Upon further inspection, it seemed that the fuel tank had remained undamaged throughout the beating and contained the desired unleaded petrol that they were searching for.

When the movie had eventually finished, Jacob led the men to the place where he had discovered the vehicle and helped them both to siphon out the sacred liquid into their trusted metal can. They then proceeded to take the petrol back up to the motorway again and pour it out into the Dodge. With the newly acquired petrol from the 'Ka', they had now filled the tank almost three-quarters of the way full.

They now had more than enough fuel to make the trip down to the Brighton clinic, and plenty for them to get back again as well. But Tom was still nervous about the trip and insisted without compromise, that they wait until the tank was completely full.

Despite the temporary delay, the plan to travel down to the Tremoline clinic seemed an absolute certainty now and would be the first proactive thing they had attempted in a very long time. The mere thought that this may bring them closer to a resolution began to fill them all with excitement and hope of the possibility that one day they could return to some degree of normality.

They knew that the plan was far from a Biblical mission to save the world. They had no delusions about being able to reverse the effects of the green cancer themselves, or being able to repair much of the destruction either. They were just six people striving to survive the harsh world and searching for a better place to live; a place where scientists and engineers would have already commenced reconstruction, and a place where the cure for the green cancer was just about to be perfected. They were searching for a place of hope, a place where the strength and determination of the human spirit still lived on.

The world had been riddled with conspiracies and secrets since the very beginning of history, from the cryptic mysteries of the pyramids to the very existence of extraterrestrials. There were some things that could never be explained in any logical fashion and some things that would just never be known. But there were certain questions and mysteries that could certainly be answered and explained, if only it was thought appropriate to do so. The governments of the world had always held the responsibility of keeping their citizens under firm control, and if knowledge would cause riots, then maybe secrecy was indeed the best policy.

So after this long history of keeping secrets, it seemed reasonable to think that just because the group had no knowledge of a big survival plan, it didn't by any means rule out the possibility of one. Out of the billions of people that once inhabited the earth, surely there were still a few geniuses alive, grouped together in a big bubble somewhere out at sea maybe, working hard on a way to prevent our extinction.

Hope and faith are powerful human emotions. They keep people striving on, fighting back, and giving them the courage and determination they need to survive. But none of the group could start to think about the big picture with any sense of clarity at this point in time. The best they could do was to just keep things simple and immediate, taking things one step at a time. They would fill up the truck, drive to the clinic and then start to think about what came next.

By the time they had finished fuelling the truck, the sun had already started to fade away and they all began to feel tired. They decided that it would be advantageous to drive the truck closer to the house and so they revved up the engine and began to make their way off the motorway slip road. While they had been away Karen had fallen asleep on the couch again and Susan had decided to go upstairs and start reading her copy of *War and Peace* for the third time over. After a mere few pages into the book she found herself thinking about Tom's medical report once again. She pulled it back out from under the bed and stared aimlessly into the text, trying to think of reasons Tom would keep it a secret from her.

Steven was sitting in his bedroom at this point, moaning to

himself that he was bored once again. He was tempted to go downstairs and watch another one of his new films, but was scared that he would get into trouble if he woke up Karen with the noise. The sound of the front door closing broke the deathly silence and immediately attracted Steven's attention. He eagerly jumped to his feet and rushed down the stairs to greet them, to find Jobe standing on his own with the petrol can and tubes in his hand.

"Alright Jobe, where's the others?" Steven asked.

"Hey bro', they gone off to watch the sun going down, or some girly rubbish like that." Jobe replied to him, pulling off the oxygen equipment. Steven responded with a snigger and shake of the head.

"What the hell's the big deal with that? I never understood why they bother." Steven asked, having pondered the question for years.

"Well, it's a nice sight I guess, beauty of nature, and all that stuff."

"Yeah, but it's not really that impressive is it? I mean, the sun rises and sets three hundred and sixty-five times in a year, hardly a once in a lifetime opportunity."

Jobe chuckled a little in complete agreement with Steven's opinion, but not wanting to sound too disrespectful to the others.

"Each to their own, hey kid." He finally replied and paced into the living room. Steven followed him in a few seconds later carrying a bowl and helping himself to a bowl of mush. Jobe walked up to Karen, asleep on the couch and couldn't help but think how beautiful she looked, peaceful and quiet like a sleeping beauty. She was lying near the edge of the couch, so he slid himself down behind her and gave her a gentle snuggle, planting kisses on the back of her neck.

"I bet you really miss your family hey, Jacob?" Tom asked him as they perched on the rubble, staring into the semicircle of red glow upon the horizon. The wind had now turned bitter cold, and Jacob's hands were firmly in his pockets. The question deserved an answer, but Jacob knew that his hands would turn to ice cubes before he could finish typing on his machine, so he merely nodded instead.

"Yeah, I bet you do. It's sad when people leave us, people we love, people who become part of us. I miss my family too Jacob." He continued. He fingered around in the breast pocket of his leather coat. All he could feel for a while was the bindings of his little black book and he started to panic, until his fingers finally felt the touch of metal and he let out a sigh of relief. He started to pull out a crimson ribbon, like a clown pulling out a ream of tied up handkerchiefs, before it reached the end and carried with it the glorious Victoria Cross. He sat and stared at it for a while, rubbing its impressions with his thumb and smiling like he always did.

"Have I ever shown you this?" Tom asked, turning his attention to Jacob. Jacob shook his head in response and looked down curiously at the medal.

"It was my Grandfather's medal. He left it to me when he passed away. He died of natural causes a long time before any of this mess started, but out of all the people I've lost in my lifetime, I think I miss him the most." Tom continued, as the medal glimmered in the amber rays of the sun.

"It's called the Victoria Cross, Jacob. It was awarded to certain men in the first two world wars, men that displayed courage in the face of the enemy. My grandfather hid from the Nazis under an enormous mound of corpses for more than a day, drenched in other people's blood and surrounded with the stench of rotting bodies. I've often imagined how it must've felt for him in that mound. I'd feel completely hopeless and filled with utter despair, like there was no way out, no way of escape, no hope for victory. That's kinda how all of us have felt at times, like there's no light at the end of the tunnel. But my grandfather had pride, will power, and determination. He was not about to let those Nazi sons of bitches get the better of him, so you know what he did?" Tom asked him, having completely captivated Jacob's attention by this point. Jacob shook his head in response, eagerly awaiting an answer.

"He crawled out from the pile when they had all gone, and killed every last one of the bastards. He even had an arm blown off in the process, but still he carried on. He was a brave man my granddad, and I loved him to bits." Tom continued and then paused for a while, smiling down at the medal again. He held it up by the ribbon, so it dangled free in the air, and gestured it over. Jacob finally took his hands out his pockets this time and cupped them under the medal.

"Here, I want you to have this Jacob, and take good care of it. Think of it as a reminder, that nothing is impossible, no situation is too dire, and that all you need to prevail, is courage." He smiled down at Jacob and released the ribbon. The medal fell gently through the air and landed softly in the palm of Jacob's hands. He looked up at Tom with unexpected delight and started to type into his machine.

"Thank you for taking care of me Tom." It eventually read out and Tom appreciated the acknowledgement.

By the time Tom and Jacob eventually arrived back at the house, most of them were already fast asleep. Jobe had carried Karen up the stairs to bed and Steven had taken her place on the couch. He had finally been able to sit and watch another film, but had fallen asleep a few minutes into it. The living room was surprisingly warm that evening, so Tom switched off the television and decided to leave Steven where he was. He sent Jacob to bed, helped himself to a glass of water and ascended the stairs to his own bed. Susan was still awake and sitting up in the bed reading her book. She greeted him with a smile and a wave and continued reading. Tom hung up his coat and sat on the bed to untie his shoe laces. Having taken off the shoes he suddenly felt a smooth surface through his socks. He bent down to look and his face turned completely panic stricken. He stood up and grabbed his black book from out of his coat pocket and sat back down again, briefly giving Susan a look, trying to read her expression. 'Had she read the report? What if she knew?' He thought, but her face showed no emotions and remained glued to *War and Peace*. She'd surely have something to say if she'd read it. She'd have questions and accusations, he continued to think. It must have fallen from the book that morning and landed under the bed. She probably hadn't noticed it. It was too far under the bed to notice it from a standing position. He decided that he must have gotten lucky, and inconspicuously slid the paper back into the book again.

"Was there much petrol in the car?" Susan asked casually, still not looking away from her book.

"Yeah a little bit. The Dodge is almost full now."

"Oh that's good, so when are we leaving?"

"Couple of days I should think, I do wanna make sure that we've got a full tank first though, just in case."

"Yeah I agree Tom, can't put the kids in danger."

"That was my thinking too. We've parked it outside the house now, so we don't have to keep trekking up the motorway all the time."

"Good idea. We'd better start packing soon then, hey?"

"Yeah, won't be long, I'm not sure how much stuff we'll fit on the back of the Dodge though."

"No, I know. I think I'll only take a few spare knickers and clothes. We should probably take a supply of clean water with us too."

"Yeah, I hadn't thought about that actually. We should take the kettles and stuff with us too then."

Susan nodded in response, and her attention returned to the novel. Tom opened his black book and started to write down the day's events. He hadn't previously intended to write anything at all that night. He was quickly running out of pages and wanted to save them for when there was a revelation, but Susan would surely get suspicious if he had taken out the book for no reason. He wrote down a few brief sentences and then clipped the book shut again, before returning it to his coat pocket.

CHAPTER SIX

IT WAS obvious to everyone that Tom had suffered another nightmare that night. His terrified screams woke up the whole house. Jobe sat up straight in bed, startled by the noise. It was quite unusual for someone else to wake up Jobe, as it was normally the other way round with the continual banging of the bedposts. The room was pitch dark and had a slight chill in the air. Before long, he realized that he was alone in the bed and could hear the faint sound of music coming from downstairs. He wiped the sleep from his eyes and gave his face a rub. 'What the hell was Karen up to?' He thought to himself and threw off the duvet. He had just gotten to his feet when there was a knock on the door.

"Jobe? Hey Jobe you awake?" The voice asked. Jobe staggered over to the door and opened it up to reveal Steven standing in the archway, a worried expression upon his face.

"Alright bro'? What's going on, you alright?" Jobe replied, still rubbing his face to wake up.

"I'm alright man. It's Karen; she's acting a bit weird."

"Weird? What do you mean Steven?" Jobe asked him, as Steven's look of worry began to contaminate him too.

"Well I was fast asleep on the couch until Tom woke me up a minute ago. I found Karen sitting on the other couch, watching the television. I said hello to her, but she didn't seem to see me." Steven explained to him. Jobe gave him a confused look and abruptly made for the stairs.

The television was playing the Madonna DVD that they had acquired before. It showed her wearing a sequined dress and singing a rendition of 'Like a payer' to a massive audience. Karen was watching attentively and smiling. Her skin was pale and cracked, her eyes were red and sore, and her lips and chin were covered in patches of wet crimson blood. The window above the couch had been pushed wide open, letting the carbon dioxide gush into the room and forcing the mush machine to work overtime to keep up the oxygen levels. But the bulky machine was obviously starting to struggle, as it vibrated violently against the wall, making a low pitched humming noise that was only just audible above the loud volume of the television. Karen began speaking, asking questions and pausing as if she could hear someone responding.

"Oh I love this one, do you remember the music video?"

"Yeah that's the one, was amazing huh?"

"Eh?"

"No, no luck on the job situation yet I'm afraid dad."

"Nah don't worry about me, something will come up."

"No don't be silly, I'm fine with money. I get my dole cheque each month, and Jobe helps me out."

"Yeah Jobe, you remember Jobe don't you mum?"

"That's right, that guy from school. He's back from the army now."

"Yeah it's quite serious, thinking about moving in together."

"Ha! No, it's a bit early to be thinking about that!"

"One day mum, I'll buy you a hat for the occasion."

"What you doing us for dinner mum?"

"Hmmm, sounds good to me, been ages since I had beef stew."

"Yes please, and don't be shy with the dumplings either."

Karen smiled over at the other couch and her attention then returned to the television. Jobe stood in the doorway, completely speechless for a while, until he came to his senses enough to close the living room window.

"Karen? Who are you talking to baby?" He asked gingerly.

"Hey Jobe you're here, you're just in time for dinner." She replied with a cheerful grin.

"You alright Karen, what's up?"

"Nothing's up Jobe, just watching Madonna with Mum and Dad. Mum loves Madonna almost as much as me. Aren't you gonna say hello?"

"Karen…there's no one here, babe."

"Eh? What you mean, they're sitting right there so don't be rude. Mum, Dad, this is Jobe."

"Karen, you're starting to freak me out a little."

"I'm sorry I didn't tell you they were coming, I thought it would be a surprise."

"Well you're right, I'm very surprised." He replied carefully.

"Well, it was about time you met them. Mum's going to cook us beef stew and dumplings for dinner. You like beef don't you?"

"Um, yeah I like beef Karen." Jobe responded, walking over to Karen and looking into her eyes with confusion.

"Tell dad about your time in the army. He fought in World War two ya know."

"Yeah, maybe later Karen." He humoured her, and wiped the blood from her lips with his sleeve. He then bent down on his knees beside the couch, and gave her a kiss on the forehead.

"You're going to be alright Karen. As soon as we get to the clinic the doctors will be able to sort you out no problem." He explained.

"What you talking about Jobe? I feel fine. Little bit of a sore throat maybe, but it's just something that's going around. Mum was saying a few of her friends from the W.I were a little poorly, isn't that right mum?"

Jobe could feel his eyes starting to swell with tears but managed to shake it off unnoticed. He stood up and looked away, clueless of what to do or say to Karen. At that point he noticed Tom and Susan peering in through the doorway, both of them looking shocked and worried. Jobe quickly paced out the room to join them, and pulled the door firmly shut.

"Hey Jobe, what's going on? Who's she talking to?" Susan asked him with a mixture of confusion and curiosity.

"She's lost her mind Susan! She's hallucinating!" Jobe rambled in a panic.

"My God, poor girl," Susan muttered.

"She looks really sick Tom. I think she's on the way out. What am I supposed to do?" Jobe asked him desperately.

"I don't know Jobe, I'm sorry." Tom replied with regret.

At that point Jobe's tear finally erupted and streamed out like a river down his face. He tried to sniff them away, but it was useless. He slid down the wall and sat on the floor with his head in his hands.

"I don't wanna lose her Tom. She means everything to me!" He blubbered out in between the tears. Neither of them could respond as they stood with their heads hung low. They tried hard to think of something appropriate to say to him, but the words just never came. Susan eventually knelt down and wrapped her arms around him. He hugged her back and continued to sob uncontrollably. Tom stood there for a while longer, still not knowing what to do. He found himself thinking that it was probably the first time in Jobe's life, that he had been reduced to tears. He was such a tough guy and the expression on his face looked out of place and strange. He walked past them into the kitchen and poured out a glass of water from the jug. It was intended for Karen, but he ended up drinking it himself with anxiety and nerves. He retained his composure and poured out another glass. Opening up the living room door he could immediately feel the increased levels of carbon dioxide in the room, as he walked over to the couch. Karen was sitting down slumped into the arm of the chair. Her eyes were half-open and looked glazed, as she continued to stare at the television screen in a trance.

"Hey Karen?" Tom whispered, and got her attention. She looked up and managed a little grin, as blood started to trickle down from her nostrils.

"Hello Tom, what you doing here? Have you met my parents?" She asked, gesturing to the other couch.

"No, I haven't. Nice to meet you both," He spoke into the empty space to humour her.

"I was telling them what a nice man you are, Tom." She replied and tried to wipe the blood away from her top lip. Her hand became drenched in the blood as she wiped it clean on the arm of the couch. But it continued to trickle down from her nose, engulfing her mouth and her chin.

"I've brought you a glass of water Karen." Tom explained and passed her the glass.

"Oh you are a good man Tom, Susan's a lucky girl." She struggled to say, taking the glass from him and taking a sip.

"You're pretty cool too Karen, I'll leave you alone now." He replied, trying to force a smile and walked back out of the room.

Jobe was just managing to regain his composure, when their attention was drawn to a humming sound from outside the house. The noise gradually became more audible over the television, a vague surging sound like the murmur of electricity in the distance. It slowly became louder and more defined, sounding more like the sound of an engine from a vehicle.

"Hey, shhh— do you hear that?" Tom asked Susan, concentrating on the noise.

"Yeah, what is it?" She quickly replied, looking up at him with the same look of concentration.

"I don't know, can't be another car, surely?" He replied, as the sound increased its resonance. It wasn't long before Steven and Jacob both appeared at the top of the staircase looking down, displaying the same puzzled expression on their faces too. Jobe wiped the tears from his face and slowly became transfixed on the noise as well.

"Nah, that don't sound like a car to me Tom." Jobe replied with composure.

"THAT'S A TRAIN!" Steven cried down with a look of shocked realisation. The look of comprehension quickly spread to the rest of them, as the chuggady sound of the locomotive then became obvious.

Back when Maidenbower was still a thriving little village, the sound of the passing trains was only sometimes audible above the ambiance of the traffic and people. But now that the place had become deathly silent, the sound appeared loud and clear, as if the train was just a few yards away. The noise of the engine and wheels upon the track grew louder, and seemingly closer. Soon it was interrupted by a sudden and abrupt screeching of brakes, and then silence again.

"That's not possible." Tom muttered to himself with a dropped jaw.

"Nah, that can't have been a train." Susan added with disbelief.

"Who the hell would be taking a train?" Jobe contributed.

Silence then returned for a few seconds more, while they exchanged ambivalent looks of foreboding, bewilderment, and excitement all at once.

"It's gotta be a rescue party, someone's come for us at last!" Steven finally shouted out, breaking the silence with optimistic exhilaration.

"But why now, after all this time?" Tom asked with uncertainty.

"Who cares? We gotta get down to that train station before they leave again." Susan insisted.

"Alright then, I'll go down and check it out with you Susan, but everyone else stays here." Tom responded. Steven let out a sigh of annoyance and Jacob remained blasé. Jobe gave him a nod and rose to his feet once again.

"Be quick Tom, maybe they can help Karen." Jobe said solemnly.

"Sure." Tom agreed with a smile and a nod.

"I'll get the canisters then." Susan announced, and ventured into the living room. She found Karen in the same position on the couch, the glass of water on the floor in front of her and diluted a pale red colour with drizzles of blood trickling down from the rim.

"What's all the commotion?" Karen asked in a drowsy slur.

"We're just popping down to greet some guests Karen, we won't be long." Susan replied, trying to sound cheerful but avoiding eye contact. She grabbed two oxygen canisters that lay down by the couch and started to make her way back to the door.

"You'd better not be back late for dinner Susan, mum's been cooking us beef stew you know." Karen called back at her before she could leave. Susan stopped in her tracks and turned to face Karen.

"I'm sure your mum cooks the best beef Karen, and I wouldn't miss it for the world." She responded.

Karen gave her a grin of agreement and her dry lips cracked open. It was the kind of sight that you couldn't bear to look at, but didn't want your disgust to be known. She turned round again with the canisters in her hands, and walked back out of the doorway.

"She still . . . um?" Jobe started to ask, unable to think of the appropriate words.

"Yeah, maybe you should go and sit with her for a bit." Susan replied carefully, passing a canister over to Tom. Jobe agreed and returned to the room.

"You ready for this then Susan? You haven't been out there in a long time now." Tom enquired with concern.

"No reason to until now Tom, I'll be fine." She replied reassuringly.

"Alright, just remember to keep your breathing steady. Don't fight with the mask, and head for home straight away if the buzzer goes off." Tom informed her motheringly.

"Quit your fussing," she replied with a grin, and slid the mask over her face.

"OK, let's do it then." Tom said to her positively, and slid his own mask on, catching it slightly on the tender part of his bridge but resisting the urge to yelp.

"Take care of everyone Jobe," Tom muffled out through the mask, as the two exited through the front door.

They set off on the expedition down the street with a sense of urgency in their stride. It was pitch dark, with only the glimmer of moonlight to guide them. Tom couldn't help but wonder why anyone would plan a rescue mission in the middle of the night, when people would be asleep and unaware of their presence. Eager for an explanation, he pushed his anxieties aside, as they started to mount the remains of the college for a better view of the station. They squinted through the darkness and could indeed make out the silhouette of a train parked on the tracks. There were no lights at the station, no sounds coming from the train, and something just felt a little strange. They continued their journey with caution, down the other side of the mound, past the shopping parade and down to the end of the street. The front entrance of the station was now in their sights, but its appearance still did not satisfy their uncertainties. The seven-foot iron bars that made up the enormous gates had now been prised wide apart, but had revealed no one in sight. Paranoia started to set in, and the pair became sheepish and nervous, flinching at the slightest movement of debris in the gentle wind. Susan looked at Tom for some kind of comfort or reassurance, but only received a shrug of the shoulders.

"Come on, we'd better take a look in the train then." Tom suggested, and gestured towards the platform. Susan returned him a look of unease, and shook her head in refusal.

"There must be someone about Susan. Shouldn't be hard to find them." Tom continued.

"Something's not right Tom, this all feels wrong." She confessed, stuttering with nerves.

"I know what you mean." He muttered gently and scanned the area for signs of life. But there was nothing, nothing at all. It almost seemed like the train had come on its own, or had been conducted by a fleet of commuting ghosts. There was a faint rattle, and a fleeting glimpse of motion from behind Tom. He spun round to catch sight of it, but there was nothing. A collapsed street lamp, a burnt out van, rubble, ash and nothing else there. He then caught the movement again. There was a dark figure behind the van and Susan saw it as well this time. He started to gingerly walk over to the van, trying to peer over to see what it was shielding, when Susan grabbed his arm firmly.

"Let's just get the hell out of here Tom, I'm petrified." She pleaded. He turned around to reassure her with a smile, but the smile soon dissolved when he suddenly realised what was happening. Dark blurry figures had crept up on them from all directions and blocked their every escape. The look of fear upon Tom's face made Susan too afraid to turn and look herself. She could tell by that look, that something very unpleasant was impending and she had a pretty good idea what it was. Tom turned back around and the figure behind the van had stood and made himself known, joined by several more of them that had seemingly appeared from nowhere. The figures remained motionless and stern as the pair could just distinguish the glimmering of light that reflected from their menacing eyes. Susan clung onto Tom from behind, wrapping her arms around him tight and cowering behind him for protection.

The figures started to close in on them and formed a large circle around them. Tom could make out at least fifteen of them, each of them ghostly pale and wearing long, dark hooded robes. One from the group then stepped into the circle and his sculptured features became visible in the moonlight. His eyes were glazed over and red raw around the lids. His complexion was bleached and wrinkled and the closest thing to a mouth was a mere remnant of a faded scar.

Tom watched the figures intensely, nervous of their every motion and soon became aware of the sharp objects that each of them held tightly in their hands. Tom discreetly scanned the immediate area for something that he could use in retaliation, but there was nothing. He gave Susan a little squeeze and started to step back a little when his foot knocked against something metallic. Tom gave the object a quick glance and realised it was a segment of iron railing. It had obviously been snapped from the gate at some point, and the end looked reassuringly jagged.

The menacing front man then rested his evil stare upon Tom and rolled up the sleeve of his robe. Attached to his lower arm was a 'Text Talk' machine. It looked old and battered and most of the buttons had fallen off. He reached down and held the 'Q' key, for the machine's first pre-stored message. The voice of the machine sounded deep and evil and the lack of solar power in the night made the voice seem to slur.

"As the end of days draws closer, we come to you in the name of our lord Jehovah, to aid in the final stages of his retribution against the wicked and unrepentant sinners. By doing this, the good and the loyal may be free from impure blood, and be reborn into eternal life in a new world of earthly paradise. We implore you sinners to lay down your lives and remove yourselves from our paths to greater enlightenment."

"You can stick it up your fucking arse, you prick!" Tom screamed back in return. He bent down and grabbed the iron railing from the floor, Susan still clinging onto him for dear life, her nails starting to dig into his skin.

"Then we shall be forced to assist you." The machine shortly replied.

Steven and Jacob were sitting around the dining table at this point, tapping their fingers impatiently and gazing from the living room window with naively hopeful expressions. The wait had seemed like an eternity now and Karen's psychosis was starting to irritate them immensely. Jobe had tried his very best to keep her calm, giving her kisses and telling her it was OK, but she could not be subdued. She had previously given Jobe a vicious slap for apparently ignoring her Mother, and had snapped at the kids for not eating all their beef stew. She had now worn herself out, and lay across Jobe's lap sleepily.

"You're going to be alright my love. Help is on the way now, just hold in there a little longer, OK?" He whispered gently, petting her like a cat.

"I'm fine Jobe, stop fussing." She replied in a breathy slur, struggling to keep her eyes open.

"You want some of this?" He asked, taking out an oxygen inhaler from his pocket.

"I don't have asthma Jobe, you know that." She replied

"Huh? No, it's oxygen Karen."

"Why would I need that? You think we live in space or something?" She replied with a shrug, followed by a childish giggle. Jobe clenched his teeth and kept his composure, though he could feel his eyes starting to well up again.

Steven's ears then perked as the uncomfortable silence was breached by loud footsteps coming up the path and then an aggressive thumping on the door, sending him into a confused panic. He stepped into the hallway just as the door was smashed wide open and the hideous robed figure entered.

"Oh fuck!" Steven cried, as he ran back into the living room and threw the door firmly closed.

"What the fuck's going on?" Jobe asked.

"Fucking Jehovah Witnesses, that's what's going on Jobe!" Steven replied, as the carbon dioxide started to seep through under the doorway.

"You're fucking shitting me!" Jobe screamed in disbelief, as the handle started to turn on the living room door. Steven ran to the door just as it started to open and slammed it closed with all his might, trapping the assailant's fingers in the gap. A faint groaning of pain could just be heard emanating from the figure's partially functioning vocal chords. He yanked forcefully at his hand and eventually managed to pull it free, leaving behind scrapings of skin and blood upon the doorframe. Steven quickly pushed the door completely closed and held up the handle with all his might.

"Does it look like I'm shitting you?" Steven replied to Jobe, struggling to keep the handle up.

"Are the guests here then?" Karen asked sleepily.

"Looks like it babe," Jobe replied, standing from the couch and gently resting Karen's head back down on the cushion.

"I can't hold this door much longer Jobe!" Steven told him, the strain becoming obvious on his face.

"Let me take that. You sort out the oxygen masks. I can feel the gas coming in." Jobe replied and took the handle. Steven then pelted to the other side of the room where the three oxygen canisters were sitting side by side against the wall.

"Hey Karen, you gotta put this on I'm afraid." He told her and slid the mask gently over her face.

"Christ, this fucker is strong!" Jobe groaned, as he could feel the handle starting to turn. He gritted his teeth and wrenched the handle back up, his muscles bulging to the point of explosion. Steven set one of the canisters down by Jobe's feet and put the mask on his face for him, before throwing the last canister upon his own back and sliding on the mask. Jacob had been paralysed with fear during all of this and stood with his back against the wall, desperation and panic covering his face.

They could then hear the front door closing again, then footsteps, then a loud squelching sound and a thud against the floor. The resistance to the handle had vanished and Jobe let out a sigh.

"Hey guys it's us!" Tom's voice came through the door.

"Thank God for that." Jobe replied, and opened the door immediately.

Tom and Susan stood in the hallway, panting and sweaty from their ordeal. Susan had lost one of her shoes in the escape and her foot was now blistered and cut. Tom's shirt had been sliced open down his left side and was smeared with blood. In his hand he still tightly clenched an iron bar, blood dripping heavily from the jagged edge. The assailant lay face down on the hallway carpet, a massive gaping hole through his spine that gushed blood like a smashed fire hydrant.

"We're in trouble guys. The shit has seriously hit the fan." Tom told them in between pants, as he quickly secured the front door with the deadbolt and removed his mask from his face.

"How many of them Tom?" Jobe asked.

"Dunno, fifteen maybe?" Tom replied.

"My damn foot hurts like a bitch." Susan sobbed. "And let me have a look at your side Tom, it looked nasty."

"It's fine Susan." Tom replied, dismissing the wound.

Before any of them had the chance to catch their breaths or devise any resemblance of a plan, the rest of the psychotic group arrived at the house and started violently bashing against the doors and windows.

"Take Karen and the kids upstairs Jobe and find yourself a weapon." Tom ordered him frantically. Jobe slid his mask on his forehead and lifted Karen up from the couch.

"I'd leave that on if I was you Jobe." Susan advised with a frown. She limped further into the room, leaving bloody footprints behind her. She sat down on the couch and examined the underside of her foot. She had acquired a massive blister on her heel and a smaller one on her sole. There were also various cuts and grazes inflicted on the foot, some quite deep and gaping and all of them filled with grit and dirt. She brushed away the excess dirt with her hands then proceeded to try and pick out the bigger bits of grit with her nails.

"I ain't hiding away upstairs Tom. Gimme a knife and I'll slice the fuck out of them!" Steven shouted aggressively with the facemask dangling around his neck.

"Do as you're told Steven, and get that damn mask on!" Tom replied, dashing into the kitchen and raiding the drawers.

"Come on kid, I need you to look after Karen for me." Jobe called to him from the foot of the stairs. "You too Jacob," he added and started to mount the stairs. Susan hobbled into the kitchen to join Tom and grabbed one of the jugs of water.

"What the fuck we gonna do Tom, there's so many of them!" she cried, pouring the water over her foot.

"We'll do the best we can, can't do much else." He replied as he stared at one of them through the kitchen window. The hideous face stared right back at him and started to punch at the window.

"Where the fuck are all the sharp knives, Susan?" Tom screamed at her aggressively.

"Ask Jobe! He threw them all away!" She screamed back with equal aggression.

"What? Why the hell would he do that?" Tom snapped back in disbelief.

"I don't know, alright!" She snapped back.

The thumping continued all around the house, the front door, the back door and the windows in the living room and the kitchen. Tom turned and grabbed the iron bar again, deciding it was probably the best weapon in the house. The violent punching against the kitchen window finally resulted in a slight crack, then a bigger one.

"Keep that mask on Susan, the glass is gonna break!" He told her and ran back into the hall as Jobe appeared from the staircase once again.

"Susan!" Jobe called out as he was reached the bottom. She hobbled back out of the kitchen again and was delighted by the sight.

"Here, Karen doesn't need these at the moment." He explained, and held out a pair of shoes.

"You're a star Jobe." She replied sighing, gratefully taking the shoes and slipping them on.

"Don't you have any weapons Tom?" Jobe asked in a panic.

"Not that I can think of Jobe, where have all the damn kitchen knives gone?" Tom responded abruptly.

"I threw them away 'cos of Karen, I'm sorry," Jobe explained.

"What? Why?" Tom replied, obviously still confused.

"Why you think? Fucking slice-slice!" Jobe shouted angrily, mimicking the act of slitting his wrists. There was then a moment of uncomfortable silence before Tom nodded his head in apologetic realisation.

"I think there's tools and stuff in the garage that we could use, but we can't get out there," Tom finally explained with a frustrated frown.

"Yeah well I got a shotgun in the truck, but we have the same problem." Jobe replied.

Susan dashed back in to the kitchen and grabbed a wok from the worktop and just at that moment, the window finally gave way and shattered to a thousand shards. The gush of carbon dioxide knocked Susan back and she almost fell. The ghastly figure then started to pull himself in through the open window. Susan immediately grasped the wok firmly with both hands and brought it down crashing upon the intruder's head. The force of the blow sliced the side of his head into the jagged edge of the glass around the window frame and sent blood gushing on to the draining board. Unsatisfied with the infliction, Susan repeated the blow harder, and again harder still until his head completely smashed open like a watermelon.

"Susan!" Tom shouted at her from the hall. She rushed out the kitchen to join them and shut the kitchen door firmly shut.

"Sorry, I was enjoying that." Susan explained, as she wiped her assailant's blood splatters from the side of her face.

The deadbolt on the front door then suddenly snapped off and the door smashed open, almost falling off its hinges in the process. The open doorway revealed another seven attackers with foot long blades in each of their hands. The one at the front was the spokesman from before and Tom could now see a silver medallion around his neck, symbolising that he was an elder member of the faith. He was the oldest of them all and the only one with the 'Text Talk' machine on his arm. He scowled at Tom with disgust and his cheek muscle almost bent his lip scar into a smile. With a slight gesture from the elder, they suddenly began to close in, like a relentless zombie attack from a George Romero film. They swiped and sliced frantically at them, mere inches away from penetration when the elder suddenly plunged his blade deep into Tom's kneecap and twisted it in the wound. Tom screamed out in agony and the expulsion of air that the scream carried with it almost sent his facemask flying off. Susan then retaliated in a fit of anger and cracked the wok violently against the elder's head, knocking him instantly unconscious. He fell to the floor in front of Tom, leaving the blade protruding from the wound. Susan then dashed straight into the living room with Jobe dragging Tom closely behind. They reached the room just before the others could clamber over their leader's unconscious body and shut the door just in time.

"I'm kinda glad you just got stabbed Tom," Jobe confessed to him and pulled the knife from the wound. Tom screeched out in pain and cupped his hand around his knee.

"Sorry about that," Jobe said.

The sound of thumping and pushing on the living room door was soon replaced by that of footsteps on the stairs.

"Christ! The kids!" Susan cried.

Jobe held the knife tightly in his hand, ready for a fight and offered the other hand to Tom.

"On your feet Tom, you'll have plenty of time to think about the pain later." He shouted down at him. Tom grabbed his hand and Jobe wrenched him up to his feet.

"I'm good Jobe, let's have it!" Tom replied, holding the iron bar in two hands. Susan took a step back in hesitation and tried to gain her composure, gripping hold of the wok that had become her new best friend. Jobe gave them all a quick look of confirmation and flung the door wide open again. They were immediately greeted by one of the members waiting by the doorway, towering over them with a butcher's knife. He brought it down slicing through the air with unexpected speed and plunged it deep into Jobe's left upper arm. Jobe tried not to react and gave the intruder a stern uppercut with his blade, burying it deep between his Adams apple and his jaw. He retracted the blade and the wound gushed out like a fountain as the ghostly figure fell to the floor, dead. Jobe turned to catch a brief glimpse of a few more reaching the top step, before two more at the bottom changed their direction and started to close in on them. He dashed passed them, barely avoiding a slice and started ascending the stairs in pursuit. Tom and Susan then found themselves at the front line. Tom started swiping the iron bar in the direction of one of their heads, just missing contact each time, as his opponent backed away wielding a six-inch hunting knife. Susan swung violently at the other robed fanatic with arrogant confidence. She finally made impact and knocked the machete flying from his grip. She was then taken by surprise as the figure grabbed the hand that was grasping the wok handle and squeezed it tightly with a massive strength. Susan could feel her knuckles and fingers starting to cripple and snap against the solid metal of the handle and fell to her back. Tom could see what was happening but couldn't disable his own opponent enough to go and help her. Susan lay on the floor helpless as the menacing figure stood above her and brought the wok smashing into her own face. She felt her nose break immediately and the metal framing from the facemask snapped and became deeply imbedded in her cheeks.

"Susan!" Tom cried out desperately, breaking his attention from the fight. His opponent seized his chance and pushed Tom to the floor. He held the knife up high and prepared to plunge it deep into Tom's chest. At that point Tom noticed his attacker's robe gape open revealing his umbilical unit clipped to the top of his trousers. The knife came down crashing towards him, as he just managed to roll out the way. He then reached in and grabbed the umbilical chord that was now on display and with an almighty tug he ripped it clean from his attacker's stomach. The infliction paralysed the grisly figure for a few seconds, as a blend of stomach acid and blood poured from the flapping stomach wound. Tom then pulled himself to his feet and stabbed the jagged end of his iron bar deep into the left temple of his opponent's head.

"Get the fuck off of her!" He screamed over at Susan's brutal attacker. He wrenched his trusted iron bar from the corpse of the dead fanatic and cracked it violently across the head of the second one, just in time to prevent another vicious swipe at Susan's face. The ghastly beast was knocked unconscious immediately and dropped the dented wok to the carpet. With the iron bar still firmly clenched in his hand, Tom then proceeded to stamp at the sleepy fanatic's head until he heard the reassuring snapping noise of a broken neck.

Susan sobbed uncontrollably and lay on the floor limp and weak. Blood had gushed from her broken nose like a tap and rapidly filled up the facemask. She lay there drowning on her own blood for a good few seconds before Tom could finally assist.

"Christ Susan, you OK, my baby?" He asked, dropping to his feet and cradling her head. He pulled off the mask and the blood splashed down her face and onto the carpet. Susan's immediate reaction was to take a deep gasp of air, but this only made things worse. The air at this point was more than eighty percent carbon dioxide and it stung her throat and lungs like acid and she started to choke again. Tom quickly bent back the protruding metal framework that had been imbedded in her cheeks, and slid the mask gently back over her mouth and nose again. The blood flow had now dropped to just a trickle, which easily escaped from the edge of the mask. In a panic she panted rapidly from the oxygen supply, feeling sharp pain in her tender lungs with every inhale. She could feel her heart rate speeding away at turbo acceleration and thought she was about to have a heart attack too. She finally managed to calm down enough to breathe normally a few moments later, when her lungs recovered from the oxygen deprivation and the panic subsided somewhat. The elastic strap around her head pulled the facemask tightly on her broken nose. The tension pulling it down made the pain far worse, but she knew that the oxygen was far more important. Tears of pain streamed out of her eyes and rolled endlessly down her face, diluting the remnant of blood in its way. She found herself so consumed with pain that she was unable to muster the strength to talk, and just gave Tom a look of desperation instead.

"My God, Susan I'm so sorry," He cried down with a guilty look of sorrow. He stroked her hair and kissed her forehead, before lifting her up and carrying her through the living room to the sofa.

"Stay here my darling and rest, there's only a few left now." He told her with a reassuring smile, but her reaction did not reflect the same optimism. She was petrified, stiff and her body started to shake.

"Hey, hey, it's alright Susan. Just try and stay quiet and they won't even know you're here. It's all going to be OK." He continued, bending down to her and kissing her crippled hand, as if his affection alone would heal her wounds. He left the room quickly, clambered over the corpses and gazed out the open front door. He scanned the area for the remaining members of the cult, but could see no one at all. He knew they were out there somewhere, hiding in the shadows and around the corners, preparing to sneak up and attack them at any minute. He went to close the door and realised that it was blocked by a corpse. He grabbed the body with two hands and threw it out into the street. The body landed head first into the curb and Tom could see its neck snap at ninety degrees. He pushed the door shut expecting it to click into place, but it just bounced back. The lock and bolt had both snapped off from the force of the intruders bursting in and now dangled from the door completely useless. He pushed the door shut again and held it in place as he reached over and dragged another corpse to prop it shut.

Steven and Jacob had managed to keep the other two deranged men out the bedroom for as long as they could, but were inevitably overpowered. The door swung open with force and sent them both flying. Jacob immediately ran to the other side of the room and cowered behind the bed with fear. He felt a strange curiosity about the men too, having never met anyone else with an umbilical unit before. Their appearance was all too familiar to him, and not at all scary. He saw the ghastly sight every time that he peered into the mirror, and felt a strange urge to talk to them and ask things that had played on his mind.

As they burst into the room and first saw him, Jacob could see a moment of empathy in their faces too, a singular moment of doubt in their actions. Steven saw his opportunity and took advantage of their momentary loss of concentration, and satisfying his yearning for carnage, rammed one of Tom's black biros straight into the eyeball of the man in front, making a slight popping sound. The towering beast then let out a massive groan and dropped his weapon to try and remove the pen. The figure behind him then tried to step around and punish Steven for his actions, but Jobe suddenly appeared in the doorway and drove his newly acquired knife deeply into his back. The blade pierced easily through the black robe and crunched through the spinal chord, making a loud cracking noise like an egg breaking live on a microphone. Jacob watched the whole ordeal and found himself staring deep into the man's eyes at the very moment that the knife was inserted. A menacing scowl was replaced by traumatic shock, then pain and distress, before his eyes finally rolled back in his head and he fell down to the floor, taking his wounded companion with him.

Jacob had filled most of his life with disturbing and repulsive images from horror films, and assumed he would be immune to such a sight, but it affected him more deeply than he'd expected. He slumped to the floor and sat rocking back and forth on the spot while Jobe stepped further into the room and snapped the neck of the biro-wounded lunatic who hopelessly thrashed about on the floor.

"You all OK?" He panted out through the mask. Steven returned an unconvincing nod and slumped against the wall with exhaustion. It was a few moments later that they heard the front door closing again and Tom rushed up the stairs to join them.

Jobe pulled off his mask and dropped the canister to the floor. He let out a sigh and rubbed his face hard, trying not to breathe too hard till the oxygen levels had returned to normal.

"Hey Karen? You awake my darling?" He called gently, looking down at her on the bed. He walked closer and knelt down beside her. "Karen?" He repeated.

Her eyes were firmly closed and she looked peaceful, but suspiciously still. Jobe became concerned by her unresponsiveness and reached down to feel the pulse in her wrist. The pulse was undetectable at first, but then he started to feel the faint murmur.

"Is everyone alright?" Tom's voice called from the doorway. Jobe planted a soft kiss on Karen's cheek and turned to face him.

"We're all alive if that's what you mean." He replied emotionless and drained.

"Where's Susan?" Steven added with concern.

"She's alright kid, she's a bit beaten up, but she'll be fine." Tom replied.

"What happened to her?" Steven continued.

"She broke her nose and hurt her hand, but she's fine." Tom answered.

"So what now Tom? Is that all of them?" Jobe asked, praying for a reassuring answer.

"No," Tom replied, shaking his head solemnly. Jobe rose to his feet, with vengeful aggression taking control of him.

"What! How many more of these fuckers are there?" He shouted with anguish.

"Susan and me counted about fifteen of them at the station. Um . . . I killed two or three there I think, we killed about seven here, so there must be at least four or five about still." Tom explained.

"Well, where are they?" Jobe roared, clenching his fists.

"No idea Jobe, I've looked outside but I couldn't see them. They crept up on Susan and me at the station without us even noticing them, so they've no problem in making themselves invisible." Tom explained.

"Well they've come here to fuck us up, so they're gonna show themselves soon enough." Jobe replied, trying to calm down a little. "I think we should get Susan up here though, don't you?"

"Yeah, good idea, Jobe," Tom replied with a nod.

Tom and Jobe dashed down the stairs and into the living room where Susan was still lying on the couch.

"Hey my love," Tom greeted her and gingerly pulled the mask from her face. "The oxygen levels should be okay now."

She wiped away her tears with her good hand and cradled her broken nose. Her face was swollen and splattered with blood. Her nose was bright red and bent a little to the left.

"Is everyone else OK?" She whimpered.

"Yeah, everyone is fine." Tom replied with a smile. Jobe stepped up and gave her a smile too, before noticing how badly broken her nose was.

"Hey Susan, you alright?" Jobe asked.

"Been better Jobe," she replied with a sniffle.

"That nose is pretty bad Susan. It's gonna have to be reset I'm afraid." He told her. She didn't reply, but the look on her face showed her unhappiness.

"The sooner I do it, the less it's gonna hurt. Shall I do it now?" Jobe asked her with a look of sympathy. Tom stepped aside, unsure what to do with himself.

"Go on," Susan eventually responded abruptly. The last thing that Susan wanted at that moment was anybody even touching her nose, let alone cracking it back into place. But she figured the extra pain would appear insignificant to what she was already feeling, and she didn't want a bent nose. Jobe bent down to his knees in front of the couch and placed his palms on her cheeks. He then placed the ball of each thumb around either side of her bridge gently and firmed the grip with his fingers around her head.

"This is probably gonna hurt a bit," he told her. She let out a little sigh and nodded her head to let him know she was ready. He increased his pressure with the thumbs and with a singular sharp motion, he forced the nose straight again. An enormous crunching noise resonated through her head and she bit down to keep from screaming, except she misjudged her bite and buried her teeth through her bottom lip. The pain surged to her brain in a sudden burning wave, shortly followed by the taste of blood in her mouth. Her eyes started to water as she began a gentle high-pitched whimpering. The pain slowly faded to an ambient level and her nose started to trickle with blood again.

"I'm sorry I had to do that," Jobe confessed with an empathetic expression. Susan took in a few deep breaths and calmed down.

"It's OK," she managed to say in another panting breath. Jobe got to his feet and Tom took his place on the floor. He gave her a smile and stroked her hair.

"How's the hand?" He inquired.

"It doesn't need re-setting if that's what you mean!" She snapped at him cynically.

"We have to go out and find the rest of these bastards before they attack us again. I think it'd be safer for you and the kids upstairs." He explained.

"You be careful out there Tom, these cunts don't give up with out a fight." She replied with concern, struggling to her feet.

"No need to fret Susan, I've got a shotgun in the truck, they haven't got a chance." Jobe assured her.

"Can you take care of Karen and the kids for us? Keep the door shut up there and the air should be fine." Tom asked.

"Yeah, alright Tom," she replied and followed him up the stairs.

They arrived at the bedroom when Tom realised he'd left the kids alone with two bloodied corpses on the floor. It was hardly the most responsible thing to do, he thought. Susan's face grimaced at the morbid sight and Tom felt a little ashamed.

"Everyone OK?" Susan asked Steven and Jacob, who were standing by the window.

"We're OK Susan, are you OK?" Steven replied, removing his attention from the window.

"Well I've never had my nose broken before. It's not the nicest thing." She replied with a touch of sarcasm. Tom turned to the corpses on the floor again and started to drag them past Susan and out the door. Jacob turned to Steven at this point and gave him a poke in the shoulder, followed by a disconcerting look.

"Oh yeah, TOM?" Steven called out. "Jacob reckons that he saw some of them out the window." He then continued. Tom dropped the bodies at the top of the landing and rushed inside the room to the window.

"Where Jacob? Where were they?" He asked. Jacob peered back out the window and started to point.

"What? In Tina's house you mean?" Tom enquired as Jacob gave him a confirming nod.

"Thanks, kid," Tom concluded and gave him a pat on the back, before rushing back to the top of the stairs again. Jobe was waiting for him at the bottom, ready and eager to start hunting down the last of them.

"Watch yourself Jobe!" Tom called down, as he picked up the first corpse by the collar and belt. Jobe realised what Tom was doing and soon stepped aside, as Tom hurtled the corpse into the air. It landed at the bottom step with a bone-cracking thud, and then Tom launched the second. It landed between the first one, and the other corpses that were littering the hallway and starting to form a bloody mound.

"We need to get that shit outside before it starts to stink up the house." Jobe told him, looking down at the bodies.

"Yeah alright, let's just sort the rest of these bastards out first though." Tom replied, descending the stairs.

"I'm ready for it Tom. If the coast is clear then I'm gonna grab that shotgun from the Dodge."

"Alright then. Jacob said he saw some of them in Tina's house, so just be careful and I'll keep a look out for ya, OK?" Tom told him.

"Cool with me bro'," Jobe confirmed, as they approached the front door and slid their facemasks back on again. The front door was still being propped shut by the body of the elder member, whose head was swollen like a balloon from the impact of the wok. Jobe reached down and grabbed the limp body by the hood, before discarding him to one side. Jobe felt inside his pocket for the keys to the Dodge and gave Tom the thumb's up.

They opened up the door with caution and tried to scan the street for signs of movement. The night was still pitch dark and uninviting, which made spotting them very difficult. A small amount of light was beaming from the smashed kitchen window, which illuminated the far side of the house and they could see that there was definitely no one hiding there. Tom stood by the carbon dioxide unit that was by the front door and tried to keep a careful eye out for Jobe, as he edged his way closer to the Dodge. There were still no signs of anybody about, but both of them could feel their eerie presence close by. Tom suddenly noticed a vague shadowy figure walk past the living room window of Tina's house, and then it appeared again at the open doorway.

"Jobe!" Tom called discretely, trying not to bring attention to himself. "Jobe!" He repeated louder, finally getting Jobe's attention.

"What?"

"The doorway!"

Jobe immediately turned his attention to Tina's front door and could clearly see the eerie silhouette. The demented fanatic looked straight at him, his evil eyes emotionlessly piercing right through him. Jobe and the figure continued to eye each other for a few seconds, wary of who would make the first move. The figure then removed something cylindrical from his robe pocket and held it tight as he started his approach to the truck. Jobe panicked and scrambled his key into the Dodge's door lock and quickly climbed inside. He then pushed down the door lock and assumed he'd be safe while he fetched the gun. Tom then dashed over to engage the man, to buy more time for Jobe to get the gun and to try and disarm the assailant in the process. But just as Tom approached, he was suddenly jumped from behind and sent tumbling to the floor. The second attacker was unarmed, with the exception of the industrial steel toe-capped work boots that he used to kick Tom about the head with.

Jobe pulled out the shotgun from behind the driver's seat and started loading it full of shells from the glove box. He then placed the box of remaining shells into his pocket when he suddenly noticed a bright spark from outside the truck. He turned to peer from the truck's window to see the fanatic attempting to light a flare stick outside, but with the lack of oxygen to feed the spark, joined with the strong extinguishing power of the carbon dioxide which now dominated the air, the tiny spark fizzled out in an instant and left the flare completely useless. Realising his mistake, the fanatic quickly discarded the dud flare to the ground below and removed a new one from his robe pocket. Noticing the newly-fitted PGOGM pumping oxygen into the cabin of truck, he then moved closer to the Dodge where the gaps in the doors and windows of the truck would provide just enough oxygen in the air to ignite the spark of the new flare.

"Christ!" Jobe yelled, frantically pulling up the lock and wrenching open the passenger door. The robed figure then ripped open the Dodges petrol cap and re-sparked the new flare next to the hole. The fumes from the cherished petrol then gushed out into the flare and immediately sent a line of flames shooting back down into the petrol tank of the Dodge, causing the tank to explode with an almighty bang and sending the truck flying fifteen feet into the air.

The explosion sent Jobe flying through the air with the shotgun still tightly in his grasp. He landed on his back with a massive thud by the front door of the house and lay winded and unable to move. The flare-wielding figure had made no attempt to escape the blast himself and was blown apart instantaneously, sending torched limbs and body parts flying up with the truck too. It appeared that Tom's attacker was just as surprised as the rest of them, which allowed Tom the brief opportunity to break free and quickly run for safety. The truck then started to plummet back down to the ground again with intense speed and force. It landed with an enormous crumpling of metal, right on top of the second attacker. It threw him to his back and crushed down on to his ribcage. His ribs suddenly cracked apart like twigs and the weight of the truck sent them penetrating down through his organs. The impact of the crash also caused the truck's windows to shatter apart which immediately released the build up of oxygen from within the cab and expelled it out into the surrounding area. The dense bubble of oxygen immediately ignited, creating a perfectly spherical orb of blazing fire around the truck. The sight looked magical and surreal, as if a miniature sun was blazing away in the street before them.

"Hey, you alright mate?" Tom asked Jobe with concern, and offered him his hand. Jobe grasped the hand and pulled himself to his feet.

"Just got the wind knocked out of me bro'," He replied panting and stumbling.

"Christ the TRUCK! How the hell we gonna get out of here now huh?" Jobe continued in a vicious rage. Before Tom had a chance to think of a response, another hooded figure appeared from around the corner of the house. Jobe's reflexes had not been affected by the trauma at all. Within seconds he cocked the shotgun loaded and fired it at the approaching figure. The shell struck the man directly in the Adams apple and exploded upon impact. It ripped apart his throat and gullet which erupted with blood, leaving his head dangling loosely on its side, before the body eventually fell to a heap on the floor.

"God that felt good," Jobe announced with a grunt.

At that point Tom spotted another two figures watching them

from inside Tina's living room. The second they realised they had been spotted, they scurried off and hid somewhere in the house, obviously realising they stood no chance against such a weapon. Jobe had just caught them in his sights as they were running off too, and he proceeded to load another shell into the gun.

Tom and Jobe then strolled across the road to Tina's house with a sense of confidence in their strides, holding the gun out menacingly in front of them. Neither of them felt a moral urge to let any of these crazed fanatics live and considered their deaths to be a public service. They swept through the house till they found the last two in the kitchen. They were standing by the sink waiting for them and holding rusty carving knives. They held out the weapons in front of them, poised and ready for a hopeless conflict. Jobe found their persistence quite impressive, but thought they should've known that a man with a loaded shotgun had very little to fear. Jobe aimed the weapon and pulled the trigger twice. With an almighty explosion of gunpowder and a little kick back, the bodies fell to the floor and the job was done.

Upon Tom and Jobe's return to the house, they dragged the rest of the bodies out into the street and piled them up in a heap on the pavement. The poor Dodge looked a depressing sight as it lay there on its roof, burning up in smoke along with their hopes of escape. It roared away in a ravenous blaze and bellowed out thick black smoke that seemed to disappear into the pitch-black sky.

One by one the men took turns launching the bodies on to the blazing inferno and listening to the crackling sound of burning flesh on the fire. They reached the bottom of the pile and found the elder member of the group once again. Tom grabbed him by the wrist and the groin and lifted him into the air. Just as he took aim and prepared to launch the maniac on to the flames, he felt a faint pulse from beneath his skin and dropped the body with surprise.

"This bastard's still alive Jobe," Tom yelled over the sound of the roaring blaze. Susan had landed him a hefty blow with the wok, but it seemed the smack had merely knocked the man unconscious.

"Leave him. I got something good in mind," Jobe replied with delight. He dragged the remaining body back into the house by the ankle, scraping his face against the gravelled pavement along the way. Tom followed shortly behind, and propped the door shut with his oxygen canister.

"What are we gonna do with him?" Tom asked, removing the facemask for the last time.

"Lots of things Tom and none of them are very pleasant." Jobe replied with a worryingly sadistic grin. They checked through his pockets for any weapons and tied him up against a dining room chair in the living room. His wrists were tied behind the back of the chair with bootlaces and his feet tied to the chair legs the same way. He appeared completely sparked out and harmless, so they left him alone and ventured back upstairs to check on the others.

As they began climbing the stairs again they became aware of the complete lack of noise from the upper floor. They had expected to be greeted with open arms and praise for their achievement, or at least some kind of re-assurance that everything was alright. But there wasn't even the sound of a whisper or movement from up there and it was obvious that everything was not alright. Jobe reached for the handle of the isolated room and slowly pushed open the door. Steven and Jacob were staring out of the window still, emotionless and traumatised. Susan was sitting at the end of the bed with her head in her hands and sobbing.

"Hey, what's wrong everyone? We got them all." Jobe said, trying to work out why they didn't appear happier. It was at that point he noticed the duvet of the bed had been pulled over Karen's head and completely covered her. Susan pulled her hands away from her face and gave him a tearful look full of sorrow, but couldn't quite manage to voice the explanation which was plain and obvious.

Jobe stood frozen and unable to speak. He stared down at the bulge in the duvet and a mild thumping began at the back of his head. He took a few paces before dropping down to his knees and pulled back the duvet. Karen's pale emotionless face lay heavy against the pillow next to an array of dried crimson stains. He placed his hand on her cheek and stroked it gently as the thumping in his head began to increase. It consumed his whole head and started to cause pressure strain at the back of his eyes. His vision started to blur and its saturation drained away. He looked around and could see people talking to him with solemn faces. Their lips were moving but no sound reached his ears. He turned back to the motionless body and everything else in the room disappeared. He could feel her presence in the room still and imagined her calling to him, telling him she was alright now and at peace. But her lips would never say another word. They would never give him a cheeky grin and they would never kiss him again with loving passion. All hope and reason to live was gone. Their means of escape was gone, and the woman he would spend eternity with was now dead. The pain in his eyes grew to an excruciating level before the blood started to drain from his head. The bed started to spin around him like a merry-go-round and his stomach started to churn. He started to feel dizzy, disorientated and nauseous, before he finally erupted with vomit and passed out cold on the floor.

CHAPTER SEVEN

SUSAN HAD tossed and turned in the cold dark silence for hours now, while her mind tried desperately to process all the traumatic events of the night. The clock had just ticked over to 6:00 a.m. and she could see the sun beginning to rise outside the bedroom window. Tom lay motionless beside her, breaking the silence with intermittent snoring and grunts. She appreciated his exhaustion from his efforts to keep them all alive that night, but couldn't quite understand how he found it so easy to sleep at a time like this.

After Jobe had fainted that evening they were both left with the strenuous task of lifting his weighty body up on to his bed and then tending to the butcher's knife wound on his upper left arm. They then carried poor Karen's lifeless body down the stairs and discretely hid her away in the kitchen. The kitchen had now been declared 'out of bounds' to them all now anyway, due to its smashed window and the carbon dioxide that now engulfed the entire room.

It had only been a mere few days now since the arrival of Jobe and Karen, yet the loss of Karen felt so much worse to Susan, like losing a lifelong friend or a loving family member. She couldn't start to imagine what could be going through Jobe's head at this point, and felt a certain responsibility to do her utmost to keep him from doing something stupid. She recalled how Karen spoke about her own suicide attempt previously and feared that now in her absence Jobe would have nothing else on his troubled mind.

The fact that none of them had actually been killed as a result of the fanatics' brutal attack had come as a welcoming relief to Susan, yet the very contemplation of considering it a good result made her feel guilty and two-faced to Karen's memory. The fanatics didn't have a reputation for failure and the defeat probably came as quite a surprise to them too. Susan wondered how long it would be before more of them arrived to correct their previous failure. She recalled how the friendly looking anchorman had briefly mentioned the cult on the news and how his short twenty-second report was completely overshadowed by the news of the mysterious green gas and the bombings. He quickly glossed over the news of their intensions and gave the impression that the police and authorities were unable to spare the time to investigate, concentrating all their efforts on more immediate matters. She remembered thinking nothing of it at the time, and felt it was probably just a rumour or an exaggeration of the truth. She assumed that the authorities probably had a similar view of the allegations as well, but now wished that everyone had taken it more seriously.

Her broken nose and crumpled hand had continued to throb and surge with pain throughout the night, but she found herself strangely satisfied with her minimal inflictions and had now started to become accustomed to the pain. The house itself was now covered from floor to ceiling in splatters of blood and flesh and had become unsightly and nauseating to even the strongest of stomachs. She thought how it now looked like the crime scene of a huge mass murder case which surely would've made the front page of the national papers. All the house was missing were chalk outlines of the dead bodies and yellow police tape tied across all the doorways, reading: 'Crime scene investigation. Do not cross'.

She turned to look down at Tom again, gently snoring away like a baby, fully clothed and lying on top of the duvet like a drunken teenager recovering from an all-night drinking session with his mates. She then recalled Tom's own inflictions from the attack and realised that he had not yet attended to his wounds. He had endured a deep cut to the side when they were first ambushed at the station and then had a knife imbedded in his kneecap in the hallway. It then occurred to her that Tom hadn't complained about the wounds either, or even mentioned them once since they had occurred. She bent over him to look at the wounds closer and gingerly prised apart the flapping rip of Tom's T-shirt. His chest was covered in blood smears and splatters that lie upon seemingly perfect skin. She bent over more and gently wiped the blood aside with her hand. The blood had completely dried by this point and brushed away from his skin like dust. Underneath the blood stains, his skin revealed no signs of perforation at all, not a mark or a cut to reflect the previous events. She jumped back with a look of disbelief when she suddenly remembered the medical report once again.

"So it was real!" She muttered under her breath, finally receiving the confirmation that her mind needed to accept the surreal facts of the once dubious report.

She then turned to look for the little black book. She could see it poking from the breast pocket of Tom's coat which hung from the back of the door.

'Why the secrets?' She asked herself in another quiet mutter and gently slipped out of the bed to grab the book.

The book itself looked very worn around the edges and segments of the leather had fallen off over time, like a battered suitcase that had travelled around the world and reflected the countless tales and anecdotes of its journey through time. She sat back down on the bed and looked over to Tom for more assurance that he was indeed still asleep. She then unclipped the popper and curiously turned to the first page.

Tom had acquired the book shortly after he was first diagnosed with diabetes, when his life had first started to take a new and unforeseen path. As a young child, Tom had always imagined having a simple life, an easy happy existence in which he'd pretty much keep to himself without causing too much hassle on the way. He saw himself with a respectably good job and a nice house with a wife and a kid. He would provide for his family well, and install morals and ethics upon the child, raising it to be honourable and true like his Grandfather Dunn. It was a nice image, and even to this day Tom wished it had become a reality, but life had a tendency to throw you into the unexpected.

Tom started to find it increasingly difficult to talk about his problems with people, and tried his best to repress them all instead. He was turning bitter and resentful, and not even his grandfather could relate to the reasons why. He felt completely alone at the front line of a war inside his own mind. It was a civil war of emotions that relentlessly battled each other for a conscious decision. He had read on the Internet that the varying blood sugar levels within his body could cause severe mood swings and depression. These could range from 'mild grumpiness' to 'complete hopelessness and desperation.' This was exactly how it all started for Tom so he felt a slight comfort knowing that there was a reason for the way he was feeling, that he wasn't just going mad, but it still didn't make life much easier to cope with.

Tom often wished that he'd been diagnosed with the illness sooner, so that he would have learnt over time how to keep his sugar levels steady and wouldn't have to experience these moments of such despair. After sixteen years of living his life a certain way it had become routine and he thought he understood how to keep his body satisfied. So being told one day out the blue that he had to change his entire lifestyle and reassess every single action he took came as quite a shock to the system. For Tom it was like jumping into an alternative reality, where everything that he'd previously learnt about life no longer applied.

Tom started to use the little black book to write down everything he was thinking and feeling, so he could channel his bitter resentment and relieve the impending urge to act upon it. He would then read it all back at a time when he felt more stable and subdued, and assess his mind set to conclude whether or not his emotions were sensical and justified.

The depressing days of despair and hopelessness became a frequent occurrence to Tom and over time the entries in the book became more twisted and bitter to the point where there were very few days of clarity left by which he could rightfully assess his writings. The entries became increasingly malicious and resentful towards the people he had previously called 'friends,' accusing them of ungratefulness towards their normal lives and how they didn't care what he was going through. He detailed his growing hatred of them and explained in great detail exactly what he'd like to do to them all.

The book was a good inch thick and full with blank lined pages for him to write. It was bound in a smart leather skin and looked like a businessman's diary. It went everywhere with Tom, just in case something came into his head that needed to be jotted down immediately. Tom often caught people on the street looking over at him while he was writing in the book and revelled in the possibility of being mistaken for a businessman, jotting down notes for an important conference that day. But although the book seemed to serve many purposes for Tom, he realised after a while, that the constant scribbling of evil thoughts was probably making him even more isolated from the world and exacerbating his borderline psychosis. He slowly began to dedicate less time to the book, merely jotting down notes now and again as just a reminder of his thoughts and events and found that his mood started to slightly improve.

Susan read through the first few entries that talked about all this, but still couldn't understand why Tom would want to keep his miracle cure and ability a secret. If it were her that had suffered from the illness when she was a kid, then she would have been over the moon that she had been cured and would want to tell everyone that she met.

She then flicked through a few pages to the point when Tom was studying for his A-level exams and it was at this point that the entries started to take a shorthand note form which made them quite difficult to comprehend. She then started to notice a reoccurring name in the entries: 'Victoria Fielding' and then something about a vicious attack. She flicked back a few pages and began to read the entries more intensely again, trying to understand what was happening.

Victoria Fielding was a girl that Tom first encountered when he enrolled at the local college for his A-levels. She was an amazingly attractive girl and Tom felt a strong infatuation for her immediately. Victoria was also a very bright and intelligent girl who had enrolled herself in many of the same subjects as Tom, and so it was inevitable that they would become close friends. Although their friendship started to flourish very soon, Tom was unable to act on his feelings, for Victoria had come to the college with her long-term boyfriend Jason Selby. Jason had failed entry into all the academic subjects that his parents had imposed upon him, and had only been accepted in to the college to do an A-level in physical education, a subject that he naturally excelled in due to his bulging muscular physique and addiction to physical exertion.

Despite Victoria's long term commitment to Jason, she would flirt with Tom on a regular occurrence, sitting on his lap in chemistry lessons and provocatively seducing him into giving her back massages at break. The initial lustful spark she had once felt for Jason had faded to a vague twinkle by this point, but it was fear that kept her from breaking the ties. From that initial spark onwards through their relationship, Jason had become an aggressive and controlling boyfriend who constantly forced his masculine authority over her and on occasions would even strike her if she disobeyed his strict commands.

Not only was Jason a big muscular guy, but he was an intimidating bully as well and enjoyed nothing more than exerting his aggression on unsuspecting students in violent bone breaking tackles, not only on the rugby pitch, but behind the bike sheds, down the streets, and whenever he needed a little extra cash for his lunch too.

After just a few months or so into the new school year, Tom finally decided to resign his longing for her and began intermittently dating various other girls at the college. He remained good friends with Victoria throughout the year and they helped each other out with their coursework and exam preparation. Tom often noticed evil scowls from Jason whenever he spoke to Victoria but tried not to let it bother him, even when Jason cornered him in the corridor and threatened to beat him up if he didn't stay away. Although maintaining a calm exposure, Tom wanted nothing more than to give

Jason a taste of his own medicine and make him feel worthless and scared like the cowering timid mouse that Victoria became whenever Jason was in sight. But Tom always remained hesitant and withdrawn, aware of the limitations he faced because of his diabetes.

Tom would lock himself away in his bedroom for hours on end sometimes, manically scribbling away in his little black book and manifesting his malicious desire for punishment and retribution into barely readable italics, hoping that one day Victoria would find the courage to finally leave Jason and be free.

At the end of the two-year A-level course Tom and Victoria both passed their exams with straight As and Tom began his application for university. He was hoping he'd be accepted for a course at Oxford University entitled 'Molecular and Cellular Bio-Chemistry.' Victoria on the other hand, felt that further education would not be advantageous to her and just wanted to get out into the 'real' world and start making a living for herself. She knew deep down that her intelligence alone would have carried her much further up the food chain, but couldn't bear the thought being financially dependent on her parents for another three years.

The student council had discussed plans for an end of year party and decided to book one of the local nightclubs for the evening for the students to celebrate their results and say a final goodbye to their fellow students. Tom was hesitant to attend at first due to his shameful single status and the fact that he had lost most of his friends over the years through arguments and misunderstandings. He restlessly toyed with the idea for weeks before eventually giving in, on the naive assumption that he wouldn't see any of them again, so it didn't really matter what happened. So he spruced himself up for the night in his best shirt and tie and borrowed an expensive pin-striped suit from his father. 'I may as well go out in style,' he thought to himself.

Tom had never ventured to this particular nightclub before as it had a bad reputation for violence and there had even been reports of people getting stabbed with HIV infected syringes. But as the night was booked especially for him and the other students he felt it safe enough on this one occasion. When he arrived at the club he was quite shocked to see how many of the students had turned up. Without a lengthy head count, it seemed to him as if almost every student from the year had attended for one last drinking session together, with the obvious exceptions of the most geekiest of students and those who didn't even know what a pint of beer tasted like.

The lighting in the club was almost non-existent. The only illumination came from flashing '70s disco lights and the occasional strobe that revealed still snapshot images of the exuberant dancers. The music pumped relentlessly out of the six foot speakers at maximum decibels and the bass enhancer sent violent vibrations through the wooden flooring.

The repetitive drum and bass music was complete and agonising torture to Tom from the very start and made his head begin to thump like a second heartbeat from an unborn foetus growing inside his skull. He had known before he even left the house what to expect, that not in a million years would he arrive to find them playing some gentle Beatles track that he might enjoy, but he had never expected the noise to be so bad that it gave him a migraine. His head hurt so intensely that he'd rather burst his own eardrums open with a screwdriver than listen to another second of it.

He tried to block out all the noise pollution and queued up at the bar for a double Jack Daniels with diet coke. He took a large gulp of his drink and stood leaning at the bar for a while, looking out for people he might be able to socialise with. It wasn't long before he decided to give up the search and sat himself down on a bar stool. He sparked up a cigarette and took a long drag on it when he suddenly felt someone rubbing his back and a voice came from behind.

"Hello stranger," came the voice.

Tom recognised the voice immediately and spun around on the stool excitedly. He peered up at the figure with a warm smile. Victoria smiled back down at him. She looked amazing. She was wearing a tight fitting red dress that stopped a few inches above her knees and accentuated her curves beautifully. She had curled her long blonde hair and was wearing an endearing shade of red lipstick. Some may have considered it to be a little 'tarty,' like she had made too much effort and was gagging to get laid, but Tom thought she looked breathtaking and her vibrant beauty separated her from all the rest.

"Vicky hey, I was looking for you." He replied with a joyful tone, and stood up. He leaned in to give her a friendly peck on the cheek when she unexpectedly turned her head and planted her lips on his, gently slipping her tongue inside his mouth. Tom lost himself in the moment and enjoyed the kiss passionately before realising the potential danger of their actions. He suddenly broke free from her heavenly lips and took a step back, frantically scanning the club for any sight of Jason or his mates.

"Hey relax Tom, I've done it." She told him with a flirtatious grin.

"Done what Vicky?" He replied, hoping that he already knew the answer.

"He's gone Tom. I finally told him where to shove it!" She responded and slid her hands around his waist. Tom replied with another warm smile and leaned in for another passionate kiss, sliding his hands round to gently squeeze her bottom.

"Hey, calm down!" She whispered to him playfully.

They drank and shared playful jokes for the rest of the night and her womanly persuasion even tempted him on to the dance floor for a few songs. Tom momentarily felt like all his problems were gone, like there was nothing left for him to be depressed about. It was the climax that two years of flirting had built up to, and Tom wanted the feeling to last forever.

The party ended at about 2:00 a.m. and Tom was confidant that everyone in his house would be fast asleep. He asked Victoria if she would come and spend the night with him and she accepted the offer with pleasure.

"Call us a taxi and I'll be outside in a few minutes." She said, and ran off to the toilets. Tom assumed that she was off to buy some condoms from the machine, so he obeyed her without question and walked outside to call a taxi. He stood out in the cold smoking a cigarette and watched as everybody else left the club. The taxi cab soon arrived and beeped for his attention, but Victoria had still not returned from the toilets. He looked down at his watch and realised it had been a good fifteen minutes now. He didn't think too much about it at first. In his experience girls had always taken ages in the toilets. He asked the taxi driver if he would be willing to wait a few minutes while he dashed in to see if she was ready, but the man refused angrily and the fare was soon replaced by another drunken student instead.

Tom waited another five minutes for Victoria, but she had still not returned. He then realised that he was the only one left and that the club was now completely deserted. He walked back up to the main doors just as the nightclub manager appeared from the other side of the glass and pulled across the dead bolt.

"Hey mate, my friend's still in there." Tom called to the man through the glass.

"Empty mate, they must have left." He hollered back at him and walked off into the distance.

Tom was confused, not quite understanding what had happened. Maybe she had changed her mind and escaped though the back entrance he thought, or maybe she had just been teasing him all along. Tom remained confused and his depression quickly returned and was stronger than ever. 'She sounded sincere though,' he thought to himself, as he started to stroll around the building in search of her.

Just as Tom turned the corner, he noticed a black Capri pulling away from the rear entrance of the club and as the car got closer he could clearly distinguish the faces of its passengers. In the driver's seat sat Jason Selby with a fuming expression on his face. It was bright red like a beetroot and the veins were bulging out and pulsating. Sitting next to him in the passenger seat was Victoria. She had a massive red hand print on her face where she had obviously been slapped about. She was crying hysterically. Jason caught Tom in his sights and drove the Capri recklessly in front of him and slammed on the breaks. Tom pushed his fears of Jason aside and stood by the car with clenched fists. Jason threw open the door and sprung open a six-inch flick knife.

"I warned you, you fucking cunt," he raged and without hesitation he plunged the blade deep into Tom's side and twisted it around in the gaping wound.

Tom was immediately paralysed with shock, surprised that even Jason would do something so extreme, before collapsing helplessly to the ground. Jason peered down at him and watched as Tom's blood spewed out all over the concrete. He projected a globlet of phlegm down at Tom and returned to his car without a second thought. Tom pulled himself forward to sit up and watched as Victoria screamed over at Jason manically, trying her best to escape the car to help him. Jason activated the central locking of the Capri, trapping poor Victoria inside. He then proceeded to punch her square in the face with the full force of his fist and threatened to strangle her if she didn't calm down. Tom was powerless to help her and could start to feel the blood draining from his head, as he watched the Capri finally speed away into the distance.

Tom lay down on the pavement panting and scared, trying his best to stop the blood flow with his bare hand, but it was futile and the wound continued to gush. The dramatic loss of blood then caused Tom's sugar levels to drop instantly and he started to feel a hypogylemic attack approach. His mind became blank and unable to function, as his muscles became limp and motionless. He felt his eyelids suddenly become very heavy and could no longer maintain the strength to keep them apart. He curled into a ball and slowly began to lose consciousness.

Susan managed to understand most of these events from the brief scribbles in the black book and filled in the blanks with her imagination. It had started to become clearer to her why Tom was so hesitant to talk about his troubled childhood. She could empathise with him. She assumed that the last entry and the ones that followed spanning a six month time period were all written from his hospital bed. They were all disjointed and seemingly random scribblings that Tom had written while drifting in and out of consciousness. Among the few words that she could decipher from the following entries were the phrases 'sweet revenge' and 'fucking bastard planet' and she had no idea of their specific meaning or purpose.

Ironically, the blade had penetrated through Tom's side and embedded itself into his pancreas. It was then twisted and retracted which left a seeping hole in the organ. For most people, this probably would have caused irreversible damage to the organ and the onset of diabetes. In retrospect, Tom should have considered himself quite lucky, having already been inflicted with the illness and leaving him with no added long term complications, but it just made him even more angry.

It took countless blood transfusions and a lot of time for Tom's body to recover from the incident. The diabetes had also caused serious complications with many of his other organs too and his sugar levels kept persistently dropping.

Because of the persistent falling of Tom's blood sugar, he remained in a constantly fluctuating state of semi-consciousness for months. His brief patches of blurred consciousness during this time were filled with bright flashes of TV news reports coming from the television of the old man in the adjacent bed who was "zombified" from a severe heart condition. Reports of increased knife crime and gangland violence penetrated the blurry haze, and strobe-like images of hooded thugs branded themselves deep in his subconscious. The images soon conjoined themselves with the memories of his own traumatic experience. In Tom's mind the face of every single thug, bully, or knife-wielding offender turned to that of Jason Selby.

The one night of dancing with his cherished Victoria had soothed the build up of suppressed anger inside of him and left him feeling calm, happy, and worry free for the first time since his diagnosis and onset of his depression, but with the insertion of that blade into his side, they all stormed back into his mind with vengeful determination. They pushed all the good thoughts aside once again and completely consumed every conscious and subconscious thought.

As Tom's consciousness began to expand to more than a few minute intervals, the amount of news reports that he absorbed began to grow too. Warnings of how our life styles were affecting climate change and reports of the constant threat of terrorism emanated from the TV, only breaking for intervals to show depressing NSPCC adverts in-between.

Tom's anger and hatred soon spread its aim to all of those around him and all he could think about was how the world had spiralled down to a pit of disgrace, and how no one on earth deserved the right to live.

It was at this point that Tom's fragile mind finally overloaded and detached itself from the cancerous anger which grew inside his head. It then took on a consciousness of its own and spoke to Tom in a bitter, evil voice, which raged at him and demanded retribution against the world that had done him wrong.

At the demands of the evil voice, Tom immediately grabbed his little black book and jotted down every single angry word that was spoken to him, scribbling so hard on the pages that the words ripped through the paper and imbedded themselves onto the pages below. He noted down his longing for revenge against the world and how this would begin with Jason Selby, a nail gun, and a dark alleyway.

Susan shut the book with shock and disbelief as the dramatic events quickly unveiled themselves. She had never imagined that Tom could ever be so angry and vengeful against anyone. It was a side of him that she had yet to see and hoped she never would. In the book Tom did not specify what he actually did to Jason, or whether he ended up dong anything to him at all. But if he had, it was easy to assume that it wouldn't have been pleasant.

Susan placed the book down on her lap for a second and gazed around at Tom's sleepy face once again. The potential revelations in the book made her doubt her opinion of him again and the empathy that she once felt turned to that of unsettling ambivalence. Did everything she thought she knew about Tom amount to nothing but fallacy? She wondered.

Without further hesitation she returned to the book again and carried on reading from where she left off. After a few more pages of undecipherable rantings and sadistic sketches of dead college students, the entries began to calm down again and talked about how Tom had been accepted for his course at university. He wrote how the excitement of finally moving out of Crawley and into the halls at Oxford had enabled him to gain more control over his thoughts and actions. But even with the evil voice pushed to the back of his mind, he could still feel its presence and influence over him.

Tom then started to talk about a girl called Abrianna Lutish. From the entries in the book, Susan could establish that she was a young Korean girl that had taken the same course as Tom and that she normally sat on her own during the lectures in the row directly in front of him. Tom noted how this Abrianna girl always seemed lonely and isolated and how she didn't seem to have any friends at the university at all. He noted how he found this very strange, as a girl of her beauty and intelligence would normally be the most popular.

The entries then went on to explain how Tom had started to befriend this Abrianna girl and that he eventually began to date her. Strangely enough, the entries in the book that followed seemed to make more reference to Abrianna's father, than Abrianna herself. From the book it appeared that Pong-Ju Lutish still lived in North Korea with the rest of Abrianna's family, and had sent her to live in England when she had done well on her A-level equivalents.

Tom seemed very intrigued with Pong-Ju and his line of work in North Korea and seemed almost desperate to meet him. Susan was confused as to what Tom found so intriguing about Pong-Ju and carried on reading in hope of finding an explanation.

The pages that followed looked like equations and formulas that she assumed were related to his degree. They all went above her head and she couldn't understand any of it. One equation in particular seemed to crop up again and again throughout.

'$6CO_2 + 6H_2O + \text{Energy} = C_6H_{12}O_6 + 6O_2$'

Susan now wished that she had paid more attention in science class when she was younger, instead of just messing about with her friend Laura in the back row, gossiping about celebrities or discussing what outfits to wear on the weekend. Maybe then she would have had some comprehension of what Tom was writing about, but it was useless. Straining her vague memory to the maximum, she could just about remember that 'H_2O' were the molecules for water and thought maybe the 'C' stood for carbon, but apart from that it was complete gibberish to her. She continued flicking though the pages of meaningless numbers and letters until she came upon a large diagram of two plants cells that were labelled accordingly. The pictures brought back some recollection to Susan from her GCSE Biology class, but there was something labelled in the second diagram that she couldn't remember being taught about at all, though she realised it was probably just something else she had not paid attention to. Tom had labelled this item 'CGM2/E' and Susan came to the conclusion that it must have been something they hadn't taught her, and that it must be something too advanced for GCSE level. She disregarded the strange diagram and carried on flicking through the pages.

Plant Cell Before Administration of CGM2/E

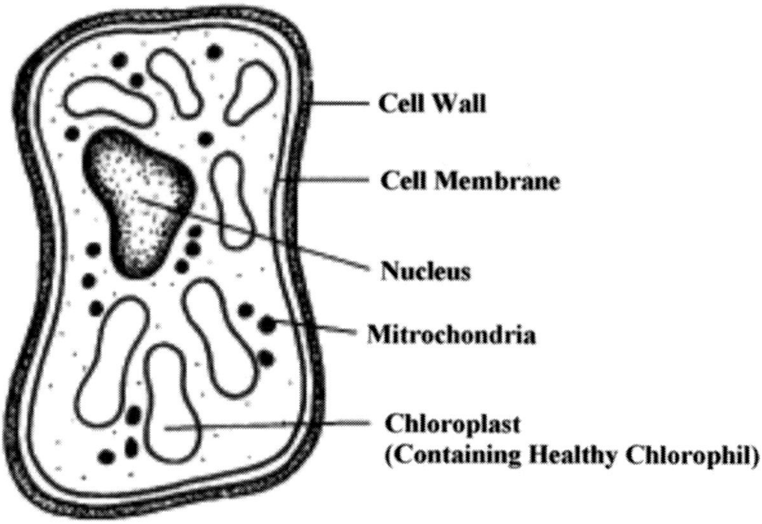

Plant Cell After Administration of CGM2/E

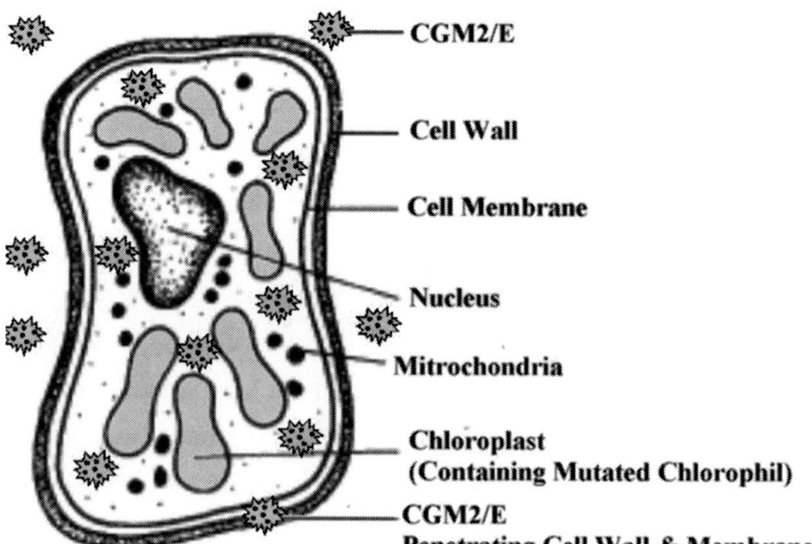

The next entries in the book referred to Dr. Richards and his stem cell research. Tom wrote how he had begged Dr. Richards to let him undergo the experimental procedure and how excited he was when Dr. Richards had agreed. Susan could see the remnants of the Pritt-Stick in the corner of the page and realized this was the page in the book that the medical report had originally been attached to. Tom carried on saying how happy he was to finally be rid of the diabetes and how he had dashed to the shops in excitement, buying most of the chocolate from the shelves.

There was then a large gap in time before Tom had started to write in the book again. Following the gap he wrote how he had proposed to this Abrianna girl and married her when they received their degrees. He then wrote how he'd moved to Korea with Abrianna to start their lives together. He wrote how he had struggled to learn the language and found it hard to settle in at first. There were then more references to Abrianna's father and something about a job that Pong-Ju had offered him in a lab, mixing chemicals and making solutions. A few entries then followed that were writing completely in Korean, with strange bold headings at the top of each page.

Susan didn't even attempt to make sense of these and carried on turning through the pages in search of an English entry. She then reached two pages that were seemingly stuck together with something. She began to gently prise them apart with curiosity and detached them with ease. She then realized that the pages had become affixed with a blood stained fingerprint upon the paper that had congealed once the book was closed and sealed them together. The entry seemed to span almost four pages in total and was the longest single entry she had come across. At the beginning of the first page was an underlined title at the top that read: 'The death of my sweet Abrianna.'

Susan felt a cold shudder down her spine and looked away from the book. It was all getting a bit much for her to digest at once and she found herself hesitant to read on. Maybe she'd have been better off listening to Tom's advice and just leaving the damn book alone, she thought. Nothing she had read so far had been to her advantage and had only degenerated her loving vision of him. She let out a gentle sigh and gulped, as she then returned her eyes to the page and read on with caution. A look of horror and disgust grew more apparent on her face as she read though the horrible events. Tom had written the entry in a way that sounded like the events were happening right then and there. He was precise and detailed to his every motion and thought, as if he had written down notes from a playing Dictaphone. The style was unlike anything else she had read in the book and made the entry even more eerie and unsettling for her to read.

The death of my sweet Abrianna

My meeting today with Pong-Ju did not go as well as I'd hoped. I told him I had changed my mind but he just became angry at me and then fired me from the lab. I now knew what I was going to have to do.

The walk home from the train station seemed to take the longest that it ever had, so many thoughts and feelings were running through my head, so many pros and cons to weigh up and so many special times that would count for absolutely nothing. I don't know if I can hold back the tears, how could I do this? She's such a sweet and lovely girl and she means the whole world to me. It's times like these that make me re-think the whole plan, to find damning justification for it. But it's no good, there's no turning back at this point. It has to be done. I wish that things were different. I wish the world was full of loving honourable people like my Abrianna, but it isn't, and that's why this has to be done.

I think I'll just stand here for a moment or two, catch my breath, compose myself, and wipe this sweat from my brow. If she sees me like this then she'll know for sure that something is up. She's seen this look on my face before, and she knows me far too well.

Deep breath. Composure. I reach into my pocket to ensure that I still have it, that it didn't fall out earlier when I pulled out my packet of cigarettes, or got stolen by some vigilante when I was on the train. The cold touch of metal against my fingertips was reassuring. I shouldn't have doubted the security of these deep pockets of my trench coat. I sometimes wonder why any coat would need such deep pockets, but right now I'm so glad that they do. Imagine if I'd have been caught with it on the way home. I'd have been in some serious trouble. Not that the guy in the pawn shop was too concerned about that when he sold it to me. He was more than happy to take my money and turn a blind eye.

There were so many different ones to choose from in the shop too, all of different shapes, sizes and colours, but I was drawn to this one immediately like a homing beacon. It was exactly the same as the one that old Granddad Dunn used to have. An instrument designed specifically to kill, but somehow all I saw was beauty in a revolver. Maybe it was just because of all the memories it triggered that made me smile, memories of my dear old granddad, the most honourable and courageous man you could ever want to meet. It was a shame that a device with such beauty and memories would now be used to do something so terrible. I now wish I'd bought a different one, one of the cheap pistols that looked like they were made of out plastic, one that I didn't associate with such pride, because there was no pride in what I was about to do.

I spun myself around to face the door and to shield myself from observation then examined the weapon under my long coat. I sprung open the barrel and inserted a single bullet into the lonely chamber and snapped the barrel shut again. I only needed one bullet. I had no plans for a struggle, no sporadic gunfire, just a single shot. Easy, painless, and quick. I assumed that it would be painless anyway; people were always saying that it was a painless way to go, though I doubt anybody had actually had a conversation with a dead guy with a bullet hole in the back of his head, to enquire exactly how his experience was. I'm sure some loopy morgue attendant from Texas probably tried at some point, but I doubt he got much response from the corpse.

I slipped the shiny metal device back into my pocket with a shaky hand. I'd never been this nervous before in my whole life. I've always had such certainty in everything I've done, but now I was consumed with doubts and hesitation. A cigarette, a cigarette would calm me down, make me think straight again. I slid one out the pack and sparked it up. It tasted so good, just like the first one of the day, or after a really nice meal. But I was just stalling things now, I had to go through with this, and I had to do it now.

I took a large drag on my cigarette, slid my key in the lock and opened up the door. The taste of nicotine in my lungs was immediately replaced with the satisfying aroma of home cooking: roasted chicken, boiled cabbage, and freshly made gravy. It was mouth watering and delicious.

I took a final drag and flicked the cigarette butt out of the open doorway and onto the path. I was normally more conscious of littering and pollution, but right now, I couldn't give a shit.

I reached forward and pushed the door shut with a little thud, which triggered footsteps from the kitchen. I gritted my teeth and prepared to act like everything was all OK.

"Hello my darling,"

I heard from behind me, in that sexy Korean accent I had come to adore and cherish. It was the kindest thing I could do, is what I kept telling myself, and considering the alternative, I was probably right. But that didn't make it any easier for me. Yes I was sparing her from a lifetime of illness, destitution, and a long hideous death— my heart was in the right place. But I loved her so damn much. No turning back now. I turn to face her.

"Hello sweetheart." I reply to her. We embraced lovingly. I caressed her lips with my own and ran my fingers through her hair.

"How was your day?" She asked, as she placed her tender hands around my waist. I fake a warm smile and look deep into her gorgeous brown eyes, knowing that it would certainly be the last time that we would ever share a moment together.

"I've had a great day my darling, how about you?" I ask her.

"Mine's been good too. I bought you some new goldfish, ya know, those speckled fantails I know you love. Oh and I finally fixed the DVD player, so I was thinking that we could snuggle up and watch a movie together later?" She asks.

"Sounds good to me love" I tell her. We're then interrupted by the whistling sound of a boiling pot from the kitchen.

"Dinner's just about ready love. I hope that you're hungry because I've cooked us a feast," she tells me.

I give her another warm smile as she turns her back and heads towards the kitchen. I reach into my pocket and feel the cold metal against my skin once again. Grit my teeth. Deep breath, and bring the revolver into the open. Abrianna's attention was consumed with the dinner, stirring one pot, and then the next. I should do it now, quickly. She wouldn't even know what's happened. That's how I want it, her to be living and breathing in ignorant bliss one second, and up in heaven the next. She never need know that her husband shot her in the back of the head, nor does she need know the reasons why. I raise the gun, my hand shaking like crazy. I aim at the back of her head, my lips starting to quiver. I close my eyes tightly and grit my teeth. I don't want to see this. But I only have the one bullet and I can't afford to miss. If I missed she would be scared, she would scream and she would run out the door, while I scramble around manically trying to find another bullet to finish off the job. I couldn't let that happen, that would not be good.

I open my eyes back up abruptly, but I'm too late, I've wasted too much time. She's looking at me. Frozen still and trembling, jaw dropped and eyes wide open. A tear rolls down my cheek. That look in her face was going to haunt me for the rest of my days— that look of pure fear and utter confusion. Her bottom lip starts to wobble, as if she wanted to say something, but no sound came out. Another tear rolls down my cheek, and another, streaming now. I re-firm my grip on the gun and re-align my aim.

"I'm so sorry my beautiful girl, I'm so…so…sorry," I tell her. I grit my teeth one final time and pull back the trigger. I wonder to myself whether her life flashed before her eyes in that split second, whether she saw all

the wonderful things we'd done together, all the love we'd shared, all the beauty in the world. Or was the image of me holding a gun at her face burned into her soul forever? Maybe the only thing that went through her head was that bullet but I guess I'm never going to know. I'm never going to know if it was painless. I'm never going to embrace my beautiful wife again.

The sound of the exploding gunpowder slowly fades into the distance and leaves me in silence, alone. There's definitely no turning back now.

The entry in the book stopped there, and left Susan completely speechless and frozen. 'How the hell could he do that to her? How could he just murder her in cold blood?' She thought. Susan's thought process was then completely shattered by a loud rattling and clunking noise of metal from within the garage below her. She had been so engrossed in what she had been reading that she never noticed the sound of Jobe descending the stairs and leaving the house. The rattling then stopped and she could hear the front door closing again. Curious, she stood and slid the book back into Tom's coat pocket. Then the sound of an electric drill started up, immediately waking Tom.

"What the fuck?" He called out with sleepy aggravation, as he sat up abruptly.

"God knows." Susan replied, staring out the open doorway nervously. It was at that point that she remembered the prisoner they had been holding hostage in the living room and suddenly realised what was happening.

Jobe circled the hostage menacingly with the cordless power tool, occasionally revving up on the trigger to install fear in his prey. The disfigured man sat there wide-awake and terrified, with sweat dripping from every pore. He shifted around nervously on the chair, desperately trying to pull the knots loose. His attempts to escape were futile though and Jobe enjoyed the power he possessed over the man. He eventually stopped circling around and bent down in front of him, looking deep in the man's eyes and squeezing down on the trigger again. The deafening noise of the drill started up again and the man could feel the vibrations through the floorboards. He clenched his eyes tightly and braced himself, as Jobe drilled the machine directly into his left kneecap. There was then a light showering of flesh and blood, before the drill bit reached the bone and continued into it like it was cement, spraying ashes of bone dust into the air. Jobe knelt rigidly and watched the discomfort in the man's eyes, as they started to water and roll back into his head. Jobe suddenly heard the mans vocal chords spring back to life and groan out through his sewn lips and glued together gums, as he continued to drill with a sadistic smile. Eventually the drill piece began to protrude from the other side of the knee and started to imbed itself into the wooden chair leg. Jobe kept his grip firmly upon the trigger and was curious to see if the man's frantic screaming attempts would eventually cause him to rip his mouth back open again, but it never did. He then retracted the drill and dropped it to the floor with a sigh. The drill lay on the floor and continued to spray out the remnants of blood until the rotation slowly grinded to a halt. It was at that point that Jobe became aware of Susan and Tom standing in the hallway, watching awkwardly.

Jobe wiped away a puddle of sweat that had built on his forehead before leaning with his back against the wall and returning his evil glare back to the hostage. The man looked back at him, weeping with agony as his eyes begged Jobe for forgiveness. It was hard for any of them to think that once upon a time, this man was just a normal guy like the rest of them. He probably had a wife and a kid and a boring job that he begrudged going to. He undoubtedly had a name too, though it was unlikely that he had been addressed by it in quite some time now.

"What could turn a man so bitter? Don't you have a soul?" Jobe muttered under his breath.

He bent down and picked up the drill once again and pulled back the hood of the man's robe. He then squeezed down upon the trigger and placed the end of the drill piece against the man's temple. The man's muffled screaming commenced once again as Jobe gently pierced the drill into his flesh, keeping the depth at about half an inch to prolong the suffering as much as possible. Jobe pulled out the drill and released a mild cackling noise, before commencing the same on the other side of his head.

"Jobe, this is wrong!" Susan said to him, finally bringing herself to voice an opinion.

"Don't you tell me what's wrong!" Jobe immediately snapped back at her. He turned and gave her an evil stare. Susan looked down sheepishly and put her hand across her mouth. She didn't want to watch any more of the torment but strangely couldn't bring herself to walk away.

Jobe turned back to the captive and pulled open the front of his robe. Underneath he was wearing a tatty pair of black trousers and a stained grey t-shirt. His umbilical unit was protruding out from in between the trousers and shirt and clipped on to the top of the trousers with a clip.

"You think you're so powerful and indestructible because of this, don't ya, you prick?" Jobe shouted at him. He grabbed hold of the machine and wrenched it away from the trousers, snapping off the clip that was keeping it in place. He grabbed the top of the umbilical chord firmly in the other hand and started to twist the machine round slowly. After half a turn the machine started to rip away from the artificially grown flesh of the umbilical chord, and after a three-quarter turn it completely detached from the chord with a low-pitched popping sound. Jobe threw it to the floor and released the chord from his grip. They all watched as the man struggled to keep conscious, but eventually fell in a slump. The chord dangled on the ground loosely, expelling blood and stomach juices from the end, forming a putrid puddle on the floor. Jobe then released his final bout of anger and punched the lifeless corpse in the side of the head, knocking him and the chair flying to the wall.

"It was no more than he deserved Susan!" Jobe growled at her and stomped past them up the stairs again.

Tom was somewhat pleased that the kids upstairs had either remained asleep, or were too scared to leave their rooms. Jacob especially would have been affected very badly by seeing the torture, or even becoming aware that it was happening.

Tom placed his hands gently around Susan's waist and tried to offer her a comforting smile. Susan looked back at him with cautious eyes, unable to decide whether or not the smile could be trusted anymore. The image of him that had been created by the book was not going to disappear from her mind with a single smile, and her new perception of him was going to be hard to push aside. She couldn't see him as the sweet and caring guy that she had once known anymore, but only the murderous and deceitful man that had been depicted.

All her love and gratitude for him had died and been replaced by fear and anxiety. She never thought that he would have been capable of doing the things she had read about, and now she feared what else he would be capable of. She feared the anger he appeared to keep inside of him, and what he might do to her if he was ever to find out what she had read.

She turned to him and looked deep into his seemingly genuine eyes before returning a smile and a hug to avoid suspicion, and solemnly followed him back upstairs again.

CHAPTER EIGHT

THE ROOM was dark and blurry and the only sound was that of the night breeze rattling against the windowpane. Tom opened his eyes and stared aimlessly at the ceiling, feeling surprisingly awake and refreshed. He was then struck by a strange feeling of surrealism.

'Why's it so dark?' He asked himself with confusion, having already seen the initial rays of the sun entering the room during Jobe's brutal torturing session. 'Is it possible that I slept through the whole day?' He asked himself.

An eerie, cold wind fluttered past him and sent a slight quiver down his spine. He turned his head to the side, hoping to feel relief at the sight of Susan lying peacefully beside him, but he was alone. A high-pitched scraping noise then reached his ears, like nails on a chalkboard. He lifted his head just in time to glimpse a dark shadowy figure walking past his open doorway and dragging a scythe alongside him. Tom immediately jumped up in bed and threw the duvet to the floor.

'Am I dreaming? It doesn't feel like a dream, not even my most lucid dreams felt like this,' He thought to himself. He then looked down at his hands and gave himself a slap on the face to test his theory. He could definitely feel the sensation and so surely he couldn't be dreaming, he concluded, though he remembered being tricked like that once before. He then stood from the bed and called out Susan's name into the eerie darkness. The sound echoed down the corridor into silence and returned no sign of reply. He then dashed out the room and into Jobe and Karen's room opposite, to find that room empty as well. He then tried Jacob's and Steven's but there was still no one to be seen. He then noticed the dark menacing figure looking up at him from the bottom of the stairs, only just decipherable in the darkness.

"Hey!" He called out to the figure, quickly reaching over for the light switch. An enormous orb of white light slowly grew from the bulb, and illuminated the room to the intense brightness of a supermarket store, making everything seem pale and washed out. The light stung Tom's eyes for a second and he clenched them tight. Upon reopening them the figure had faded away with the darkness. Tom then flew down the stairs in search of him and entered the living room.

The living room remained dimly lit by the refracted light from the hall, yet the ghostly silhouettes of people sitting amongst the couches and dinner table chairs could be clearly seen. Tom frantically scanned the faces in front of him with scary recollection. The crowd of people hung their heads low and motionless like the solemn attendants of an untimely wake, as the tall shadowy figure wielding the scythe stood with his back turned and gazing out the window.

Upon the first couch sat the unsettling images of Tom's dead parents, and upon the second sat Jason and Victoria from college. Each of them sat completely motionless like dusty stone carvings, while blood gently poured from each of their ears, eyes, and nasal cavities. Around the dinner table sat Grandfather Dunn and Uncle Bobby, equally as lifeless and still. They were sitting around a blood stained poker set.

Tom started to feel nauseous and dizzy and his mind began to overload with the confusing array of haunting apparitions before him. Jason Selby then broke free from his motionless trance and raised his head to stare at Tom with an evil look. His piercing stare fixed on Tom's eyes without a blink or flutter and remained solid and firm, intimidating and fearless. His skin appeared pale and drained, like a freshly starched sheet from the washer with heavy dark bags under each of his eyes. The eerie apparition of Victoria Fielding remained lifeless beside him with the exception of her juddering eyes which moved back and forth nervously across the room.

"You're still a fucking pussy Tom. You could never be anything else." Jason taunted him with a calm intimidating presence. He then rose to his feet and took a few steps towards Tom, invading his personal space and stopping a mere few inches away.

"Do you really think that Victoria ever felt shit for you Tom? You know she only ever felt pity for you. Pity for a sad pathetic excuse of a man—a man with no courage, no balls to fight for what he wants. You will never be a real man Tom, Never." He said.

Tom remained stunned and speechless, before suddenly feeling a strange sensation in his grip. He peered down to see that a Black & Decker cordless nail gun had now materialised in his hand. He nervously tensed his fingers with surprise and accidentally pulled down upon the trigger. A six inch nail immediately shot from the device with exacerbated force and imbedded itself deep into the floor beside him.

"Well you've finally got your chance Tom, a chance to act like a fucking man for once instead of pussying away behind that stupid black book like the repressed schizoid coward that you are! Well, do it then you fucking loser! You know exactly what you wanna do to me. You wanna jam that damn thing into the side of my head and jab a six inch nail directly into my brain. So go on huh? What's wrong? Not got the balls for it Tom?" Jason continued to rant at him.

"Well come on freak boy! You think you're so much better than the rest of us, like you're something special, but you're nothing, nothing but a coward. You're not Mr. Goody-Goody whose moral high ground prevents him from doing any wrong. You just lack the bollocks to actually do anything. The truth of the matter is that every day you wish you could be more like me!" Jason continued, pausing only to watch Tom's aggravated expression grow more fierce and pent up. The increasing anger inside of him finally summoned up the adrenalin to force his sheepish eyes to return the same menacing stare at Jason and remain fixed and confidant on him, as the purpose of the weighty nail gun in his grip grew more certain and undeniable.

"Fuck you!" Tom eventually screamed back into Jason's glaring face before violently thrashing the nail gun into his head and releasing his explosive anger with a frantic shower of speeding nails. The array of rusted nails protruded his head down one side like it was a tattered pin cushion and released trickles of blood to meander down the contours of his pale white face. The nails unbalanced his bloody head and weighed it down to a crooked sideward slant to the right. Jason's restless stare then finally relented to an emotionless gaze and he became silent once again.

"We're very disappointed in you Thomas. We thought you were better than this," said a familiar voice from behind him.

"Fuck you dad. This world is full of bastards!" Tom screamed back at the condescending apparition of his father, feeling his own reminiscent hatred consuming him. "Who do you think you are, passing judgment on me? You're nothing but the bastard offspring of a worthless whore!" Tom continued with rage and smashed the nail gun into his father's head, firing off another nail.

"And what about me Tom? Did I deserve it?" A sweet, sorrowful voice spoke.

Tom spun around on the spot to see Abrianna standing at the doorway, a bullet hole between her eyes, causing blood to gush uncontrollably down her face. She gave him that same look of confusion and betrayal and then started to cry, as the tears diluted the blood.

"Don't you try and make me feel bad either, you fucking bitch. I never even liked you. I just used you to get to your father. You mean nothing to me," he growled back at her.

She started to cry harder and started to approach him with open arms for a reminiscent hug. The image of the gushing blood was putrefying to him and he took a step back.

"Get the hell away from me you stupid bitch." He warned, as Abrianna continued to come closer.

"But I love you, Tom." She continued to cry.

Tom immediately held up the nail gun to aim it at her, but it had now turned into a loaded revolver. He pulled back the trigger without hesitation and shot another hole through Abrianna's head. The girl seemed to fly though the air in slow motion and landed with a loud thud against the wall. The smell of gunpowder in the air triggered off memories of when he had shot her the first time and the musty aroma felt strangely satisfying to him.

Tom kept the gun firmly within his grasp, as he started to notice the rest of the room's ghostly occupants becoming lucid and looking at him evilly, like a pack of hungry wolves that were eyeing their prey. Even the figure of his Grandfather was now looking ready to engage in bloodshed and brandished his own duplicate revolver. Tom stood nervous and panting, not sure whom to aim his weapon at first, when he started to feel a painful thumping in his head.

"It's good to see that anger is still alive in you Tom. I thought you'd gone completely soft over the years." A deep gravely voice emanated from the shadowy cloaked figure by the window. Tom turned to face him and held out the revolver with his finger confidently upon the trigger.

"Who the fuck are you? Why do you haunt my dreams?" Tom demanded fiercely. The figure then turned around to face him and the expected skeletal face that had appeared to him so many times before, had now been replaced with the eerie sight of his own face looking back at him.

"Do you see the things I can make you do, the things we can achieve together? You need me Tom. You like the power I can give you. You like the feeling of conquest. But yet you fight me. You deny me. Why?" The eerie doppelganger asked.

"This isn't real. None of this is fucking real!" Tom muttered agitatedly.

"I'm real Tom. Surely you know that much by now? Huh? You're not capable of anything without me. It's all me Tom, all of it!"

"What the hell do you want from me?" Tom roared back, starting to lower the gun.

"Only what I've always wanted Tom, to help you."

"Help me? All you've ever done is anger me, control me, and tell me lies! I don't need your damn help!"

"Oh yes, you do Tom. You just don't know it yet. Just take your new found 'friends' to the Tremoline clinic and I'll take it from there."

"How can I do that? The Dodge has been blown to pieces!"

"There are other means of transport aren't there, Tom? How do you think the fanatics got to you?" His ghostly double asked.

"The train?" Tom muttered to himself, as the revelation entered his mind.

The exploding ignition of gunpowder then pierced through the surreal dreamy images and sucked Tom back into reality once again, where he found himself alone in his bed. The midday sun was shining brightly through the bedroom window and the sound of screaming bellowed from beneath him. He looked down at the ragged bloody cloths upon his body and caught sight of his perfectly regenerated skin below them.

"Oh shit," He muttered to himself, as he realised his neglect to hide the once ghastly wounds. His secret would surely be exposed if anyone was to catch sight of his miraculous recovery and it was not a conversation he felt confidant to engage in. He immediately leaped from the bed and proceeded to change his clothes, hoping Susan had been equally as ignorant to the gashes as him. The merciless screaming from below him showed no signs of diminishing so he followed it down the stairs with nervous curiosity.

"Please Jobe! Put the fucking gun down, this isn't helping us!" Susan pleaded with him, as the smoke gently seeped from the end of the discharged shotgun. The mutilated corpse of the fanatic hostage lay limp and desecrated in a pool of blood on the floor. A new shotgun wound to its head had blown away any recognisable feature from its face and left behind a bloodied open mass of flesh and bone, displaying fragments of skull and brain tissue which gently trickled and fell from the gaping wound. Jobe stood towering over the rancid mess and ignored Susan's constant pleas to desist in his actions. His eye fixed sternly upon the body as if it were still alive and dangerous, as he quickly re-loaded his smoking weapon in preparation for another blast.

"Jobe stop! She was sick, Jobe. This won't bring her back." Tom insisted from the doorway. Jobe took a deep aggravated breath and finally lowered the gun slightly. He turned to Tom and violently threw the shotgun to the floor in defeat, as he shot a piercingly evil stare of disapproval at Tom. Tom sheepishly looked away as he noticed Jobe's muscles tensing with rage and sweat dripping from his brow.

"Yeah, she was sick Tom, and I coughed up half a sink full of blood this morning too. But you seem alright, don't you Tom!" Jobe exploded at him, starting to step forward towards him. "Huh? You're not fucking sick at all are you Tom?" Jobe continued, as he stepped closer and looked Tom up and down.

"I don't know what you're talking about Jobe." Tom replied nervously and looked over at Susan in confusion. Jobe then reached out his hand and gripped Tom by the throat, lifting him up against the wall and into the air.

"Huh? Answer me Tom! Why aren't you fucking sick you son-of-a-bitch? Something you're not telling us?" Jobe raged at him and increased the pressure around his throat. Tom desperately tried to respond, but the force around his vocal chords prevented any sound from leaving his mouth and he started to choke. Jobe gave him one last growl and finally removed his hand from Tom's throat, sending Tom crashing to the floor and gasping for air. He nursed his bruised larynx and aimed his sorrowful eyes at Susan, who had not responded to the attack in any way.

"You've read it, haven't you?" He asked her. She opened her lips to reply but then hesitated and looked away instead.

"Yeah, she has Tom. What the fuck is this shit, huh?" Jobe demanded, pacing up and down.

"I didn't think you'd believe me." Tom muttered in response and pulled himself to his feet.

"So why do you get to be the fucking special one, huh? My poor Karen didn't deserve to die, did she?" Jobe continued.

"I'm really sorry, Jobe." Tom responded with sincerity.

"Yeah, I bet you fucking are. Just watch your back Tom, 'cause I'm watching you!" Jobe replied with more composure and stomped past him back to his room.

"Thanks, Susan," Tom muttered to her sarcastically.

"Well, why keep secrets from me Tom? I thought we were close." She blurted out emotionally.

"It ain't the kind of thing you can just tell someone. You'd have thought I was insane." Tom replied defensively.

"Yeah, maybe I would have, but it still ain't good enough." She replied angrily. She then released a sigh and dropped herself on to one of the couches, chewing on her fingernails hesitantly.

"What else have you read?" He asked, starting to get suspicious and worried that more secrets had been revealed.

"Nothing Tom, I found the damn report on the floor." She replied cautiously.

"OK then, all I ask is that you leave my fucking stuff alone Susan. It's very personal to me." He pleaded.

"Why? What else are you hiding Tom? Huh? You're starting to look very guilty over there!" She snapped back at him.

"Nothing! It's just . . . it's just really personal stuff, that's all. I would never go through your diary and I expect the same respect. OK?" He explained to her with frustration. She looked back at him and released another sigh, before finally nodding her head in agreement. She now began to feel like the deceitful one, since she intended to return to the book as soon as she could, confident that the mysterious black book contained much more that she needed to know about him.

Tom sat down beside her on the couch and held her hand in his own. She slowly looked back at him and tried her best to decipher his thoughts through his glazed and unrevealing eyes.

She then started to consider the possibility that she had been too harsh with her judgment of him, for there were plenty of people in the world that she would have wanted to hurt in the past. Maybe if her thoughts were all down on paper like Tom's, then maybe others would have had a similar opinion of her. She began to realise that rage and the need for retribution consumed everyone at some point or another, and that the presence of a singular and uncontrollable thought didn't necessarily have to result in the aforementioned intentions. She soon began to relate the anger to her own feelings about her real father and all the evil thoughts she had conjured up in the past, all the things she would have liked to do to him for revenge. She had sought retribution and closure for years now, for all the bad things that he had done to her and her Mother, and for walking out on them all without even saying good-bye.

She then started to think about what Tom had done to his wife Abrianna again. It was a harsh thing to do to her and Susan would have never done it in a million years, but maybe Tom's intensions were good. Was it possible that Tom loved this girl so much, that he didn't want her to live in a world like this? And if so, could she really pass judgment on him for his actions?

"So you forgive me right?" Tom eventually asked, abruptly interrupting Susan's thoughts.

"Yeah, I forgive you, Tom." She decided and planted a kiss on his cheek. "So what was diabetes like then? I never knew anyone with it before."

"It wasn't nice Susan. I wouldn't wish it on anyone."

"So, you had to inject yourself and stuff then?"

"Yeah, four or five times a day. You wouldn't believe how good it is to be rid of it."

"So tell me about this stem cell treatment, then. I didn't even think that they had perfected the whole stem cell thing, let alone what they did to you."

"Well the government has a tendency to keep the public in the dark about things. I'm sure they've perfected human cloning too, but just didn't want to tell us about it to avoid controversy."

"Well where's the controversy with stem cells?"

"Well, you know where they come from right?"

"No, sorry."

"Well, they're extracted from unborn baby embryos."

"Oh, right."

"Well, to obtain enough to do what they did to me, they needed to harvest almost a hundred baby embryos, and those pro-life activists would have had a field day with it."

"So that's all they had to do? Just inject these stem cells into you?"

"I'm not really too sure, I think it was a bit more complicated than that. I think they needed to mutate the cells in order for them to stay alive in me."

"And how did they do that?"

"I've no idea Susan. I was too happy with the results to ask questions. I'm not sure that they even intended or expected this to happen to me."

At that point Steven appeared in the doorway with a distressed and tiresome expression upon his face, like he'd been abruptly woken from a pleasant dream. He rubbed his eyes and walked into the room.

"What the hell was all the shouting about? Can't you people control yourselves?" He asked in a complaining tone.

"Don't worry Steven, Jobe's just upset about Karen, it's understandable." Susan replied to him with a smile. Steven then cast his eyes down upon the bloodied corpse on the floor and looked away in disgust.

"Isn't anyone going to clean that shit up? It's starting to reek in here." Steven asked with annoyance.

"Oh God! I'm so sorry, Steven. I completely forgot that was even there. I'll get rid of it soon." Tom replied to him shamefully.

"What the hell are we going to do now Susan? Karen's dead and the truck has been blown to pieces. We're just fucked ain't we?" Steven blubbered, close to tears, and fell down onto the other couch.

"Hey watch your language kid. I know things seem a bit bleak at the moment, but you have to stay strong and positive." Tom assured him.

"Positive? Be positive about what Tom? We're stuck in an isolated house that stinks of rotten corpses, in a world in which we're the only people alive with the exception of monstrous looking fanatic cunts that want to kill us. What the hell have I got to be positive about, huh?" Steven asked him, almost shouting by this point, a single tear trickling down his cheek.

"Hey, come on Steven, I've done my best for you so far haven't I?" Susan defended herself and moved to the other couch next to him.

"Yeah, I know you have Susan, I'm sorry. It just seems hopeless, and I miss our family." He replied and buried himself in a foetal position under her arms.

"Don't worry about the Dodge Steven, I have a Plan B." Tom told him and stood from the couch.

"What plan?" Steven asked him in confusion.

"I'll explain in a minute," Tom replied and started ascending the stairs.

"Jacob? You awake kid?" He called out, reaching the top of the stairs. "Jacob?" He called again, and pushed open the bedroom door.

Tom found the room in a complete mess, like the result of a childish tantrum, with bed sheets all over the floor and clothes flung all over the place, but Jacob himself was nowhere to be seen. Tom then checked in Steven's room and the bathroom, before running back down the stairs again.

"Has anyone seen Jacob this morning?" Tom asked the two huddled on the couch.

"He's in his room isn't he?" Steven replied from beneath Susan's arms.

"No, he isn't," Tom quickly replied, and reached for an oxygen canister.

"Can you both do me a favour and make sure the other canisters are charged? I'm gonna go look for him." Tom continued and made for the door. He pulled away the dining chair that was propping the door shut and gave Susan a look to remind her to replace it once he had gone. He then opened it up and ventured out into the street.

Tom headed straight for the remains of the old college, where he immediately found Jacob sitting on the rubble in his own usual spot. He was sitting motionless, looking down at the Victoria Cross that Tom had given him. Tom walked up beside him and sat down on the rubble uncomfortably, placing his arm around Jacob.

"How's it going kid?" He asked with a sigh of relief. Jacob looked round at him solemnly and started to type into his machine.

"You all think I'm a monster don't you? Like the men that came in the night." The voice read out.

"No, not at all Jacob," Tom quickly responded with empathy. "Those men were bad people Jacob, they wanted to hurt us, and you're nothing like them." Jacob looked back at him again with the same blank expression and started typing again.

"They looked frightening to me. I was scared. I must look scary to all of you." The machine read out, as Jacob pressed down on the 'Talk' button with hesitation, and started to cry.

"Hey, look at me kid. You don't look scary to me Jacob, not at all." Tom said with a smile, trying to reassure him. Jacob tried to wipe away his tears and looked back down at the medal again.

"Your parents took you to the Brighton clinic didn't they?" Tom asked him. Jacob nodded. "And you'd remember where it is right?" He continued, and received another nod.

"Well that's where we're going Jacob, and I can't promise anything, but they might be able to help you." Tom said to him with slight hesitation, trying not to give Jacob false hope. Jacob hid the medal away in his palm and looked up at Tom with curiosity and awaited an explanation.

"I mean, they did that procedure a good few years ago now Jacob. They would have made great advancements by now." Tom continued, aware that he was going out on a limb and reaching the point of complete fabrication. Jacob paused for a second with a confused expression, before returning to his machine once again.

"How we gonna get there?" It read out.

"The train, Jacob. If those religious idiots could manage to work it then I'm sure we'll have no trouble." Tom told him with another smile. "But we need your help to find the clinic, so I need you to be strong for us, OK?" Jacob nodded back again with more enthusiasm this time and rose to his feet, placing the Victoria Cross safely back in his pocket. Tom stood up as well, pleased that he had managed to cheer Jacob up, and they both walked back towards the house again.

With three oxygen canisters charging up from the mush machine, Susan had ventured into the kitchen with the fourth mask on her face. She tried her best to ignore the rotting corpse of Karen on the floor, and wished that a sheet or something had been used to cover it up, to shield everyone else from the ghastly sight. Susan kept her eyes firmly on the jugs in front of her, as she boiled up water from the kettle and transferred it to the next jug. She then washed up a few bowls and spoons to serve the daily mush in, and turned to leave the room. Keeping her attention from the corpse, she almost tripped over Karen's limp arm and briefly lost her composure. She closed her eyes and took a few deep breaths, relieved in the fact that at least Karen's body had not yet started to smell, as the rancid stench of decomposing flesh would surely make her stomach churn. She regained her composure and pushed open the kitchen door with the bowls in her other hand. She walked through the doorway and closed the door as quickly as she could, before pulling the mask from her face and leaving it dangling around her neck. The persistent beeping of the mush machine had started to make her head pound and she was relieved to finally press down on the reset button and start to dispense out a bowl.

"Here you go Steven. You need to have something to eat." She called out to him, as he remained in the same still position on the couch.

"No, I'm not hungry Susan." He replied lethargically.

"I don't care if you're hungry or not Steven, you need to eat." She replied assertively, walking over and placing the bowl on his lap.

"Eat!" She insisted.

The sun was surprisingly bright that day and the machine was working very efficiently. It wasn't long before all the canisters were fully charged and the next bowl of mush was ready to be served. She unclipped the three canisters and placed the forth one on to charge as she poured out a bowl of mush for herself. She sat herself down at the dinner table and started to eat her way through the mush. The sloppy mess actually tasted quite nice that day, but neither of them was upbeat enough to appreciate it. In the kitchen there were only a few cans of real food left now, a tin of ham, some hotdogs, and a can of potatoes. Although tempting enough to eat, Susan wanted to be out the kitchen as quickly as she could. The thought of cooking food with a dead body in the room made her stomach start to churn over, so she decided to leave the tins for another time, a time when the body had been removed from the room and properly disposed of.

Not that she could think of an appropriate place to put the body at this point in time, a place that would be respectful and that Karen would appreciate.

She was deep in thought again as she suddenly heard the chair by the front door falling over and looked round to see Tom and Jacob appear from the hallway.

"Hey, Jacob, you alright then?" She asked him, as she walked into the hall and planted a kiss upon his forehead.

"Are the canisters all done?" Tom asked her.

"Yeah, all but one. Are you gonna tell me what's going on now then Tom?"

"We're going to the clinic Susan, today."

"But how, Tom? Our only means of transport is gone."

"Not our only means Susan. When was the last time you took a nice train journey?"

"The train? But none of us know how to work the train Tom."

"It can't be hard Susan, and I don't think we have any other choice."

"Well, you're right about that I guess."

"The train is stationed on platform five, which is the direct track straight to Brighton. All we have to do is work out how to get it going and it'll take us straight there."

"And do you know where the clinic actually is Tom?"

"No idea Susan, but Jacob's been there before."

"Yeah, of course he has."

She thought about the idea for a moment or two, chewing on her bottom lip, before coming to the conclusion that the plan might actually work. Steven then appeared beside her with a changed look of excitement that lit his face like a firework in the night sky.

"So when are we leaving Tom?" He asked.

"Today, Steven. Why don't you go and pack a few things to take with you." Tom told him with a smile. Steven replied with a cheeky grin and dashed off upstairs to start packing.

"There are rucksacks in the loft!" Tom shouted up after him.

"You too Jacob, only the essentials though." Tom added and watched as Jacob dashed up the stairs as well.

"What else do you think we'll need Susan?" Tom asked, turning to face her.

"Um…I dunno Tom, there's so much that we depend on here."

"Like what?"

"Well the kettle to make the water drinkable for a start. Then what happens if we get there and there's no breathable air?"

"Well they make all the machines there Susan, so I'm sure there'll be something we can use."

"I don't know Tom, I'm really nervous about this. I mean, what if the building isn't even there? You know as well as I do that the building may have been blown to pieces by now."

"Yeah, I know that Susan. I just have a feeling that it's going to work out."

"And what if it doesn't Tom?" She asked with agitated concern. Tom hesitated and shrugged his shoulders, having not thought that far ahead.

"I'd rather take the chance than be stuck here forever Susan. Wouldn't you?" He finally asked her back.

"Yeah, you're right Tom." She agreed.

"Do you want me to get the stuff we need from the kitchen?"

"No it's OK Tom. I've already been in there once already. What are we going to do with her?"

"I was going to put her body in one of the beds before we leave. I don't think there's much more we can do."

"Yeah OK then, you can go and speak to Jobe while I'm sorting out the kitchen, though. Tell him what's going on."

"Alright, back in a minute then." He told her and pressed a kiss upon her lips.

Tom slowly walked up the staircase, unsure and hesitant of Jobe's state of mind, or how bad his aggression may be towards him. He walked down the corridor towards the room and nervously placed a knock on the door. The knocking caused no reaction so Tom repeated it and called out his name. "Jobe?"

There was still no reply so Tom opened up the door and poked his head gingerly round the corner. Jobe sat on the side of the bed, staring aimlessly out of the bedroom window. His expression was emotionless and twitchy and remained ignorant of Tom's presence.

"Hey, Jobe, how you doing?" Tom asked cautiously and sat down beside him. Jobe's eyes briefly peered round to acknowledge him, but then quickly returned to the window without any response. Jobe gently rested his chin on his entwined fingers and started tapping them against each other nervously. He sat there trying hard to think of something to say, but found nothing to express the emptiness that he was feeling in his gut. Looking out through the glass panes of the window, he hoped to see something enlightening, to lift his spirits and give him the courage to continue with his life. Just something small and insignificant that he may have taken for granted before. Something of beauty that he could appreciate, like a bird flying through the air, swooping down to catch a worm and singing in joyous harmony. Or a commercial plane in the sky, taking its passengers away on a long awaited holiday to the Caribbean where they would lay peacefully on the beach with the tide nipping at their toes and the sun beaming heavily upon their exposed bodies. But all that was visible to him was the aftermath of destruction and the slow decomposition of the world.

"The world has nothing left to offer me Tom." Jobe finally forced out. "Take a look Tom, tell me what you see?"

Tom took a look out the window to humour him and hesitated to respond.

"The world is dying Tom, and we are the last remnants of a civilisation. The dinosaurs had their time on this earth, and I guess we've now had ours. So what's the point in fighting it?" Jobe asked him despairingly.

"Come on Jobe, Karen wouldn't have wanted to see you so depressed." Tom replied to him sensitively.

"No, no she wouldn't Tom. But she's gone, and I feel all alone."

"Yeah, I know you do Jobe. I've had that feeling before. But you need to have hope. The rest of us have decided to take the train down to the Brighton clinic, and you need to come with us." Tom explained.

"And what's that gonna achieve?"

"I don't know Jobe, maybe nothing. But it's the only thing we have left to do, and I can't give up for the sake of the others."

"I wish she was still here to come with us Tom, she had her hopes in the clinic too."

"I know she did Jobe, so do it for her."

"Maybe . . . I don't know."

"Well do it for the kids then. They could do with having you around."

"Yeah I guess. I imagine that poor Jacob has suffered ten times more than I have. Maybe I'm just selfish."

"No, I don't think you're selfish at all Jobe. Jacob has the strength to carry on because he knows that we all love him, and we consider you part of the family now too."

"Ha! Thanks, I guess we do all need to stick together on this. I'm sorry for taking things out on you earlier Tom. You're a good bloke."

"It's alright Jobe, I never took it to heart mate. I find it hard to believe it myself sometimes, like I'd just imagined it or something. So you can imagine why I would be hesitant to show off about it to everyone."

"Yeah, if I'd have known you were indestructible I would have let you fight all the fanatics by yourself!"

"Well, I wouldn't say that I was indestructible Jobe, but I do have a slight advantage I guess. It's like I get a strange feeling inside me, like I can actually feel my metabolism speeding up and my wounds just start to heal in front of me."

"So if I cut off your arm, are you gonna grow back another one, then?"

"Ha! No I don't think so Jobe, and I don't really wanna try that one out if that's alright. Besides, I think I'm beginning to lose it a bit now."

"Oh? Why's that?"

"I dunno Jobe, it just doesn't feel quite the same as it used to. It's like, it's taking longer to heal and afterwards I feel completely drained and weak, like I'm hung-over. And there are these weird dreams too."

"Dreams?"

"Yeah, I'm not sure if they are related or not to be honest, but they're just strange."

"Nightmares?"

"Yeah, nightmares. Like memories I want to forget, mixed with my fears and paranoia and . . . and something else too. Look, I don't really wanna think about them right now Jobe."

"That's alright Tom, another time. So when are we all leaving?"

"Soon. I've got the others packing at the moment. You got anything you wanna bring?"

"Just my shotgun and I'll be fine."

"Yeah, might come in handy. Don't know how many more of those freaks we're gonna encounter."

"I was thinking of another reason actually Tom. We all used to carry cyanide pills with us in the army, you know, in case the enemy wanted to torture us for information. I was never tempted to use them once, but it was comforting to know the option was there. Well, it's kinda like that, you understand?"

"Yeah I understand Jobe, and I guess I can live with that. Get everything you need and I'll see you downstairs in a bit, yeah?"

"Yeah, alright, Tom . . . just one last thing?"

"What's that?"

"Karen?"

"She's in the kitchen Jobe. Before we leave I was planning on tucking her away peacefully in one of the beds, unless you have another idea?"

"No. No that sounds fine to me Tom, but I will be the one to do it. I need to see her one last time."

"Sure Jobe. I understand."

Tom gave him one last friendly smile and walked out of the room, shutting the door closed behind him. He walked across the hall and into his own bedroom with a chuffed feeling of achievement for his efforts, and started looking around for things he would need to take. He grabbed a few pairs of underpants that were relatively clean, along with a jumper and his disfigured old toothbrush from the en-suite and threw them all into a black rucksack that he kept under the bed. He unhooked his coat from the door and slung it on, ensuring that his black book was still safe within the breast pocket and made his way back down the stairs again to join the others.

Jacob and Steven were sitting on the couch with excited anticipation on their faces. Next to them were two more rucksacks, each of which were full to bursting point and appeared overly heavy for the children to carry.

"You sure you need all that stuff?" Tom asked them with sarcasm.

"Yeah, just some clothes, a pillow, and a few books." Steven replied nodding.

"Books? Since when have you ever read a book?" Tom asked him.

"Well I think I'm gonna start, seeing how I couldn't fit the TV and DVD player in my bag!" Steven replied humorously.

Tom peered round to see the three oxygen canisters on the floor beside the dinner table, fully charged and ready to go. He then noticed a bowl of mush on the table with a spoon poking out the top.

"This for me?" Tom asked, turning back round to Steven and Jacob.

"Yeah, Susan poured it out for you. Actually tastes quite nice today." Steven replied.

Tom dropped his rucksack on the floor and sat down at the table to eat the mush, just as the kitchen door opened and Susan appeared from the doorway. She was carrying out three big shopping bags worth of supplies from the kitchen which she placed on the table and then returned her facemask to its dangling position around her neck.

"Hey!" She greeted him and pressed her lips against his forehead.

"Hey to you too. You got everything we need?" He asked her in between gulps of mush.

"Got the food, the kettle, and a few other bits, so I think that's everything from the kitchen. I just need a few more bits from upstairs and then I'm done. Where's Jobe?" She asked.

"He's just coming in a minute. He's calmed down a bit now but he's still very depressed." Tom explained to her.

"Alright well, I'll look after him." She replied.

She rested for a few moments to catch her breath, before removing the heavy canister from her back and making her way up the stairs and into the bedroom. She packed a few pieces of clothing and a few items from the bathroom, along with her copy of *War and Peace* and walked back onto the landing just as Jobe emerged from his room. She stopped and offered him a friendly smile and held his hand for comfort, as they walked back down the staircase together. The others were waiting anxiously in the living room with their canisters on their backs and luggage in their hands, like a family going away on a camping trip to the forest.

"You all leave without me and I'll meet you at the station in a minute or so," Jobe asked them, giving Tom a little nod to remind him of his plans.

"Sure," Tom replied with a nod to show he understood.

"But don't go without me, I don't think I'll be able to catch the next one!" Jobe continued jokingly.

Jobe cupped his hand tightly around his nose and mouth as Tom reached for the door handle and let the carbon dioxide gush into the house once again. The rays of the sun shone down brightly from the clear blue sky and the warmth on their skin kept their spirits high and hopeful. It was like a sign from God that the journey would be fruitful and lead them to a place of happiness, as they marched out of the doorway in single file and into the street.

Jobe watched them all leave from the doorway and felt a small grin force its way onto his face too, as the same strange feeling of hope fluttered in his mind as well. He closed the door back up and propped it shut with the chair again. Then he walked into the living room and leaned his head in close to the blowing fan of the mush machine for a gasp or two of breathable air, like steeling a shot of whisky from a pub optic while the barman ventured into the cellar to change a barrel of beer. The euphoric feeling of joy then fluttered away as quickly as it had arrived, as Jobe's mind fixated back on the present job at hand. He paused for a while and contemplated how he would cope with seeing the body of his beloved Karen again. He tried to tell himself that it was just a body, like a shell or a casing that once held her loving spirit captive inside it, and that now the shell had been cracked open and released her spirit to the heavens above, where it would float around in peace and harmony at long last.

He equipped himself with the oxygen gear and tried to keep the pleasant thought in his head. He held onto it as tight as he could and tried with all his strength not to let it slip away. He opened the kitchen door with closed eyes and took a final deep breath to reinforce his composure, but as his eyelids slowly opened and rested on the motionless corpse on the floor, all memories of that happy thought vanished from existence, and left behind a sad bitter pain in the back of his throat. He bent down at the knees and grasped the body firmly with two arms before lifting her up and finding his balance. He could feel a tear forming in his eye and his lip started to quiver but shook the feeling away angrily and gritted his teeth. Jobe knew that his strength and determination were qualities that Karen had once loved and admired to the point that she felt safe and secure with him in any situation, and he was determined not to let her down now. He carried her weighty body with delicate care, like cradling a newborn baby, making sure not to scrape her head or feet against the walls or door, and took her up to the bedroom. He laid her down gently upon the bed and covered her to the neck with the soft fluffy duvet, just like he used to do after a drunken Friday night, when she had fallen asleep during the taxi ride home. He knelt on the floor next to her and lovingly stroked her cheek and smiled. She looked so peaceful to him, like it was the end of a long journey and he only hoped that her destination had turned out to be everything she had hoped it to be.

"We'll be together soon my baby." He whispered softly into her ear.

"But these people need me now, so I have to go." He continued, before rising to his feet, and slowly walking away.

CHAPTER NINE

THE GROUP seemed to reach Three Bridges train station in almost no time at all, as if the hope and enthusiasm they all shared had consumed their thoughts to the point where the journey had become nothing more than a flash. They passed the bodies of the dead fanatics that Tom had previously slain and entered the station through the tall iron gates. A long fenced alleyway led them past the old red ticket machine that now lay dented and dusty on the littered floor. Then they passed through the ticket check point that the ticket inspectors used to man, standing proud in their uniforms like security guards or bouncers from a nightclub. Tom remembered the grief that he used to cause these men when he was a kid, running past them in a frantic dash as the train arrived on the platform. Avoiding paying the fair was a regular and fun game to him back then. He didn't do it because he couldn't afford the fare. He did it because it gave him such an adrenaline rush to be rebellious that he just couldn't resist the challenge.

One at a time they took turns climbing over the rotating barriers and made their way onto the main platform where they stood for a while and looked at the gleaming locomotive over on platform five at the end. It seemed to glisten in the bright rays of the sun and beckon them towards it. Tom smiled in appreciation before starting to wonder how the fanatics had actually got the train up and running again in the first place, and what station they had started their journey from. The locomotive had control cabs at both ends of it for ease of driving, so it was impossible to even tell the direction it had come from. The possibility had already occurred to Tom that the fanatics may have actually come from Brighton themselves and that if the clinic was indeed still standing, then the insane fanatics would have surely taken it over and set up camp there. It was a possibility that he felt inappropriate to share with the others, as it would have surely dampened their spirits and made them hesitant and fearful of the journey. It was equally as possible that the cult had begun their sadistic adventure from the north and that they were travelling down the track one station at a time, wiping out any survivors on the way with Brighton being their final destination. The platform that the train was currently stationed at was also the line that led directly into London Victoria in the other direction. From there it would have been possible to obtain another train that led to Birmingham, Manchester, and Liverpool. All were major cities on a much larger scale to Brighton, and all of which had a high population of Jehovah's Witnesses at the time of the incident. The thought also occurred to him that if these fanatics had based themselves in Brighton, then the attack on them would have surely come a lot sooner than this, since these fanatics had been on their bloody rampage for quite a few years now and Brighton was only a mere few stops down the line. It was equally possible that these people didn't even have a main base, that they were scattered all over the country in little groups, making it more efficient to conduct their mission.

Susan gave him a little nudge to break his thoughtful daze, and gestured her head to the far platform with a smile. Tom replied with another nod and then led the group down into the subway. The bright halogen bulbs that had previously lit the passageway to a deceivingly daylight hue had long been smashed and left it in a state of complete darkness that felt eerie, damp, and cold. If the group had found themselves in the same situation back at the turn of the millennium when day to day life was at a state of normality, they would have discarded the thought of even entering the tunnel, for fears of muggers and rapists that lurked within the darkness, ready to pounce on their prey like lions with an exacerbated hunger. The absence of these possibilities should have lifted any fears or concerns regarding the darkness, but still the passageway gave them that uncomfortable feeling of uncertainty. They stepped through it as quickly as they could, until daylight shone down upon them once again and they ascended the metal staircase onto the last platform.

The sight of the train in front of them lifted their spirits once again, like finally reaching the pot of gold at the end of the rainbow.

The train was now close enough to touch and feel and any possibilities that it was merely a mirage were all gone. The illuminated 'open' button on the train's door gained Steven's attention and drew him to press it. The mechanism sprung to life like waking up a sleeping tiger and slid the door open to the right with a metallic clunk. One by one they stepped up onto its carpeted floor and placed down their heavy luggage before pressing another brightly illuminated button to close the door once again. Susan let out a sigh of achievement and reached up to grasp a hold of her facemask. Tom briskly grabbed hold of her wrist tightly and stopped her from going any further. He looked up at the train's on board PGOGM fans that were mounted on the ceiling and gestured for Susan to look up as well. The fans were completely motionless and still and Susan felt herself lucky to have been stopped, as a gasp or two of pure carbon dioxide would have been far from pleasant at this stage. She then remembered how the fanatics had no need for oxygen and understood why they had not bothered to activate them.

"The switch must be in the front cabin, I'll see what I can do." Tom called to her through the facemask and started walking along the carriage.

"I'm coming with you." She insisted and followed behind him, leaving the kids to rest on the cushioned seats.

More illuminated 'open' buttons led them from carriage to carriage through the train until they finally reached the front cabin a while later. The control carriage was missing a similar 'open' button on the door and instead was locked and protected with a sturdy metal keyhole and handle. Tom tried his luck at the handle at first, on the off chance that the fanatics had not bothered with conformity, but was left disappointed by clunky resistance to his efforts.

"Oh shit," He muttered to himself, realizing that the key was probably with the elder member that Jobe had tortured to death previously. If Tom had thought about it before then he could have searched the man or demanded to know its location, giving reason and purpose to the sadistic torture that they had inflicted upon the man. But the thought had never occurred to him that these men would go to such lengths to protect their ride home.

"So what we gonna do now then?" Susan asked him with a frown.

"Dunno Susan, guess I'll have to go back to the house and search the body for the key." He replied with a look of disappointment.

"Can't you just kick it in or something?" Susan asked him. Tom looked back down at the chunky looking lock again and shrugged.

"Alright, step back then Susan." He reluctantly replied with an unconvinced grumble.

She stepped back obediently and watched as Tom attacked the door with all his might. Tom was convinced before he even started that the door was not going to budge an inch, but was equally fond of the idea of not having to go all the way back to the house again. He kicked the door over and over again but couldn't even manage to inflict a dent in its sturdy metal structure. He carried on with all his might until eventually he caught the door awkwardly and twisted round his ankle. The pain was obvious in his face immediately, as he hopped away from the door cradling the afflicted ankle and sat himself down upon a nearby chair.

"Well that wasn't very successful was it?" He said to her, trying to stay light hearted about the situation.

"What you moaning about Tom? I thought you were special!" She replied jokingly.

"Yeah, maybe I can heal a little bit quicker than you, but I can still feel pain thank you very much!" He responded, as his ankle started to swell.

"Wimp! You want to stay here while I go back to the house then, huh?" She asked him.

"Yeah, alright then, and while you're out could you grab me a packet of fags and a paper from the corner shop?" He asked back with a cheeky grin.

"Yeah, only if you let me do the Soduku puzzle." She replied playfully.

Tom pulled himself to his feet and hobbled back with her to the carriage they had first entered and sat down opposite Jacob and Steven. Jacob peered up at him and gave him a confused slant of his eyebrows.

"Don't ask Jacob!" He said to him with a defeatist grin.

"No air then?" Steven pried further, not satisfied with the vague smile.

"Not yet!" Susan replied to him as she pressed her fingers back on the door release button. The door slid open once again and stopped with another metallic clunk. She stepped back down onto the platform and headed back towards the entrance of the dark eerie subway. She braced herself and took a deep breath before descending into darkness once again.

The tunnel now seemed somewhat longer than it had before and the absence of companions made it seem even more daunting and eerie. She gave her lungs another deep gasp of the sweet tasting oxygen and proceeded down the tunnel with caution. A light breeze in the air started to emerge and seemed emphasized down in the tunnel as it whistled past her, bringing a cold chill along with it and sending shivers down her spine. She carried on walking and placed her hands out in front of her slightly when she suddenly stubbed her toes on something hard on the floor and almost lost her balance. Her toenails pushed back into her flesh, sending a sharp pulsating wave of pain through her. She stopped in her tracks and bent down to finger the object with curiosity. Her fingers touched a cold rough surface, like a brick, or lump of cement when her ears then tuned in to a tapping noise from the other end of the tunnel. She looked up startled, but could see nothing there but darkness as the noise become louder and closer. She picked up the object firmly in her grasp and stood with her back against the wall, as the sound got closer and she could finally distinguish that they were footsteps. She could feel her body begin to shake with fear and held out the object ready to attack. The possibility then occurred to her that there were more of these demented fanatics lurking about. After all, it was a long train and could have easily carried at least ten times as many of them than they had encountered so far. The footsteps carried on at a steady pace towards her, and echoed through the tunnel. They got louder and closer with each one, until she could feel the presence of someone right next to her. She swung with the heavy object and felt it connect with a soft thud, and prepared herself for a second swing. There was a crash upon the floor followed by a deep groaning of pain as she suddenly realized the reality of her hasty actions.

"Hey stop!" shouted out a deep voice.

"Jobe? Christ, I'm so sorry!" She replied, dropping her weapon to the floor.

"Yeah it's me, who were you expecting for God's sake?" He replied, pulling himself to his feet.

"I'm really sorry! This tunnel was just freaking me out, did I hurt you?" She asked regretfully.

"Yeah, you did! You almost broke my arm! What was that?" He replied in between painful groans.

"I dunno, a brick or something."

"That fucking hurt! I hope that I never get on your bad side!" He said to her with a slight chuckle, seeing the funny side of it. "Where's everyone else?"

"They're all on the train, but we can't get into the control cab, it's locked." She explained.

"So where were YOU going?" He asked with confusion.

"Back to the house, see if the key was on that body in the living room." She explained.

"Oh right, well I wouldn't worry about that. I'll get the door open." He replied with certainty.

"Well let's get out this bloody tunnel first. It's giving me the creeps!" She insisted and started to walk back towards the light again. She walked back up the stairs again with Jobe closely behind and the change of brightness stung her eyes for the second time. Upon re-opening them she could finally see Jobe clearly and noticed the shotgun in his hand.

"So that's how you're gonna get the door open then!" She said, looking down at the weapon.

"Well, it might help!" He replied with a smile.

They walked along the platform and Susan stepped onto the train through the open doorway. Tom and the kids were still sitting there waiting for her. They were surprised to see her back so quickly. Their attention was then drawn to Jobe as he boarded the train behind her, blood seeping through the sleeve of his shirt.

"Hey, what the hell happened to your arm Jobe?" Tom asked him with concern. Jobe smiled back and looked at Susan.

"I think Susan mistook me for a big hairy monster or something!" He explained light-heartedly.

Susan turned to him and suddenly noticed the blood.

"Christ! Did I do that?" She asked with surprise.

"Yeah! I think you ripped my wound back open again, but don't worry." He replied with a shrug.

"I feel really bad Jobe, I'm so sorry!" Susan pleaded sheepishly.

"I said don't worry about it, girl. I'll live, won't I?" He replied reassuringly.

"You didn't get the key then?" Tom asked the pair with a vague expression.

"Nah, don't need a key when you got one of these!" Jobe responded and held up the shotgun.

"Fair enough Jobe. Try not to blow up the train though please!" Tom asked him and hobbled to his feet.

"I'll try not to. What's wrong with your foot?" Jobe asked back, noticing the hobble.

"It had an argument with the cabin door!" Tom explained with an embarrassed grin. Jobe shook his head in comical disbelief, and gestured down the carriage with the gun. Susan and Tom followed him back down through the carriages while Steven and Jacob sat watching them all leave again, enjoying the humour of the slapstick-like events.

Jobe cracked open the chamber of the shotgun and fed it a shell from his trouser pocket.

"Stand back then," he told them, as he snapped it back into place and fixed his aim on the metal keyhole. The deafening sound of the igniting gunpowder resonated in their eardrums as the door flew open instantaneously and crashed against the inside wall of the cabin.

The opening revealed a large black control panel containing a vast array of buttons and levers, a single chair sat in front of the panel, and on the floor sat a large brown cardboard box labelled with big black letters: 'Explosives.'

"Christ! That was lucky!" Tom exclaimed. "If that shell had hit that box then we'd all be gone!" He stepped into the cabin.

"That was more than luck Tom. That was a bloody miracle!" Susan added as she peered down at the ominous box. Tom let out a sigh of relief and turned his attention to the control panel as the task of getting the train running now seemed even more taxing. He suddenly noticed a small green button on the right of the panel that contained the writing O_2 upon it. He reached over and confidently pressed the button all the way in with a reassuring beep. A gentle grinding noise then commenced from above them followed by a loud clunk and Tom could start to feel a slight breeze of air on the back of his neck.

"I think that's done it bro'," Jobe told him, walking back into the previous carriage and nodding in confirmation.

"Well at least that's something I guess. Just give it a minute to bring the levels up though." Tom advised.

"So what do you think those freaks were planning on blowing up?" Susan asked, bending down to take a closer look at the box.

"I don't know Susan, but I guess we put a halt to their plans." Tom replied vaguely. Susan peeled back the brown masking tape that was keeping the box closed and opened up the flaps.

"Hey! Be careful Susan, we don't know how volatile that stuff is!" Tom snapped at her abruptly. She stopped in her tracks and looked down at the contents of the box. Jobe peered over into the box as well and nodded in agreement.

"Tom's right Susan, I'd be careful if I was you. We used to use a similar stuff in the army for our training simulations and it's fucking powerful stuff!" Jobe added.

"Right, so to need all this, they must have had something big in mind, yeah?" She asked him back.

"Oh yeah! Used properly, that amount could probably bring down a skyscraper!" Jobe informed her.

"So that's plenty to bring down the Tremoline clinic then right?" Tom asked attentively, chewing on his bottom lip in contemplation.

"Yeah, would be more than enough. You reckon that's what they were planning on doing then?" Jobe asked him, thinking of other possibilities.

"I dunno Jobe, but it seems like a logical thing for them to do. I can't think of any other big structures they'd want to demolish." Tom replied with a shrug.

"Well if that WAS the case, then these freaks obviously thought the building was still standing too. And if it was important enough to destroy it, then there must be something there, right?" Susan pointed out and closed the box back up again.

"Yeah maybe, maybe not," Tom replied.

They stood listening to the fans spinning around above them for a moment, while Tom returned his attention to the control panel and tried to scan through all the buttons again. Just below the green oxygen button was a keyhole with three notches for turning. There was a key already placed inside the hole and the position was turned to the first notch. Tom assumed the concept to be similar to that of a car ignition and immediately turned the key to the third notch. He was half expecting to have to hold it there for a few seconds while the engine revved itself up, before remembering that it wasn't actually a car. There was no sound of revving, but instead a mild humming noise started to emanate from the engine of the locomotive.

"You know what you're doing then Tom?" Jobe asked him, leaning over for a closer look.

"Nope, I haven't got a clue Jobe!" He replied with a playful chuckle.

The pressure of the elasticated facemask had only caused mild discomfort to Susan's fragile nose at the start, and she had been able to easily blank it all out with her mind. But as it became increasingly irritable, the pain had slowly increased and turned into a severe pulsating throb. She decided that the oxygen levels must be breathable by now and pulled the mask away with a pleasurable exhale. The others looked around at her with questioning frowns and awaited an approving response.

"The air's fine." She confirmed to them with a nod. Tom and Jobe then proceeded to do the same and dropped their heavy canisters to the floor.

"Why don't you go and check on the kids Susan. I'll see if I can work this out." Tom asked her with a smile. She smiled back, nodded and turned back down the carriages again.

She strolled back down to the first carriage to find Steven in the same position that she had left him in, though his face now showed expressions of agitation and impatience. He peered up at her while tapping his fingers on the arm of the chair. "So? Are we going or what then?" He asked her.

"The guys are just trying to work it out Steven, give them a chance!" She replied, and sat down on the chair next to him. "You can take off that mask now." She then added. Steven immediately pulled it away from his face and propped his feet up on the chair opposite him.

"It can't be that hard surely?" He asked her with a sigh. She replied with a shrug and a half smile and turned her attention to Jacob who was now sitting on the adjacent isle of the carriage, staring aimlessly out the window. He was twiddling his thumbs nervously like an old lady watching a TV game show, with his luggage placed on the seat next to him.

"You alright Jacob?" Susan called over to him inquisitively. Jacob slowly turned his attention around to her and gave her an apathetic nod. Susan was about to think of something reassuring to say to both of them when suddenly they felt an unexpected judder and the carriage started to move.

"Ah you see! Here we go!" Susan perked with enthusiasm. She sprung back up from the chair and landed a kiss on Steven's forehead.

"Get off!" He cried light-heartedly and wiped away the wet patch with his hand. Jacob watched with humour before Susan turned her attention to him and smiled. She planted another wet sloppy kiss on Jacob's head and ruffled up his hair. He cringed at her and leaned away, turning his attention back to the window. He then watched as the station slowly disappearing from view.

"Are you both going to join us at the front then?" She asked chirpily, gesturing a hand out to each of them.

They ventured down the train together hand in hand and sat themselves down in the first class seats at the front carriage. The acceleration then began to increase and the noise of the wheels chugging on the tracks grew louder and louder. With the exception of Jobe, it was the first time that any of them had left Crawley for a very long time now, and they found their attention glued to the passing scenery on either side of them. They looked onward into the distance, hoping to see some signs of life through the grease-stained windows of the carriage. They shot past mountains of rubble and scattered debris on either side, but not a movement in sight.

The small village of Balcombe rushed towards them on the left-hand side, but all that had survived the bombings was the old clock tower and the peak of the church that now protruded out from the surrounding rubble. The train then entered a small tunnel and emerged at the other end into open countryside that had once boasted endless fields of yellow and green like a patchwork quilt that spread out for as far as the eyes could see. There were crops of barley and wheat and wild poppies that grew between, with the sweet smell of pollen in the air and baby rabbits dashing around the fields. All that now remained of this once beautiful land were brown sloppy quagmires of rotting mass and even the mud itself looked diseased and putrid.

In the distance they saw a small grouping of trees to the right of them, and for a second their eyes lit up at the sight, hoping maybe the trees were still alive. The trees had begun their lives in the lush nutritious soil hundreds of years before and stood towering over them forty feet into the air, but as they got closer to them it became obvious that their branches had long since shed their leaves and now stood brittle and rotten, ready to snap and plummet to the ground at the first strong wind that attacked them. Tom's attention was drawn to the trees for a second too, with the same hopeful gaze as the others, but as he returned his eyes back to the train track in front of him he was confronted with the sight of a fallen tree trunk upon the tracks ahead.

"Hold on!" He screamed out in a sudden rush of panic, fearing that the hefty looking trunk would derail the train and send them crashing hopelessly into the mushy swamp of the surrounding quagmires. They all shut their eyes and held on tightly to the rails, as the train burst into the rogue fallen trunk at top speed. There was then a brief juddering of the train which would have probably gone unnoticed had they not been expecting it, before they quickly opened their eyes again, in mild confusion at the non-eventful impact. To their relief, the train had exploded straight through the trunk as if it was just a mirage, causing nothing but a small puff of rotten sawdust to gently disperse into the air and gracefully flutter down on either side of them like a blanket of wooden snow. Tom released a sigh of relief, pleased that none of them had been harmed, but at the same time strangely disheartened by the outcome, having now received complete confirmation that all the trees were indeed dead.

Jacob sat with his forehead and nose pressed up against the glass of the window and could feel every vibration of the carriage echoing through his bones. He watched out into the distance in a sleepy daze as the scenery passed him by. His warm breath hit upon the cold glass panes of the window and turned it frosted and cloudy. He reached up with his hand and with his index finger he drew a smiley face in the condensation. He returned the smile before slipping his thumb back into his mouth and sucking on it nervously.

"Hey Jacob, how you doing?" A sweet tender voice beside him said. He turned to her and presented a twitchy grin. A beautiful young woman with long curly blonde hair and glossy pink lips looked down at him with a loving and reassuring smile, as she reached down for his hand. She grasped it gently and caressed it soothingly with massaging strokes of her thumb.

"No need to be nervous Jacob, everything's going to be fine, OK?" She continued.

"I don't wanna go mummy." Jacob replied in a desperate groan, trying to stop himself from bursting out in tears again.

"Come on boy we've talked about this. It's for your own benefit." A deeper, less comforting voice from above told him. Jacob peered up hesitantly in the direction of the voice and then looked away again sheepishly.

The man stood beside them wearing an expensive business suit with a black tie and gold cufflinks and he looked down at Jacob with a look of annoyance. The man was surrounded by a crowd of busy commuters who were crammed onto the train like sardines, and talking amongst themselves loudly. They all shared a similar pale complexion with sore red eyes and depressed expressions, as the sounds of coughing echoed above all the commotion. The suited man continued his piercing stare at Jacob with stern, unforgiving eyes that demanded his attention.

"Not everyone's as lucky as you Jacob. Most of us will never have this opportunity," he continued.

"But daddy!" Jacob cried.

"No buts Jacob!" The man concluded abruptly and turned his attention to the passing scenery.

"Marcus, maybe we should think about this a bit more." The woman with the curly hair asked him gingerly, and looked in his direction with a tentative frown.

"Look around Sylvia, what do you see?" He replied, gesturing to the people surrounding them in the carriage. Her eyes scanned the carriage discreetly before nodding to him in agreement. "Look how sick everyone is, diseased, weak, dying. I don't want that for my son."

"But I don't want to!" Jacob shouted at him, starting to cry uncontrollably and thrashing his arms about in a childish tantrum. A flying arm then struck Sylvia in the face before she grabbed him firmly and shook him.

"Behave yourself Jacob! Stop making a scene!" She shouted abruptly. Jacob turned his attention away from them again and continued to sob into his hands.

Graffiti-covered brick walls quickly appeared on either side of the train marking the entrance of Brighton. The train soon entered the tall glass structure of the station and slowly grinded to a halt by the side of the platform.

"Jacob? You awake?" Susan called gently, tapping him on the shoulder. "Jacob? We're here kid."

Jacob shook himself from his cloudy daydream and tried to reply. His gums opened slightly and a faint ripping noise was clearly audible. Memories of his life before the operation had faded over the years to the point where he could remember nothing at all, but the train journey had now triggered something in the back of his mind and it had all come flooding back to him.

Reality soon replaced the childhood images as the sharp pain in his gums pulsated through him and the taste of blood drizzled down the back of his throat.

"Jacob, you alright?" Susan asked again, watching Jacob cradling his mouth in pain. Jacob shook it off and peered up at her with a nod.

"You sure?" She asked him, sounding confused and concerned. He nodded back at her again, looking more comfortable as the pain slowly drifted away.

The once amazing glass structure of the station had survived throughout most of history, since before the Nazis had even started to attack from the shores, and even now it had retained most of its glass panels on the roof. It was almost like the hand of God had preserved the great architecture for a reason or a purpose. The small array of shops housed within the structure had all been looted and vandalized as they had come to expect, and the floors were covered in litter and broken glass.

"We all ready then?" Jobe asked as he turned to face the others in the carriage. Susan gave him a nod as she handed Steven his canister and lifted her own on to her back.

Once they were all equipped with their oxygen masks and luggage in their hands they opened up the doors of the train one last time and descended onto the edge of the platform. They clambered over all the obstacles in single file and made for the exit. A ceramic archway led them out to the street where they found themselves at the peak of a hill that descended down into Brighton's main high street, and towards the sea.

It was clear at this point that Brighton had not been targeted in any attacks at all and that the only damage and destruction that could be seen was the result of vandals and looters. It then struck Tom that the chances of finding more survivors here were great and that the destined Tremoline clinic should almost certainly be standing. They stood in silence for a while and looked around, all sharing Tom's unspoken optimism for survivors and hoping to glimpse a sighting of someone peering down at them from the flat windows located above each of the shops.

"Hello? Hello? Is there anyone there?" Tom bellowed out into the silence, hoping to attract someone's attention. But his voice echoed away into the distance and the deserted city became silent once again. Tom stood for a while longer, hoping for some response from his calling and pondering the situation again.

"Maybe everyone's congregated in the clinic or something?" He told the group, trying his best to remain hopeful.

They then began to descend the hill and veered off down one of the lanes, still keeping a tentative eye out for survivors, when Jobe suddenly stopped in his tracks and turned to face an old dusty shop window. He took a few steps back and looked up at the shop sign. It was completely covered in dust and spray paint, but the embossed lettering was still clear: 'Penetrations' read the sign.

"Hey Steven!" Jobe called over to him and gestured at the shop.

"Yeah?" Steven replied and walked over to his side. Jobe then rolled up the sleeve of his shirt above the blood-stained bandage of the butcher's knife wound and up over his shoulder, revealing the bulldog tattoo that Steven had previously looked upon in envy.

"That's where I got it done Steven!" Jobe told him.

"Really? Oh cool!" Steven replied and rushed to the shop window, wiping clear some of the dust with his hand. Through the gap in the dust Steven leaned in for a closer view through the window and scanned the room for anything of interest. Upon the walls he could just make out a selection of pinned up sketches and designs of the various tattoos available, along with photographs of the tattoo artists' latest victims. Bringing his attention back to the front window again he could see a selection of strange and random piercing rings and bars that were on display. The jewellery was labelled 'Nipple,' 'Navel,' 'Eyebrow,' and 'Labia.'

"What the hell's a labia?" Steven asked curiously. Jobe and Tom looked at each other trying to think what to say, but it wasn't long before they both burst out into immature chuckles.

"What's so funny?" He asked them with annoyance.

"Wait a minute Steven." Jobe finally replied, as he returned to the window and started to clear away more of the dust. To the left-hand side of the window he revealed several porcelain models that displayed the various piercings available. There were nipples, a face with rings through the tongue, eyebrow, and nose, a belly button, and at the end were a pair of spread legs showing a woman's private parts.

"Oh right," Steven finally replied, looking sheepish and embarrassed.

"Real mature guys, well done!" Susan announced with a little smirk.

"Come on, let's keep moving," Tom told them, trying to calm down.

"So how's your memory doing Jacob?" Tom asked him, trying to change the subject. Jacob responded with a nod and pointed down the hill.

His memory of Brighton and the clinic were all coming back to him as clear as day, but he couldn't help wishing that some of them would stay forgotten. He had walked down the same road with his parents all those years ago with his Mother holding tightly on to his hand. He had wriggled and tried to escape from her grip the whole way down the road until he finally succeeded when they had stopped at one of the traffic lights. His mother's hands had become sweaty in the heat and Jacob slipped his hand free. He ran for his life through an alleyway and round the meandering paths of the north lanes. The sounds of running footsteps were close behind him and the deep angry voice of his father calling out his name. Jacob had soon become out of breath and slouched to the ground, crying, in front of an old record store where he was finally apprehended once again. His father grabbed his wrist fiercely and wrenched him to his feet again before smacking him around the behind with all his might. His father then aimed some strong words in his direction and waved his finger at him angrily before practically dragging Jacob the rest of the way to the clinic.

The group quickly reached the end of the long road and found themselves leant up against white painted iron railings that looked out into the crashing waves of the sea. The strong smell of seawater penetrated through their plastic oxygen masks and left them feeling nostalgic and reminiscent of happier times. They stared far out into the sea, listening to the tide swishing in and out with almost hypnotic pleasure. They could almost imagine the sounds of laughing children running along the pebbled beach with brightly coloured kites in their hands, and the busy hustle of people walking back and forth along the road, indulging themselves with freshly battered fish and chips from greasy paper.

Tom gazed deep into the sea as well, thinking not about joyous memories of his childhood, but contemplating the meaning of life once again. He remembered one theory that his old biology teacher had told them about the origins of life on earth, and how we had all evolved from the organisms from the sea, back when the earth was nothing more than molten rock and lava. The Earth's atmosphere at the time was made up of mostly water, hydrogen, and carbon dioxide with the odd molecule of nitrogen about, but not a single molecule of oxygen to be found. The first forms of life had started to form in the cracks of the ocean floors, feeding off hydrogen and carbon dioxide created from the volcanic activity. These life forms thrived harmoniously without the need for oxygen and were actually poisoned and killed when the earth first started to cool down and molecules of oxygen started to form.

Tom found it curiously strange how things had gone back to square one in a way and wondered whether these single celled life forms had now started to flourish again at the bottom of the sea, surviving in conditions that would leave everything else dead and rotting. 'Maybe the world is not coming to an end at all. Maybe it's just a new beginning', he pondered curiously.

It was during Tom's pondering that he started to feel the ache of his bladder muscles telling him that he needed to pee. He had been holding back the mild urge since they had first left the house that morning, but now the feeling had become too overwhelming to ignore and he needed to go urgently.

"Just wait here for me a second would ya, I need to pee." He told the group and proceeded to descend the nearby staircase down on to the pebbled beach below. He then dashed behind the staircase out of view, unzipped his fly and released the pressure with a sigh. He was then suddenly struck with the strong, sickly sweet smell of his own urine, piercing through the facemask and into his nose. The smell was vile and putrid and made Tom start to heave until the flow finally stopped again. It was at this point that Tom then realised how dehydrated he felt and how his palms and forehead had become hot and sweaty.

These three symptoms were all too familiar to Tom and their occurrence would have previously only meant one thing to him: that his blood sugar had started to rise again and that his body needed insulin to counteract it.

"No, no that's not possible!" He muttered to himself, desperately trying to think of alternative possibilities that could explain the feeling.

"No, no I'm cured, it's gone. I'm just tired and stressed out. That's all it is, it doesn't mean anything." He tried to assure himself and took in a few deep breaths to calm down.

"Are you alright down there Tom?" Susan called down from the railings, becoming impatient by the wait.

"Yeah, I'm just coming." He quickly replied to her, before taking in a few more deep breaths and wiping away the build up of sweat on his brow.

Tom composed himself and ascended the staircase again to join the group, giving them a friendly smile and gesturing that they should keep moving. They then turned east and carried on walking along the seafront in the direction of the marina. They soon reached the entrance to the Palace Peer on their right and gazed over at the vast array of snack food stalls on either side of the main gate. They stood sturdy and proud in front of them and Steven found himself longing for a fresh hot doughnut covered in sweet tooth-rotting sugar.

They carried on past various nightclubs and casinos that were to the left of them and before long Brighton's marina was clearly in their sights. A tall building peaked above the horizon in the distance and with the glare on the sun reflecting from its glass windows it seemed to twinkle at them like a homing beacon.

"Is that what we're looking for Jacob?" Jobe asked with his eyes glued on the building. Jacob nodded in return, before realising that everyone else was gazing at the building too. He then reached down and began typing into his 'Text Talk' instead.

"That's it." His little machine read out.

Their pace quickly accelerated with childish excitement until they were all practically running towards the glistening building and Jacob struggled to keep up with them.

"I bet I can get there first!" Steven shouted out to Jobe with a bragging grin and an eyebrow gesturing an invitation to race.

"Oh yeah?" Jobe returned with a playfully competitive chuckle.

"GO!" Steven yelled and broke out into full sprinting mode towards the building. Jobe reacted with strange determination and pelted along the pavement next to him, not prepared to let his years of army training be shamed by a cocky teenage boy. Susan laughed out at the sight of them running neck and neck into the distance as she carried on at her steady pace with Tom and Jacob beside her.

The building stood tall and towered above them into the clouds, with the familiar 'Tremoline' logo embossed on the top floor. Jobe and Steven quickly reached the front doors and stood panting for a while, waiting for the others to catch up and arguing about who got there first. The others carried on towards the building at a triumphant marching speed, like medieval knights approaching an enemy castle to save a damsel in distress.

Jacob reached up and pushed a small green button alongside the large glass doors and they slid open to reveal an elevator-sized glass compartment. They stepped inside and triggered a sensor which caused the great glass doors to slide shut again. The noise of a powerful turbine then powered up above their heads as the carbon dioxide was briskly sucked out from the compartment and replaced by sweet tasting oxygen. Tom was impressed by the efficiency of the building, 'like a decompression tank' he thought. Once a few minutes had passed there was a high pitched beep and the glass panels on the opposite side of the door slid open to tempt them inside. Tom decided that it was only right for him to be the guinea pig and he removed the oxygen mask from his face, taking in a deep breath and exhaling with pleasure. The oxygen in the room was even more refreshing than he ever remembered oxygen to be, and far superior to that of the oxygen in his mask. He gave the group a smile and a thumbs-up and ventured further into the building. To the left of him was a large waiting area, furnished with large comfortable sofas and plasma television screens. To the right was a long reception desk with leaflets and stationary on one side and a computer and telephone on the other. Any signs of life that the group had hoped for were completely missing and the eerie silence was only broken by the echoes of their own footsteps down the long corridors in front of them. Tom looked around, confused by the emptiness and approached the reception's counter.

"Jesus Christ!" He suddenly cried out with a look of pure horror on his face. He turned back around, trying to stop himself from heaving.

"What? What is it Tom?" Susan asked, stepping towards the counter.

"Stop there Susan. You don't wanna see this." He quickly replied, holding out his palm forcefully like a policeman diverting traffic. It was at that point that Susan smelt the scent in the air. Jobe could now smell it too, but stepped up to the counter regardless and peered over the top. The seat of the leather chair was drenched in congealed blood and on the floor by its swivelled wheels laid the dismembered body parts of the receptionist. Most of the parts were too small to recognize as anything more than just chunks of bloody meat with ripped apart clothing scattered all around them. The head of the receptionist was the only part that revealed to Jobe that the body was that of a woman. It lay upon the floor a few feet to the right of the mess, torn raggedly from the neck and stuck to the floor like glue amongst its own sticky puddle of blood. Her eyes were wide open with shock and her jaw bone locked in place. Jobe quickly turned away too, reaching his hand up to his mouth and taking a few deep breaths, trying to think of something to replace the ghastly images in his head.

"We're too late guys. They've already been here." Jobe then informed the group with a look of regret.

CHAPTER TEN

HANNAH JENSEN had been a loyal employee of Tremoline since the Brighton Clinic's grand opening. She had attended her interview in a smart business suit and starched white blouse and gave the interviewer all the right answers with a smile. She immediately got the feeling that the job was already hers and walked from the office with a euphoric grin on her face. It was probably the best job she had ever landed in her whole career and she turned up every morning thereafter with energy and enthusiasm. Besides the great salary deal and the holiday perks that the job had to offer, Hannah assumed that her health would be in good hands too, that she and her family would be well taken care of by Tremoline when things started to go bad. The thought had never occurred to her that one day she might end up as a pile of rotting flesh upon the reception floor.

It was Hannah herself who had greeted the Stevensons the day of Jacob's operation. Her warm and inviting smile made them feel relaxed and comfortable as they sat patiently in the comfy chairs, waiting for the doctors. Jacob however, could not relax and sat fidgeting on the chair nervously and chewing his fingernails. He was the only child in the building that day, and sat amongst a room full of big muscled men with shaven heads and battle scars. These were the first batch of soldiers that had volunteered to undergo the ground-breaking surgery. They were the kind of men that sat with emotionless iron faces, showing the absence of fear of anyone or anything even when deep inside they were probably just as nervous as Jacob. Their surgery was to be fully paid for compliments of the British government with an additional financial gesture towards the soldiers' families on completion of the surgery. It would have been a tempting offer for anyone who had been given the opportunity, but the financial aspect of the deal was not the reason these men were convinced. These were the kind of men that would fight the enemy with every last breath in their body, not because of their dedication towards the queen and country but for the strange satisfaction that arose from causing death and destruction to others and the victorious self-satisfaction of knowing they were superior in the art of killing. They were the kind of men that would surely be tried for savage war crimes afterwards (if civilization had lasted long enough to put these proceedings into action) and sent away for a long time to protect the safety of innocent civilians who may fall victims of their addiction. There was a time when Jobe himself was at risk of turning into one of these obsessed killing machines, before his subconscious moral stand point exploded into his conscious thoughts and made him finally realize the reality of war. He knew from that point on that he needed to get out.

The doctors emerged shortly with warm friendly smiles and took them away to a consultation room down the main corridor. They explained all the details of the procedure to Marcus and Sylvia while Jacob sat there confused by almost everything the doctors said. Eventually the doctors turned to Jacob and told him that everything was going to be OK before escorting him off to an adjacent room to change into a hospital gown.

"Right, if you can just jump up onto the bed for me please, Jacob." The doctor asked him, as two nurses and an anaesthetist then appeared by the bedside. Jacob obeyed without question and jumped up onto the bed.

"OK, now lay back and relax." The doctor continued, as Jacob lay back with his head softly cushioned against the pillow. The doctor then stepped aside and walked off into the distance to check some of Jacob's notes and to inform the surgeons that Jacob was being prepped. The anaesthetist then took the doctor's place by the side of the bed and gently reached down for Jacob's arm with a smile.

"Now you're going to feel a short little prick Jacob. But just try to stay calm OK?" He told him, and without hesitation he pierced a needle straight into Jacob's vein. Jacob gritted his teeth in pain, thinking 'that was more than a tiny prick!' He felt the needle rummaging around inside of him.

"Now I want you to count backward from ten please Jacob. Before you reach one, you will be fast asleep." The anaesthetist told him with another friendly smile and gestured for Jacob to begin. Jacob nodded his head in return and then started to count down. As he started he could feel a strange cold fluid flowing down his vein.

"Ten, nine . . . eight . . . seven . . . six . . . five . . ."

Jacob slowly regained consciousness hours later to the sound of beeping machinery all around him. A few seconds later the immense pain in his body first started to kick in. He gently began to try and prise apart his sticky eyelids and then continued to blink away the opaque blurry tint to his vision. He then tried to muster the strength to lean forwards in the bed, but his body was exhausted and weak and he immediately fell back down again with a cushioned thud against the pillow. His entire body seemed to be throbbing away with stabbing pains in places that he had never even felt sensation in before, as he slowly reached his hand up to his chest and began to finger along the bristled stitches down his breast bone. He then cast his eyes down to the wound with curiosity, and could see that it was still fresh and sore, with blood gently oozing out from between each of the stitches. He continued fingering the stitches down to his stomach and then brushed the strange umbilical chord that was now attached to his belly. It felt slimy and unnatural and the touch of it caused a nauseous feeling to churn up in his stomach. At that point he tried to scream out with an uncomfortable yelp, but found that his jaw was firmly locked in place. He started to cry and groan uncontrollably before he could hear the sound of nurses rushing over to help him.

"He's awake guys. Can I have some more morphine over here please?" Was the last thing he remembered hearing before drifting off into unconsciousness again.

There were three intensive care units on the ground floor of the building, along with five operating theatres and four consultation rooms. The first floor of the building consisted of a research lab where they would carry out experiments and conduct research into the effects of the green gas that had caused the whole mess, along with storage facilities for biological and genetic material that was used in the experiments and the surgeries. Various offices for the doctors and staff were housed on the second floor of the building, along with a large a call centre at the end. The call centre was where people could call in for information on Tremoline products and to discuss and arrange the surgery. All three of these floors were now in a similar state to that of the reception area where they had first come in, with blood and body parts scattered all over the floor and up the walls. It was a sickening and ghastly sight even to Tom and Jobe, who had volunteered to inspect the building whilst the others remained safely downstairs in the waiting room.

The blood and horror that now surrounded them in every direction had taken away any hope that they were desperately clinging to. It was discarded to a distant forgotten place in the back of their minds. It was a place in Tom's mind where the dark and sadistic figure from his dreams had been safely locked away behind stern bolted doors. But with the feeling of hope slowly drifting away he had started to feel like those bolts were gradually coming loose again. The deep menacing voice of the figure had now started to echo out to him from the dream world, and release its infectious secretions into his waking consciousness, forcing its influence upon his judgment once again. It was a feeling that he had felt regularly when he was younger: the feeling of being controlled by a bitter and twisted voice inside that fuelled his anger and frustration at the world. It was a voice that told him to do things, very bad things, giving him ideas and thoughts that were not his own, and influencing him to take actions that only now he could fully understand.

Since the cure of his diabetes the voice had slowly faded away to obscurity, leaving behind the fruits of its incarnation. Only occasionally would it make appearances in the darkest of Tom's dreams, but now that the dreams had become a regular occurrence, the voice inside was fighting desperately to escape.

'You're a failure unless you do this Tom, a pathetic excuse for a man who's going straight to hell.' The voice began to echo down at him, over and over again inside his head, pounding violently until he could feel the pressure behind his eyes build up and explode into a purple poker dot migraine of blinding agony.

Jobe could clearly see the agonising pain on Tom's face, as he walked alongside him with the shotgun firmly in his grip, not for fear of being ambushed by these religious fanatics again, but for the comfort of knowing that his last resort was still available to him.

Tom squinted his eyes as hard as he could and forced the voice away again, knowing full well that his attempts would only keep it back for a short while, and that when it returned it would be louder and stronger and would take far more than just willpower to silence. His bladder by this point was also starting to feel full again and had started to ache with muscle strain. His brow and palms had continued to sweat and he was now starting to feel very tired too. The thought that his diabetes was causing all this occurred to him again and again and it now seemed like the only possible explanation for it. The only way he would know for sure, was to try and find a blood tester within the clinic somewhere to test his sugar level and pray for good results. He knew that if the results turned out to prove his suspicions, that he would only have two options available to him, either to pray that somewhere within the clinic there was some insulin that he could inject himself with, or, to hope that his inevitable death was as quick and painless as possible.

With Tom's paranoia temporarily pushed to one side, they continued with their inspection of the building. They strolled through various rooms and laboratories where the scientists had previously done experiments, desperate to find a cure for the green cancer that was killing the world. They saw test tubes and Bunsen burners on the tables with racks upon racks of various different coloured chemicals and solutions that they were testing for any reversible effect.

The bodies of theses poor scientists now lay completely dismembered and drenched in blood, with ghastly segments of limbs and organs scattered randomly around their own equipment. Upon the floor of the lab, the men quickly spotted a few dead fanatics too, and the thought that these scientists had managed to kill at least a few of these bastards was mildly enlightening to them, even though it was obvious that they had not fought a good battle.

Upon the walls of the room, the men then glanced up at a large white board which contained various different equations and formulas scribbled upon it in messy 'doctor-like' handwriting.

"Any idea what any of that crap means then bro'?" Jobe asked him with a curious shrug, finally breaking the silence and tension that had engulfed them for over half an hour now.

"Um, yeah I do understand most of it actually Jobe." Tom responded, looking up at the lettering and pointing to the main equations in the middle of the board;

'$6CO_2 + 6H_2O + \text{Energy} = C_6H_{12}O_6 + 6O_2$'.

"That's the most important equation of them all, that's what all this mess is about." He continued.

"That means nothing to me Tom, explain?" Jobe asked in return.

"Well, carbon dioxide, plus water and energy, equals oxygen and glucose. It's the process of photosynthesis Jobe. It's what plants do to keep the gasses in even balance. It's the fact that none of that is happening anymore that's fucked everything up." Tom explained to him.

"How the hell do you remember all this shit Tom?" Jobe quickly replied, slightly annoyed that Tom's intelligence obviously outweighed that of his own.

"Well I did do biochemistry at Oxford Jobe, but you should have read about photosynthesis at GCSE?"

"Yeah, well I never really paid attention in class Tom. Too busy going off the rails, ya know. So you like all this science stuff don't ya? You said you worked in a lab didn't you?" Jobe continued, enjoying the change of subject for a second.

"Yeah, well science replaces religion for me. Science can explain things and prove things that religion doesn't even touch. It gives facts and doesn't just rely on faith." Tom explained.

"Well science doesn't seem to have done the world much good now. It couldn't save us." Jobe replied with mild defensiveness.

"You say that, but we're both alive because of the PGOGM technology. Without it we would all be gone by now, like the dinosaurs." Tom pointed out.

"And how much longer do you think we're going to last Tom? Huh? At this stage, I'd rather have God behind me than science." Jobe answered with another shrug.

"Well I can't really argue with you on that one." Tom concluded with a vacant smile and a shrug of his own.

As they continued their inspection of the lab they soon came across a large refrigerator with a glass door that was emanating a gentle humming noise and vibrating from side to side. Jobe leaned in for a closer look through the glass but his view was obscured by frosty mist from within, so he reached down for the handle. The gasses quickly escaped out into the room and the view inside then became clear, displaying stacks of cylindrical glass tubes that lay side by side along each of the glass shelves. Jobe reached inside with curiosity and carefully slid out one of the mysterious cylinders. He held it loosely in both hands and peered down at its contents. Inside the tube was a long and slimy organic chord, submerged in clear preservative fluid. Jobe was confused at first and thought the chord looked like a big worm or an eel. He was just about to turn and ask Tom's opinion of it when he suddenly realised what they were: genetically engineered umbilical chords. He felt his stomach start to churn again as he was bombarded with images of his old army friends with the slimy chord attached to their stomachs. He imagined what they must have looked like with their mouths and nasal cavities sown up and being completely reliant on a small device that fed them though a tube. He took a deep breath and blocked out the image, quickly sliding the glass tube back in the refrigerator again and shutting the door firmly.

"You alright Jobe?" Tom asked, noticing the disgusted expression on his face.

"I don't like this place Tom, not one bit." He replied, walking away from the refrigerator shaking his head in disgust.

"Seems like a wasted trip, huh?" Tom announced with a disgruntled frown.

"Yeah, you're telling me Tom. So what's the plan now? Do we even have one?" Jobe snapped back in frustration.

"I don't know Jobe. Guess we can just snoop about and see what we can find. Then if there's nothing I guess we'll just have to go home again." Tom answered him, his eyes fixed glumly on the floor.

"I'm not going back where we started Tom. What kind of life is that? If we find nothing then that's it for me, the end." Jobe told him.

"I'd like to stop you, but you're the one holding the big gun. Just hold out a bit longer though would ya? We might find something here. After all, these guys had some of the best minds in the world. They must have found out something, right?" Tom replied.

"After all the shit and false hope we've had, I'm not holding my breath Tom." Jobe responded with a sigh. "Come on then, let's go and see what's on the next floor." He continued with a disgruntled exhale.

Susan and the kids were still sat in the clinic's waiting area at this time, patiently awaiting the return of Tom and Jobe for reassurance that the building was safe and that the kids would not come across any gruesome surprises. The room was engulfed in complete silence with the only exception being the rhythmic tapping of Susan's fingers on the chair's armrest. It wasn't tapping through impatience as much as it was a distraction from the fact that she was bursting to use the toilet. Occasionally she would move her head around and stare at the bathroom door for a while, wondering to herself whether the place had any toilet paper or not, before discarding the thought and returning back to her tapping once more. She crossed her legs and squirmed even more in the chair and it wasn't long before her needs were obvious to all of them.

"You can go to the toilet if you like Susan. We're not going to run off anywhere you know." Steven tried to assure her with a slightly patronising expression. Susan looked down at him and then again at the toilet door thoughtfully.

"Alright, but don't move from your seat OK?" She told him quite sternly.

"I promise." He replied, starting to sound somewhat offended by her distrusting tone. Susan then looked round at Jacob too before giving them both a nod and dashing off towards the toilet.

Susan just managed to burst into a cubical and pull down her knickers in time before her bladder muscles finally gave up and the pressure was replaced by pleasurable relief.

An uncomfortable tickling sensation in the back of her throat had also been growing stronger over the past few hours and was now about to erupt too. She braced herself as the cough-hybrid-sneeze abruptly escaped into her cupped hands, causing an aching pain to manifest at the bottom of her lungs. She swallowed in discomfort before the sensation quickly returned to her and she released another chesty cough, this time more painful than the last and leaving behind a resonant feeling of croakiness.

The firm cupping around her face had also placed unexpected pressure on her broken nose, causing sharp stabbing pains to shoot through her sinuses, so she quickly released them. She shook off the pain and took a few deep breaths before she started to realise the wet feeling upon her palms. She looked down expecting to see globlets of phlegm or mucus, but was presented with a puddle of crimson red blood instead. She stood up in a panic and pulled up her knickers, before dashing out the cubical to look at herself in the bathroom mirror. She prayed to God that the sneezing had just caused her nose to start bleeding again, and that nothing else was wrong. Her pale drawn reflection stared back at her through the greasy smearings of the mirror, but her broken nose had remained congealed and dry.

She ran the tap and started to wash off the blood from her hands when the feeling returned again without warning this time and she spluttered out blood all over the pale reflection in front of her. She swallowed again and tried desperately to hold back the tears. She knew that her health had remained too good to be true over the past few years and that it was inevitable that the carbon dioxide poisoning would get her sooner or later. But the slow delirious death that had consumed Karen and many others was a thought she had tried to block out.

The blood drops ran gently down the mirror until they reached the basin at the bottom and she could block out the fear of death no longer. Death was now staring her straight in the face and she knew that this would be the beginning of the end and exactly what horrors would be awaiting her. Her tear ducts started to well up with rapid expansion and there was nothing she could do to stop them. They burst open with an eruption of downpour that meandered down her face and dripped down into the sink below. She felt her body start to tremble and grabbed hold of the basin tightly as she took in a few more deep breaths and struggled to regain composure.

'Pull yourself together girl,' she told herself forcefully. The downpour eventually subsided, so she scanned the room for something to sort herself out with. To her left was a white plastic paper towel dispenser affixed securely to the wall and to her pleasant surprise it was fully stocked with white quilted paper towels. It was a luxury that she had gone without for years now and the sight of it brought a slight grin to the corner of her mouth, as she pulled out a crisp new sheet and started to gently mop away her tears.

The waiting room had remained in complete silence during Susan's restroom stop, but Steven had begun to get very restless and agitated with the uneventful wait. He stood up to stretch his legs and started to wander round in circles, kicking his feet along the ground. Eventually he sat back down again with his head in his hands and a look of pure boredom on his face. He started to give serious consideration to reading one of the books he had brought along for the trip and unzipped his bag for a closer inspection of them. He quickly scanned through all the titles on the spines and then zipped the bag back up again with a sigh, having decided that he wasn't quite that bored yet.

It was at that point that Susan eventually returned from the toilet. Steven turned in her direction to give her a smile and it was plainly obvious to him that she had just been crying. Her eyes were red and sore and the smile she offered him in return looked forced and unconvincing. Steven pretended he hadn't noticed and returned his head to his hands again.

During this time Jacob had sat with a similar look of apathy and was also getting frustrated and bored. He started to feel a desperate urge to get up off his behind and do something to occupy his mind, something to stop him from constantly thinking about his past and his last visit to the clinic. He was overwhelmed with images of mean looking soldiers in all directions, queuing up for their mutilation and month-long semi conscious recovery that awaited them. He wanted to get away from the memories of that moment when he first woke up with glued jaws and the inability to scream, and the expressions on his parents faces when they first saw him. These memories were followed by those of the complete humiliation he felt leaving the clinic, looking like a freak and communicating through a cheap tacky box elasticated around his wrist. The waiting room held far too many bad memories for him and the sight of it flooded constant reminders to him. He eventually decided to close his eyes firmly shut so that he could see the room no more, and could pretend that he was still at home, in his bedroom where he felt safe and secure.

The silence that still engulfed the room allowed the noise of a faint beeping to echo its way from down the corridor behind them, followed by a light clunk as the lift doors suddenly slid themselves open. Susan and the kids turned their heads round towards the corridor with eagle-like reflexes and awaited the familiar images of Tom and Jobe to re-appear in front of them. As the sound of footsteps added to the ambiance Susan could wait patiently no more and jumped up from her seat, pacing quickly towards the noise with anticipation.

Tom slowly paced down the corridor towards Susan feeling shy and hesitant on how to greet the awaiting group again. He wished that he and Jobe had returned with better news for them, news that there were surviving scientists upstairs that had found a cure to the whole mess, and that everyone was saved and that life would be good once again. The news would bring a smile to everyone's faces and they would jump up in joy and start celebrating with hugs and kisses, knowing that it had all been worth the effort. But he couldn't even bring himself to greet them with a smile; for fear that the smile would bring them false hope that he had any good news at all. He eventually appeared from round the corner with the disheartened look of despair that had now become the norm throughout all of them. It was a look that answered all their impending questions at once without the need for explanation, and left them all with nothing to say at all. Tom followed the expression with a sorrowful smile and a shrug, before mouthing an apology to Susan and wrapping his arms around her tightly.

He planted a gentle kiss upon her neck and released himself from the embrace, as Jobe then appeared beside him and started to explain their disappointing findings to the group.

Tom's discreet search for a glucose tester had also been unsuccessful and left him with the continuing uncertainty of what exactly was happening to him. He was sure that if he had been searching more intensely for the machine that he would have had success, but he knew that explaining his concerns to Jobe would make him look weak and feeble, an image he detested with a vengeance. His increased perspiration that emanated the sweet smell of pear drops had seemed to have gone undetected for now, so he decided that he would try and keep his cool and continue his search at a later time when the group were all asleep or pre-occupied with something else. That way he would know for sure, and wouldn't be saying something to them prematurely which may or may not be true and cause unnecessary distress and worry.

It was decided shortly after they were reunited that the group would venture up to the second floor of the building where the carnage appeared to be at a minimum. In fact, they had only found one bloodied corpse on the entire floor. It was the body of a doctor who had been hiding away in one of the offices up there, hoping that these menacing fanatics would somehow miss him, but they hadn't. Jobe had concluded that the lack of office workers on the floor must have been due to them fleeing the building prior to the attack, running away like cowards as the dedicated scientists and doctors carried on working, desperate to get results. Or the possibility also occurred to him, that they had all been laid off at some point. Considering that the war and disease had killed most people in the area, the need for these workers may have become obsolete.

The second floor of the building also housed a large staff lounge, furnished with oversized comfy sofas and TVs, and it was here that the group set up camp. The corporate grey toned décor gave the room a dingy depressing feel and the TV screens just played fuzz at them. It wasn't long before they were all slouched around again in silence and Jobe started to stare at the barrel of his gun again.

In the corner of the room was a small kitchen type area with sinks, water dispensers, and two different types of mush machines screwed to the wall. Between boredom and curiosity, Susan stood to give the machines a closer look and was pleasantly surprised with her findings.

"Hey, have you seen these Tom?" She called over to him with an unrepentantly cheerful tone.

"What's that?" He replied to her, barely turning his head in her direction.

"These mush vender things," she continued.

"No why? What's so special about them?" He asked back, finally looking round at her and the machines.

"Well, they seem to have made them into flavours." She told him, continuing the pleasant tone and looking around for an appropriate bowl.

"Flavours? Really?" Tom replied, sounding surprised and intrigued enough to stand up from the sofa. "That's clever."

"I didn't know that was possible." She responded as she began opening up various cupboard doors, still searching for a bowl.

"No, nor did I. They must have started playing around with the equation." Tom told her, trying to sound clever and technical. Susan hesitated for a second before replying, knowing that she would probably sound stupid, but asked anyway.

"What? What you talking about?" She said.

"Photosynthesis and the glucose product created from it." He explained.

"Nope, sorry I'm still lost Tom." She confessed.

"Well, if you arrange the glucose molecules differently, you get a different product. Like, if a banana tree photosynthesises, its by-product is bananas, and an apple tree makes apple, etc . . ." Tom continued.

"Right, but this isn't an apple tree, it's a lump of metal." She returned.

"Yeah I know. That's why I'm impressed." He told her.

Susan finally reached her last cupboard and was greeted by a large stack of white porcelain bowls.

"They had to be in the last damn cupboard didn't they?" She said with a sigh and took them over to the machines. She looked up at the first machine and started to read through the buttons. Tom had now reached her side by this point and eagerly awaited her selection.

-Rainbow

-Strawberry Mousse

-Citrus Slush

"Come on then, choose one." Tom prodded her, trying to hide his mild excitement. She eventually placed the bowl underneath the steel nozzle and pressed her finger on to the green button adjacent to the words: 'Citrus Slush'. A cold orangey liquid then drizzled out through the nozzle, and landed in her bowl with a dense glug. She took a large mouthful of the stuff and swallowed it with a pleasing grin.

"That's actually really nice Tom. Tastes strange, a little bit like a slush puppy maybe." She told him and nodded her head with approval.

Tom took a mouthful of the Citrus Slush too and was equally impressed with the taste, licking his lips afterwards and releasing an agreeable humming noise, momentarily ignorant of the consequences that the sugary slop may have on his diabetes.

He then turned to the adjacent machine which only had the one option, which simply read 'Savoury.' He quickly reached for another bowl from the cupboard and poured himself out a serving of that one too. A white and fluffy looking substance oozed its way out of the nozzle and into Tom's bowl. He cupped a spoonful of the stuff and emptied it out into his mouth, unsure of exactly what to expect. He started to chew it round in his mouth, trying to savour the flavours with a look of intrigued curiosity, before swallowing it and starting to smile again.

"Mashed potatoes!" He abruptly announced with his mouth full of the mushy white cloud, and projected out fluffy clumps of it into Susan's face. He raised his hand up to his mouth shamefully and swallowed the rest in one large gulp. "Sorry!"

An audio amalgamation of chewing and swallowing noises echoed over to Jobe and the kids in stereo sound and perked up their attention. Up to that point, the grotesque and bloody images of Hannah Jenson, laid out in gloopy dismembered heaps, had stolen away any feeling of hunger from them and left behind an uncomfortable churning feeling in their stomachs. But as the agreeable noises continued, the images started to slowly fade and they realised just how hungry they were. Their heads turned in the direction of the machines and they finally gave in to their urges.

Jacob however, had remained in his seat looking glum and deprived. He understood how easy it must have been for the rest of the group to take their basic pleasures for granted, but he expected them to at least notice him sitting there in the corner by himself while they stuffed themselves silly with the mush.

Like anyone presented with a disability in their life, Jacob had adapted over the years to compensate for his lack of smell and taste, and tried to draw pleasure from his remaining three senses. His eyesight and hearing had grown far superior since his operation and he could now see and hear for miles with crystal clear accuracy, but it was nothing in comparison to his memory of what a big juicy burger tasted like. He turned his attention away from the group and found himself staring aimlessly out of the staff room window. The view from there looked straight out into the churning grey sea and the trajectory of his view meant that he could see everything around him, far out into the distant horizon. The waves of the sea continued to crash violently as they had previously, with the rest of the beach and streets remaining completely motionless, with the exception of small pieces of litter that danced about gently in the breeze. He looked down at Brighton's infamously pebbled beach and followed it along until he laid eyes upon the various boats that were docked within the harbour below them. There were boats of all different shapes and sizes, some great, some small, ranging from tatty old fishing boats that were now consumed with rust and falling apart, to great white yachts that continued to retain their glimmering robust images. It was a pleasant sight to him and fed his imagination of long holidays in the sun without a care in the world. The thought even brought a little smile to his face as he imagined what it would feel like to swim around in the sea amongst all the friendly fish and wildlife. After a long dip he would lay down upon a fluffy white towel, while the sun beamed down upon him, turning his skin a gentle shade of golden brown. He would have a strawberry ice-cream in his hand and an icy cold glass of lemonade on the side. His father would stand proudly at the helm of the ship, staring out into the never-ending ocean with the controls in his hand and a contented smile spread from ear to ear. His mother meanwhile would be down below in the galley, filleting up all the fresh fish that they had caught previously and preparing a leafy side salad to go with it.

The noises of pleasurable consumption continued for a while longer, joined with smiles and laughs between gulps. By the time the novelty mush had ceased to captivate their attention, Jacob was long gone, vanished from sight without making the slightest noise or commotion. Tom's smile suddenly slumped into a desperate frown as he realized the boy was gone, and he suddenly felt immense guilt over neglecting him. His eyes dashed about the room in a manic frenzy and his heartbeat accelerated to a violent thudding, as if desperately trying to escape from his chest. A clenched fist and a long deep breath prevented him from bursting out into a panic, so he turned to Susan calmly.

"Don't worry hun, he couldn't have gone far now." He tried to assure her with a smile. She looked back at him and felt the contradictory uncertainties emanating from his eyes.

"JACOB!" She cried out and started to walk away from the group.

"Hey Susan, relax, please. Me and Jobe will go and find him, it's no problem." He assured her, and then turned to Jobe, demanding a nod of agreement from him with a stern look. Jobe looked back with annoyance and a long breathy sigh before delivering the expected nod and reaching out for Susan's arm.

"Hey, look. Everything's going to be fine, hey? You and Steven stay here. We won't be long." He told her and handed over the shotgun.

"Take this just in case. Just pump and shoot, simple. Just don't kill us when we get back. You seem to have it in for me at the moment!" Jobe finished and suddenly started to feel naked without the big strong weapon in his grasp. Susan looked back at him with a ginger smile, still embarrassed about attacking him in the subway.

"Yeah, I know how it works Jobe. Just find him OK? I'm too stressed out to be dealing with this right now."

The men walked away again, out of the staff room and back down the corridors towards the lifts. Tom reached forward and pressed the button on the metal panel and initiated the mechanism which pulled up the lift. The digits on the neon display read 'G, 1, 2' and then opened abruptly in front of them.

"Well at least we know he went down to the ground floor Jobe, narrows the search a little."

"Well maybe it does, maybe it doesn't Tom. What if he left the building? Huh? He don't need oxygen or anything out there, he could have just fucked off out into the middle of Brighton!" Jobe replied, immediately putting a halt to Tom's optimism as they both stepped into the lift.

'*Stupid cunt of a boy doesn't deserve saving anyway*,' a deep mutter resonated from within Tom's head. The voice was loud and took Tom by surprise, but he tried his best to shake it off and told himself that he had heard nothing.

'*Just leave the little prick Tom*'

"Shut up!" Tom grunted aloud.

"Hey! Keep your hat on bro,' I'm just trying to be realistic here." Jobe replied, looking slightly taken back by Tom's sudden outburst.

"What? Oh . . . no, not you, sorry, don't worry." Tom sheepishly apologized, not realising that he had actually spoken out loud.

'*What do you care Tom? Why the act? He'd have only grown to be scum like all the rest, a thug, a vandal, a bully! Just let him die! They should all be dead Tom, EVERY LAST MOTHERFUCKER!*'

Tom's brain felt like it was being thrown against the walls of his skull with the resonance of the voice. Visions materialized of a face screaming down at him with anger and defiance. He felt a pain in his chest and the taste of blood in his throat. Tom shook his head violently about, in an attempt to exorcise the demon from his mind, but the shouting just got louder. He quickly glimpsed the sight of Jobe looking down at him in confusion, saying something to him, but nothing audible could penetrate the demonic violent screams. The screaming quickly grew louder and more intense, now adjoined with high pitched ringing as well. Greasy dribbles of blue and purple oil then started to dribble down through his blurry vision and like paint thinner, they seemed to melt away reality with them, leaving behind a murky black hole of emptiness. The black hole created a vacuum which sucked Tom deep into its suffocating anti-matter as the deep menacing voice returned, screaming, cackling, taunting. Tom's limbs ripped from their sockets. His skin dried and cracked, bones buckled, blood dripped. Before Tom could even realize it, it had already happened and there was nothing left to see. No hands, no feet, no nothing. He was just alone with his consciousness through an endless sea of anti-matter.

'*What is this place?*' He asked.

CHAPTER ELEVEN (A)

SINCE JACOB'S disappearance the sky outside the building had quickly become dark and gloomy, with the clouds turning black in preparation for an inevitable downpour. The men had been gone for what seemed like an eternity now and Susan's mind had begun to drift between various scenarios of where on earth Jacob could have gone, and why he would want to run away like that (having still not realized the offensiveness of her eating habits).

She had paced back and forth across the staff room so many times now that her feet had begun to swell and ache in her shoes, but her nerves and anxiety had still not been subdued. During this time Steven had eventually given in to his increasing boredom and had started to read one of the books that he had brought along for the journey, but after a mere few pages of *Stephen King's Pet Semetery* he had fallen fast asleep on the sofa, leaving Susan all alone with her thoughts.

'Why was it taking so long to find him? Is he dead?' She asked herself, but quickly shook off the morbid thought and tried hard to think about something else. She soon found herself curious about the dead doctor Jobe had found in one of the offices on that floor, and started to wonder which office it was.

'What was he doing in his office anyway? Hardly filling out his tax returns or sending an e-mail to his mistress, huh?' She asked herself, and started to think up different scenarios around that mystery too. She soon decided that with the absence of anything better to do, she may as well seek out the body herself and try and solve the mystery from there. She turned to double check that Steven was still safe asleep on the couch and then grabbed the shotgun from where it had been safely propped up against the wall. She carried it in one hand and ventured out the staffroom, closing the door securely behind her.

'Steven will be perfectly safe in there,' she told herself, 'there's only one entrance to the staffroom, so anyone would have to come past me.'

She followed the corridor down from the staffroom and took a right turn adjacent to the lifts, where she was then presented with a stream of glass-walled offices on either side of her which led down to a wide open space with desks and telephones. The inch thick glass of the office walls contained intricate frosted patterns which intertwined and swirled around like vine leaves upon a trellis and obscured the contents of the offices from view. The doors of each office were reinforced with stainless steal frames and on each of the doors hung shiny silver plaques with the various doctors' names on them. Susan gingerly edged her way down the hallway, pushing open each of the glass doors in turn, anticipating the sight of the body.

Upon peering in through each of the office doors, she could see that they were all furnished immaculately throughout, with modern and stylish décor. They had silver plated mirrors, marbled flooring and solid dark red mahogany desks, each with state of the art computer systems with shiny peripherals she had never even seen before. She passed four or five of these offices when she suddenly saw one up ahead that caught her eye. It was the only one along the row with an open door and on the inside of the opaque glass she could see the distinct remnants of blood splatters which had run down the wall, congealed and dried. She quickened her pace towards the office and read out the name upon the door plaque: Dr. Brown.

She slowly entered the office with her eyes firmly shut and her hand over her mouth in anticipation of what she would find inside the room. She was almost certain that she would find the corpse in the same state that they had found Hannah Jenson down in reception, but as she slowly opened her eyes, she was pleasantly surprised to find the doctor's body completely intact and laying face down upon the marbled flooring. A small crimson puddle of blood had formed from an exit wound on the doctor's left temple and a few inches from his right hand lay the small black pistol that was responsible for it.

She paused for a moment or two and looked down at the body, telepathically asking the doctor for an explanation of what had happened to him until the most plausible scenario became apparent to her. She removed her hand from her mouth and carefully stepped around the body towards the window. She peered out and down and could see the main entrance to the building and the company car park two floors below her. She imagined how the noise of the Jehovah's Enforcers storming towards the building would have probably still been audible from all the way up here. She then looked around to her right to see the left hand drawer of the mahogany desk pulled fully open. She bent down for a closer look and could see an empty gun case and a box of extra ammunition, along with a set of keys to some kind of vehicle, most likely the doctor's expensive car that remained in the car park below her. She imagined the doctor standing there with the pistol in his hand, frightened for his life as he listened to all the scientists and doctors on the lower floors getting slaughtered, knowing that they would soon reach him and that there was no where left for him to run.

On the desktop next to the plasma computer screen was a photograph of the doctor's wedding, taken on the beach in the Caribbean. His beautiful wife stood next to him and smiled euphorically into the camera without a care in the world as the sun shone down and glistened upon her golden skin. She imagined the poor doctor taking one last look at the photograph and shedding a tear, before finally holding the gun to his head and pulling down hard upon the trigger.

She propped the shotgun down against the wall of the office and sat down on the doctor's leather chair. It was at that point that she first noticed the strange looking paperweight that sat next to the photograph. It looked like a snow globe similar to one she used to have as a child. She picked it up and gave it a closer inspection. The paperweight seemed to depict an island encased in a strange looking glass dome. On the island there appeared to be various houses and shops and they were all surrounded by luscious green grass and trees. The model seemed very detailed and the closer she stared into it, the more details she could make out. There seemed to be solar panels and vents on the top of the dome, strange water filters around the edges of the island, and one of the buildings inside had a large plaque above it which read: 'Tremoline Farm.'

Susan liked the thought that maybe Tremoline had built a facility like that, like a modern day Noah's Ark that would save enough of them to eventually repopulate the earth. But she immediately dismissed the possibility that it was a reality. It occurred to her that if the dome was real, then surely she would have heard about it by now. Someone in the world would have surely discovered it and started to spread the word of hope to all of those around. Surely they would have set out to save people by now to take them away to salvation. But they hadn't. She gave the pretty model another smile and placed it back upon the desk where she had found it.

She then turned her attention to the computer and reached over for the shiny optical mouse. She gave it a little tap and the computer immediately sprang back to life again, greeting her with Microsoft's pleasant start-up tone. Displayed on the computer's desktop screen were several yellow folders which sat on a peaceful background photograph of the deep blue sea, with starfish and seahorses surrounded by a shoal of orange and yellow angel fish. The folders on the desktop were named:

'Analysis,' 'COMS,' 'Dome,' 'Misc,' and 'Product list.'

Amongst the yellow folders were the usual expected desktop icons, along with a shortcut to Microsoft Pinball ™. She momentarily contemplated clicking on the familiar icon to kill some time while she waited for the men to return and distract her from the stress and worry that was starting to consume her, but then she looked back at the yellow folders again and began to ponder their contents. She read through the names of the folders once more and it then occurred to her what pivotal information she might find within. The folders could contain research files, test results, and explanations, and who knows what else there could be stored on the doctor's hard drive too. It also occurred to her that she probably wouldn't understand any of the information she did find, but she couldn't take the risk of missing something important.

She immediately moved the cursor back up to the 'Analysis' folder again and opened it up with excitement. Within the folder there were dozens of document files that were all named by date and spanning through several years. She opened up the first file dated 10/09/2013 and read through it carefully, followed by the second one, 23/11/2013.

Analysis report of unknown gaseous substance

Date: 10/09/2013
Completed by: Dr. S. Brown

Aim:
To decipher the molecular structure of the gaseous substance sample taken from a crop field in Sussex, and to determine any detrimental effects of it.

Procedure:
Gaseous substance to be condensed to liquid form and processed through the molecular analysis equipment

Results:
The results of the analysis show that the gaseous substance was a vaporised version of CGM2/E. CGM2/E was a test substance used in the research for a potential cure for cancer in humans. The substance was originally designed to locate cancerous cells within the body and to form a wall around these cells to prevent mutation of further cells and allow healthy cells to regain majority. Tests were quickly halted as it appeared that the substance exacerbated the cancer to a level that it was able to easily break down these walls and continue spreading.

Conclusion:
CGM2/E has no direct detrimental effects on non-cancer sufferers and is merely passed through the system. The purpose of dusting this substance is still unknown and investigation continues.

Report Update of CGM2/E

Date: 23/11/2013
Completed by: Dr. S. Brown

Update:

Further investigation into the effects of CGM2/E show this substance to have severe detrimental effects upon plant cell anatomy. As the substance was originally designed for human medical treatment, effects upon plant life were never officially researched.

After comparison between a healthy plant cell on file, and a sample cell taken from the exposed area, it appears that during the process of photosynthesis the plants cells have absorbed this substance through their membranes. CGM2/E has then attached itself to the cells' chloroplast glands and caused mutation within. The effects of this mutation have been observed as the inability for the cells to perform further photosynthesis, resulting in the death of the cell and the plant.

As a result of this, oxygen levels within the atmosphere are predicted to dramatically fall over time and research has now commenced as to how this can be reversed.

Authorities have been informed of these effects and advised to investigate the original medical team at Cancer Research UK that were responsible for the research of CGM2/E, including ex-students of Oxford University who aided them in the original tests.

Susan paused for a second to ponder, trying to recall where she had read about that substance somewhere before. It was more than just mere deja-vu, she knew.

"C-G-M-Two-Slash-E?" She repeated over and over again in her head, trying to locate its significance somewhere in her memory. It was on the tip of her tongue when suddenly her thoughts were interrupted by an almighty bolt of lightning from outside the office window. She jumped up with fright, as if someone had crept up behind her and plunged a knife deep into her spinal chord. She shuddered and shook off the eerie cold feeling before turning to the window and watching as another shocking bolt shortly followed. The bright lights exploded into the dark night sky and seemed to illuminate the whole of Brighton for a mere few seconds. The lightning was immediately followed by the downpour that she had already predicted and her thoughts turned once again to poor Jacob, praying that he was somewhere safe and that he had found some shelter from the harsh weather outside.

As time passed, the relentless rain only grew stronger pelting down harder and fiercer with every splash until it solidified with the impending cold and grew into golf ball-sized hail stones that seemed to impact the ground with malicious intent. By this time, Susan had finished reading through the first ten 'Analysis' documents and was no further enlightened as to the cause of it, or any potential reversal to the effects. She closed down the folder with a lethargic sigh and began to read through the 'COMS' files instead. After numerous meaningless e-mails to and from Dr. Brown's boss and staff, she finally came across a fax from the metropolitan police sent to Dr. Brown back in March 2014.

Facsimile

Date received: 30/03/2014
Sent from: 01293884628
Subject: CGM2/E

Dr. Brown
Firstly, we would like to offer our gratitude to you and your team for your continued help and advice in this investigation.

FOR YOUR INFORMATION ONLY
We have concluded our investigation of the employees of Cancer Research UK who were involved with the CGM project. Investigators and forensic teams have found no evidence that any of these employees have come into contact with this substance since the original tests. Investigations into the ex-students of Oxford University have also returned a similar conclusion, although two of the students that were registered on that course could still not be accounted for. They are

Miss Abrianna Lutish

Mr. Thomas Harvey

These are now our prime suspects in the investigation and any information you may have about these two suspects would be pivotal to us. Upon background checking, it was found that Abrianna Lutish is the daughter of Pong-Ju Lutish, who is believed to be part of the North Korean military and a close aid to Kim Jong-Il himself. The prime minister has been advised to place the nation on red alert, while U.S. military stationed in South Korea have been deployed to infiltrate into the north and find the suspects.

Your facilities have now been ordered to focus all efforts in reversing the effects of this substance, and all other projects must halt until this is resolved.

We thank you once again for your co-operation and await further updates from you in the near future.

Yours gratefully,

Chief Constable Hadland

Susan reached up to cover her gasping mouth before scanning through the fax document again to ensure that she wasn't jumping to any rash conclusions, and she wasn't.

"Tom? No way!" She blurted out in baffled confusion. "He can't have been involved surely?" She continued, but after a few moments of denial and an uncomfortable lump in her throat, it all started to make perfect sense to her. It was like a thousand pieces of a jigsaw puzzle coming together with crystal-like clarity and once again turning the image of her faithful companion into that of a soulless monster. It was at that point that she suddenly recalled where she had read about the CGM2/E substance before. It had appeared on the pages of Tom's mysterious black book, along with that weird diagram of the substance attacking a living cell.

The more in-depth she contemplated her suspicions the more it became apparent that there were clues she should have noticed before, like Tom's bio-chemistry degree from Oxford University and how he had always avoided questions about his time working in the lab. She then remembered what the friendly anchorman had once told them about the Korean planes that were spotted on the day of the green gas, and how she had read about Tom moving to Korea with his wife.

It was then clear to her why Tom needed to kill Abrianna. With the Unites Sates military searching for him in Korea he had to make a quick get away and cover his tracks. He knew that her father would take the information to his death, but Abrianna was a loose cannon. She would have caved in. She would have talked.

"But then how did he manage to get back into the United

Kingdom undetected?" She asked herself, and contemplated the possibilities. It was possible that he could have used his connections within the Korean military to get flown in by private jet or helicopter maybe, but even then, with the police and army and everyone else desperately searching for him, how did he hide? Surely his parent's house of all places would have been the most obvious place for them all to look? They would have searched there straight away, interrogated his parents, and demanded answers. His parents would have known from the start what Tom had done. So then why would they take him back in and hide him? Was the love for an only son that strong that they would forgive him for bringing the whole world to the brink of Armageddon?

It then occurred to her that maybe they hadn't even agreed to take him back at all. Maybe he just assumed that they would forgive, but when he arrived it was a different story. Maybe he killed them off like he had his wife. The scenario now seemed much more likely to her than the chance that they were killed in a bombing attack when Tom just happened to be out of the house.

Thoughts and questions flooded her mind with confusion and anger. Just as many things became crystal clear to her, others just began to make less and less sense.

"Why would he even want the end of the world? Was his life that bad? Was he that evil? Or was he just completely insane?" She contemplated further. "Or was it just his own intelligence and knowledge that drove him power hungry and spiteful? Why on earth would he do this?" She continued to think.

Her own thoughts started to make her feel dirty and betrayed like a battered rape victim slowly regaining consciousness in hospital, only to recall the memories of her ordeal. The thought of him touching and kissing her repulsed her deeply, so much so that she felt herself starting to heave and had to concentrate hard to stop herself regurgitating the flavoured mush from her stomach.

Another crack of thunder then struck outside the window, sending vivid flashback images into her head of that infamous day back in 2019 when she lost her family. She tried to block them out, but they were too strong. The images of her beloved sisters and parents blown to shreds in the blasts, their flesh and blood raining down on her like a blood-drenched thunderstorm from hell. Tears began to stream down her tired face and as another bolt of lightning shortly followed, her sadness turned to anger and she no longer cared for an explanation. She stood and peered out the window just in time to catch sight of Tom and Jobe casually strolling back into the building through the main doors and she immediately reached down for the beckoning shotgun. She cracked it open to make sure that it was loaded and sure enough there were two shotgun shells ready and waiting for her. She cracked it shut again and cocked it loaded. She would take revenge for the sake of her mother, sisters, and everyone else that she once held dear to her heart; every life that this demented bastard had taken away. She would make him pay for what he'd done.

CHAPTER ELEVEN (B)

OXFORD UNIVERSITY had many inspirational talkers and lecturers visit them during the time that Tom studied there. The first was a group of research chemists from Cancer Research UK. They came to the university in Tom's first year in the halls and asked for volunteers to help them test a new batch of chemicals upon cancerous human cells, to analyse and study any signs of the cancer receding.

The university allowed the research group to use one of their spare labs and all the students studying medicine or chemistry were urged to take part for extra credit recognition. With evil thoughts still swimming around at the back of Tom's mind and the absence of any new friends at the university, Tom decided that taking part might help him subdue his psychosis. He enrolled in the testing immediately. It was during the first session of this testing that Tom noticed Abrianna a few rows in front of him and immediately recognised her from his Bio-Chemistry lectures. She looked around at him and smiled, having recognised him too, and they soon paired up to do the testing together.

The head scientist from Cancer Research UK was a friendly looking woman in her early forties. She stood at the front of the class and explained to the group of eager freshman that they had recently discovered a new chemical called 'CGM.' She was not specific as to where the chemical had come from or how it had been discovered, but said that initial testing upon it had shown evidence that it could affect the spread of cancerous cells. She then proceeded to hand out different strains of the chemical around the class and it was at this point that Tom and Abrianna were first introduced to CGM2/E.

The testing was due to last two to three weeks and required the students to attend for an hour each day, testing the chemical on human cells in progressively deteriorating stages of cancer. They would vary the concentration and temperature of the chemical and keep meticulous notes of their findings and observations under the microscope.

As the days went by, Tom and Abrianna began to enjoy each other's company even more. They began to share stories with each other of their past experiences and feelings. Tom told Abrianna all about his diabetes and what had happened with Victoria and Jason at the college and how the evil voice inside his head kept telling him to do bad things. But instead of scaring Abrianna away (as Tom expected his unsettling revelation to), his openness and honesty about his unstable mind actually drew Abrianna to him. It also tempted her to reveal her own dark secret, when she finally let slip what her father did for a living. She told Tom all about her father's relationship with Kim Jong-IL within the Korean military and explained how he ran a chemical and biological warfare research lab. She continued to explain how she was forced to leave Korea for her own safety and that her father Pong-Ju had sworn her to secrecy over it. Tom was equally as passive to this news as Abrianna had been to his own and they enjoyed the closeness that arose from these intimate revelations.

The same day that Abrianna revealed her secret to Tom was also the day that the CGM2/E chemical revealed a secret of its own. Tom had accidentally spilt some of the chemical into the soil of a nearby potted plant a few days prior and had curiously watched the plant slowly die during the days that followed. It was at this point that Tom finally stripped one of the dying leaves from the plant and took a closer look at it under the microscope. He immediately noticed the presence of the chemical inside the plant cells and could see exactly what it was doing to them. He then grabbed his little black book and sketched down the diagram that Susan had already discovered. The evil voice in Tom's head then demanded that he take the chemical, knowing exactly what Pong-Ju could do with it and knowing that his own desire for bitter revenge could finally become a reality. The evil voice inside him was far too fierce and demanding for Tom to ignore so he quickly slipped a bung into the end of the test tube and inconspicuously slid it into the draw-string Nike bag where he kept his insulin needles.

The CGM testing ended a few days later and it was concluded that the chemical was unsuitable for cancer treatment. The friendly woman from Cancer Research UK then thanked all the students for their time and hard work and left the university completely unaware of the stolen test tube.

It was almost two years after these events that the university was visited by Dr. Richards and his team of stem cell researchers, who took Tom in and successfully cured his diabetes. The evil voice from inside Tom's head seemed to vanish at this point too, leading Tom to believe that his psychosis must have been the result of a physical brain defect, a defect which the flowing swarm of mutated stem cells had also now repaired.

He immediately started to feel refreshed and clear headed again for the first time in ages, but his miracle cure and change of mindset had come far too late to stop the upcoming green cancer infection.

Tom had already made initial contact with Pong-Ju shortly after the end of the CGM testing, and had sent him samples of the CGM2/E chemical. They then heard nothing more from Pong-Ju for a long time, but when the friendly news anchorman reported that North Korea were detonating nuclear devices in the ocean, it was obvious to Tom what they were really doing: infecting the sea algae with their new biological weapon.

It wasn't until the end of their degrees that Tom and Abrianna next heard from Pong-Ju, when Abrianna received a package from her father in the mail. The package contained a lengthy letter from Pong-Ju, mostly congratulating Abrianna on her degree, along with two plane tickets to Shenyang Airport, China. Abrianna had now been apart from her family for almost five years and she was overjoyed to find the invitation to go home. Tom was nervous over Pong-Ju's intensions with him, as Abrianna had already explained his intense hatred of all westerners, but was equally intrigued by what he might find there and decided to take the risk.

They took the lengthy flight to Shenyang Airport where they were met by one of Pong-Ju's associates in the military. They then travelled southwards through China towards the border and crossed over the Yalu river into North Korea via the world famous Dandong 'Friendship' Bridge. It was here that Abrianna was finally reunited with her loving family who greeted them both with open arms and smiles.

It was shortly after this that Pong-Ju offered them both a big house and a car if they were to stay in North Korea, along with a job for Tom in the lab, helping to make up more of the CGM2/E chemical that they were now replicating by the tanker-load. Although appearing like a kind gesture, Tom knew this was Pong-Ju's way of keeping a closer eye on him, ensuring that the secret they both shared remained a secret. Tom toyed with the idea for a while and came to the conclusion that if he declined Pong-Ju's kind offer then he would most likely find himself silenced in a much less pleasant way. Tom also knew that working closely with Pong-Ju would give him the opportunity to learn the scale of their intensions with the green cancer, so he accepted the offer with a smile.

Tom soon learnt the full intensity of Pong-Ju's hatred towards America and the western world, but it wasn't for another year that he started to pay attention to his conscience, as it screamed down at him with anger at his shameful actions. The guilt of abandoning his own loving family back in the United Kingdom and the knowledge of what was about to happen to them all became too overwhelming for him not to take action. Tom quickly arranged a meeting with Pong-Ju and pleaded with him to exclude the United Kingdom from their evil plans, but this just enraged Pong-Ju and he screamed at Tom with outrage.

"All westerners will suffer at our hands Tom! No-one will be spared!" He screamed over and over again in Korean.

It was the day after this that Tom made his secret arrangements to flee back to the United Kingdom again, to spend Earth's remaining period of humanity with his loving parents. Before departing, Tom made one last stop at his Korean home again, to execute his beautiful wife. It now seemed as if nothing he could do would stop Pong-Ju's evil plan, but what he could do was make sure that his beloved Abrianna never suffered a minute of it. He stood over the body of his dead wife with the smoking pistol in his grip, and wondered whether her life actually did flash before her eyes in the split second before the speeding bullet reached her brain. Tears then began to flood down Tom's face at the sight of her cold dead body in front of him, and he knew from that moment on that he was damned to hell.

CHAPTER TWELVE (A)

"DON'T WORRY about Jacob, Tom. He's a smart kid. He would have found himself somewhere to shelter." Jobe tried to assure him as they strolled back through the reception area, their oxygen masks hanging loosely around their necks and the heavy canisters still upon their backs.

"He is indeed Jobe, and I'm sure you're right," Tom replied in an effortless monotone slur, his eyes not once shifting from their forward emotionless stare.

"You alright, Tom? You been acting a bit weird, like there's something on your mind, something other than the obvious I mean."

"No Jobe, now what would make you think that? Huh?" Tom asked with a hint of sarcasm, finally turning to face Jobe and aiming a cold judgmental stare in his direction.

"Well, you had some weird psychotic blackout thing in the lift, and then, when I finally wake you and we go out to look for Jacob, you act like you begrudge the effort, as if you couldn't really care less about him anymore. It's just not like you. That's all."

"Yeah well, why should I give a fuck about him, Jobe? He ain't my kid is he? If he wants to run off like a stupid little prick then fuck him, let the cunt die!"

"Well he ain't mine either, Tom! But who else have we got left? What the fuck's the matter with you all of a sudden?" Jobe demanded sternly and grabbed a hold of Tom's arm to halt him from strolling away.

"Get your damn hands off me, Jobe!" Tom growled back at him in a deep gravely tone, a husky menacing tone that resonated through the ground and vibrated back up through Jobe's bones, sending a cold shiver down his spine. He then rested his icy cold gaze right through Jobe, as if looking directly into his soul as he aggressively shook the rogue hand from his arm.

"What the fuck's ya problem bro'!" Jobe screamed down at him, projecting his stale breath into Tom's face.

"Ain't nothing wrong with me you stinkin' nigger! I feel better than ever."

"What the hell did you just call me?"

"I called you a stinkin' fucking nigger! You got a problem with that?"

"Yeah I got a fucking problem with it." Jobe replied with shock at Tom's obscenities, before reaching up and firmly grabbing the scruff of Tom's coat. "You'd better watch your fucking lip Tom before I smack the shit out of you!" Jobe continued.

"Yeah? Well be my guest, Jobe. I ain't scared of you . . . nigger." Tom answered back with a calm smile, sticking out his chin for the threatened blow. Jobe exploded with rage at this point and without hesitation his adrenalin took over and he plunged his clenched fist into Tom's face with all of his might. The fist impacted like a solid brick on Tom's mouth and nose with a brittle crunching noise and projected him momentarily into the air. He tumbled backwards and landed with an almighty crack, striking the ground and his spine curled around the bulky metal canister behind him.

"Now, you gonna pull yourself together or what?" Jobe roared down at him, hoping the blow had shaken some sense back into him. Tom gritted his teeth firmly to hide the pain and rolled over onto his side, releasing the canister from where it had imbedded into his tender back.

"Why don't you just go and fuck your dead girlfriend you sonofabitch!" Tom growled back at him in a panting breath, as he reached into the breast pocket of his jacket and unclipped his black pen from the cover of his diary.

"Oh, fuck you!" Jobe cried in outrage and plunged his foot hard into Tom's stomach. The foot struck just below Tom's rib cage and momentarily winded him, but not enough to prevent Tom from grasping hold of Jobe's leg, removing the pen from his pocket, and stabbing it fiercely into Jobe's groin, penetrating cleanly through his trousers and skin and burying itself directly into a main artery with a faint popping sound. Jobe's face lit up like a firework and his jaw locked open as if to scream, but the agony of the infliction took away too much breath to allow any noise to come out. Pins and needles started shooting through his body in cold flooding waves as he desperately tried to wrench the leg free from Tom's grip, but Tom clung on to it tightly and firmly as if it were a buoyant life preserver saving him from drowning. The pen slowly started to buckle and crack as Tom continued to exert force on the pen. He pushed it further and further into the gaping wound, twisting it round psychotically with a menacingly orgasmic smile from ear to ear until he finally caught the beautiful sight of blood gushing out from of the end of Jobe's trouser leg.

One final wrench and Jobe finally pulled his leg free of Tom's grip and fell backwards onto the floor. The pen remained stiffly in Tom's hand for a second, drenched in blood which dripped gently down his hand and arm. He watched it run down his arm intensely before letting out a relaxing exhale and sucking off the remaining drops of blood from the pen. He then lay down on the floor gently, breathing in and out deeply and peacefully, as he listened to Jobe's panic stricken groans with a contented evil smile.

Tom continued to enjoy the groans for a few seconds longer until the point arrived when they seemed to beckon his attention like a stray duckling calling out for his mummy. Tom couldn't ignore it any longer. He couldn't just lay there while the poor duckling got itself more and more distressed, and so he finally pulled himself to his feet to save the duckling from its misery. He looked down at Jobe rolling around below him, as the pool of blood grew bigger by the passing of each second.

"You rot in hell, Tom!" Jobe panted out between the thrashing and squeals.

"I'm sure I will." Tom gently whispered back to him, and slipped the oxygen canister off of his shoulder. He spun it round by the strap and held it firmly with both hands before giving Jobe one final smile and hammering down the heavy canister on top of Jobe's head. The full force impacted Jobe's lower jaw bone and completely shattered it, tearing it away from the top. Jobe spluttered and convulsed, coughing out blood and pieces of broken teeth as his jaw bone flapped around independently. Tom expelled a childish giggle as he stared down at the gruesome sight and lifted the canister back up again. The second blow of the canister crashed edge first in between Jobe's cheek bone and nose and caved his face in like a ripe watermelon, splattering blood and flesh tissue all over the ground like a squashed fly. Tom raised the canister into the air once more and strained to bring it down as hard as his pulsating arms would allow and cracked it right into Jobe's skull, sending a stream of brain tissue and blood-stained skull fragments swishing down the corridor like a burst dam.

Tom finally dropped the canister after the third and final blow and stood appreciating the glorious blood bath below him. He rubbed his blood stained hands on his face, smearing the blood all over him like a sadistic victory ritual and sucked off the last of the crimson red candy from his fingertips.

The mental exhaustion of the brutal attack caused Tom's fragile mind to slowly flutter in and out of sanity again, recalling his banished soul from its purgatory abyss to struggle in torment with his unholy possession. His multiple incarnations violently battled for supremacy and dominance of the mind until the ambivalence finally toppled the equilibrium and his mental intruder finally retreated to its home at the back of Tom's head. Reality soon merged into full focus again, allowing Tom a few brief moments of clarity. The evil voice in his head cackled down at him hysterically as the shocking images of Jobe's ghastly mutilation smacked him in the face like sulphuric acid, burning away at the back of his eye sockets. Breathless and repulsed, Tom began to taste the blood in the back of his throat and immediately knew it was not his own. He felt the wet blood covering his face and dripping from his hands and was completely paralyzed with the realization of what he had just done. His jaw froze apart and his lips began to quiver, as his head pounded with the resonating cackles from within.

"My God, what have I done?"

"God? What the fuck's God got to do with anything? Huh? Where the fuck is your almighty lord now?"

"No! What have I done?"

"You? What have I done you mean! It's always me that has to step up to the mark when you can't stomach it!"

"NO! GET OUT MY HEAD YOU SONOFABITCH!"

"You make me laugh Tom. You'd be nothing without me, NOTHING! JUST ANOTHER PATHETIC LITTLE CUNT!"

"Jobe!"

"Ha! Nice work hey, even if I do say so myself. Can you taste his blood Tom? How fucking nice does it taste?"

"I'm sorry, Jobe."

"Sorry? Why the fuck are you sorry Tom? Six billion people have died slow and painful deaths because of us. Are you sorry for all of them too?"

"That was you, not me you bastard!"

"And where the hell do you think I came from Tom? Huh? All those years of pent up anger and hatred has to manifest itself somewhere. You made me everything that I am, just so that you could distance yourself from your own human emotions and live a pathetic depressing existence, exempt from these bad thoughts. Well, it didn't really turn out the way you planned it, Tom!"

"SHUT UP! SHUT UP!"

"Getting angry now? That's what I like to see, Tom. You just wait and see what I do with the rest of these inferior pricks! I'm gonna make them suffer! Starting with that pathetic little bitch up there!"

"YOU LEAVE HER ALONE!"

"Ha! I don't think so Tom. I'm gonna rip her apart, real slowly, before I arse-rape her cold dead body and guess what Tom, you get to watch every last second of it!"

"I'll kill myself!"

"Oh you're gonna die soon enough Tom. There's a whole heap of fun waiting for you in hell, but not before we finish what we started!"

"I won't let you."

"You don't have a choice!"

Tom's head began to swell up like a pain-filled balloon of incoherence as his vision blurred and his ears began to ring again. The voice drew its evil strength back from Tom's increasing anger and once again invaded his body, taking full control and banishing Tom to a powerless point of spectating paralysis.

He flexed his back muscles and rotated his shoulder blades around as if warming up for a vigorous workout in the gym or doing that morning stretch that everyone does before they make the coffee. He then turned to the lift and pressed down on the button when he suddenly heard a crash from behind, and turned back to see little Jacob on the floor in front of him. He smiled down at Jacob sadistically and began to step towards him slowly.

"What's this I see? Another poor duckling that needs my help?"

CHAPTER TWELVE (B)

JACOB'S INCREASED sense of hearing had amplified the constant chewing and slurping noises which bounced around inside his head with exacerbated annoyance, like obnoxious bagpipes would do on a peaceful Sunday morning. He turned his attention from the group and found himself staring aimlessly out of the staff room window, desperately searching for some means of distraction.

The trajectory of Jacob's view enabled him to see pretty much everything around him, far out into the distant horizon. He watched the waves of the sea continue to crash about violently as they had been for a while now, and then looked down at Brighton's infamously pebbled beach. He followed the pebbles along the meandering coastline until his eyes stopped on the various different boats that were docked within the harbour below them. He closed his eyes and imagined himself far out to sea with his family, laughing and having fun. But the obnoxious sounds of gulps and slurps from behind him pierced through the dreamy images like a warm knife through butter.

More than anything else, Jacob wished that he could be normal once again, not just a freak, a mutant, an outcast. He wished he could taste that mush so badly he would have gladly sacrificed his superior ears and eyes for the chance. Even the smell of the euphoric sugary slush would have been mildly satisfying to him at this point, at least then he would have known what the others were making such a fuss about. He opened his eyes as a build up of tears forced their way out between his eyelids and streamed their way down his twitchy emotional face.

'How could they do this to me?' He thought to himself. 'Surely they would realise my frustration? Were they really THAT ignorant and self obsessed?'

He raised his hand to wipe away the tears from his face and continued to stare longingly out into the harbour.

There was one boat in particular that suddenly stuck out to him as an oddity from all the rest. It was a large white yacht with the infamous Tremoline logo on the back in large black print. It was moored separately from all the other boats on the far right hand side of the dock and glimmered out to him with its crisp pristine condition.

'Why would Tremoline have a boat?' He then asked himself and stared at it for a while longer. It suddenly occurred to him that maybe there was more to Tremoline then what he had initially realised. That maybe the company was concerned with more than just butchering up innocent people. It then occurred to Jacob that the large empty docking spaces on either side of the great white yacht had probably moored many more of these yachts at some point, and he started to wonder where they had all gone.

He quickly turned to face the others and began typing into his little machine, when he suddenly stopped in his tracks, having second thoughts. He looked up at the group with a begrudging scowl, as they stood with their backs to him, stuffing their faces like ravenous obese gluttons. He then shook his head in disapproval and quickly erased all the text from the machine's display. 'Why should I even tell them, huh?' He thought to himself. 'They don't even know I exist. They don't give a damn!' He continued to think, as the obnoxious slurping and gulping almost drowned out his own thoughts. He finally stood from the chair in defiance and walked straight through the staffroom's double doors completely unnoticed. He strolled up to the lifts and pressed down on the button, shaking his head again in disbelief of their insensitivity. The lift doors quickly sprung open in front of him and he immediately stepped inside.

"JACOB!" He finally heard Susan calling out hysterically as the lift doors began to slide shut, but it was far too late for their redemption. The pain had been caused and he no longer felt the urge to please them.

He travelled the lift back down to the ground floor again and made his way out into the open air. The sea breeze felt nice upon his face. It was cold and harsh but at least it made him feel somewhat human again. He quickened his pace away from the building and headed off towards the harbour in the distance, not once stopping to look behind him or to reconsider his rebellious actions.

Jacob seemed to reach the harbour in almost no time at all and jumped over the surrounding railings in search of the enigmatic vessel that he had spotted. He strolled past all the old rusted fishing boats and made his way to the far right hand side of the harbour where he finally caught the glimmering white yacht in his sights again. He quickened his pace towards it even more before leaping over onto its varnished wooden deck, causing the boat to gently rock from side to side. He smiled at his achievement and sat himself down with his legs crossed and looked attentively ahead towards the sea, like he was sitting down for a school assembly in front of a stern headmaster who was about to lecture them all about their poor performance in class.

He continued to stare out at the open water for a while longer and then started to imagine the blissful cruise with his family again. The chopping water began to crash harder and louder around him and it wasn't long before the sky turned gloomy and overcast with the clouds growing darker by the second. At first the increasingly cold winds couldn't deter Jacob from his hypnotic stare into the sea. Even when goose bumps began to cover his pale skin he merely lay down on the wooden deck and gazed dreamily up at the sky.

He closed his eyes peacefully and was beginning to drift off to sleep when the first crackle of thunder startled him from his peaceful rest and he suddenly realised just how cold he really was. He quickly stood up and rubbed off the shivers from his arms and turned to approach the cabin door behind him. He reached down for the handle hoping he would find it unlocked, but he was not so lucky. 'Damn,' he thought to himself, and quickly walked around to check the other side, to find that door locked as well.

He then thought for a while before realising that his only option was to break into the ship somehow. After thinking about it, it was actually quite logical that Tremoline would keep all the doors and portholes to their boat firmly secured and couldn't quite understand why he was immediately so surprised by it. He began his break-in attempt by trying to ram in the door with his shoulder blade, but after several failed attempts he realised he was getting nowhere fast and his shoulder was starting to pulsate and throb with agony. He then came to the conclusion that he would have to smash one of the windows instead, and open the door from the inside.

Jacob had never been much of a vandal in his lifetime and the idea of smashing anything was new to him and slightly exciting too. He climbed back on to the shore and made his way down to the pebbled beach to find the biggest, most destructive looking rock he could find. He sifted through the endless heaps of tiny fish-tank sized pebbles for ages until he came across something vaguely suitable for the job at hand: a tennis ball-sized brown stone. The tide had been rounding off the sharp edges of the rock for centuries now and it felt smooth as silk in his grip. He strode back to the boat quickly and as soon as he was close enough he launched the rock into the air with all of his might. The throw felt very satisfying to him, and even more so as he watched it smash right through the glass pane at the top of the side door with a shattering explosion of glass.

Jacob momentarily forgot all of his worries again at that point, and started to feel young and free with the exhilaration of adrenaline charging through his veins. He felt like a normal kid again for the first time in a long while, acting rebellious and care-free, and as he got caught up in the moment he tried to scream out "Woo Hoo" with immature joy. He immediately felt the pain in his jaw and lips and realised his hasty mistake, but managed to block out the pain and resorted to a strange contented smile instead.

He skipped back to the boat and approached the shattered pane, reaching inside and unlocking the door from the inside. He stepped inside the cabin door and stood in amazement at all the controls and buttons that were displayed before him, and ran his fingers along them all gently in awe of such beauty.

He sat himself down at the captain's chair and it was at this point that he first noticed the thin white booklet which lay on the dash of the yacht's controls. He reached over and grabbed it, suddenly remembering the question that had drawn him to the ship in the first place: why did Tremoline need such a boat moored in the dock? He started to flick through the fifteen page booklet and it all started to become crystal clear to him. The strange contented smile then returned to his face once more and his eyes lit up wide, as if he'd just unwrapped a Christmas present that he had pleaded for his entire life. Finally the group would have a goal and a course of action, finally they would have a reason to strive on, and finally there was a plausible reason to have hope.

[Excerpts from the booklet]

TREMOLINE

BIO-DOME PROJECT

LOCATIONS AND STATS FOR BIO-DOMES

Dome 1
Location : Atlantic Ocean, 500 miles east of Florida coast, USA
Capacity : 1500 Class B Housing
250 Class A Housing
% Split : American 55%, Canadian 25%, Other 20%
Investors : Bill Gates, Jim Walton, Larry Page

Dome 2
Location : Indian Ocean, 650 miles west of Perth, Australia.
Capacity : 850 Class B Housing
125 Class A Housing
% Split : Australian 45%, New Zealand 25%, Other 30%
Investors : Frank Lowy, Richard Pratt, Kerry Packer

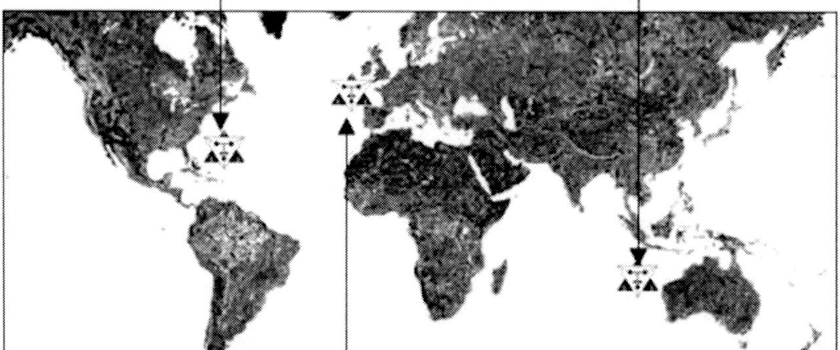

Dome 3
Location : Atlantic Ocean, 215 miles west of Brest, France.
Capacity : 1150 Class B Housing
200 Class A Housing
% Split : European 40%, British 40%, Other 20%
Investors : David Reuben, Sean Quinn, Richard Branson

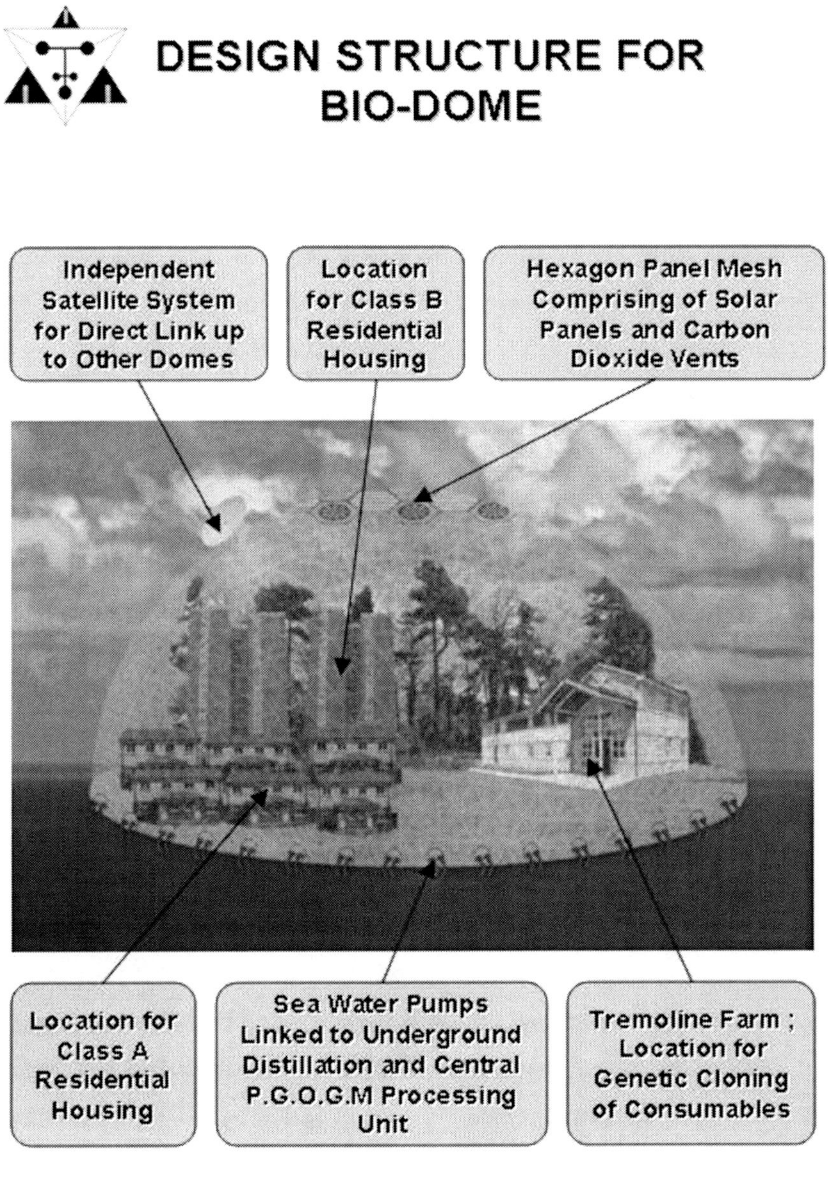
DESIGN STRUCTURE FOR BIO-DOME
Independent Satellite System for Direct Link up to Other Domes
Location for Class B Residential Housing
Hexagon Panel Mesh Comprising of Solar Panels and Carbon Dioxide Vents
Location for Class A Residential Housing
Sea Water Pumps Linked to Underground Distillation and Central P.G.O.G.M Processing Unit
Tremoline Farm ; Location for Genetic Cloning of Consumables

With another loud crack of thunder, the heavens finally opened up and commenced a savage downpour of rain. The cold violent winds then started to increase in speed and power and soon the crashing waves of the sea also became increasingly more vigorous. A large swell began to rise from the sea and viciously crashed into the dock, knocking the Tremoline boat back and forth relentlessly. But despite of all the harsh weather and the gloomy depressing sky outside, Jacob's spirit still retained its warm and fuzzy feeling. It was like no other feeling that he could remember and it made him feel enlightened and hopeful and blissfully ignorant of the rumbling thunder and bright sparks of lightning from outside.

Another violent wave then crashed against the side of the boat and as Jacob tried his best to counterbalance the shake, he suddenly felt something sharp dig in to his thigh. He steadied himself again and reached into his trouser pocket in search of the offending item. As soon as his fingers touched the smooth metal surface, he immediately remembered what the item was and removed it from his pocket for a reminiscent glance.

He stared down at the Victoria Cross in his palm and immediately began to think about what Tom had told him. He remembered how Tom had described his beloved grandfather as the most honourable man you would ever meet, and how Tom wished that the world was full of these honourable men. Jacob then began to think about what Tom had done for him over the past years and concluded that he was a good man too, a man of honour. If it wasn't for Tom's continuing kindness and patience towards him than he would have died a long time ago, along with Susan and Steven too. Tom was now like a father figure to Jacob and he would be forever grateful for his love and companionship.

It was at this point that Jacob began to think about his own recent actions. He immediately began to feel guilty and ashamed for running away from them all like that. Maybe they were all guilty of a little ignorance, but they were all good people and none of them deserved to be made to worry about him, especially at a time when they all felt run down and depressed at their hopeless situation.

Jacob took one last thoughtful gaze at the prestigious medal before carefully wrapping it back up around the red silken ribbon that suspended it. He then stood up from the captain's chair and stared out through the shattered hole in the glass, watching as the rain outside gradually morphed itself into hail. He then suddenly realised the reality of what his hasty destructive actions had caused. The shattered glass in the window had now broken the air tight seal in the helm of the boat and the P.G.O.G.M machine that hung securely above his head was now completely useless. He was now guilty of the same insensitivity that had offended him in the first place and he realised how easy it was to forget the needs of others.

He rubbed his face with his hands and tried to think of a solution. He turned round to the flight of stairs behind him and followed them down to the lower deck. To his great relief, at the bottom of the stairs stood another sturdy air tight door which sealed off the galley and sleeping quarters of the ship. The room was complete with another P.G.O.G.M machine hanging above the inside of the door and would supply the room with all the oxygen that they would need.

'But who's going to sail the boat and man all the controls?' He asked himself in a festering fluster, completely unaware that the ship actually housed an advanced auto-pilot system which used satellite navigation to guide the ship to its destination. The coordinates of the three Tremoline Bio-Domes had already been stored within its hard drive memory.

He dashed back up the small staircase again and stared intensely at the intricate controls in front of him, desperately trying to establish which buttons did what. The more Jacob stared deeply into the array of buttons and tried to work it all out, the more confused and worried he soon became. In his flustering panic he completely missed sight of the large green button at the bottom of the panel which clearly read: 'Enable Auto-Pilot Navigation'. 'I guess I'll just have to work it out!' He continued to think, trying his best to calm down. The group had come so far now that he knew it would be silly to give up at such a small hurdle, especially when they had overcome so much more to get where they were now.

He carefully stuffed the Tremoline booklet down the front of his trousers and took one last look at the fierce hailstorm that eagerly awaited him outside. It was far from a pleasant sight to him and he knew that the angry hailstones would hurt like hell as they struck him down with hurricane ferocity, but the excitement of sharing his good news with the others was too strong now and he wasn't prepared to wait all night for the weather to subside.

He mentally prepared himself for the pain he was about to receive and quickly dashed out onto the deck, before taking a running leap from the boat and safely landing back on the dock again.

He fought against the wind and hail with relentless determination, as he climbed over the railings once again and stared out at the Tremoline building ahead of him. It was at that moment that he suddenly caught a blurry glimpse of Tom and Jobe in the far distance and immediately jumped up waving his arms for their attention. Unsuccessful with his efforts, he then began to run after them and watched as they entered into the 'decompression' chamber of the main entrance. He chased after them as fast as he could but the building was further than it had seemed on his departure and the painful hail striking him down made the journey even more of a struggle.

He finally reached the doors a few minutes later and entered with the joyful excitement of his news. He waited while the entrance chamber sucked out the carbon dioxide and wiped some of the rain and hail from his frozen earlobes and cheeks. He then caught another brief glimpse of Tom and Jobe as they walked though the double doors towards the lift, but couldn't escape from the chamber entrapment until the timer had released the lock of the inner doors. A minute passed while Jacob impatiently jumped around on the spot excitedly and as soon as the doors began to open, he was off like a bullet and shot through the reception area and through the double doors.

The putrid bloody images of Jobe's desecrated lifeless body then bombarded his young innocent eyes and froze him dead in his tracks. It was like a gory climatic scene from one of his horror movies, but no amount of exposure to these images could desensitise him from its harsh shocking reality. He quickly turned his head away from the gruesome sight and firmly clenched his eyes shut, but the ghastly images had burned themselves on to his inner eyelids and shook every last memory of joy and excitement from his exhausted body. The warm fuzzy feeling that he had felt within his heart now felt like it had been sliced into two halves and left it throbbing and broken.

He cautiously began to open his eye again and it was at this point that he noticed Tom standing behind the bloody corpse and facing the lift doors. He appeared to be somewhat mesmerized and unaware of Jacob's presence, as he stood flexing his muscles and rotating his shoulder blades around. Jacob looked up at Tom with the same confused, fearful look of betrayal that Abrianna once had and his hands started to tremble. He saw the blood dripping from Tom's hands and covering his face and knew immediately that he was responsible for the ghastly act. Tears soon began flooding down little Jacob's traumatised face uncontrollably and his entire body now started to shake with fear.

Jacob gingerly began to step back, ready to run out the building for dear life when he suddenly slipped on a puddle of blood and landed head first into a mound of Jobe's brain tissue on the floor.

Jacob felt the moist warm substance smearing his face and began to feel his stomach churning. His body immediately began to heave and convulse with the increasing repulsiveness of the slimy feeling and his stomach began to feel like ingested grenades were detonating inside of him.

With the noise of Jacob's fall, his presence was finally brought to Tom's preoccupied attention. He immediately turned to face little Jacob on the floor and slowly began to pace towards him, looking sinisterly pleased that he had returned.

Jacobs convulsing continued violently inside of him and with the inability to expel the vomit through his mouth, it became entrapped in his oesophagus. Little Jacob could feel the vomit travelling up and down inside of him until his own stomach acid began to burn away at his insides with an intense scorching sensation.

Tom stood towering over poor Jacob, staring down at him with sadistic pleasure, as he watched him rolling around the floor in agony and clutching his stomach tightly as tears continued to stream down his tormented face. The pain inside Jacob seemed to increase by each second until his stomach acid finally began to back feed down his umbilical cord and seep into his umbilical unit. The acid began to ooze and bubble from the metallic seams of the unit until it completely burnt through the insulating seal that surrounded the solar electricity compartment. The little machine immediately began to short circuit and spark and black smouldering smoke began to pour from its CO_2 vent.

Tom's evil smile soon grew even larger as he watched the random sequence of events unfold before him. With the evil mentality of Jason Selby, he then projected a globlet of phlegm down into Jacob's face, before stomping with all his might onto the malfunctioning device.

There was then an electric blue explosion from the device and Tom could feel the electric current bouncing off the rubber sole of his shoes and through Jacob's body to the wet conductive puddle of brain tissue below his head, sending sizzling shocks through the boy's beating heart.

Jacob spasmed with sudden electrifying shock and his body began to glow intensely like a hundred watt light bulb. His body's immediate reflex reaction was to scream out in agony and after all the strain Jacob had forced upon his surgical wounds in recent days, they finally split apart with the intense force of a reversed bear trap. Electrified sparkling blood viciously gushed from the gouging wounds of his damaged gums and lips and his vocal chords sprung back to life just long enough to release a bellowing agonised scream of terror to accompany the humming electric ambiance.

After a brief few seconds of vibrating electric blue flashes, the umbilical unit's solar energy was all consumed and Tom's entertainment was over. Jacob's tattered body remained stiff and rigid on the floor, perfectly preserving its look of agonising terror. His skin lay charred and smouldering and his fragile heart would never beat again.

Tom released a satisfied cackle into the air before turning back to the open lift doors that awaited him, stepping inside and pressing down on the button. The metallic doors quickly slid shut, enclosing him amongst his infinitely repeated reflection on the mirrored walls that surrounded him. He then smiled at his own ghastly images and they all smiled back at him like an army of evil clones. He cackled out again in his deep sadistic voice, the sound echoing all around him until it eventually faded into obscurity.

The lift took Tom up to the second floor as he stood blissfully unaware that Susan was eagerly awaiting his arrival from the other side of the metallic lift doors, the shotgun locked and loaded in her hands, ready to seize her revenge.

Beads of sweat gently dribbled down the sides of her flustered brow as she firmly gritted her teeth to steady the nervous quiver of her top lip. With her finger twitching nervously on the trigger, she listened carefully to the sound of the arriving lift. She sighted along the barrel of the shotgun, aiming directly for the centre of the lift doors as they suddenly began to open.

CHAPTER THIRTEEN

BEFORE TOM even realised what was happening, before he could have a chance to talk his way out of the situation or somehow overpower Susan, he found himself deafened by the sound of exploding gunpowder from the shotgun. But there were no sudden images that flashed through his mind, no sudden memories of his childhood or his family, just the feeling of a skipped heartbeat and the loosening of his bowls.

He tumbled backwards and fell into the corner of the lift floor, fingering the bloody wound where the shotgun shell had scraped past his rib rage and spared his life by a mere few millimetres.

Susan's intense stare never flickered or flinched once during the shot and as Tom began to fall she was already pumping the shotgun loaded for a second shot at him.

"Susan, wait! Please!" Tom pleaded from the floor, actually sounding sincere and repentant.

"There's nothing you can say, Tom, I know! I know everything you've done you fucking bastard!" She yelled down at him aggressively and set her aim on his forehead.

"You know nothing you stupid bitch!" He screamed back at her, his sincere voice now returning to its husky demonic growl.

Without any further hesitation she pulled down on the trigger once more and took her last remaining shot at him, but Tom's reactions were faster this time and he managed to escape another impact. He leaped over to the lift's control buttons just as the shotgun shell exploded into the rear mirrored wall of the lift, sending a cloud of razor sharp reflective shards of glass dashing through the air. Tom punched his hand violently at the control buttons as the piercing shards penetrated into his back like a point blank nail bomb. The light illuminated from within the first floor's button as Tom released a groaning of pain from the imbedded shards. Before Susan could do anything more, the lift doors quickly slid closed again and the lift began to move downwards.

"FUCK!" Susan cried out in anger and threw the empty shotgun at the closed metal doors of the lift.

It was at that moment that she noticed Steven standing in the doorway of the staffroom, looking over at her with stunned confusion and disbelief.

"S . . . Susan?" He stuttered over to her with a quivering lip.

"Oh Steven, come here!" She called and ran over to embrace him.

"What the hell's going on?" He cried out from within her warm embrace.

"Tom's bad news, Steven. We've got to get out of here before he comes back for us!" She told him, quickly breaking loose from the embrace and looking him sternly in the eyes to reinforce her sincerity.

"But I don't understand Sue. What's he done? And where the hell is everyone else?" He replied with continued aggravated confusion.

"I've no idea where they are Steven and I don't understand what's going on either, but Tom's responsible for all this. That much I do know."

"Responsible? Responsible for what, Susan?"

"Responsible for everything, Steven! The green gas, the wars, everything!"

"But how? How is that possible?"

"I'll explain everything later, Steven. You just have to trust me. But right now we have to find a way out of here!" She demanded, and ran towards the fire escape with Steven's hand firmly in her grip, practically dragging the boy along like a defiant dog on a leash.

"No wait!" She cried, stopping in her tracks as she suddenly remembered the pistol she had found in the doctor's office.

"Come with me, Steven," she then continued, and dragged Steven along the office corridor.

"My arm, Susan! PLEASE!" He pleaded with her as he began to feel it pull from the socket.

"I'm sorry, Steven. Just wait here OK? Don't come in. Don't even look inside here OK?" She insisted as she left him by the door of Doctor Brown's office and ran back inside. She bent down and grabbed the gun next to the doctor's cold dead hand and stepped around the body to the mahogany desk again. She then released the magazine clip from the gun and began to load it with bullets from the desk drawer. She once again noticed the vehicle keys next to box of bullets and decided that finding the doctor's car would be worth a try. She locked the magazine back into the pistol and grabbed the keys from the drawer, flinging them into her trouser pocket and dashing back out of the office again.

"What are you gonna do with that? Are you gonna kill Tom?" Steven asked as his stare fixed on the loaded weapon in her grasp.

"Yeah, Steven, well I'm going to do my damnedest to anyway. If I don't then he's going to kill us, so I don't have much choice about it do I?" She replied and fiercely grabbed a hold of his hand again without waiting for him to answer.

Ever since their last attack by the fanatics, Tom had suspected that something was not right with his extraordinary healing ability. His wounds had taken much longer to heal than usual and the process had left him feeling drained and weak like he was hung-over from a long drinking session. He had also started to suspect that his diabetes had somehow returned but what he didn't understand was how. Dr. Richards and his team of researchers had once concluded that these genetically modified stem cells had evolved within Tom's body into asexual self-replenishing entities that would presumably stay alive along as he did, and continue their healing processes until the very end. The initial tests upon Tom had indeed verified that these stem cells had shown little or no evidence of depleting or ever dying out, but after declining Dr. Richards's strong requests that he undergo further testing, Tom was ignorant to the actual truth of the situation.

The fact was that his inherited diabetes was keyed into every strand of his DNA, and the continuous repairing of his malfunctioning pancreas was merely a temporary fix, while the disease slowly returned to kill it off once again. His pancreas had now died a hundred times over and each time that the stem cells rushed in to repair it, they had become weaker and weaker. The strain of repairing Tom's injuries inflicted during the last fanatic attack had now completely killed off the last few stem cells that still remained within him, and from that instant his body had started to deteriorate very quickly. After a mere few minutes of their depletion from his body, his pancreas had become weak and began struggling to secrete the required amount of insulin into his body. And within a mere few hours it was completely dead again and this time it had no chance of repair.

Now, with every mouthful of the glucose-rich flavoured mush that Tom had stuffed himself silly with, his sugar levels had begun to rise exponentially. Within minutes of digesting this, his body had become completely hyperglycaemic to the point of advanced DKA, which had blurred his eyesight and weakened his body enough for his mental demon to take full control of him once more.

The shotgun wound in Tom's side grew increasingly painful and blood continued to gush down his side, showing no signs of ever healing at all. The lift quickly reached the first floor of the building and he stumbled out on to the floor of the lab, confused as to why his body was feeling so weak and feeble, but determined to finish off the job regardless. He summoned up all of his remaining energy to pull himself to his feet and staggered his way deeper into the laboratory, slowing the bleeding down with his bare palm and desperately searching for a weapon—a gun, a bat, a knife? At this point it really didn't matter much to him. Anything would do the job just fine.

"Just wait to the side, Steven," Susan whispered to him as she gently pushed him away from the lift entrance and summoned the lift back up again, holding out the loaded pistol, ready to fire as she had done before. Her finger remained confidently touching the trigger as the lift doors flung open, but it was empty. She released a sigh of relief and then gestured over to Steven that it was safe. She reached out for Steven's hand once more and gripped it tight and firm as she nodded for him to press the ground floor button. The lift took them gracefully down to the ground and opened up to reveal the ghastly surprise bloodbath that Tom had left for them both. Susan immediately released Steven's hand and quickly reached her hand up to cover his eyes, praying that he hadn't already caught sight of the horror that lay before them. She breathed in and out calmly and did everything she could to keep herself composed.

"Oh my God," she muttered to herself, barely managing to hold back the tears as she stared down at the fried and bloodied corpses of her dead companions.

"What? What is it?" Steven demanded fiercely, starting to smell charred flesh in the air.

"You don't want to see this, Steven. Trust me on that alright?" She replied to him as calmly as she could, before reaffirming her grasp over his eyes. She then took another deep breath and began to guide Steven's footsteps around the mutilated bodies and pools of blood and brain tissue until they eventually made it to the double doors of the reception area. Susan pushed her way through them and finally removed her hand from Steven's eyes. She then checked the room thoroughly for any signs of Tom then turned back to face Steven again.

"Just take a seat, Steven, and I'll be right back in a few seconds OK?" She told him insistently.

"Why? Where are you going now Susan? I'm really scared!" He confessed to her.

"I know you are, Steven, I'm pretty scared too you know. But I will be right back in a second, I swear to God." She told him and began to edge away. He reluctantly obeyed her wishes and started to make his way over to the seats, looking back at her with a look of complete terror in his eyes. She turned back around and pushed open the doors again to catch sight of the bloody massacre once more. She reached up to cover her mouth and nose and gently bent down next to Jacob's poor frazzled body and this time the tears could not be stopped.

"My poor boy!" She gently sobbed, as she slipped the pistol down the front of her trousers and reached over to gently stroke the boy's cheek. But as her hand began to approach him, a static spark suddenly leaped from the boy's skin and she felt the strange sensation enter through her finger. She quickly retracted her hand again and tried to shake off the eerie shiver that travelled down her spine. She then stood up to leave again when she suddenly noticed the booklet protruding from Jacob's trousers. She bent back down with curiosity and confusion and carefully pulled the booklet free.

"What's this?" She gently muttered to herself, as she began to flick through the pages of the singed booklet. She then set eyes upon an image of the doctor's snow globe again and the sudden realization of its potential existence hit her square in the face. She then flicked to a blueprint of the Tremoline yacht and the existence of the dome became even more plausible to her. She then removed the doctor's keys from her pocket and began to study them more closely. Upon closer inspection of them she then noticed a Tremoline key ring attached to the hoop and suddenly realised that they were not car keys at all, they were boat keys.

"So that's where you ran off to then, Jacob." She gently whispered down to the body, as her flow of tears increased and began to splash down on the side of Jacob's face.

"You rest in peace my sweet boy." She then continued and rose to her feet once again, wiping the tears from her face and dashing back into the reception with the booklet still in her grasp.

"Steven! Come on, get your oxygen pack on and let's get the fuck out of here!" She called over to him.

"Why? Where are we going Susan?" He asked, quickly standing from the chair and reaching over for his pack. Susan flicked through the booklet to the picture of the snow globe once again and held it out in front of her for Steven to see for himself.

"This is where we're going Steven!" She told him with a crooked shaky smile. He carefully studied the picture and remained confused for a while longer, but Susan's smile soon spread to his own face as he began to understand exactly what he was looking at.

"Here, you can take this for me." She told him, as she passed over the booklet and removed the pistol from her trousers once again.

Susan then grabbed her own oxygen pack from the floor, swung the canister onto her back and gently placed the mask over her fragile broken nose again.

"Ready?" She mouthed over to him from under the mask. He replied with a smile and a thumb's up as they proceeded onto leave the building, completely oblivious to the sound of an arriving lift behind them.

Susan held firmly onto Steven's hand once more as they fought their way through the wind and the hail, heading straight for the harbour that beckoned them in the distance. The hail was fierce and painful, striking them like metallic ball bearings from an air gun and bouncing off their skin as if it were made from jelly, but still they carried on.

The glorious vessel was just coming into their sights when Susan suddenly felt a sharp slice to her left hand, forcing her reflexes to immediately drop the pistol to the ground. She gasped with surprise and turned around to receive another deep slice, this time to the side of her face and ear, narrowly missing her oxygen tube. She fell to the ground with shock and smashed her head onto the solid concrete below her, looking up to see Tom towering over her with a blood drenched scalpel in his grip. He smiled down at her sinisterly, before turning his attention to Steven beside her. Steven quickly released Susan's hand from his grip and began to run as fast as he could, and

Tom began to chase him. Tom forced all of his remaining strength into his running legs and belted off towards Steven with demented determination, but from his immense blood loss and his extreme state of hyperglycaemia, his attempts were futile. He collapsed to the ground with an almighty thud a few seconds later, panting for air and desperately trying to stop his bleeding wound.

The echoes of his fall travelled through the concrete to Susan who was still lying, drowsy with a concussion. She released a sigh of relief that Steven had not been harmed, before finally managing to pull herself up and catching sight of the fallen pistol in front of her.

"Go ahead, Susan! Do it you fucking bitch!" Tom taunted her, as he gripped his bleeding chest tightly and watched as Susan's eyes fixed down upon the weapon. He then followed his taunt by releasing a deep demonic cackle into the air, mixed with gargles of blood that spurted from his weak degenerating lungs and splashed against the insides of his facemask.

Susan immediately grabbed the pistol without a second thought and gingerly walked over to where Tom's wounded body was lying. She towered over Tom like he had her and pointed the pistol down directly into his face.

"Why, Tom? Why would you do all this? Why?" She cried at him hysterically.

"Why? Because the world fucking deserved it, you stupid bitch. That's why!" He growled back at her.

"Well then let me put you out of your fucking misery you piece of shit!" She continued to scream and without any further hesitation she pulled down on the trigger and finally put an end to it all.

The speeding bullet struck between Tom's eyes and continued through his skull and brain before embedding itself deep into the concrete pavement below him. It immediately set Tom's world ablaze with flames and molten rock and unleashed a flooding swarm of fiery demonoid hell-spawn from below the smouldering cracks of the concrete. A mash of bloodied teeth and claws grasped hold of him tightly and sunk deep into his tattered flesh, as his skin pulled away from muscle and muscle pulled raggedly from the bone. His pain turned from red to white until it became the only feeling he could remember.

It was at this point that Tom finally began to feel the saturation of his evil infection begin to recede. He felt it being fiercely extracted from all of his thoughts, along with all remnants of its bitter incarnation. His immense white pain then suddenly stopped in an instant and he found himself amongst the peaceful cornfields from his dreams.

The air around him smelt fresh and clean and his skin felt warm and sunkissed. He then suddenly heard the welcoming voice of his beloved grandfather, beckoning him from the log cabin ahead and Tom ran towards it in joy, knowing that his terror was finally over. Never again would the cornfields burst into flames before him and never again would the ground crack and crumble underneath his feet.

The birds chirped joyously from the azure blue skies above him and the squirrels ran about the treetops without a care in the world. This was Tom's heaven, and his tormented soul would finally find peace here, never again to be invaded by the evil thoughts of the devil.

EPILOGUE

THE VICIOUS thunderstorm that consumed the angry sky of Brighton had relentlessly continued throughout most of the night. Bright flashes of fierce white lightning pierced through the gloomy darkness at regular thunderous intervals and the hurricane-force hail-infested winds blew mercilessly into anything that got in its way.

The violent choppy waves of the English Channel crashed angrily into the sides of the Tremoline boat and threw it about the ocean as if it were made of nothing but flimsy cardboard, persistently trying to capsize the vessel with unappeasable determination. It was almost as if the skies were cleansing themselves free of their own anger and wrath, and by the time the cleansing was finished, the seas had become calm and gentle once again.

Steven had fallen fast asleep on the soft duvet-covered double bed of the sleeping quarters whilst the storm was still at its strongest. But Susan had remained awake throughout. She stared out through the smeary porthole of the quarters and directly into the eye of the storm, determined that she would outlive it. She watched as the crashing waves of the sea finally subdued and then stared out longingly into the distant horizon. She tightly clenched her teeth together to stop the chatter of her increasing anxiety and prayed to God that the journey would be fruitful, that it would finally bring them the salvation that they had strived so hard to find. As Susan's nerves and anxiety began to peak, her mind quickly became flooded with morbid possibilities that filled her with doubt and despair.

What if her previous perception of the dome had been correct all along? What if it was nothing more than a nice idea or a pipedream project yet to reach completion? What if they arrived at the co-ordinates to find nothing there at all? What would they do then?

What if the Jehovah's Enforcers had already taken a boat of their own out to the island and taken over? What if they had already killed everyone? What would they do then?

What if they arrived at the island to find it fully occupied? With no space left for her and Steven? What if they were not welcome there? What if the islanders became hostile? What if they immediately tried to blow them out of the water? What would they do then?

What if the boat's 'Sat-Nav' had become corrupt and unable to find the co-ordinates? What if the boat ran out of fuel before it even got to the island? What if they found themselves completely stranded somewhere in the middle of the English Channel? What on earth would they do then?

Susan quickly began to work herself into a panic over all the possibilities and started to hyperventilate. She leaned over to the onboard PGOGM and took in a few deep breaths of the sweet tasting oxygen to try and calm down again.

Her racing heartbeat eventually began to drop back down to normal again and it was at this point that her jittering eyes became settled upon the pistol which lay on the bedside cabinet. She then looked across at her sleepy brother. The sight of his peacefully sleeping form made her smile, before her eyes returned to the gun again. She leaned forwards and nervously picked the gun up, checking that it was still loaded and thinking about what Jobe had said before about 'last resorts.'

She then began to think about her own family again, and how dearly she missed them all. She remembered the divine taste of her mother's cooking, and how it had never been beaten once in her entire life. She imagined the sight of little Shelly and Jayne fulfilling their childhood dreams of performing in a cabaret, dancing about the stage in skin-tight pink latex with fluffy feather bowers and cute little headpieces. She imagined Melissa finally up on a Boeing 747, standing in the aisle in a cute airhostess's uniform and performing the famous emergency procedures mime. The images made her feel nostalgic and sad and eventually caused a single tear to roll from one eye.

Maybe fate actually did have something good in store for them this time, she thought. Maybe these negative possibilities were nothing more than irrational paranoia brought on by her stress and her fatigue. Maybe everything would work out. But either way, this would be the end of their long journey together, that much she would make sure of.

THE END

Lightning Source UK Ltd.
Milton Keynes UK
176135UK00003B/4/P

9 781608 602032